The Secret Lives Of Librarians

a novel by 44

The Secret Lives of Librarians: a novel by 44
© 2011 by Crow's Flight Publishing
@44theWriter

This is a work of fiction. Names, characters, places, and incidents are either the product of the author's imagination or are used fictitiously, and any resemblance to actual persons, living or dead, businesses, companies, or events is entirely coincidental.

All song lyrics are quoted by permission.

For the empire of Dusk
and a sexy little schoolmarm,
right from the start.

Thou art the book,
The library whereon I look.
-   Henry King, *The Exequy* [1657]

Chapters

1.

<u>Sol Isistrato</u>

"I remember when the librarian was a much older woman;
kindly, discreet, unattractive.
We didn't know anything about her private life. We didn't want to know
anything about her private life. She didn't *have* a private life!"
- Officer Bookman, "<u>Seinfeld</u>" television show
Larry Charles, writer ('The Library' episode) 2003

"'Librarian' might be a dirty word.
Use 'information professional' to be on the safe side."
- Karen Elliot, '<u>What I Really Learned At Library School</u>'
Papers on Library and Information Studies Education
Congress on Professional Education, July 26, 2006
American Library Association

He had hoped so long, once even found himself praying to a god he didn't believe in, for an orderly, peaceful and quiet life. And for three months in the spring of 2003, he had almost known it.

After all those years of personal struggle, of competition, forbearance, sacrifice, and, ultimately, disillusion, he had come to realize that all he really wanted was to be left alone, to continue his studies undisturbed. He still believed in the *principles* of Law, at least, and so when he was offered the desk of county law librarian he'd been more than glad to accede.

A schedule set in stone, a noiseless office, a decent (and guaranteed) salary, an unbeatable three-block walk from home, health benefits, paid vacations, and a pension, no less; normalcy at last. The visitors to the law library were almost invariably paralegals, lawyers, or judge's assistants. They knew what they were looking for and how to find it and how to use any of the machines or software. Thus, Sol was rarely put upon to actually assist anyone or to perform any real work aside from keeping the holdings in their proper places and the occasional purchase order or expense report. It was perfect; it left him free to spend the workdays reading or transcribing his personal notes on the office computer, conspicuously busy behind two glass walls overlooking the entire small library, humming along until closing time. There was some kind of contentment in a daily routine, an easy rhythm he'd let himself slip into.

That didn't last long. The day he convinced himself he might have finally secured the beginnings of an ordinary life was the day the real trouble began.

* * * *

Calisthenics and cardiovascular early that morning and he walked out of the ex-cop's low budget gym on Newark Avenue with something on his face that was dangerously close to becoming a smile. It was mid-June daybreak in the northeast, the air was delicious mist, the sun met him at the door for a race. He bolted toward the waterfront and the financial district, cooled as he ran by the vain satisfaction of not being one of those he saw already commuting to work.

He mused that even the journey to your day's work should be a pleasure, as he took in the shining new skyscrapers exclaiming a brand-new downtown. He sprinted past the light rail cars toward one of the oldest neighborhoods in the country, cut away, rounded past the block of City Hall and going west along Montgomery Street began the slow climb up the eastern slope of the long, giant humpback hill that is Jersey City.

By the time he reached Summit Avenue he was dripping sweat and laughing softly to himself with runner's high. A right onto tercentenary Bergen Avenue took him to Journal Square, after what used to be a world-class newspaper, where hundreds of people from hundreds of countries buzzed toward the trains and buses that would take them to other Jersey towns or across the river to Manhattan. Once a sparkling theater district of a bright metropolis, the vibrant colors here had faded to pale yellows and awkward browns. But there were some in town, locals, who were working toward a restoration of a former vividness.

Four blocks from his place and the second half of breakfast, the notion occurred to him that he was in a good mood. He was a sharp-looking bachelor at a prime age, owned his home, called his own shots now. At last, his future was in his own hands and that future was broad and gleaming. He thought he might even find it inside him today to be pleasant to those around him. He'd completely forgotten the evil inherent in Monday mornings.

During the week Sol wore thick-framed black eyeglasses of a light prescription and what amounted to a uniform: black jackets and slacks, white button down (sometimes grey), black ties with minimal other colors, if at all, and officer's shoes. This arrangement worked to create enough space between him and others that he was immediately rendered neutral.

It was as he crossed the street approaching his office building that he started feeling the descent of a fine day, a submersion of some kind. Maybe he just hadn't noticed it before, but there it was: a droning intensification of the regular cacophony of car horns, occasional shouted complaints from drivers; the line-up of glum and irritated faces at the bus stop; the slowness with which everyone seemed to be moving today. Suddenly there was gloom without even rain clouds. He stepped onto the curb between two parked cars and the guy on roller blades gliding sleepily toward him dropped his take-out cup coffee right by Sol's right foot, splashing him from the knee down. The skater was already crossing at the corner, shouted behind him, "Sorry!" and kept going.

Sol cursed some and stormed up the pale stone stairs to the entrance of the green-grey Sixties box of glass and steel of the County Administration Building, hurried through the security gate and straight to the nearest restroom, on the first floor, to try to clean up a bit. This delayed him enough that he was already three minutes late in opening the library. He always arrived five minutes early.

When he got to the fifth floor he saw his boss, David Vendi, leaning against the wall outside the law library entrance reading from an open manila file folder cradled in his left hand. The bald, humorless Israeli American smiled with a frown and absentmindedly took Sol's proffered handshake. Pale with deep blue eyes and circumstantial evidence of hair at the base of his skull, the County Administrator only visited the library when it was absolutely necessary. After the greeting his superior ordered him present in a conference room on the third floor at start of the next hour.

At ten o'clock Sol walked into a small meeting room where his boss was seated at a long, thin lacquered teak table along with County Executive Steven Riley and two men who Sol pegged for law enforcement types. The two strangers were dressed too similarly casual and plainly to be anything else. The jackets were, of course, large enough to conceal weapons. There was a small tape recorder on the tabletop. *Curious…* thought Sol.

Vendi spoke first. "Sol, you know Mr. Riley…" (winning blue eyes, magnanimous smile)

"Of course, good to see you, Steve."

"Nice to see you again, Sol." (Sol, the black-haired former legal hound)

"This is Special Agent Robert Pines and Special Agent Al Macy," Vendi continued, "of the F.B.I."

Now what? thought Sol. He had figured law, just not Feds.

"They have something they want to discuss with you after I finish what I have to tell you." Vendi explained gravely.

Okay... "Alright..."

"We have to record this by the way." Vendi switched on the recorder and made the protocol opening statement of persons present, date, authority, etcetera. "As I'm sure you're aware, Mr. Isistrato, [this was getting formal now] the court system in Hudson County operates on a much lighter schedule during the summer months. This building, in particular, is practically empty in summertime and the Board of Freeholders has decided that it simply isn't cost-efficient to keep it open during that time. Accordingly, we'll be opening a satellite unit for the law library at the main library building downtown."

"*The PUBLIC library*?!" Sol blurted out.

"Yes, Sol, the public library. Is that going to be a problem for you?"

Aw, no, no, no! Please, no! "No... No, of course not. But would such a setting be adequate?" A feeble attempt at objection, visions of uncontrollable, noisy children and too many indignant, uniquely scented half-crazy homeless people flooding Sol's mindscape. It felt as though he were being punished for something he didn't even do.

"We're expecting you'll make sure that it is adequate. The decision's been made. You can choose to work with the situation or, if you find the setting disagreeable, you can take an eight-week layoff. There are student interns available right now to cover for you for the duration. Either way, we'll need your answer by this time tomorrow. I do apologize for the short notice, but the Board is under extreme budgetary pressure from all around. We'll need to make the necessary arrangements and transition by the end of the week. Your schedule would remain the same except that you'd have the option of substituting Saturday for a weekday."

That's supposed to be an option? He was stunned.

"I'll be available throughout the day to answer any questions you might have, Sol, but that's the way it's going to be. Gentlemen..." Vendi rose and excused himself, taking the recorder with him..

Riley stood and jumped right into his pitch without giving Sol a chance to think.

"Mr. Isistrato, what may seem an inconvenience right now might actually turn out to be an unexpected opportunity." Here he flashed the wide politician's smile. "You see, Mr. Pines and Mr. Macy are with a unit of the FBI that investigates art crime."

"Art crime...," repeated Sol.

"Thefts, mostly, you know..." the young blonde man, possibly late thirties and obviously the agent in charge, explained amiably. "Like what we're here to talk to you about today, Mr. Isistrato."

Sol simply looked at the man, allowing him to continue.

"As it happens, the fourth floor location of the library where the annex is to be set up was, until recently-"

"-A museum."

"You're familiar with it."

"Somewhat. I used to visit from time to time. I haven't been to the new building, yet."

"It's only been open eight months. What concerns us, though, is that at some point during the relocation there occurred a theft of some fairly valuable artwork. We have strong reason to believe that there is a librarian involved. If not the actual thief, then acting as an intermediary between the thieves and potential buyers of the stolen items. Right now there's an ongoing investigation in which you could play a vital role, if you chose to. We're able to offer you the equivalent of your regular salary in addition to your normal county pay. But we would be asking for a small amount of your time apart from your normal duties."

Macy, the curly brown-haired other agent, chimed in.

"Mr. Isistrato, as in your previous line of work, what we would require of you is basically just the recording of observations and interviews with the subjects. Except that in this particular case you would be working specifically in an undercover capacity."

They had been poking around in his background. Sol mulled, slowly growing irritated. "So, you want me... to spy... on a bunch of *librarians...?*"

"Well, there's not a whole lot of surveillance work required by yourself," quick parry by Macy, "we'll take care of most of that. Plus, you'll be partnered with a member of local law enforcement if there is any cover work requiring movement outside the library."

Why would I need that?! Closing his eyes, his hand drawn to his head, Sol let escape an involuntary chuckle. He opened his eyes and looked at all of them, the two wholesome Middle Americans, the usually jovial East Coast Irish American, and asked in disbelief, "You've got to be kidding me..." He chuckled again.

Riley reached his hands a few inches outward on the table. "Sol, we're being sued by the Royal Dutch government for the loss of what they're claiming belongs to them. For a whole lotta money. We'd have to make some serious cuts if we lost the suit." A pause. "You're a county employee now, you know, and we're counting on you to take one for the team. And the royals have even offered a reward for recovery, Sol."

"How gracious. How much?"

"Twenty-five thousand. Supposedly only a drop of what it's worth."

Sol did the math in his head and wondered why they couldn't just get a regular investigator for this job. "And it's just a coincidence that I'm being shuffled downtown?"

Pines answered. "Your availability is coincidental, but our investigation has been in operation for three months now. You're a local and legit all around. You wouldn't raise any eyebrows or tip anyone off. We're just asking you to be an observer for a couple of months, ten weeks or so, make some easy money and you're out at the end of summer. And yes, we could have gotten someone else."

Sol wondered if he really needed the money and if he shouldn't just take a long vacation. Then he remembered his newly purchased building and its mortgage, the plans he had for it, and the things he could do with a windfall like what was being offered. But his calm life was being interrupted… And yet, it was just some boring librarians, wasn't it? One or two had gone bad with the taste of real money and Sol could round them up quickly enough and maybe even collect the reward. No long nights, no violence. How terribly difficult could that be? He'd hang out on the fourth floor that nobody ever visited, wrap this thing up early and take a vacation anyway. Screw 'em all. But then, what was to say they wouldn't just impose on him whenever they felt like it?

"Let me guess. You need my answer by tomorrow."

"We're under some time constraints, yes. Also, the general briefing is scheduled for Wednesday." Again answered Pines.

His last weak objection: "But, I'm a librarian myself, now…" delivered with just the slightest less conviction than he probably should have mustered.

Macy smiled sympathetically. "We've renewed all your licenses and permits and paid the fees, as a courtesy."

"Oh, you did, huh?" Now, at last, he was completely pissed off. "I'm that easy, am I? Well, how 'bout I just let you know if I *feel* like doing this? As a courtesy, of course. I'm actually thinking of taking that vacation." And between gritted teeth, "You gentlemen have a good day."

And he stood up, firmly closed the door behind him and walked somewhat stiffly to the stairwell and down to the street. As he walked around the corner, he called the main receptionist to inform her that the law library was closed for the day and that signage needed to be posted.

He cut through a small Italian neighborhood, past Little India and along JFK Boulevard for almost an hour ruminating over his situation, the hassle of it all with impromptu inconveniences, a change of schedule, annoying co-workers and once again having to report to someone. After some time, he felt hungry and paused to take a better look around. He realized he'd wandered all the way into the Heights neighborhood almost as far as Union City and that he'd have to take a cab or a bus back home. Nearby he recognized an old tavern taken over by a Spanish couple. He had an exceptionally large plate of paella and even cake for dessert. Sol normally had a healthy appetite but also took to food when he was tense or nervous. He'd even had two large glasses of burgundy. By one o'clock he was at home via taxi, pacing around for another hour until he sat to rest on a lounge chair and promptly fell asleep, his hands clasped on his enlarged lunch hour belly.

It was almost six when he awoke, a little disoriented, as he was unaccustomed to napping or wine in the daytime. The afternoon rush hour din was winding down and the sun was shining blindingly through the west windows. He noticed he still had his tie on, loosened it and undid the top two buttons of his shirt. He lowered the blinds halfway and took a cursory glance at the street below. After five-thirty the neighborhood became a lot quieter; there'd be some stragglers leaving work in the judicial district, a few local kids playing sometimes. The area had a nice mix of long-timers and immigrants. Sol liked it because it was usually calm by seven or eight.

Except tonight; tonight he noticed a big young black dude hanging out about twelve feet away from Sol's building casually making drug sales. Sol became amply annoyed.

Sol was a fair-minded man, he felt. He made a point of not being too quick to judge, of not being blind to all the aspects of modern reality, especially in cities. He had a deep loathing of these street powders which ultimately only destroyed people, but if some people wanted to destroy themselves it was none of his business. The danger was to those around them and that's where it concerned him. There was always too much violence involved. Any violence was too much. People were always fighting over the drugs themselves, or the money involved, or they were influenced by whichever particular drug to act violently. And that was aside from the wicked internal bodily damage that those drugs cause.

In any case, Sol figured, naively enough, it was a momentary thing and the dealer would simply move along elsewhere while Sol busied himself with some chore or other.

That didn't happen. Instead, it seemed the corner entrepreneur was actually setting up shop basically in front of Sol's door.

This, Sol knew, he couldn't allow to happen. *This is my home*, he said to himself, *and I will defend it.*

He had to act calmly, now, and with reason. The man didn't appear to have a gun, but Sol would be ready for that nonetheless. This guy was large, but out of shape and looked lazy. Moreover, he would never anticipate Sol's approach.

He took off his glasses and his shirt, leaving an undershirt like the guy outside. From his bedroom he retrieved a 9mm pistol and prepped it as he walked slowly downstairs. From the storage closet under the stairs he pulled out a nightstick and set it against the wall by the front door. The gun he placed on the exit shelf near the doorjamb and covered it with one of the newspapers he had everywhere. He checked for wallet, keys, and phone and took a deep breath. Making sure the door was unlocked, he stepped outside and let his anger flood him.

The dealer had a customer. No matter, any buyers would also have to know that this was no drug spot. The shriveled junkie hurried away at seeing Sol's menacing gait. The dealer turned to face him and visibly stiffened. Sol came within two feet of the guy's face and stood for a second.

"I don't care what you do, it's none of my business. But you are NOT gonna do it here… You understand me?"

The guy just stood still, staring.

"Or do you think you can beat me?" Sol added.

Naturally there was adrenaline rushing through Sol's veins; you never know what your opponent will do…

The man just turned away and started walking slowly. He looked halfway behind him and casually shouted. "E'rybody know yo' shit up and yo' back wide…"

And he kept strolling away defiantly until he turned the corner.

What did that mean? That Sol was built? It wasn't like he was trying to keep it a secret. Whatever, the important thing was whether or not this guy was coming back with weapons and/or friends. If it were going to happen, it would be within the first hour or some incalculable hour in the night.

Sol quickly looked up and down the street, at all the nearby windows and into the closest parked cars to see who might have witnessed the encounter but aside from the crackhead no one had seen him come out of his building. He casually walked back to his door, still checking around him.

Once inside he immediately retrieved a hunting rifle from his basement, checked and loaded it, collected the house phone, a magazine, some leftover pasta and a bottled water and headed all the way upstairs to the roof. On the roof he had set a few patio chairs and a table for himself and occasional visitors. He pulled the table and a chair close to the ledge and settled in to wait.

* * * *

The sun fell, it became dark, and no thugs arrived to shoot at him or his place. At this point, the only damage they could inflict would be to his building or they'd have to wait until they saw Sol on the street. That was assuming there even was a "they" to worry about. Since the dealer had initially arrived alone there was a strong possibility that he mainly operated alone. Chances were good that the hood would assume Sol was some kind of cop and this guy, at least, would think twice before coming around there again. Still, Sol would have to be on watch for the next few hours. No relaxing tonight and he had to stay in motion. Now this began to bother him as well.

Could it be that unless one is wholly isolated from other humans we are never truly in control of our own lives?

Perhaps music would help, as it often did. Something mellow was called for. Cool jazz? Some form of folk music? Classical? He settled on a CD of Indian flutes and tablas. It was rare that he was truly in the mood, or need in this case, for this eclectic pleasure. But it always calmed him down. It was music from the other side of the world and Sol found himself wondering if there wasn't some poor schlep somewhere over in Asia, perhaps even a librarian like himself, who was also wishing he were somewhere else, like New York or some other American city. And then the phone rang.

It was his lawyer friend Paul calling to ask if Sol wanted to come out to a Manhattan nightclub party that night to help him celebrate a victory in court. What he really meant was that he wanted Sol to be the designated driver for him and his fellow lawyer friends while they got drunk and acted like fools. He knew Sol didn't mind since it always meant a free gourmet dinner and being around plenty of attractive women. Once in a while Sol would even meet someone halfway interesting. It was Monday night, but he wanted to get out for a while anyway. This time though, he didn't want to take his own car into the city, so he told Paul he needed to be picked up.

He changed into black jeans, casual shoes and a long-sleeved navy-blue pullover and returned to the roof, this time with the guns back in their storage spaces. He was still somewhat tense after having had to pull them out.

A waste of his time, he thought, but better than having had to *really* pull them out. Now he had all this unused energy that would keep him wired for hours. He paced back and forth along the ledges looking for either of Paul's cars (as well as keeping an eye out for thug life). It was a clear, warm night and a half-moon was rising over Central Avenue.

After a long hour he saw the familiar black SUV crawl around the corner on Cook Street and his cell phone began buzzing in his pocket. He walked downstairs and grabbed a light blazer.

In the truck were the usual suspects: Dan Grainger, Andrew 'Andy' Philips and Tommy Zhào. They were all hotshot attorneys, all corporate. All except Paul, who worked for the District Attorney's office and who was already out of the driver's seat, motioning for Sol to take over.

"I have to make some calls," Paul said, smiling mischievously. His green eyes were already celebrating. His light brown hair was carefully smoothed and he was dressed as if he were in Miami. They shook hands and Paul thanked him for coming out.

"What're we having tonight, Sol? Italian? Middle Eastern?"

"Chilean. There's a place right across from Christ Hospital I've been meaning to check out. I heard they give big portions."

Sol had met Paul at Columbia law school eight years ago, Paul having originally come from Long Island before moving to Jersey City in ninety-eight. The others were Paul's friends mainly, whom he'd met at the lawyer hangouts here and in next-door Hoboken. They accepted Sol as one of their own inasmuch as he had a law degree and could keep up with the jargon of court life. Sol didn't talk that much anyway, and it was just left at that. The routine was usually that they fed Sol first at a place of his choosing so long as it had a bar or at least served alcohol. The others might order light fare but that was only to line their stomachs. The driver duly prepared, the revelers abandoned themselves to a carefree night of imbibing and imbecility. It wasn't that Sol disliked Paul's friends, it was just that one gets to see how silly people can be when you're the only one sober in a group of drunken partiers.

These guys were sowing their oats and it's a natural thing so more power to them. But Sol had gotten all of that out of the way early and these days simply adopted a bemused observation of human behavior. Besides, Paul was one of a small number of people he still counted as friends, so he hung out with him when he felt so inclined.

When they got to the club, an old theatre building in Tribeca, the alpha male group found the party people just too freaky for their liking. Wacked out club kids, drag queens and downtown hipsters made the Jersey boys nervous. The woman that Paul had been hoping to meet there, and who had invited him, had changed plans and headed to Brooklyn with her friends. He wasn't about to go chasing after her. There were a good number of pretty and stylish women around, but they immediately made it clear that they weren't "into lawyers or suits". It being a Monday, none of the guys could think of anywhere else in the city to go. Declaring the night a bust, the men decided to trawl the Jersey City bars before going home. Sol took the Holland Tunnel again and by eleven o'clock they were downtown. They speed-surveyed the regular circuit, The Sand Lot, AJ Dooley's on Marin Boulevard, but everything was dead. Andy Philips suggested a place he had just heard about, The White Spur, off Mercer Street, which was supposed to be popular with the hospitality industry crowd, waitresses and bartenders. And that's where they hit the jackpot.

The place had a cattle ranch theme, ala Coyote Ugly, but with a sepia-toned self-mockery. Local artists hung on the walls and there were candles on the café-style tables. But most importantly, there were chicks *everywhere*; in groups at tables, at the bar, smoking cigarettes outside. There were a handful of other men present but of the four, two worked for the bar and one of two in a group near the door was definitely queer. All were quickly disregarded, as there were so many women to choose from. The guys felt like they were giddy fourteen-year-olds again, raiding a slumber party. Here the women weren't objecting to free drinks and there was an air of casual mingling throughout the room. Paul's group commandeered two tables in a corner and made themselves comfortable.

After a half hour of macho posturing and distance-flirting they connected with a group of women on the other side of the bar and it became a party. Booze flowed, the CD jukebox greedily sucked in dollars and grew louder right along with the crowd. These women were from out of town, here for a marketing convention. They were staying at a nearby hotel and had ditched their male co-workers to raise hell in a new town.

Sol was as sociable as his personality allowed, which in truth wasn't all that much, but when it became apparent to the women that he wasn't drinking he was largely, if politely, ignored. While looking around the bar he noticed a raven-haired woman at a nearby table casting not-so-furtive glances in his direction. She was with two other women but seemed aloof of their animated conversation.

He was sure of it: she was checking him out. She was very pretty, too, beyond the gothic girl look she wore. It wasn't heavily done, like with the New Wave vampire makeup, but she was dressed in all black with subtle Victorian touches. Sol sensed her attraction yet wasn't quite sure what to make of it. He certainly didn't look like the tattooed and pierced rocker someone like her might favor. Or maybe he was stereotyping her and selling himself short.

She met his eyes and demurely looked away again. He began to think of how to make contact and couldn't decide on anything. The only thing that was certain was that now he was turned on.

She got up from her table and walked toward the bar, affording Sol a long look at a deliciously curved body in a short skirt and black stockings. He nearly knocked over his own table getting up to follow her. No one in his area noticed him leaving.

"You look like you're having about as much fun as I am," he said when he reached the bar. She turned toward him and smiled perfect wine-red lips. Eyes like blue flames seized him.

"I really didn't feel like coming out tonight. My best friend's sister is visiting and I'm helping her entertain. Barely." She laughed unselfconsciously.

"I'm baby-sitting," he told her.

"I knew there had to be something decent about you if none of those airheads is paying attention to you."

"You noticed."

"You know that I did."

The noise had increased in the place, and they had to raise their voices accordingly. He introduced himself and she told him her name was Rebecca. He asked her to linger at the bar with him for a bit as he was in no rush to return to his non-party. She gamely agreed on the condition that they talk about anything except what they did for a living.

"Believe me," he said, "work is the very last thing I want to talk about."

"Steller's Jay songs," she offered.

"Pardon? Never heard of him."

"Not a person, it's a bird. Steller's Jay, or *Cyanocittastelleri*. It's a western bird, related to our eastern Blue Jays. Your friends reminded me of them. Their songs aren't very melodic and include a jumble of low gurgles, pops, snaps, whistles, and other harsh sounds. Sorry, not to be mean, but that's what they sounded like." She smiled beautifully.

He grinned and turned to look at his company.

"Wow. You're right."

They shared a small laugh.

"Ulrich Schnauss!" he volleyed dramatically with a sitcom European accent.

She'd had a couple drinks already and guffawed slightly. "Who?!"

"German ambient composer I heard for the first time yesterday. He's worked with Robin Guthrie of Cocteau Twins."

"I love Cocteau Twins!"

"His music stayed in my head all day and what you said made me think of his song 'Monday – Paracetamil'. If it's melody you want you might like his work, though you might find it a bit strange."

"I like strange. What's a paracetamil?"

"I'm pretty sure it's a pharmaceutical drug, exactly which I don't know but I'd bet a relaxant. For Mondays. Something I could have used today… Anyway, …"

"Why don't you have a real drink?" she said neutrally.

"You know what? I think I will. Just to be wild and crazy," he deadpanned.

She smiled again and he ordered a vodka cranberry along with hers. They went on joking and talking of random things for a good half hour until Paul came swaggering over. It was so noisy now everyone was nearly shouting.

"Hey! You're Rebecca, right? I'm Paul, Sol's friend. Your friends told me your name. They're hanging out with us now, as you can see…," and he swept his arm grandly. "Guess what, Sol? You're fired!" Paul was having a good time now. "The girls from the convention have a hotel shuttle van and a driver *at their complete disposal*! Party bus, dude! You don't have to drive! Go ahead and let yourself chill out for a change, man! Live a little! We're all headed to the hotel bar in about a half-hour, they're open all night. Rebecca, your friends are coming, too. That's what I came over to tell you guys. They've got a karaoke stage!" And he strolled away bopping to some Smashmouth song that was playing.

Rebecca and Sol looked at each other with mutual apprehension and then shared gestures of mock dread and a laugh.

"I'm having a much better time just talking to you," he told her. "Would you like to go somewhere quieter?"

She looked at him for a long moment but didn't speak.

"I'm definitely not staying out all night," he said. "I have work in the morning unlike these rock stars."

Still, she only stared into his eyes as if looking for something.

He smiled at her reassuringly. "We're just talking, Rebecca. I know this cool little lounge nearby and I was on chauffeur duty anyway. I'd be glad to drop you at home, or wherever, if you're not driving."

She turned and looked at the rowdy bunch of people who were already collectively belting out Top 40 songs. She returned her gaze to Sol, a serious and responsible man, it seemed to her.

"Let's get out of here," she said. And they discreetly made their way out the back door.

* * * *

The Side Bar on Newark Avenue had originally been planned by its owners as a draw for the attorney crowd, but it was just that much too far from both the corporate environs of downtown and the courts buildings on the hill that their vision never manifested itself to reality. Instead, it became popular with the area's recent young arrivals who couldn't afford the fashionable "loft-style" condos which had mushroomed around town and who also had little or no interest in exploring any of the city's other, less trendy neighborhoods. Some six months earlier, a popular neighborhood woman had been hired as the manager and she'd brought in all of her female friends as bartenders. They'd begun low-key promotions with themed nights, local DJ's and artsy events. When it wasn't too crowded, it was one of the few places that Sol might stop into occasionally on the weekend. And that was mostly because it was close to home for him. By now he was a familiar face.

When he and Rebecca walked in, he was greeted by name and one of the bartenders even reached across the bar to give him a kiss hello. This friendliness was not lost on Rebecca, and she was now even more comfortable with her new acquaintance.

They sat at the bar for a while sipping their drinks and conversing until about one o'clock when a sort of bohemian crowd started drifting in. The music changed from a downbeat thread to livelier trip-hop. When it became slightly crowded up front, they moved to an area in the back sectioned off by translucent white curtains.

By now the first two drinks had taken their effect on Sol and he'd loosened up considerably. She was at ease as well and their dialogue was fluid, moving easily from one topic to another. Their knees met often, and their hands conspired to frequent touches. People had started dancing casually throughout the lounge, not limiting themselves to the area provided in the center although there were some there.

She had started swaying to the music as well and he could tell she was enjoying herself. Subtle looks toward the dance floor told him she wanted to move around some. He was no dancer by any stretch of the imagination, but he wasn't afraid to serve as accompaniment, either. At some point he stood, took hold of her hand and led her to an area between their table and the dancers.

They let the beats rock their bodies together in sultry undulation. Neither cared about perfect moves.

Almost imperceptibly the songs slid into deep house, drawing the couple closer to each other in increasing arousal.

She allowed herself a sensual freedom. He wasn't pawing at her. He wasn't giving her the googly eyes. He wasn't trying to talk while dancing.

She pressed her body against his and felt a solid form of muscles. He inhaled her scent of lilac and womanhood.

The two didn't even realize they had been joined in dancing by a small throng of others.

The music intensified and so did the heat between them. Pheromones were flying and they were both perspiring slightly. She wanted him completely. He was raging with desire.

She led him back to the seats they'd left, their drinks mostly ice now. They slaked their thirst and then they started kissing in the corner.

She whispered his name. He had never really liked it until then.

"Come home with me," he said, "I live nearby. You can hold my keys."

She took his hand and walked him out to the car.

"Alright if I drive?" she asked.

"This is Paul's car. But, here, you can open my door while I park this thing around back." He escorted her through the front door and returned to the truck.

Upstairs, she had taken off her shoes and played Cat Power on the stereo. She seemed to know and enjoy that there were no neighbors. She prowled his living room. Everything was neat and minimal.

He stepped in, she walked up to him and grabbed him by his hair and they started kissing again.

They pressed and they kissed and they tore at each other. They slammed into walls and fell onto the floor. She bit at him gently in places and he tried to devour her.

They were naked in the hallway. She pinned him against the wall. They started having sex upright.

They pulled each other into his bedroom. She said everything, she said it all. He gave his all to please her, the most fascinating woman he'd met yet.

They banged and kissed and howled. They pushed each other to their limits and then pushed more. They kept at each other until a silent truce was understood and they fell to rest. Curiously enough, she was actually a blonde.

* * * *

They lay in bed purring and cooing. They murmured half-phrases to one another. She whispered something about the sheer ecstasy of sex without details. He laughed a little but when he opened his pulsating eyes some four hours later, shocked awake by a violent storm of nausea and throbbing pain in his head and limbs, she was gone. He was able to move his neck a little and if he only used one eye at a time he could look around and see that she'd left nothing whatsoever to indicate she was ever there. For a second, he thought he might have dreamt it all, but he knew he hadn't. He'd just had too much to drink. The one clear thought that flitted across his blurred mindscape was that while love may be fleeting, lust is eternal.

The glowing symbols on the alarm clock slowly solidified and showed that the time was 8:19. That would mean he had to be at work in half an hour. He told his body to rise but nothing happened. He strained mentally to will motion but only physical anguish was the response.

Somehow his left hand completed the journey to the phone on the nightstand. Dialing by feel, he called his department's reception number for the second time in twenty-four hours.

Explaining that he'd had some dubious seafood last night and couldn't even make it past his bathroom door, he said he'd be taking a sick day, and someone would have to cover for him. Sol never took any days off, so he absolved himself of the guilt of the lie. His boss would be suspicious but so what? Oh yeah, him. One last thing, he told the receptionist. He asked her to leave a message for Vendi: that he would be taking care of the annex project on schedule starting the next day. To himself he told he would call the FBI offices in Newark later on and agree to the other thing, too. And he retreated back into oblivion, to wait for his body's return.

2.

<u>Lorelei McSherman</u>

"If she intends to remain fully feminine,
it is implied that she also intends to meet the other sex
with the odds as favorable as possible."
- Simone DeBeauvoir, <u>The Second Sex</u>, 1952

"Turn yourself around, you weren't invited.
Turn yourself around, you weren't invited.
Good, good things happen in bad towns.
Good, good things happen in bad towns.
Runaway! Runaway! You want it.
Runaway! Runaway! You want it."
- Karen O of Yeah Yeah Yeahs
"Honeybear", <u>Show Your Bones</u>, 2003

She had started wondering, quite unexpectedly, about the meaningfulness of her life, wondered if maybe she hadn't settled for safety and surety instead of striving for something more important, somehow, something more dynamic, maybe. She wasn't so sure of herself now, she was restless, and it was beginning to show.

Things were more serious these days, not like the playful decade that had just passed. And though she tried not to be, she was cockier now, too, almost as if she had something to prove again. She couldn't help it; she was a tough girl, tough daddy, big brothers, and so on. Dad and just about everyone else in the family had been in local law enforcement since forever it seemed, and she'd never really thought twice about it until recently. It had come naturally to her, being a sheriff's deputy, even if she was the only woman in the family to do it since her aunt Helen in the seventies. Her father had objected but he knew better than to try to change her mind. She was a pretty woman, too, Lorelei; all Irish red and athletic. She could have just done pretty stuff, but she never really believed it or spent too much time thinking about it. She was aware that men were obviously attracted to her, yet she was just fine with the guy she was with.

He was a cop, too, city, very handsome and moving up swiftly. They made a good couple, and both had strong local ties so this was where they might make a life together. She had just made detective two months ago and would work in that capacity for the sheriff's department until, probably, about the time they would be having their second child if things proceeded well. She'd felt happy with the way they had talked and spent so much time together through the winter but now something had changed with them since then. Maybe it was just her, maybe she was going through a phase or something, but lately she questioned the direction her life was taking, how *everything* was going, actually.

She couldn't help feeling, knowing, really, that she was getting passed over on assignments, and yet the town seemed to be getting more and more violent every single day. It was enough to investigate the occasional industrial burglaries, once in a while assist on inter-agency drug busts, transport prisoners to court, maintain the local peace and all, but now there were a lot more murders, shootings, gangs evident, an influx of all kinds of new people (even terrorists among them as was recently revealed). There was that and all the other law enforcement pains that came with a growing city.

It was that day she considered quitting the sheriff's office that things got interesting.

* * * *

There are those mercifully rare days when you feel like hell and people around you insist on telling you that you look great. Irrelevant compliments, flirtations, offered time to share when there's none to spare. Are you graceful, smiling, or do you bark like a sleepless dog? You love your fellow humans, just not this morning, nothing personal. It is one of those days. A long, uneasy night due to someone else's problems and it would be nice to have a day of rest.

No such luck. Yesterday was the usual Monday chaos, today it's picking up a wife-beater who's violated a restraining order and, thusly, parole by swinging by to pick on his two children's mother, yet again. As an officer of the court enforcing a court order she was accompanying two state parole officers, females, by the way, to escort one mister Michael Crandon (age 30, 5'9", 165 lbs., medium slight build, Caucasian, dark brown hair, brown eyes, multiple tattoos on arms and neck, 2-inch scar on left shoulder) back to his favored lodgings at one of the state prisons.

Her own man had canceled on her last night, said he had a family situation to attend to. What was so terrible about waking up alone? One becomes accustomed to some bodies.

This other man, the one she was here to arrest, came by yesterday to punish his soon-to-be ex-wife for not wanting to have to wake up to his misery anymore. The woman had called the sheriff's office when she first sought out the restraining order and did so again early this morning after Mr. Crandon had gotten drunk last night and invited himself to stay over. Because his mailing address was constantly changing, he still did not know there was a restraining order against him. The woman was too scared to tell him.

Lorelei had met these other officers and been briefed at the state parole offices on Summit at Sip Ave. Though the call and initial action was through the sheriff's office the state assumed authority and she was coming along as interdepartmental cooperation aside from her role as an officer of the court. Whereas she was in uniform, stiff navy blue and black, very similar to city police, the parole officers were plainclothes: jeans and the oversized, gun-concealing tops. The season's warmth was hinting at its arrival.

It was routine, or supposed to be… nothing more than an escort. The other women were friendly enough, much more accustomed to constant daily interaction with the criminal kind. One was a bit butch but nice. Lorelei didn't have a regular partner at the moment, as her position was currently undefined. Basically, she was a floater until she joined a detective squad and, in the meantime, remained a detective-grade general duty deputy.

Even if stretched out this whole thing would only take an hour or two. Usually the subject was cooperative, very familiar with the process. Lorelei would serve him with the violation of the restraining order, his parole officer would state his violation of parole and they would take him into custody. All four would proceed to the county jail, where Crandon would be placed in a holding cell until the paperwork and other reception procedures were completed and he was transferred to the general population to wait a few weeks for transport to a prison. Most of the time, when nothing violent is happening, the jail is a social place where cops and criminals all catch up with associates they haven't seen in a while. But today Mr. Crandon wasn't feeling very sociable, and he went rabbit.

The three women walked up the wooden steps of the old house in an everyday fashion. From his file they knew he had no weapons offenses and that he tended to direct his violence against females. His parole officer, a tall shorthaired and healthy brunette with ocean blue eyes, rang the doorbell with an air of Southern style relax. Less than a minute later Mr.

Crandon pulled aside a yellowed white lace curtain to look out the small glass window on the wooden door. It took him an instant to process the blue uniform and his parole officer's accompanied presence in his mind's program and he jerked into a reaction.

There wasn't a second to lose and he went running for the back door. The way he dropped the curtain and turned made the women realize he wasn't going to open the door. Instinctively, Lorelei dropped over the side of the porch banister and called out, "I've got him!" and started for the back of the house. Crandon's parole officer, a Ms. Kersh, had to call it in and her partner, the butch beauty, bounded down the stairs to join the pursuit.

Hurtling the usual alley obstacles, the sheriff's deputy swore to herself as she set her mind to the task at hand. Men are often excused for being eluded or bested but a woman is usually blamed for her being a woman in any failure. It made Lorelei try harder. She knew this and she always made sure it was her pushing herself first. It was always that way, no matter what people say. But this one, this one was all hers as she was the first to move and everyone knew what he was; another scumbag abuser that had to be put down again. And she was just the one to do it.

Crandon jumped the back fence and cut through the opposing yard, tearing off north on Hoboken Avenue with Lorelei behind him at thirty yards or so.

This was his neighborhood and Lorelei lost a few seconds coming out of the alleys and figuring out what direction he'd taken. Generally ignored in this city is a massive, raised railroad embankment, long abandoned and greatly overgrown, and which cuts a great swath a full city-block wide and a half-mile long west to east at the northernmost quarter of the town. It was through this urban thicket that Mr. Crandon thought he could lose his pursuers. But Lorelei was only getting warmed up.

She found the stone staircase entrance he'd taken and followed. At the top she had him in her sights and radioed her position. There was a wide path parallel to where the tracks lay nearly buried. While Crandon imagined he was moving fast he was actually a heavy smoker incapable of any real speed and Lorelei would soon overtake him. He looked behind him and saw her barreling down on him. So, he started considering his options. He had no weapon on him, and this she-cop seemed to sense that.

Lorelei eased into position alongside him to his left. He was already starting to wheeze.

"I can make you stop, but it's gonna hurt!" she shouted at him as they ran in tandem.

He gave her the finger and poured forth the last reserve of breath he had to sprint forward. She sped up as well. He stopped abruptly and swung his right elbow around and square into Lorelei's mouth knocking her feet out from under her.

"Now, bitch, what?!" He slouched forward, panting to catch his breath and then started running again.

It took Lorelei almost a whole minute to come out of the clanging and blur in her head. Luckily, she hadn't landed too badly and she was able to shake off the blow and the fall. There was Crandon ahead at twenty yards. So much for showing him mercy…

She went at him full steam, fueled by a hot rage. She caught up to him even quicker this time. He could hear her approaching behind him and tried speeding up again. But she was already next to him.

She spiked her right heel into his left ankle and he tumbled, sliding forward on his face for at least twelve feet. This time Lorelei stopped to regulate her breathing. Crandon grabbed his ankle and howled in pain. She started walking purposefully toward him. He hobbled up on one leg, threw his hands up as if to fight her and hurled all the filthiest insults he could think of. She could have drawn her gun at this point and procedure dictated that she should. But she had already decided to teach this guy a lesson. Without breaking stride, she drove a straight jab onto the bridge of his nose. There was a spurt of blood and a yelp from Crandon. He fell back a few feet, almost stumbling to the ground.

She spoke loudly, "Michael Crandon, you are under arrest for violating a restraining order and parole. We'll add assault on a police officer and eluding. Go ahead and kneel down with your hands on your head. Please…"

He lunged and swung at her, just as she had hoped. She merely leaned back to her left and threw her right knee deep into his abdomen and he dropped like a rock. That did stop him. He flailed a little but could scarcely take in air. With him on the ground, she placed herself over him, her left knee on his back to hold him down. Then she easily pulled his arms together and handcuffed his wrists. He began cursing at her again and even tried to spit behind him at her. She gave him a swift slap on the back of his head. "That'll be enough. You've got resisting arrest now, too," she said. She read him his rights and waited for the others to get there.

The parole officers caught up to them within a couple minutes and they quickly assessed the situation. Crandon began crying out about his rights having been violated. Disgusted, his parole officer assured him he would get his one phone call. As they were walking him down a different stairwell, she couldn't restrain herself and added that she wondered how all his buddies in jail would react when they found out he got beat up by a girl.

When asked down on the street, Lorelei insisted she needed no medical attention but only wanted to fill out the paperwork necessary to get this guy out of her sight. Her hair was a wild mess, she had a busted lip, and the entire back of her uniform was dirt-covered. She was in a truly foul mood now.

Then the back-up arrived, both hers and the parole officers'. Out of the Sheriff's Department car jumped Deputies Mitnaul and Carlotti. Mitnaul was a very large African American man who had appointed himself Lorelei's keeper, a Northern Baptist's chauvinist but benevolent disapproval of women on police forces. His partner was a diminutive second-generation Italian, fierce as a wild animal but with the mellowest exterior. Mitnaul was shouting before his door had even opened.

"Laura! Where the hell have you been, girl?! Why do we have to find out where you are from the parole office? The boss is going ballistic looking for you! Do you have any idea what kind of drama he's giving us? Why do I have to get all the crap?..." He saw her lip. "Damn! What happened to *you*?! Did this little?... I will..."

Lorelei rushed toward her friend and raised her hand against his chest.

"Relax, Mit. It's all over. What does the boss want?"

The hulking deputy looked quickly back and forth between Crandon and Lorelei's reassuring glare and decided to calm down.

"You weren't at roll call."

"I was pre-assigned! I had to meet State at 7:30."

"You had a half-hour to stop in."

"I don't have to check in when I'm already scheduled. That's not procedure..."

"C'mon, Laura..." He gave her a knowing look. "You know better than that. You know he likes to see everybody's face in the morning. Ain't nothin' changed. You're not even in a regular unit yet."

"Are you serious?"

"Yes, I'm serious, and he's pissed. Says he wants you in front of him *right now*. We'll take this guy in with State."

"But I still have to fill out the reports."

"Now, Laura, please. I don't want to listen to any more of his nonsense today and you can do all that later. Okay? Byyeee!..."

Lorelei walked to her patrol vehicle feeling like a scolded child. Her boss, the sheriff, was a good guy. He cared about people greatly and treated her with the utmost respect. But he could also be overbearing and far too fatherly. That was because he actually knew her father, of course. She chalked it up to 'the way it works'.

She dusted herself off, smoothed her hair and checked herself in the mirror in the car. A disaster she was. She wiped and brushed herself as best she could, but it was still obvious to anyone that she'd just been in some kind of scuffle. And now her wannabe uncle boss was about to unload some completely disconnected frustration on her yessing, lower-rank self.

The radio crackled. "This is headquarters. Deputy McSherman, are you out there? Repeat, this is base."

"Yes, Donna, this is Laura. I just got back to the car and I'm headed over there. Five -ten minutes, okay?"

"Copy, Deputy. Sheriff Cottington is looking for you."

"Yes, I know, dispatch. Thank you."

"Hurry up, Laura, please. He's driving us crazy."

"I'm…on…my…way, Donna. Out."

She took a deep breath and started the engine.

* * * *

She hurried across the little plaza in front of headquarters, aware that her boss's office looked out directly over it and he was probably watching her arrive. He really was like family to her, but he never hesitated to remind her that he was her superior first. Him and his bushy pushy eyebrows.

"Where have you been?!" he immediately asked crossly.

"You already know where," she replied.

"You know what I mean! Why didn't you check in with me this morning?" He must have been rehearsing this in his head.

"I had my assignment already."

"Oh. I see. So, at this point, you're able to tell your station and your commanding officers where you'll be…"

Something was wrong. She knew this man well and right now he was acting like a complete jerk. Smaller than average height but with an

24

immense spirit, he had seen plenty, good and bad. And now his gray hair was ruffled and his pointy face more pinched than usual.

"Sheriff, what is this really about? What's the matter, Dan?"

"I have bosses and so do you. I'm your boss, right? So try to show a little respect."

"Yes, sir. I apologize if I sound disrespectful and for breaking protocol. I went straight to the State Parole offices. Now please tell me what you needed to see me about that is so urgent."

"I have a regular assignment for you for the next two months. It's short notice and I don't have anyone with, uh, more seniority to fill the spot. I've got the County stressing me on this and I most *definitely* don't want to hear anything from you about me trying to keep you out of the action. I'm serious, Lorelei. I'm not going to lie to you and say that I'm not pleased that this assignment will get you off the streets for a while, but you know very well that I don't like to be pushed around. They want a single detective from us for county jurisdiction."

"What is it?"

"Security guard at the public library, but you'll be undercover at the same time."

"What?"

"There's a theft investigation being conducted over there by the F.B.I. You'll be the security guard on the surface but simultaneously working the case for them and the county."

"Really? Well, that sounds like fun!" *A working vacation!* she thought.

"Glad you think so. Anyway, I'm out of the loop. You'll be reporting to a federal agent, Pines is his name, since the sheriff's office is too small for you these days."

"Aw, stop it, Dan. You made your point, and you know I love you. When do I start?"

"Your briefing is tomorrow morning at six, fourth floor of the library. You're being partnered with some kind of P.I. That's all I know. Here, this is for you: preliminary letter of hire. You're getting some federal money for this on top of your salary. Feel free to thank me with some tickets to Shea Stadium. And maybe you can find it within your busy schedule to let us know you're okay once in a while. Now go clean up whatever you have here, including yourself, and take the rest of the day off."

"Yes, sir. Thanks, Dan. I'll call you tomorrow to let you know how it goes."

* * * *

It didn't take long for Lorelei to close out all the details she had pending at headquarters. She had no unfinished casework, a few court dates that had to be reassigned and the reports for the morning fight took about an hour.

Sitting in the parking garage in her own car, a maroon Wrangler, she allowed herself a tired smile. She was excited about the job she'd just been given. Any change of pace was welcome at this moment. She tore open the envelope Cottington had given her. It didn't have her name on it nor did the letter inside. It was addressed: Officer of the Law. And it read like a conscription to military service, replete with twenty-first century legalese.

Whatever, she had the basic information already. Tomorrow she could get it all in English. Right now, the only thing she wanted was a hot shower. Dirty, sweaty, tired, hungry and grouchy, she just wanted to be home.

Her little apartment on the first floor of a colonial house off West Side Avenue seemed like Paradise at the moment. The neighbors upstairs, who were also the owners of the house, were an adorable elderly Polish couple who cherished her presence and were nothing if not respectful of her privacy. Both yards, front and back, were large enough and perfectly foliated to allow her to find peace in them when she wanted to sit outside. The neighborhood was just that, a place where people knew and looked after one another. She would miss it if she moved. Her boyfriend, Anthony, fiancé now, had already been talking about moving in together to a larger place. She'd been single so long that it had become difficult to consider giving up her independence, but he really did seem like the right man.

There was no bread at home and the dog food was running low. She figured she would make a quick run to the supermarket and get some take-out as well. There was a Philippine place on the same block as the A&P where the owners let Lorelei mix and match entrees and appetizers if it wasn't too busy. She figured she'd also pick up a bag of snacks for her black Labrador, Mister.

She found a parking space near the restaurant and walked down the street to the supermarket, where she strolled along the aisles finding more items than she had planned to get. As she walked out with a number of bags, she noticed a couple right outside the restaurant arguing. Young Filipinos, late teens, early twenties, maybe. When she got closer, she saw the man grab the woman's arm and her trying to pull away. She was considerably taller than him, but he was obviously the dominant. Lorelei was within fifteen feet of them when the man noticed her and muttered something in Tagalog to his girlfriend.

"Are you alright, miss?" Lorelei asked.

"She okay," the man replied.

"I was asking her!" Lorelei snapped.

The girl looked nervously at her boyfriend's scowl and then at Lorelei and smiled saggingly. "I'm okay," she said with sad clown lipstick.

"Are you sure?"

"Yeah, yes, I mean. Thank you, though. We're just gonna go home now. Thank you." And she hurried to open the passenger side door of a silver Mitsubishi Eclipse parked in front of them. The man pointedly looked at Lorelei's lip, met her eye and turned and walked around to his side of the car. He looked at Lorelei smugly again as he opened the driver's door. They glared at each other for a second and he got in. As they drove off Lorelei made a mental note of the license plate and immediately wrote it down once she'd set her bags down in the restaurant.

She was greeted boisterously by the couple behind the counter and Lorelei asked them if they knew who the young man was that had just left. They immediately negated, which made her suspect that they did know him. In these small ethnic communities, everyone usually knows everyone else. Lorelei let it go and turned her attention to picking out her lunch. Every once in a while, she caught an urge for this salty fare.

As she neared her house, she saw the Wielwowskis out front pruning and clipping. Mister, the dog, was lazing on the porch when he saw her approach and jumped up with two hearty barks in greeting then ran around back to the garage to meet her. She parked halfway down the driveway, gathered all the bags from the car and walked to the front to say hello to her friends. Mister lavished her with attention, as he knew she was home early and could smell food all over her.

They were in full gardening gear and since they hardly saw Lorelei lately, they dropped their tools to receive her. They were among the few who called her by her full name.

"Lorelei! What a wonderful surprise! How are you? We never see you anymore!" Mrs. Wielwowski exclaimed mildly.

"Hello, Deputy!" Mr. Wielwowski beamed.

"Hiya! Only a half-day today! Gotta grab 'em when you can…" she answered with a smile.

"Oh, no! What happened to your lip, hawny?!" Mrs. Wielwowski missed nothing.

"Well, I had to beat up a boy today. You know how it is, Elena…," she winked at the elder woman.

Mrs. Wielwowski huffed sharply and turned to her husband. "You see what savages and despicable creatures you men are?!"

"Savages," he repeated.

"Why aren't you helping her with her groceries, then, Frederick?"

He immediately moved to take Lorelei's bags, but she stopped him. "No, Mr. Wielwowski, thank you. I've got them. I'm just going inside to pig out on some take-out. I already know you guys don't like the salty stuff or I'd offer you some. Let me get Mister inside before he has a conniption, okay?"

"Of course, hawny, of course! We were just getting ready to go out ourselves," lied Elena. Her husband's surprised eyebrows gave it away.

From inside, she could hear them bickering lightly in Polish. They only pretended to argue to keep themselves amused and you never saw one without the other. Lorelei had lived with them long enough to discern that they were once again debating who was going to drive.

It always made Lorelei smile when she thought of their marriage. They were young lovers with no one but each other when they escaped the German and Russian invasions at the onset of World War II. Fiercely devoted to one another, they survived the hardships of immigrant life to raise two children through college and now lived off savings, his pension and the rent from the first floor of the house. Lorelei once again found herself wondering if she and Anthony would reflect that devotion at that age and mentally brushed away the thought. Mister was haranguing her for his payoff.

The dog lay at her feet punishing a large piece of rawhide as Lorelei picked at her food at the kitchen table, washing it down with a kind of ginger soda the restaurant imported from the Philippines. In repose she began identifying certain points of pain around her body, developed from the earlier conflict. She decided she would run a hot bath instead of taking a shower.

She located a mix tape a friend had made for her of a slew of Lorelei's favorite bands and popped it into the waterproof player in the bathroom. Picking out a rose scented bubble lotion, she drew out all the hot water in the tub. Mister asked to be let out to the yard again and she gladly liberated him. She lit one of the large candles on the bath stand and settled in for at least an hour of complete relaxation.

* * * *

She opened her eyes to find her fiancé, Anthony, sitting across from her with a bouquet of flowers along his arm. He had a subdued look on his face and smiled gently as her mind focused. He was still in uniform.

"Hello, beautiful." His dirty blonde hair was tossed from wearing his cap all day.

"Hi, babe," she said drowsily. "How long have you been there?"

"I lost track," he teased.

"What time is it?"

"Couldn't tell you."

She started to say something but just smiled instead. She blushed when she realized the bubbles had dissipated and she felt a sudden warm tinge all over her body.

"Get out," she told him. "I'm going to dry off before you see my wrinkles."

"I saw you had lunch already, but I'll be right back with dessert." He knew where all the Italian bakeries were in the area and which were closest to her apartment.

By the time she'd finished changing into shorts and a t-shirt and had dried her hair, he was back with an assortment of pastries and a bottle of Sauternes. He was spoiling her; Mitnaul had probably called him immediately to tattletale, as he did with everything else. Anthony walked over to her and kissed her lightly on the lips.

"Mitnaul's got a big mouth, doesn't he?" she complained.

"He sure does, but I like that about him," he replied.

"I'll bet you do. He's like your nanny for me."

"He's just tending to his flock, Lorelei," he smiled at her beatifically, pressed his palms together in a gesture of prayer and looked up at the ceiling. Mitnaul was an ordained minister and preached in his church on Sundays. "Don't worry, I got mine, too. You know, how I *allow* you to do such dangerous work, and how I should have you at home making babies, and so on. But anyway, do you want to talk about what happened?"

"No. I was sucker punched." She paused. "And I took him down, that's all."

"Good for you. Listen, I'm all sweaty from work. Gonna take a quick shower, okay? You go ahead and treat yourself. I'll be out in a few minutes." She had set aside a closet for him in the hallway near her bedroom and he kept some basic items of clothing there.

He was back in less than ten minutes but obviously refreshed. She was contemplating a frosted biscotto as she nibbled on it and he kissed her again lightly as he helped himself to a glass of the dessert wine. He stood behind her and started to massage her neck and shoulders.

"Oh, my god, I think I'm going to melt off this stool," she moaned gently.

"Well, melt onto the couch because you're getting the full treatment." He nudged her toward the sofa. He rubbed her back, her arms, legs and her feet. She felt she was beginning to dream when he suddenly stopped. Delicately, he coaxed her to turn around. He finished his attentions with the front of her arms and legs. She tugged on his shirt and drew him close to her.

"You awful, awful man," she whispered. And she began kissing his face, then his neck and his chest. Slowly, leisurely, they rubbed against each other with small wet kisses. They petted and caressed each other. He slid to the floor, knelt, took her in his arms, rose and carried her into the bedroom.

They undressed each other leisurely, lovingly, moving over each other's bodies with the freedom of a summer afternoon. They made love on a desert island.

* * * *

He lay beside her sleeping quietly as she gently stroked his hair. She found herself thinking about the future again and, despite reminding herself to appreciate the present moment, she was wondering where she would be in that nagging standard prognosis of five years. An hour passed and he awoke. They talked for a while and she told him of her new assignment. He laughed in genuine amusement and, speaking of which, why don't they see what movies are on cable tonight? She told him not to make fun of her and that if he wasn't careful, she'd make him watch a chick flick with her. They settled on a sci-fi thriller and ordered a Chinese food delivery.

3.

<u>Generalities</u>

"Every artist undresses his subject, whether human or still life.
It is his business to find essences in surfaces,
and what more attractive and challenging surface
than the skin around a soul?"
- Richard Corliss, On Andrew Wyeth's studies of Helga Testorf, Time 18 August 1986

"Card, stocking, and drink
Cause many to sink;
But right use of the same
Has never brought shame."
- Dutch proverb

The Jersey City Free Public Library, on Jersey Avenue between Montgomery and Mercer Streets, was a latecomer to the American library movement of the mid 1800's. It was founded at the start of the twentieth century (really 1889, when they first began discussing it) by a group of local businessmen and professionals forming a library company, inspired and led primarily by one Doctor Leonard J. Gordon at a time when the city was at the forefront of American industry and culture.

Designed by the premier team of architects Henry Bright and James Bacon in the Beaux-Arts Classicism style (all solid stolid Greek temple-like on the outside, the inside full of walnut-and-brass rails, marble walls, columns and floors) the building, cornerstone laid August 16th of 1899, was completed in December of 1900 and the opening ceremony was on January 14th of 1901, when still mostly only men were librarians.

It might have interested Sol to know that it was the second largest library in the country at that time, after the New York Public Library, of course, and that the city's first law library was in fact originally at the main public library. But at this time, he would not have been able to care less. He was consumed by the feeling that he'd already served the general public to a good extent and that he was now entitled to some private time and any other rewards for his efforts. He'd paid his dues, and it was all about him now; number one. After all, if you don't take care of yourself first, how can you ever possibly help anyone else?

And yet, he'd rented himself out again just the same. Only for a little while, anyway, he reasoned. It seemed not even his revered librarians

31

were above naming a price for themselves so why should he be any different? It felt like a punishment to have to work with the public again but Sol would complete this assignment and collect his just desserts. Why not?

* * * *

The briefing that Wednesday had had to be held sufficiently before opening hours that no one would notice. Both Laura and Sol had had to skip their morning workouts and report to the fourth floor of the library at sunrise, right around six that day. The only person on the street was some slight guy on Newark Avenue who looked like he'd been out all night, still in button-down shirt and tie, and who was now waiting for the first bus anywhere. At 575 Jersey Avenue a discreet federal security officer was at the front door to receive them when each arrived, Sol a few minutes early and Lorelei right on time.

At the top of the stairs Sol noted that the two former art galleries had been altered into the Historical Projects/New Jersey Room and into the Government Documents Room, the latter of which he presumed would now become or incorporate the new satellite law library. The meeting was in the New Jersey Room, the walls covered with old maps and pictures. Only Special Agent Pines was there.

When Lorelei arrived, dressed in a dark burgundy business suit, she opened the old wooden door to find a mid-thirtyish blonde man in casual business attire leaning against a desk and facing a seated man in his late twenties or early thirties who seemed to have been plucked out of a 1950's newspaper photo, but somewhat bulky under his jacket and with a very serious demeanor.

"Good morning," she smiled at them. Agent Pines came over to her lightly returning a smile and extended his hand. The stranger with the glasses stood but remained where he was. Agent Pines introduced himself and then Sol.

"Laura, this is Sol Isistrato. Sol is currently the county law librarian as well as a former legal investigator. Sol, this is Detective Lorelei McSherman of the Hudson County Sheriff's Office."

Sol reached out for Lorelei's hand but did not smile. She was gorgeous and he had to remind himself to maintain a professional stance. "Hello, Ms. McSherman. Miss?" *She seems rather young to already be a detective,* he thought.

32

"Hi, Sol. Yes, it's Miss, but I'm engaged. And everyone calls me Laura, by the way." *He's kinda stiff,* she thought.

Pleased to meet you." *Is that a fat lip she's got?*

"I'm giving each of you a folder with the other's dossier," began Agent Pines. "I suggest you discuss them with one another as soon after this briefing as possible. We need to be out of here before seven so you'll have to forgive me if I get right to it. Please, take notes and I'll answer any questions as soon as I'm done."

"You are both county employees and while you'll be working with that authority you are also acting as temporary employees of the federal government because of the jurisdiction and international factors involved. To that extent, I strongly encourage you, and officially instruct you as much, to conduct yourselves according to the guidelines for temporary agency laid out on the second page of this next set of papers I'm handing you. You are being partnered only for this one case assignment, meeting at least twice weekly to gather your information, and reporting to me directly as needed, at a minimum of once per week. Sol's had plenty of interaction with federal offices but he's never actually worked for us before. Also in these folders are a number of other forms, including disclosure and confidentiality agreements, which will all need to be completed before we leave here this morning. Sorry 'bout all the legal formalities and paperwork but I'm sure you can understand why it's necessary. Any questions so far?… Okay, on to the case history."

As young as he might be, Agent Pines gave the impression that he'd held hundreds of these briefings, probably always with the same fresh-faced efficiency that bordered on zeal.

"The Jersey City Museum, now at 350 Montgomery Street, originally occupied this fourth floor of the library. It was part of the library from 1901, when they both first opened, until 1987, when they became separate fiscal entities. During the fifties, the city suffered from sharp economic declines and the museum was forced to store its Permanent Collection and severely limit its operations. In 1993, the Jersey City Redevelopment Agency donated the current building to the museum but it was in such a state of disrepair that it wouldn't be ready for occupancy for another seven years. The renovation was completed in December of 2000, and in January of 2001 the museum organization began the slow work of moving into its new home. The grand opening for the new museum was on October 19th, 2001, but because of the terrorist attacks the previous month it went largely unnoticed.

"In February of this year, the Dutch Royal family of Queen Beatrix, House of Orange-Nassau, received a letter of offer by an unidentified party to sell an oil painting by Jan Steen, a Dutch painter of the mid-seventeenth century. The seller claims the piece is actually of Dutch Royal property and 'improperly obtained' by entities in the United States, further claiming to be able to prove as much. As a quick side note, American law, unlike the majority of other countries, dictates that you can't sell what was never yours. That and the old rule of *caveat emptor*, or buyer beware, provide redress for an individual to reclaim any property they can prove belongs to them. So the royals immediately contacted the American government through their embassy, demanding that we conduct an investigation or pay the ransom for the stolen painting. On top of that, they got their own bureaucratic machine riled up to file suit against Hudson County for damages.

"The fact of the matter is that art crime has always been an increasingly lucrative enterprise. One might think diamonds or bank heists, but the organized theft of artifacts and fine art is now third in place behind drugs and guns, and the FBI has had to keep up with its practitioners. My unit at the Bureau is a prototype for an art theft program currently in development. We were assigned the case in March and at this point in the investigation we needed to hire a couple of locals. I'll be your liaison and handler for the duration of your involvement, available at all times and meeting with you on a regular basis, just not in this same manner. I cannot stress enough that we will no longer have these exposed meetings in this area and you are never to call me at the FBI offices unless it's an absolute emergency. You'll have a dedicated mobile number that is always within my reach and available for any particular needs. Equally important is that the two of you are never seen together outside near this building, either, for obvious reasons. Inside, your contact should be limited to Laura's security patrols and normal passing. And, if you feel the need to surveil any of the subjects it will be coordinated through me. There will of course, come the time when you're ready to conduct the formal interviews. All clear still?"

The recruits both nodded.

"So now to the make-pretend part: It's pretty simple and easily confirmed in case anyone feels the need to go snooping around behind either of you. My partner and I have already interviewed all the subjects. They'll remember our faces and know what we're doing here. As far as they all know the case has moved into the courts. However, we've had a minor break recently and we're anticipating some serious activity in this building in the very near future. We need eyes and ears moving around in here from top to bottom and from open to close. We'll also have active surveillance of the building outside at any and all times if and when we feel it becomes necessary.

"The library employs both city police and the county sheriff's office for its security guards and you, Laura, will be taking a varying forty-hour schedule here plus some overtime, if necessary. A cakewalk: mostly sitting at the desk at the entrance and occasional patrols to stretch your legs, say hello to your partner when you get to the fourth floor. The gaps in your post will be parsed among officers looking for extra work and who have no knowledge whatsoever of our investigation. Ordinarily these positions are assigned to officers approaching retirement or as the aforementioned random supplemental income. In your case, you're a graduate student with an erratic schedule and you've been given this detail as part of your training with the Sheriff's office. Fortunately for all of us, you had already decided to seek out the detective grade as soon as you entered the department. Since you haven't actually worked any cases yet, though, no one outside your department and your circle of family and friends actually knows that you're a detective. Congratulations on your first case, by the way."

Sol groaned internally at this. *Wonderful. They're giving me a complete amateur for this. Does it get any richer?*

"Sol, being the actual law librarian, will be taking charge of the newly opening law library annex. Since the Courts Administration and not the library system employ him, he didn't have to apply for the job or submit any information to the personnel director, who is also the head librarian. Nor does he have to report to anyone here and he is completely autonomous in the law library, which includes the cleaning schedule by the building's maintenance staff. The law library will have forty set hours that Sol will determine and the two of you will be the only ones with keys to his door.

"I just want to point out that there won't be any immediate gratification here so you'll have to be patient and think in the long term. So that we're completely clear and there's no undue pressure, the Bureau is not expecting you two to break this case alone. Not that you couldn't, either, and by all means we would not have specifically approached both of you if we didn't feel you were entirely capable of doing just that. But for the most part and the time being you're mainly observers taking notes as part of a larger investigation. As such, you're not to take any direct actions before clearing them with me first. Understood?"

Yes, they said.

"Right now, the most important objective involves an upcoming meet. We just need to know who, when and where. We want the meet to take place smoothly so we can find out how to recover the artwork most efficiently. You'll be looking for anything out of the ordinary: unusual patrons, maybe one of these librarians has a peculiar visitor, that sort of thing. We estimate it will take two to three weeks for you to get a grasp on the general daily workings of this place. As a precaution, I won't tell you who our leading suspects are so that you can achieve impartiality. The last item I'll give you now is a folder with data sheets for each of the twelve librarians. I don't think I have to tell you not to bring any of these papers with you when you're scheduled to be here. Get familiar with these files so you know who you're dealing with.

"There are a few more specifics I need to get out of the way today, I'll answer your questions and then we'll do the paperwork.

"The perpetrators of the theft are trying to unload a single piece to the Dutch royals but they've alluded to other paintings being available. To be precise, there was no indication they were referring to works by the same artist but paintings, quoting, of a 'similar nature'.

"And so now I have to tell you exactly what that nature is… Do either of you know anything about erotic art?"

"I barely know anything about art in general," answered Sol.

"I'd have to say the same, Agent Pines," said Lorelei.

"You can call me Robert, Laura. And Sol, I know for a fact that you've work a few cases involving stolen art."

"*Only* a few."

"Alright then, the basics. In this third folder you'll find a photo print copy of a picture sent to the royals with the ransom letter. As you can see, it's a sexually oriented painting but we'll concentrate on the composition and coloring in the event we have to identify the piece.

"Broadly speaking, even inside the art world the subject of erotic art is rather hush-hush. A great many famous artists have produced countless sensual works either for profit or pleasure but it's not widely discussed, much less very well documented. In the ancient world, Chinese, Greco-Roman, and such, there are countless examples. In modern history, however, it's been widely regarded as pornography and illegal in most countries. European countries have much laxer definitions on what qualifies as pornography but the U.S. has always been a bit stricter. Technically, this painting we're looking for is still restricted material. And aside from the base criminal aspects of the theft, there are more delicate details which you'll both be able to appreciate.

"The second most important aspect is that of provenance. Because we've been dealing with the preliminaries of the case we haven't been able to dedicate much time or effort toward establishing the line of ownership for this painting. Sol, you can see this is right down your alley. Not only are we conducting a theft investigation but we also have to build a legal defense against the suit by the Dutch government. We have to trace the movements of this piece and make absolutely sure that the Dutch actually have a case to bring forth. And then, of course, we have to determine how the work was removed from the museum in the first place, who took it, where it is now, and how we can get it back. Hence, your assigned partnership. So, questions…"

"How do you know it's a librarian involved?" asked Lorelei.

"The letter of solicitation I mentioned is signed 'Keeper of the Books', the method of response is directed through actual books in the library. It doesn't get any more obvious than that. Again, you'll see all of the evidence very soon. We just want a blind reconnaissance from the two of you right now."

"Is there an actual timeframe for the meet?" Lorelei again.

"The suggestion was Bastille Day, the French holiday of independence. Don't ask me why, it was specified in the letter and falls on July fourteenth. Yeah, Sol… "

"Not to be crass about it, but what exactly will be my payment schedule?," Sol asked. "I budget myself."

"Of course… I, uh, I guess it would be bi-weekly. I'm not really sure. I'll check with accounting and get right back to you on that, okay? Anything else?"

Neither Lorelei nor Sol had any more questions.

"Alright, then. Let's… um…. fill out the paperwork, shall we? Oh, I almost forgot. The nephew of the queen wants to meet the investigators. He's invited you for lunch at his penthouse at Harborside, twelve sharp. Just remember it's business, not social. And be discreet, please."

The forms completed, Special Agent Pines began to wrap up the meeting. He gathered all his papers, slid them into a dark tan leather briefcase. He saw that his two new hires were also ready to go.

"Well, welcome aboard. Thank you both for taking this on and joining our team. You're on duty now, but it won't be as strict as next week when you're in place here. Work your schedules out and get them to me by Friday. I'm going to walk you out to a rear exit closer to where I asked you to park."

A delivery area in the back of the library had a small bay door and a side entrance for personnel. Pines reminded them to contact him in a couple days and ushered them out, closing the door behind them.

There was a shy moment on the street as they knew they had to move away from the building quickly but didn't know where they were to go.

Pines knew this would happen and had directed it as though a brief scene in a short play. Sol truly resented being handled. He liked Pines somewhat, easily enough a good guy, just not the circumstances under which they'd met. He knew the man was just doing his job, but that job was to tell Sol what to do and what not to do. And to not tell him certain things that Sol felt he might want to know. Such as what the big rush was. Apparently there hadn't even been enough time for a formal introduction between their two supposedly select investigators. They'd been thrown together like a pair of dice. Lorelei took the lead.

"Hungry?" she asked.

"Always," he replied.

"There's this great diner in Secaucus on Route 7, it's in an industrial zone and out of the way, if you want."

"I think I know it. I'll follow you, I'm in that black four-door over there."

"That's my Jeep."

* * * *

At the diner, the coffee was strong and rich. The morning customers were only now trickling in. Sol noted that the kitchen looked especially well kept and indulged himself with a stack of pancakes. Lorelei said she loved the place's egg-white omelet rancheros.

"So you used to be an investigator?" she asked.

"Mm hmmm…"

"What was that like?"

"Most people usually mistook me for a cop."

"What kind of cases did you work?"

"Everything from insurance claims to criminal negligence."

"Did you like it?"

"At first. Then I noticed it was the same conclusion over and over."

"Which is…?"

"People will rob their own mothers for money."

"I'll bet."

He ventured a guess. "You've got family in law enforcement."

"Yes, I do. How did you know?"

"Just a hunch. You look like you've got it in your blood."

"Really?..."

"Sure." He took a few forkfuls so he wouldn't have to elaborate and she probably wouldn't ask further. Then he looked around for the waitress. There was bebop playing on a transistor radio next to the toasters at the back counter. Sounded like Dizzy or Bird, you couldn't hear it too well.

She was studying his face and his movements. Economic motion, like a cat. Handsome, but almost without facial expression. Features of some vague European stock. The glasses obscured his eyes.

He turned to her and asked if she wanted to order anything else. One more coffee she answered.

"What's your take on all this, Laura? From what you can tell so far, really, right now. Because I'll be up front with you and tell you I feel like we were invited to the party at the last minute just to help clean up the mess afterwards."

"What do you mean? It's just a stolen property investigation with a damages claim. You must have done this kind of thing before…"

"Yeah, but usually the stuff has a halfway decent chance of being recovered. These high price items very rarely get returned. That much I know."

"So you're saying we shouldn't even bother trying?"

"No, not that. We have to try. I just have this nagging suspicion that maybe they're just using us and our job titles to close out the case and a settlement, sort of fill the blanks and we sign off on the last lines on the last day."

Her lightly auburn eyebrows furrowed the tiniest bit, her bright green eyes became a little darker and he could tell he'd just taken some of the joy out of all this for her. Her lower, half-swollen lip rose up.

"That's kind of a pessimistic way to start off, isn't it? What about the meeting Pines was talking about?"

"How are we supposed to know what we're looking for without having seen that letter? I don't like walking into anything blindly."

"Maybe you're just being impatient."

"Maybe. Or maybe I know the Feds are always playing chess, making moves weeks and months ahead of time. They've got these little scripts for us to play out, so I'll play it out. Sounds like free money to me."

"Uh, huh… So you're saying you're just going to be going through the paces on this?"

"Look, I'm a professional and I'll do everything required of me in this case, as with any work I do. But I'm not going to delude myself that we're going to crack an international stolen art ring and collect a reward in the span of eight weeks. It takes years to do that. Moreover, to do my job properly I need all the information at the start of things and I resent it when it's withheld. So, until I do get that information, I'm not gonna work myself up over it. Besides, I have to somehow magically squeeze two large rooms of books, files, periodicals and equipment into some corner of one room on the fourth floor within forty-eight hours and then sit in that corner eight hours a day twiddling my thumbs and *afterwards* have to work on this thing in my private time. So you'll forgive me if I'm not exactly overjoyed. I assure you, Laura, I will do everything I know how to the best of my ability. I didn't want this job but I do need the money. And if they want me shuffling papers for two months that's what they'll get. I'll just be happily collecting the paychecks."

How callous! She didn't know exactly how or why but she felt offended. What kind of attitude was that? How could she work with someone like him? And was there any substance to what he was saying?

"Okay, well," she replied, "we all have our personal styles. You know this is my first case and I'm going to take it completely seriously and objectively, despite your view of it. I appreciate your opinion and I hope I can count on your assistance, if I should need it."

"Fair enough. You have my complete and unconditional cooperation. Where do we start?"

The waitress walked over with Sol's order of eggs over easy, sausage, toast and home fries and Lorelei's coffee.

"Review the files."

How about tomorrow night?"

"What?!"

"I missed my workout this morning. I don't feel right when that happens. Plus we still have that lunch with Prince Frou Frou later. That by itself should count as a day's work."

"That's four hours from now."

"Three. We should reconnoiter an hour beforehand to go over what you learn from the files."

She started to give him a piece of her mind and stopped herself. There are all kinds of people out there, she reminded herself, and once in a while you find yourself forced to work with one of the difficult ones. If there was a personality clash, there was still a job to be done.

"Alright, Sol. I can see where you're coming from. Here's my card. Call me around eleven, whenever you're ready." She finished her coffee, put a ten-dollar bill on the table and left.

* * * *

Harborside is what it sounds like, except that in Jersey City it's surrounded not by quaint seashore shacks but by towering steel office and luxury residence towers which reductively mirror the older skyscrapers of Manhattan that they gaze across the river at. This and Exchange Place was where a large number of financial companies had relocated in the early nineteen-nineties to save money off New York rents. There are no actual docks or marinas in this neighborhood; all the boat slips and launches are a quarter mile north at Pavonia-Newport.

Knowing the scarcity of parking in the area, they'd agreed to take one car and he picked her up at home. He couldn't help admiring how lovely she was in a classy white skirt ensemble. She noticed he had changed his tie for one with tiny blue diamonds. While they were driving Sol mentioned that he'd taken a cursory glance at the case history and noticed that the 'Prince', as he'd referred to him, was actually a Duke, as well as the person who'd taken charge of the matter on behalf of his aunt, the Dutch Queen. She'd seen that as well, said Lorelei.

They had a half hour to kill when they got to the waterfront and sat on a bench at the piers below the duke's building. There was a yacht lazing in the river and a ferry farther south approaching Ellis Island but otherwise no water traffic. Even the clouds were taking their time crossing the sky.

She asked if he'd taken a look at the profiles of the suspects and he answered 'no', that in this case he preferred to meet them in person first, and then review the collected data. She mentally checked it off to methodologies.

"Well, they're definitely a… uh… I guess a wide assortment would be the best way to put it."

"Good. So we know they're not clones."

"I read your file, too, Sol. But you probably figured I would."

"And?"

"Not bad for someone with no family."

"Do what you can with what you get."

"Exactly. Lotta huge gaps, though…"

No reply. They sat in silence until it was time to head upstairs. In the lobby the doorman was waiting for them. By name, he asked each of them their shoe sizes. He explained that the housekeeping staff maintained a supply of velvet slippers for the Duke's visitors, at his royal behest. The slippers were discarded after each use, he assured them. A security guard escorted Lorelei and Sol to the elevator and up to the penthouse.

Inside they were led by a sturdy fortyish East Asian man to an expansive great room in the center of which was an assortment of priceless-looking chairs and lounges all facing a gigantic wall-ensconced television screen. The majordomo disappeared. There in front of the TV was a twenty-something man sprawled along a large chaise, dressed only in dark red silk pajama bottoms and robe, with a big bag of potato chips munching away happily. Good looks but somewhat doughy, he was completely engrossed by whatever he was watching and didn't notice them until they were standing directly in front of him.

"Oh, hello! Is it twelve already?" he wondered aloud.

"'Fraid so, sir," Lorelei answered him. "Must be a good show," she added.

"I record all the reality TV shows. I can't seem to get enough of them. Or these salt and vinegar chips. Would you like some?" He extended the bag and then immediately withdrew it. "No, no, of course, you don't. Well, if you'll excuse me, I'll go get dressed."

"Of course," said Sol.

The duke shouted out into the open: "Harold! Harold, why the hell didn't you tell me they were here already?! You think that's funny, do you? We'll see how funny you think it is later. Get out here and show my guests to the terrace, you witless clod!"

He smiled at them and spread his hands out in a gesture of helplessness.

"I'll meet you on the terrace in a few moments," he said and hurried off.

Harold walked in smiling and asked them out to the terrace, the entrance to which was only one room away. He sat them at a wrought iron patio table set where three places had been set. He handed them each a sheet of cream stationery paper on which was printed a daily household lunch menu. An old grayed man appeared with a tray of water and cut lemons and Harold told them that his name was Edgar and that he'd be bringing them whatever they desired. Edgar spoke English fairly well, just in case, he explained. Edgar stood attendant and Harold removed himself somewhere again.

Lorelei asked for a salad and an iced tea and that was all. But Sol, naturally, had a field day giving Edgar a variety of instructions on a full-course luncheon.

The Duke emerged after some ten minutes and soon after was followed by Edgar and their food.

"Thank you for meeting me on such short notice," he said to them.

"Not at all, this is great, your Highness," Sol said irreverently, and leaned back in his chair.

"Actually, I'm not so high on the royal ladder, so please just call me Chase." He turned to Lorelei and extended his hand. "It's a pleasure to meet you, Detective McSherman."

"An honor, Chase," she replied.

The Duke then looked at Sol and smiled ambiguously. "And you must be Mr. Isistrato, the librarian." And again extended his royal hand.

Sol became serious again and said "Yes," receiving the Duke's gesture.

After they had some bites and niceties about the food, the Duke turned to the business at hand. "Perhaps you're wondering why I wanted to meet with you right away," he said.

"We would have had to meet eventually," Sol answered. "But the sooner the better."

"Definitely! But I also wanted to personally express a sense of urgency. You see, my aunt, the Queen, has entrusted me with representing our interest in this matter until some resolution is achieved. Unfortunately, that seems to be taking quite a bit longer than we'd originally anticipated and, frankly, it's starting to make me impatient."

"Special Agent Pines and his partner, Agent Macy, are obviously very capable individuals but neither they nor the venerable FBI are getting anywhere with this. Contrary to what anyone may think, our family is not interested in money damages. We simply want the piece back in our possession."

"But, Chase," Lorelei began, "if you'll forgive me, it seems to me that no one in your family noticed this piece missing in the first place. At least not for a long time, anyway. Why is it so important to retrieve it now?"

"Well, Detective, it's a matter of national pride, now. I don't know how much you know about Dutch history, but I'm sure you're aware that we were the first Europeans to explore and settle this area of America. The Oranges of your neighboring Essex County still bear our family name, even.

"I mention this because if, as the thief claims, this painting was originally our property and it was stolen here in Jersey City, which we essentially founded, it's imperative that such a valuable work by one of our national treasures be restored to its rightful place. Despite the fact that it most likely won't ever be displayed in public, it nonetheless remains an important part of Dutch heritage. But, of course, we obviously have no jurisdiction here and so must rely on your government's actions and resources to achieve its recovery."

"So you sued Hudson County to give us an incentive…" Sol said.

"It was the only recourse our attorneys could suggest. The FBI agents out of the Newark office are not locals and their art theft program is only in its inception. What was needed was an investigation by persons who know this terrain and its people as well as someone who can find their way around such archaic records as that of a hundred year-old library. And so here we are," he smiled boyishly.

"Well, that would explain a lot," remarked Lorelei. "Wouldn't it, Sol?" She gave him a pointed look.

"It's a start," he muttered. "But just out of curiosity, let's say we do get this painting back for you. Are you still going to seek damages?"

"We're not short of money, Mr. Isistrato. The suit would be dropped once we have the work in our possession."

"And what do you have besides the thief's assertion to prove that this piece really is originally property of your family and country?" Sol continued.

"I'm glad you asked. We have our archivists digging for the appropriate documents as we speak. Between what they find, what your offices will produce and what the thief claims to have, it should all balance out. We already hold a good number of Jan Steen's works. One more won't come as a surprise."

Lorelei interposed. "Whatever the outcome, I assure you we'll be doing our best to arrive at a satisfactory conclusion for everyone. Lunch was wonderful but we really should be getting back to work."

"You're more than welcome, Detective. Feel free to stop by whenever you like. Half the time I'm bored to death around here. You, as well, Mr. Isistrato. If I can be of any assistance at all, please don't hesitate to ask. You can always leave a message for me through the lobby staff."

* * * *

Descending in the elevator they didn't speak until they were halfway down.

"So what do you think now, Sol? Still think the Feds are pawning us?"

"Absolutely. They're giving the royals exactly what they asked for to cover themselves."

There was some sense to this, she thought, but it didn't change the fact that there was a stolen painting out there that she'd been ordered to help find, whatever people's personal motivations were.

"Everything is politics, you know. I just know I have a job to do."

"Me, too, Laura. And for the next three days it means being a mover. So I'm going uptown to start packing. Where can I drop you off?"

"The museum. I'll immerse myself in art for a while then get a list of the staff. I can take a taxi home."

4.

<u>Caleb Soter</u>

"The great artists of the world are never Puritans,
and seldom even ordinarily respectable."
- H.L. Mencken, *Prejudices, First Series, 16*

"See, I'm stuck in a city
but I belong in a field"
- The Strokes, 'Heart In A Cage', <u>First Impressions Of Earth</u>, 2006

The first day of summer was one of Sol's four private holidays. More than any traditional occasions or even his own birthday, it was this day, the other solstice and the two equinoxes that were the days of his years that he felt anything close to celebratory. Maybe it was some old pagan blood or his having lived his life in a temperate zone, but the four markers for the change of seasons were his special days. It was a solitary life. The festivities planned consisted of an immersion in books and creative meals for himself and his pets.

It was still cool in the early morning and he sat in the back yard with a cup of coffee listening to birds rising. In that one quiet hour before the day's noise began he drew out his line of research.

Despite what he thought he knew before, this new project showed Sol how very little he actually did know about art as a whole. Forgetting the thousands and thousands of contemporary and recent artists, there were all these innumerable unknowns in the times of the masters on into antiquity. He could cite and describe the major movements and name examples of the principle works and artists, but that, he realized, was merely a glimpse upon the greater expanse. And, that was just considering Western art.

As far as erotic art in general, he was even more clueless. He remembered the Kama Sutra pictures and the odd naughty strays at Japanese exhibits, but here was this vast hidden world of erotic masterpieces dispersed among the wealthy nations that he had never imagined. He couldn't even begin to guess at the unspoken millions of dollars involved, both in legitimate transactions and in the underworld.

46

Fortunately for him that wasn't his job; he'd been hired to track down a single piece by a distinctive painter. Because he was no expert, Sol figured he needed a crash course on Mr. Jan Steen. And since the main library happened to have the largest art history collection in the area, he figured that would be the most logical place to start. No one there had seen his face yet in connection to the law library and he would be in and out without anyone noticing him. That was his first mistake in the case.

Clever as he was, Sol thought that the after-school hour would be the best for him to move about unnoticed, what with all the traffic. Sure enough, there they were: school uniforms and no uniforms, chewing gum, electronic noise amplifiers, loud, squealing conversations about nothing and plenty of them. But in the fine arts section there was no one. It seemed like the one area that no one was interested in.

He'd checked ahead, of course, found the numbers he needed and headed straight there: the 759's, about Dutch painters, decimal .9 for Jan Steen. Seemed the guy was a lover of life. Took on his father's craft of brewery, painted joyful scenes and loved his family. Had two wives, lived out last fifteen years with the second and her sister. But what Sol needed to know was about his patrons and his painting methods. He was making his way down the aisle when he was caught by surprise.

"Can I help you find what you're looking for?" came the male voice behind me.

Sol turned sharply to his left. Out of habit, he quickly sized the man up. A little more than his own height, longish dark brown hair, a medium-light beard, academic clothing and, sure enough, he was carrying a stack of books. It was a librarian.

Contact. Already. Sol had to employ redirection.

"I thought I remembered where the symphonic transcriptions were… Tchaikovsky No. 4." he improvised.

"Well, technically you're in the right section. But we have so many of them there's a special area in the back by the over-sized books. I can help you look through them."

"Oh, that's alright. I can find it once I get there. Thank you, though. Thank you very much." Sol turned and headed straight for the back wall before the other man had even finished saying 'Okay. You're welcome'.

The guy had moved up on Sol so quietly and easily that it, of course, irritated him. He made it a point to always be aware of, at minimum, the twenty-foot radius around him. And still this librarian had spooked him. Was it the bookshelves and carpet, old and thinned as it was, acting as buffers of sound? Was it a librarian thing to move about in silence like that?

No matter, he reasoned, he'd probably just been distracted by the books themselves.

At the music transcriptions he thumbed through the Russian composer's works, noticed two versions of the 'Pathetique' but didn't pull either. For the lie, they were simply not the one he'd been looking for. He made his way out of the building, this time successfully unnoticed. But that would be the last time he could use that library for any work on this case.

* * * *

Earlier that day Lorelei had decided she wanted to see some results right away. Yesterday afternoon she'd spent a leisurely hour surveying the museum and discreetly observing what she could of its activities and personnel. Then she'd gone home straightaway to the files of the case and reviewed them for the second time since she'd received them. She called Pines on their direct line and said she needed to look at the recent and current security schedules before she could finalize her own. He agreed that it made sense to do so and said there was no reason she couldn't get an early start by visiting the library as a preliminary.

She'd arisen feeling keen and powerful. It was a glorious day and she'd taken Mister for an invigorating run through Lincoln Park. If it was true that the case was now dragging, it was all the more imperative that she not take Sol's laid-back approach but dive right in.

She, also, had a double duty. She was now, if only temporarily, the security of the building (safe as it might be) as well as sharing their secret objective. She decided firmly that she would get the job done and just maybe even enjoy the experience while it lasted.

She dressed business casual with mid-sized heels, black slacks and a white button-down but left her hair loose. A playful wind was dancing through downtown and it hurried her through the doors of the library where a young Hispanic rookie cop jumped to attention at the security desk when she breezed in. He turned into a puppy when she told him what she was there for.

He explained that he was just picking up overtime and that he'd only had this detail once before, but he'd be happy to show her around. The regular guard, who Lorelei would be replacing, he told her, had left a number where she could be reached during the day. Lorelei immediately called the number from the desk and spoke to an Officer Murray, who happened to be nearby and amiably agreed to meet her in a half-hour to go

48

over daily procedures. In the meantime, Lorelei asked the younger officer for a full tour. He didn't really know the full layout of the place but the resourceful young man made it up as they went along.

On the first floor was the staff lounge (which they skipped), the literacy program room (unoccupied at the moment), and the Domenico Benedetti Children's Room, where an African American woman somewhere in her forties was reading to an enraptured group of pre-school children.

The rookie, Ramirez, suggested they take the elevator to the third floor, the highest it could go, then walk up to the fourth floor and work their way down. The library's janitor, an older man of indecipherable origin, doubled as the elevator operator. He didn't speak. The elevator was the original Miami Elevator Co. model 1215 with only the fewest mechanical improvements since its installation. As she took in all the old wood, the brass scissor gate, the antique glass, it occurred to Lorelei that she'd been using the Five Corners branch of the city's library system for so long that she couldn't even remember the last time she'd been to the main building aside from yesterday's briefing. Listening to the loud hum and creaking of the old lift she fully understood now why Agent Pines had instructed them to use the stairs.

The fourth floor is part of a trapezoid roof and doesn't accommodate elevator shafts as in modern buildings. Even the stairwell leading up to it is the narrowest part of the whole. Suddenly Lorelei remembered a grade school field trip to the museum some fifteen years ago. She didn't remember much except that the class had had to walk all the way up those four floors.

The two rooms there still had the ornate trappings, complete with buttoned-leather doors, but were now occupied with tome-filled shelves, file cabinets and research equipment where once there had been art and artifacts. They peered in each briefly so as to not disturb anyone and walked down to the third floor where all the administrative offices were, including the public information desk and the MIS department. It was lunch time so they decided not to bother anyone just yet.

The second floor was the heart of the library itself as there were the lending and reference rooms, as well as a store/gift shop. Lorelei and her guide, despite his willingness to spend more time with her, agreed that she would have ample chance for a more thorough instruction when her actual tour of duty commenced. He'd been away from the security desk a full half hour now and they could expect Officer Murray at any moment.

When she arrived, the woman filled out the rest of Lorelei's orientation as they walked through the basement and all the other areas hidden from the public's view. Lorelei noted a large file cabinet labeled 'Library Records Pre-1960'.

Murray confided that it was a very cushy job and that the worst she'd have to contend with were loud groups of kids and the occasional vagrant challenge. A police radio was standard and the south precinct was only three blocks away for any emergencies. Lorelei asked to see the scheduling for the post and the two worked out a schedule for the next two weeks, to begin tomorrow. Officer Murray was more than happy to take an extended weekend. Officer Ramirez gallantly offered to be on hand at all times and Murray cracked that he'd never been so available while she'd been in charge. They all shared a laugh when he stammered and blushed. Lorelei thanked them for their time and made her exit.

* * * *

No big deal, Sol thought, *they'll have to see enough of me in the coming days as it is.* He was about to head south on Christopher Columbus Drive when he decided to just begin getting the whole thing over with and turned around to go back uptown.

At the law library he called two office moving companies and asked for estimators to stop by that very afternoon for a job order to be scheduled for the following two business days. He poked around the aisles and began making a list of the essential items for a compacted collection. He began pulling out the state and federal statutes and their addendums, the journals, dictionaries and commentaries. Anything not in this barebones transfer would have to be placed on next-day delivery order and Sol would have to come by and pick these titles up himself. More joy.

He walked over to the back of his office to the window that looked out onto downtown Manhattan from the highest point in Jersey City. He blew out a big sigh, thinking of the non-view he would endure the next couple months. He picked out some acid jazz tracks on the computer and started cleaning out his desk.

The salesmen were prompt and Sol went with the second of them, arranging for a crew of four to begin the packing and moving at eight o'clock next morning. After closing the library he gathered enough books for a good start. He looked around and realized that a few machines would also have to be carefully wrapped for the ride downtown. It was six. The rest of the details could wait until tomorrow. He left.

* * * *

The sun was setting somewhere over the Hudson River as Caleb Soter walked home after work. It blazed up all the avenues he crossed with a brilliance that contrasted sharply against the streets darkened by building shadows.

He took his time, strolling, taking in all the details; the children playing in Van Vorst Park, the young woman walking a furry little gray dog on Barrow Street, a small group of teenagers goofing off in front of a defunct diner at Bright and Grand. It was one of those days that simply made you feel glad to be alive.

Two years earlier, he and his girlfriend had scored a great little walk-up on River Street before the real estate sharks had come swimming around. After the first year they'd gotten a great price to buy and now all of a sudden the numbers around them were skyrocketing. They laughed at their luck because they had only been investing in each other.

For the moment, though, their budget was still tight as they were both still paying off their student and auto loans. Just one more year and they'd be clear. *What the hell,* he thought, *I think I'll take her out tonight, anyway. We'll go to that little French place downtown.*

* * * *

Sol reasoned that he'd more or less met this first librarian already so it was time to check out his file.

Caleb Soter: Twenty-eight years old, born in Jersey, but decided to go to school all the way out west. First California, then Oregon, finishing his M.L.S. in Portland. In Jersey City since 'ninety-nine. No mention of his parents or other family. Volunteers at a couple of local senior centers, though. A note about a recent home purchase with a corresponding note from the federal bean counters that it was a clear deal. The picture showed an amiable young man with penetrating eyes.

Okay, then. Pleased to meet you, my fellow librarian. He moved on to the general file and reviewed the case history, making notes on a legal pad. And then he took out the picture of the painting.

It shocked him, to his own surprise.

Not for the explicitness, but because it was so damned beautiful.

The drawing was impeccable, lines perfect, jubilant and vibrant colors pulled you in and the raw emotion held you. This was nothing gratuitous: there was love in their eyes. Could these two people have actually existed? (There was so much detail!) A naked fortyish man held in his powerful arms a luscious, giving woman in a moment of shared ecstasy, her thick crimson gown almost still on her body. They were not strangers. Husband and wife, maybe? Was it a commissioned work?

One thing was sure: there would be no mistaking *that* work if and when Sol ever came across it. There was even music in it, in the form of a discarded lute in a corner of the room. Steen definitely seemed to enjoy the music of his day, Sol noted. And to think that he was known to have completed around five hundred undocumented works. Could many of them have been erotica?

* * * *

Lorelei set out her freshly pressed uniform, shined her policeman shoes and checked her equipment, just to start the following morning on the right note. Anthony was with friends and Mister had had a full day and was now sprawled out on the carpeting in her bedroom. The Wielwowski's were winding down their usual early evening and even the traffic outside was light. She had the whole sofa to herself.

She was thinking about thieves. If this particular thief she was looking for really was a librarian, how odd was that? Or was it true that every single one of us is capable of committing a crime?

* * * *

It was night, and he had an appointment. Very few people would mistake Sol for a jazz musician but that only illustrated peoples' preconceptions. For Sol, jazz was not a dirty word. Jazz just meant free. Play any way you feel. Despite the history, the media, the mainstream, for him jazz was a non-term. Somebody called it jazz when they were feeling free and it still worked for Sol to invoke that ideal state. And jazz was blues and blues was rock and rock was funk and punk, disco and house, rap, hardcore and techno. It was all just release. When classical composers shocked society with passion and doubt, when swing made the room go wild, when rock 'n' roll drove everyone crazy, and the music at the end of the twentieth century let people lose their minds, it was really all just jazz. And jazz was what had gotten Sol banging the drums when he was thirteen.

Today he could play with just about anyone. The hardest stuff was double-bass heavy metal and odd global syncopations but he could still hold his own with these. When he had been scraping together funds through college he'd been able to hire out as a session drummer. It was just one of a dozen ways he'd found to make money in his youth. Though he was very good at it, he'd never considered drumming as anything more than a hobby and extra cash. He still played with a few groups once in a while for relaxation, and for occasional release.

One of these was a regular session, every other Thursday night. It was mostly for the purpose of keeping everyone in practice but occasionally they played before live audiences under a name of convenience. They were simply a band of musicians who had met along the way and enjoyed each other's styles and skills.

There was Frank Sorrento on keyboards, Mike Richards, who switched off between guitar and saxophone and Sol's old friend Eddie Dawes on bass. Back in the racially tense years of their youth and in a mostly white high school he was too often referred to as Black Eddie. He was the only friend Sol had kept from those days. He was a little crazy but still fun to play music with.

They would all meet at a rehearsal studio out at the end of West Side Avenue near Route 440 at eight o'clock and play until ten. Each would bring material they wanted to work on and in the second hour after a short break they would amuse themselves with improvisations. It was always something to look forward to and often they had surprise visitors join in.

** * *

Friday morning Lorelei was all business. Just for the first day she didn't joke around once. She saw Sol come in with a large box and they merely nodded at each other. Later in the day she had to clear the movers for loading of the law library through the rear of the building. She and Sol had stood side by side for nearly twenty minutes without either uttering a sound.

53

5.

<u>Rebecca Goode</u>

"I conclude that musical notes and rhythms
were first acquired by the male or female progenitors of mankind
for the sake of charming the opposite sex."
- Charles Darwin, <u>The Descent Of Man</u>, 1871

"Music and women I cannot but give way to,
whatever my business is."
- Samuel Pepys, Diary, 1666

All cities have ghosts. The older the town, the more lost souls haunt its streets.

For the past year she'd often been waking up deep in the night, morning actually, at almost the same hour, somewhere between three and four. She tried not to think about the fact that a lot of the times it was at exactly three thirty-three; that was the stuff of movies. Still, she knew very well that there was much more to life than meets the eye so she simply accepted that something new was happening in her own life. She reasoned that since she'd only been living in this new apartment building, which was rather noisy, for less than a year, her mind and her spirit naturally sought out the quietest times. And if it weren't for the dreams that inevitably preceded her early rising she could write it off to biology.

They were strange, sometimes even scary and violent. And for someone who lived as ordinary and uneventful a life as she did, it made her wonder. She didn't watch TV much, not as many movies as she used to watch, and also didn't go out much, either. So why all the hyperactive sub-consciousness? Was it what she was reading these days? The times? She thought she knew the answer but didn't agree with it. Half of it was psychological, the other half biological, all natural, she concluded.

Whatever the explanation, she arose in the dark between midnight and dawn. It had been that way often throughout her entire life and now was one of those times. The silence was priceless. She could hear herself think uninterrupted for a few hours.

54

Fitting that it was a Monday morning and a new moon. She could feel a sense of regeneration within herself. She lit a few candles and heated the teakettle. She looked out onto an empty street washed clean after last night's rains. She opened a window in her living room and let in the fresh air. This morning she would again take a new look at her life.

* * * *

Today was his first official day at the public library. Not a life-changing event but he would make the best of it.

The owner of the gym always grumbled whenever Sol arrived before him in the morning. So what if he was a few minutes late? Everyone else had the decency to wait until six so he could enjoy his coffee and paper. Sol was a non-cop and unfriendly, but paid his dues on time for a couple years now and the schedule did say five-thirty, so the retiree merely harrumphed behind his desk and reading glasses on those days.

Sol gave all his apprehensions and discomforts to the punching bag. When he was warmed up he hit the weights as hard as he could. When he couldn't lift anymore, he limbered up and ran one of his favorite routes home through the warehouse district on the Hoboken border and up the sharp incline from the Holland Tunnel entrance to 139. A long hot shower and he was at peace with the world again.

* * * *

Rebecca would skip the black today. It was a blue Monday. She picked out a rich blue ensemble that set off her eyes. White blouse and black heels finished the set. She wore her hair up in a sexy little bun.

Outside the streets smelled like a river. She left earlier than she needed to and woke everyone up as she walked. Decided to get a light breakfast at the Korean place, sit in a corner and watch the world get ready for work. It kept things in perspective.

Where was she in this swirl of living? Alone, to begin with. That didn't bother her as much as her family being so far away. But she did have her friends from work which was great and the next best thing. Sometimes actually better.

She'd been in this city three years now and had grown to love it. If she wanted the big city and all its glories, it was ten minutes away and always within sight. This was a comfortably smaller version. There was nightlife and a quietly happening arts scene. She was never bored. But it might be nice to have a boyfriend to enjoy it with sometimes.

* * * *

When Sol walked in he saw an elder woman at the top of the lobby stairs standing with an equally older man in a maintenance uniform. They were both smiling. Behind them and to the right, seated at a large office desk was Lorelei in uniform. She looked up at him, serious as a tombstone.

"They said you were punctual," the lady greeted. They moved forward to walk down the stairs but Sol was at the top in seconds.

"I'm Mariette Savoy, the head librarian.

She had an accent, European of some sort. She was dressed elegantly without any extravagance, a prim violet suit, regal white hair and pearl earrings. No glasses.

"Sol Isistrato," as he cradled her hand, and she grasped his firmly.

"Yes, of course. And this is Mr. Klein. He's in charge of the building's maintenance."

The man didn't speak but smiled again and offered his hand.

Savoy resumed, "You have some separate plumbing on the fourth floor and a dumb waiter and brand new lighting. Just in case, you have his extension on your desk phone."

"Excellent," Sol said, "Thank you, Mister Klein. Hopefully I won't have to trouble you much at all." Still the man just smiled.

"I'm sure you have plenty to do and I don't want to take too much of your time, I just wanted to introduce you to the other librarians. I know it's only temporary for you but we do want to make you feel welcome."

"I already do, thank you," he replied.

"Everyone's upstairs in the circulation room. Let's take the elevator." The three started to walk toward the lift when Savoy suddenly stopped.

"Oh! I'm so sorry! I almost forgot!" She took his elbow and gently drew him toward Lorelei.

"This is Lorelei McSherman, a sheriff's deputy. She's in charge of security. She's *also* new here. I'm so sorry, Lorelei, Officer Murray used to insist on being left alone." Lorelei stood and walked around her desk. *Wow, she can even make a uniform look sexy*, Sol thought.

"Not a problem, Ms. Savoy. I didn't even notice." Sol and Lorelei shook hands.

In the elevator Savoy waited a few moments before speaking again.

"I'm aware that you are autonomous in the law library but we have a tradition, if not an official procedure, here that you have the choice of participating in. Everyone has their individual niches in the library but the Reference and Information desks are the only two that we all take turns at covering. The only other area like that used to be the law books and government documents which you'll now turn in to the law library. Frankly, it was the one section that no one liked to be in, so now that you're here there's a slight sense of relief." They stepped out onto the second floor. "While we're all trained for general research, no one really knows much legal research. That, and it's very rare to have a patron up there...." Sol grinned smugly inside of himself.

Through the glass doors of Circulation Sol could see a group of people seated and standing around one of the larger reading tables. He opened the door as Savoy led him in.

"I told you he would be on time," she announced. "People, this is Sol Isistrato, our new law librarian. Sol, this is…"

And she began naming everyone left from right. A man here, a woman there, and, whoah!, a hot redhead!, ouch!, a large man slumped over, next to him a young, thin man with glasses similar to his own, then a small young cutie with big brown eyes and silky brown hair, the man from the other day... The head librarian was talking but Sol couldn't hear her. Lorelei downstairs, these hotties up here…all these beautiful women already, he thought, *Who let the fox into the henhouse?!* A thin, older white man with wire-rim glasses; a pleasant looking African woman, a man who looked Indian, and then her! Rebecca! From last week! She's a librarian! Her eyes went wide behind her glasses. They locked on each other. Geek love! Savoy finished at Rebecca and Rebecca raised a meek hand. Sol smirked.

"So, I told Sol about Reference and Information and I'm sure he'll be willing to pitch in. Won't you, Sol?" asked Savoy.

"Eh? Oh! Yes! Reference and information. Absolutely! I'd be glad to start tomorrow, even. I'll have the law library set up by the end of the day."

"Wonderful!" exclaimed Savoy, "The information desk is a perfect introduction to the library! And you can start getting to know everyone right away."

"I'm looking forward to it." He looked at Rebecca. She was squirming in her seat.

"Alright, then, let's get back to work." Savoy gestured toward the locked door where there were three people already outside waiting to get in and peering at the meeting. "I hope everyone has a great day." Since Sol was closest to the door, he raised a hand and waved toward all the librarians, turned and hurried to let the patrons in. He bid them good morning and flew upstairs.

Ain't that something?!, he was thinking. How would this work out? Would she pretend it never happened? Or worse, would she pretend he didn't even exist? Or was there a chance they could pick up where they left off?

He went about his work on auto-pilot, organizing, cleaning and arranging, but he couldn't stop thinking about her. Her aliveness, her lovely body, her voice and humor and smart conversation. And then she walked in.

"Hi, Sol," only taking a few steps inside.

"Hello, Rebecca." He put down the cables he had in his hand and also took a few steps toward her.

"Look, I just wanted to apologize and explain for the way I left. I lost control of myself and I'm not used to that. You're a very nice guy and I was a little embarrassed that I jumped into bed with you so fast but it had been sometime since I'd been with anyone and we were having so much fun and the liquor had me acting like someone I'm not and I honestly thought I'd never see you again and I really did like you but guys are so weird about sex sometimes and you were sound asleep and I was suddenly wide awake and leaving a note seemed so cliché but-"

"-Rebecca. Take it easy. It's the twenty-first century and we're both single. Don't sweat it."

She closed her eyes as she turned her face upward and exhaled a long whoosh. "Thank you, Sol. You really are a sweetheart." And she walked up to him and quickly kissed him on the cheek and backed away.

"I was just hoping maybe we could go out some time, like on a regular, normal date, maybe…," he gambled.

"Oh… No… I'm so sorry, Sol. I can't do that. I never date anyone I work with. I learned that one a long time ago. It just doesn't work."

Sol felt like his heart had just jumped down into his stomach but never let it show.

"Just my luck," he said smiling, "This gig is like a cruel joke by the gods."

"But that doesn't mean we can't hang out!…" she offered earnestly. The trouble with this woman was that she was sincere. It might have been better for Sol if she'd been a cold-hearted man-eater.

"Sure thing," he replied, knowing full well he would never attempt it. He walked over to his desk, opened a drawer and pretended to fumble for something. She looked around, slightly uncomfortable. She caught him staring at her.

"What?" she asked.

"Just wow. You've really got that whole sexy librarian thing going, don't you?"

"Oh, please. Don't you know by now that it's a myth? Those are either just chicks who read a lot and wish they got laid more or chicks who get laid a lot and wish they read more."

"But you're real."

"You're damned right I am." She smiled at him that beautiful smile of hers.

"So you're not mad, okay?" She pleaded.

How could he possibly be mad at her? "I'm all grown up now, Rebecca." He assured her.

"Perfect! We'll have fun working together! You're the thirteenth librarian!"

"Really. And that's supposed to bode well?"

"Of course. Don't be superstitious. Thirteen is a good number."

"If you say so."

"It is. I'll tell you more later. I asked Isobel to cover me just for five minutes." She held out her hand in friendship.

"Friends it is," he said.

He couldn't help himself but gaze longingly at her backside as she walked away. And she knew it.

6.

<u>Johannes Claasenburger</u>

"Jazz came to America three hundred years ago in chains."
- Paul Whiteman, *Jazz*, 1926

Sol was trying to organize his desk when he heard a rumble coming up the stairs. It grew louder as it approached and he could make out two voices; one feminine and loud, and one masculine and considerably louder because of its depth. But they weren't arguing. They seemed to be debating something passionately. Sol, as usual, would mind his own business. But it blew open his door.

A woman with long loose graying hair and a flower-print dress hopped in, turned behind her and yelped, "Ha!" She turned again and smiled a mischievous smile at Sol. And then a giant of a man filled the doorway, raising his right hand in greeting as he ducked in.

"Hello," Sol said.

"Hi!" said the woman.

"How you doin', man?!" said the man. A huge frame, barrel chest and dangerous arms.But a face that made you think you knew this person when you knew you didn't. A big, wild brown beard and neatly cut and combed brown hair on top. Blue-beige eyes that welcomed and challenged simultaneously.High cheeks that laughed with you, and at you.

Sol stood. *And our first contestants are…*

"We're here to introduce ourselves personally. I'm Phoebe, and I'm all over this place. But if you ever need me for anything someone usually knows where I am."

"Sol. Nice to meet you. You'll always know where I am."

"Well, then, I'll have to make a point of coming to visit once in a while." She had a genuinely friendly face, wise eyes, no makeup.

"Of course." *Actually, dear, you needn't trouble yourself…*

"John," said the large man, his hand enveloping Sol's. "I'm your neighbor across the hall. But I'm never there. It gets so quiet on this floor you fall asleep. So I go play racquetball withthe local businessmen instead.

There's a great gym in the Town & Country Bank buildingwith a bunch of courts. Do you play?"

"Um, no. I don't think I ever have." *At least it'll be quiet up here…*

"And in the afternoons," interjected Phoebe, "he sneaks off with the other boys for beer and pizza."

"Geez, Marin, what are you, a news reporter?" John's voice boomed naturally. "It's not every day!... And anyway, beer is good. Civilization was built on it. That and guns. And a lot of sitting around talking.With beer and guns. Maybe Sol would like to come along some time."

"Sure, some time…" *Not gonna happen, bud…*

"There you go, soldier! I'll warn you now, Sol, in this in place, we men have to stick together. We're outnumbered and the women are actively working to overthrow the balance of power!" He gave Sol a Santa Claus wink.

"Maybe that's not such a bad idea..." Sol suggested.

"I told you!" Phoebe nearly shouted gleefully.

"You don't' know anything, Marin," John countered, "He's just saying that to make nice on his first day. All men instinctively fear a woman's world. Except, of course, men who wish they were women..."

"Oh!" Phoebe raised her left index finger, "You don't want to go there! Because we can get Greek right now."

"Um..." Sol began. They both looked at him. There was a pause.

"Right," said John. "I forget I never get anywhere with hippies. They're too damned accepting." He grabbed at all his pockets until he found a small spiral notebook and then a large brown-and-silver fountain pen. Tearing a sheet from the pad he leaned his bulk over Sol's desk and scribbled a phone number along with his initials, J.C. "In case you need me for anything, I'm never too far away. And if Savoy comes looking for me, I can be here in seconds. You'll cover for me if anybody ever does venture up here, won't you, old man? You seem like you have a good grasp on place and time."

"Got you covered, captain." Sol confirmed.

"Good man! And now, because it's Monday, I actually have some work to do before I can escape. Welcome aboard, Sol. Later, Phoebes. Much later..." And he jaunted off.

7.

<u>Phoebe Marin</u>

"Come sing me a bawdy song, make me merry."
(Falstaff) – Shakespeare, Henry IV, Part One III iii

"Don't let the theatrics fool you, we're actually great friends," she explained. "Rub his belly and out comes the kitten. Just like all of you." She flashed a naughty grin and placed a hand on her hip.

Sol's eyebrows twitched upward. She laughed heartily.

"Well, it's good to know you're still young enough to have some innocence left."

Sol tried to remember how to smile pleasantly. He was wondering if all the rest of the librarians were going to be parading through today.

"So I really just wanted to let you know that while everyone else will probably be keeping their distance from this room, at least at first, because they all dread the feeling of exile, I was pre-law in college before I made up my mind. I know my way around these materials and I'd be more than happy to cover for you if and when you need to run out for any reason. And you will at some point. Mariette will tell you this also since she knows it doesn't bother me to be up here."

"You don't say. Well, that's very kind of you, Phoebe. I might just have to take you up on that one of these days. Yes, I just might."

"And I'll be there for you. Do you need any help now? I can just let Mariette know where I'll be for a while."

"I've got it covered, but thank you."

"So you're only here for the summer..."

"That's what I'm told."

"But this set-up you've made in this room will stay the same way..."

"Well, I'd have to take these things back with me. I don't even know if anyone will use them this summer. Come the end of August I just have to move it all back uptown."

"Must seem like a waste of time for you."

Sol was struck by the statement and the woman now seemed more matronly than impish. "A job is a job," he said.

"No, it's not," she answered flatly. "It's a calling. One way or the other."

"I suppose you're right," he conceded.

"You don't seem the type to just settle for any old desk..."

"You'd be surprised." Now he felt like he was being interviewed.

"Great, I love surprises."

"Most women do."

"Excuse me?"

"No, excuse me, please. I'm sorry if that sounds sexist at all, there's none of that. It's just something I've observed over the years. Most women like surprises, most men don't."

"Uh huh..."

"Mars and Venus?" he pleaded. "Never mind, Phoebe, sometimes I talk too much."

"Hmmm... I think I'm going to have to keep my eye on you, Mr. Isistrato." She pointed her finger like a pistol and said, "See you later..."

* * * *

At the end of the day, as they say, you still have to face yourself in the mirror. And the only thing you can ever really hope for in this life is a peaceful sleep. Nightly, and at the end of that longest of all days.

Sol was feeling a little dirty, so he took yet another shower. Back in the days when he was in the thick of it he would sometimes have to shower up to three times a day.

Like them as he might as persons, one or more of these people was a thief. A thief he was being paid to catch. He turned on the news and pulled out the files.

Rebecca Goode: Age twenty-nine, at the library since '99, straight out of library school in Massachusetts. *Probably the closest she could get to Manhattan.* Runs the literacy program here, registered Independent voter, single, no dependents. Protestant descent but no religion specified currently. Lives downtown, the newly popular Hamilton Park area.

Johannes Claasenburger: Forty-five, ex-Marine (as if they ever stop being Marines); one tour in Eastern Europe, one in the Middle East, late '79; latecomer to his profession; former cartographer in New Hampshire, where he's from, apparently; member NRA *and* PETA? *Really...* Been at the main library six years, after two in the Greenville branch. Married, no kids. Lives in the suburbs.

Phoebe Marin: Age fifty-two, librarian since the early seventies in Baltimore, then Berkeley, then Chicago, then Prescott, AZ, then Gainesville, Florida, and finally Jersey City for the past five years. *Talk about someone who couldn't stay put...* Divorced twice, two grown children: one in Maine, one in Oklahoma, same last name. Greenpeace, Sierra Club, WWF, PETA. *No surprise there, Phoebes... Wonder if Claasenburger goes to meetings with her.* Lives next door in Bayonne.

Fine. Everyone is suspect. A job is a job, *just like I said*. Having begun to meet them, it became harder to believe. But such is life. No one is ever who they seem.

He called Pines and asked to see the incriminating letter of offer, the actual original. Sure, said Pines, but was Lorelei coming also?

"Didn't think to call her...," Sol puzzled.

"Well, would you please? We'll count it as the weekly meet. I'll call you with a location in fifteen minutes."

Anthony answered Lorelei's house phone and there was a mildly uneasy exchange between them before she came to the phone. He asked her to wait for Pines' call for the location, they'd be meeting in about an hour.

Bergenline Avenue through Union City and North Bergen is one of the most densely traversed main streets in the region. An already packed population and countless immigrants mix up and down this thin boulevard, one lane each way and at points even a one-way street. There was a very strong Latin American flavor, from Argentinians to Uruguayans. There were plenty of people on the street at all times.

Pines chose a large and popular restaurant at 39th. He was seated at a small table far in the back. He was dressed down, with even a baseball cap, Brewers. When Sol sat, the agent immediately slid over a thick sheet of paper contained in a clear plastic envelope; the letter. Using a dainty font it read:

(*No headings at all*, thought Sol.)

Your Majesty,

I have something that belongs to you and your family.

It is a painting by Dutch master Jan Van Steen.

I must warn you that it is one of his more explicit works.

If I didn't need the money I wouldn't ask. I also have dated proof that it was improperly acquired all along and I am no hero. I am asking 50,000 US dollars. Have your staff look into it and you will agree it is worth much, much more. The photo is a direct shot and I've included the negative. There are available others of a similar nature. Below is contact info through the main branch of the Jersey City Public Library, New Jersey, USA.

Signed, Keeper Of The Books

N 352.96 v.2 p.98

Pines handed him another plastic sheet protector with the envelope.
"It originated out of Aruba and was delivered by courier service to the Queen's Office in The Netherlands. The return address is non-existent."
"Can I feel the corner of the paper? Just the corner," Sol asked. Pines nodded. The fabric felt nice and expensive. Lorelei walked in and was shown the items. After ascertaining there was nothing else to cover, Pines asked them to wait at least fifteen minutes after he left before exiting themselves.

8.

<u>Information</u>

"One becomes a critic when one cannot be an artist,
just as a man becomes a stool pigeon when he cannot be a soldier."
- Gustave Flaubert, Letter to Madame Louis Colette, Oct. 22, 1846

Until about the late 1990's Jersey City was commonly referred to as "the sixth borough" of New York City. This was natural enough, since they were all settled by the Dutch at the same time as part of New Netherland and grew up together.

Back in 1609, when the Half Moon delivered Henry up his Hudson River he looked left and right, liked what he saw on both sides and recorded as much. Despite the fact that it wasn't what they had sent him for (that elusive shortcut to the East Indies) his Netherlands benefactors came as fast they could when they smelled money to be made off the abundance of forest and furry wildlife.

They seized upon the river's mouth as the ideal setting for a colony. A man named Michael Pauw was granted by the Dutch government a chunk of the west bank and he drew lines around the areas now Hoboken and Jersey City for a promise of no fewer than fifty settlers that he ultimately failed to produce. The Dutch East India Company bamboozled the locals for the island of Manahatta, where they set up headquarters and a fort, calling it New Amsterdam.

Pauw was the original and first of a long line of slumlords in the region. Because of his mismanagement of the colony and its people he was forced to relinquish his patroonship within three years. The Dutch sent a steady stream of authoritarian superintendents who built great houses for themselves and their families but all of which were unable to sustain a hard-won peace between the native neighbors and the poorer homesteaders which had previously been achieved in twenty years of early trading.

The unrest culminated in a slaughter of more than a hundred Lenape people on February 23, 1643, by newly arrived Director William Kieft who ordered a raid on a camp of refugees seeking shelter from tribal wars in the North. The attack was unauthorized by Kieft's superiors and unwanted by

66

the long-time colonists, but about a hundred twenty Dutch soldiers went about hacking up babies, throwing them into fires and the river, and forced the juveniles to watch as their parents were all drowned. The massacre set the stage for another two hundred years of hostility and bloodshed between locals and immigrants.

In the late 1660's, after decades of simultaneous fighting among Europeans in the Old World, the English finally succeeded in wrangling the New Netherland territory from the Dutch and created New York and New Jersey. Bergen Square in Jersey City was Jersey's oldest town.

And while Manhattan, being the city of the world and all, enjoys regular decade cycles of rebirth, her gimp, red-headed step-brother's fortunes drag up and down the hill in much longer time frames, more like generations-wise.

* * * *

Sol left a lunch cooler in his car and reported to the information area at 8:55, having passed an eager-beaver young Hispanic-looking security guard with only a wave. There were two rolling chairs and no one else around. A little after nine, some obvious regulars sauntered in.

He poked around the massive half-circle desk and tried to imagine what would be most useful. There were the little plastic cube trays with slips of scrap paper and short pencils, less than half of them sharpened.

He checked behind him at a case filled with an assortment of directories, reference manuals and alien bindings. Suddenly he felt a bit under prepared.

He heard a shuffling up front and turned to see the scrawny guy with the similar style glasses as his own. His clothes, a short-sleeved button-down, t-shirt underneath, dark blue slacks, a black windbreaker in his hand, all looked like they'd had to put him on when they all woke up together. Sol wasn't sure if the man's wavy black hair was a new style or simply uncombed. The man was grooming himself apishly and tightening his belt.

"Don't worry about that stuff, it hasn't been used in over a hundred years." He crashed
into the other chair and after a long sigh sat for a few minutes silently with his eyes closed before jumping awake again. "Okay! I'm up! Sorry 'bout that, needed a power nap. You must be the new guy. Sal was your name, right?"

"Sol."

"Oh, man, that's right, my bad. Mariette shouted it to me in passing. I'm Pete Roque, like the game." They shook.

"Rough night?" Sol asked scientifically.

"Every night is rough in this town," the kid replied. Sol couldn't help but think of the man as a kid, so small and couldn't be more than twenty-four. "No, nothing fun. I work another job at night."

Now, a librarian's salary isn't all that great, but it's not string peas, either, Sol thought. Why would such a young man have to work two jobs? None of his business, yet.
"So when do you sleep?" was the polite conversation question.

"I don't sleep, I drink coffee instead..," was the wide-eyed answer. Sol believed him for a second.

"Ha, ha, just kidding. I sleep on Sunday and Wednesday nights. The best nights for clubbing, so I always miss out." This time he wasn't kidding.

"Well, Pete, I hope I won't disappoint you or be too heavy a weight, but I should tell you I have never worked an information desk before in my life, of any kind."

"But Mariette said you had your library master's..."

"I do, but I've never really had to use it. It was a means to an end."

The young man smiled widely and devilishly. "Oh..." He looked at his watch. He chuckled and shook his head slowly. "Let's just let you handle the first few questions so you can get a feel for it... You've got about five minutes to review your stuff, Sol, 'cause that's when they start coming in."

In 2002, library catalogs were still just beginning to go fully online. The required computer systems and their druidical technicians aren't cheap now and were relatively more expensive at that time when they were still shiny new. The less money a library network had, the longer the wait for automation. Right after 9/11 the American economy had screeched to an unsteady stall that lasted a bad eighteen months. Even playgrounds like Miami and Los Angeles were respectfully solemn. But nowhere was the drop more acutely felt than the New York City metropolitan area and, as was too often the case, the Jersey City Free Public Library was already strapped for cash beforehand. Nonetheless, progress meandered forth and antiquarians like us all over the country, perhaps the world, were mourning the death of the card catalog. The once-holy chests that indexed a library's treasures, from the antique ornate wood styles to the industrial purely functional metal, all with their long, narrow drawers and empirical label frames, were being auction blocked at flea markets, library fundraisers and scrap metal pounds. Those endless rows of mantic lottery cards, confounding to some, delightful to others, were being recycled, sometimes just dumped, and (rumors abound) they were even in some places secretly burned at ritualistic bonfires by gnostic revelers.

For our story, though, it needs to be understood that the Jersey City system was in transition. Many people never really got the Dewey Decimal system to begin with, many were still not computer savvy and a lot more people still just don't want to have to work for something they're looking for when they can get instant gratification from a paid servant. So they went to the information desk.

"Where can I find books about astronomy?"

"Who was John Muir?"

"What is the Southern Poverty Law Center?"

"Where do I find the great essayists?"

"Do you have books in Latin?"

"What is nanotechnology?"

"How do I look up the colonization of New Caledonia?"

"Does this library have the Wall Street Journal on microfiche and, if so, how far back does it go?"

"Did Jesus have a brother?"

And so it went, steadily, Sol and Pete being assailed by random inquiries until lunchtime, when there was a crush and things got a little crazy. The two fielded a frantic press of lined-up patrons like traders on the stock exchange floor or Saturday cashiers at a dollar store.

Around 1:30 Pete announced he would take lunch first, along with a nap in his car. Strangely enough, everything became quiet. *Did he know exactly when to take his break?*

There was nothing to do now, so Sol tried tidying up and organizing a bit. It was eerie. He was accustomed to an absence of other persons, but not in such a large space. There was no one around. The ceilings were high, light came in from windows everywhere. The building seemed to breathe quietly.

Without a sound the head librarian appeared before him. She seemed pensive. They'd barely said their hello's when a hefty, mustachioed man in a brown leather trench coat came storming in.

"You Savoy? How you doin'? I'm Detective Sanders."

"Yes."

"The reason I called wuz I needed the lending history of one of your, eh, customers. He's a suspect in a major crime investigation."

"Oh, but I'm afraid I can't help you, Detective. Even if I had been formally notified of your request, which I was not, I, we, the library cannot divulge a patron's private information. Even their lending records are protected under the First Amendment."

"Lady, what are you talking about? This is a known criminal who may have been accessing dangerous information through this place and putting it to use! Now I need to see what he's been up to in here and you're gonna show me!"

"No, sir, I won't. It is not within my prerogative."

"What?!" He flashed a look at Sol and muttered to Savoy, "Is there somewhere we can talk about this in private?"

"Sol is a librarian and he knows what I'm telling you also. I prefer to have him with us."

The man loomed over the small woman with his index finger shaking. "Do you have any idea how much trouble I can make for you and this place, lady? Do you know who I am?"

"My name is Mrs. Savoy. And I am not afraid of you. Whoever you are."

The man looked as if were about to implode, his face swelling up crimson. Sol tried to intervene. "Excuse me-"

"Stay outta this, Poindexter," the man cut him off without even looking in his direction but now pointing that trembling finger at him, "before I walk over there and put my foot up your ass."

"You could try..." Sol offered.

Now the man dropped his arm and looked at the floor. He took a deep, angry breath and started walking slowly over to Sol.

"Hey! What's going on here?" It was Lorelei. She'd come upstairs unnoticed.

The detective looked at her and at the librarians and realized he was making a scene.

"None 'a yer goddamm business!" He thrust out his badge at her like the shield it resembles and bulled past her. He turned and pointed at Savoy one last time. "This ain't over!" he shouted, and was gone.

"What was that about?" asked Lorelei.

Sol exhaled, "Just another cop trying to push his weight around..."

"Nothing to worry about, dear, he won't be back," Savoy assured her. "This is not the first time. When these officers find out I'm telling them the truth they don't bother to show their faces again."

"Well, I don't appreciate his rudeness and might have to take it up with his boss," she answered. She looked at Sol. "Did he make any kind of verbal threats?"

"Forget it, Deputy McSherman, please. Like Mrs. Savoy said, we won't see him around here again and if we do, then we'll deal with it. Okay?"

Pete came back from his break looking entirely refreshed. "What did I miss?" he asked, sensing that something had just occurred.

Mrs. Savoy answered him. "You can't have all the action, Peter." She smiled affectionately and patted him on the shoulder. "Now you should probably let Sol take his lunch. I'm sure he's had a full morning." And she calmly walked off.

Lorelei waited a moment and then turned to leave without a word.

"Wow. Is that not the hottest security guard you have ever seen in your life?!" Pete could barely contain himself and smacked a fist into his palm.

"She's alright," Sol replied.

Pete looked at him with his head cocked sideways. "Alright? Are you crazy? That's like, every man's fantasy walking right there!"

"I'm going to lunch..."

"Uh huh..." Pete squinted at him and returned to the newspapers he had discreetly lain open on a shelf under the desktop.

* * * *

Later that afternoon when Sol was driving home he noticed heavy traffic coming in from the Turnpike and 1&9 and decided to cut across downtown and go up Hoboken Avenue. Zigzagging around the blocks of industrial buildings and loading docks he chanced upon an immense mural painted on the side of an empty warehouse. He ran through this area all the time and wondered how he had never seen this before. So he pulled over and got out to admire it.

There were two tropical islands in the forefront and a mainland in the background. Old colonial ships all around. In the center of the picture, aboard a schooner, there was a black-skinned leader urging his brothers and sisters on other small boats on toward the mainland. There were white European pursuers on both islands. Must be Haiti and Cuba. Obviously the painting was a statement about American slavery.

But the artwork went far beyond the message. The attention to detail was mesmerizing. The size of the work was stunning, the colors kidnapped you.

Sol stood like a small child staring at a magic wall. How long did it take to complete this? Who was the artist, or artists?

Amazed, he walked pensively back to his car, noted the location and some thoughts and jumped back into the stream of people trying to get somewhere.

9.

<u>Pete Roque</u>

"We work in the dark – we do what we can – we give what we have. Our doubt
is our passion, and our passion is our task.
The rest is the madness of art."
- Henry James, The Middle Years, 1893

The City Journal's morning headline read SENSELESS DEATH. A
boy of twelve had been robbed, shot and killed bringing groceries home
yesterday evening. The prime suspect was a thirteen-year old.

It was unusually quiet at the newsstand. When Sol went to pay for
the paper, the clerk he was familiar with only looked down at the counter
and shook his head as he was giving him his change.

The slain child had been an excellent student and deeply loved by
his family, neighbors and teachers. As anyone could guess, it had been a
gang initiation. The byline had Pete's name on it.

There wasn't the usual noise on the ride downtown. Yesterday had
been the last day of school.

* * * *

As he had expected there were no visitors to the law library that
Wednesday. A perfunctory day. He went through the updating of the
journals without the usual small joy of timeliness. He couldn't stop
thinking about the day's terrible story. So he shuffled about for eight hours.

As he was tidying up to close down Pete bumbled in. A mess. He'd
obviously not slept in the last twenty-four hours or more; jacket and tie,
but they looked like they were trying to wrestle free of him. He was
holding up the walls of the doorframe in case they fell and then the smell
of whiskey and sweat followed him in like a weapon gas.

"I would like to be a writer of nothing," he said. "I'll be like those
obnoxious wannabes you meet at parties. I just say I'm a writer and don't
actually write anything. That way I don't have to feel anything, either."

"You'd probably write about that. I'm on my way out, why don't I
drop you off at home?"

"Wanna go for a drink?"

"No, but I'll drive you and make sure you get home okay."

"Home! What is that? Come on, let's get liquored up, raise some hell and find some whores. On me."

"As much as that sounds like fun, I think you're a bit more advanced than I am. How about a quick beer near where you live? On me."

"Pisswater? What're you, still in college? 'Sides, my neighborhood ain't exactly a fun place to hang out." He pulled out a half-pint of something Irish that was hiding in his pockets. "Sing a song of mourning, old boy! You could be next!" And he thrust the unopened bottle at Sol. The poor guy had planned this, at least in the last half-hour of drunken reasoning. He'd chosen Sol, a complete stranger, to help him reconcile within himself what he'd had to see and report last night.

"I read your story this morning. Goddamned shame about that kid. Both of them, even. But at least you're letting people know what's going on."

"Just take a friggin' shot will you?!"

The young man's lopsided glasses couldn't hide bloodshot eyes, a small mouth twisted on a small face. Sol grabbed the little bottle, twisted the cap, looked Pete in the eye and said, "To the dead."

There was that brief moment when Pete's eyes turned toward the floor in relief of human accompaniment, Sol felt the burn of mortal condition, replaced the lid and slapped his companion on the shoulder to shock him into action.

"Let's go. We're taking the service elevator so no one sees you."

"Good thinking! That's the way I came in. Thanks, Sol. Can I play with your stereo?"

Sol snuck them out to his car and upon Pete's slurred directions drove to Woodlawn Avenue in a precarious neighborhood that was unsettlingly familiar. He helped Pete in to a studio apartment and drove home, looking around at all the poverty and petty crime on open display. He couldn't help but wonder at the causes.

In his living room, his pets came welcoming. Rabbits are the hardest to housetrain but they're not nearly as dumb as most people assume. Having assured them all of his commitment, he warmed up some leftovers and pulled out Pete's jacket (or file, if you prefer).

Peter Roque: Age twenty-seven, born and raised in Virginia; two-year college journalism degree there, then L.M.S. right here at the Jesuit university; pronounced Catholic. Volunteers at a local youth center. *What would bring a Hispanic kid up north to be a librarian?* Ah. Has a grandmother just ten blocks from him. Writes the 'Night Watch' column for the city paper. We know where he lives. No other information.

And then the phone rang. It was Pines: "We have a situation."

Sol looked at his watch and growled, "What is it?"

"Relax, it's for tomorrow. There's a church in Kearny, St. Stephen's at 414 Washington Avenue. There's a banquet hall behind the parking lot. I'll need you there at seven a.m."

"Of course. Fine, I'll be there."

* * * *

In the morning, in a small building that seemed more like a staff dining hall than a banquet hall, there were two men with Pines and Lorelei. It seemed they'd all been there at least a little while before him. *Why would that be?* Of the two strangers, one was a middle-aged priest and the other was a man probably in his late thirties with slicked-back hair and wearing a finely tailored dark blue suit. *Has to be European,* thought Sol, *both the suit and the man.*

Father Jonathan Villa was from the Archbishop's office at the Archdiocese in Newark. He was serving as liaison for the clergy. But it was Mister Guillermo de la Cruz Sebastian of the Granada Archdiocese in Spain that the meeting was for. He explained that he was an investigator for the church's office of art and artifacts. Sol could see where this was going.

Pines was visibly uneasy. "It seems the people we're after have contacted the Spanish Catholic church with an offer to sell a work by an artist named Alonso Cano. As with our case in progress, the correspondence claims that the piece in question was misappropriated by the Jersey City library. It also makes reference to supposed records in the library archives of a 1921 transfer of a collection of paintings to the library from an American businessman. Mr. Sebastian has a high-level Interpol clearance and is also an expert on the artist. I've asked him to brief us all this morning."

"Thank you, Special Agent Pines. Although he is not well known in the United States, Alonso Cano is regarded throughout Europe as the 'Michelangelo of Spain'. For most of his life he was under the auspices of the Catholic Church and in 1652 he was appointed a canon in the cathedral of Granada by King Philip the Fourth. However, Mr. Cano was not always a saint and led a rather tempestuous life, particularly in his youth. He began his art studies early, under the tutelage of his architect father and then other Spanish masters. By the time he was twenty-four he'd gained fame for his figures both in painting and in sculpture. Of course you understand that nudes were commonplace then, but there were rumors, never proven, mind you, that Alonso had created some works of a possible immoral and ungodly nature. These rumors did not surface until after his death and so he was unable to deny them and no physical evidence ever manifested.

"You can guess why I've told you this last bit. I'm aware that this will make a second work of erotica that your quarry is attempting to peddle. Unfortunately, judging from the photograph accompanying the letter, there is a small possibility, however slight, that the painting is a genuine Cano. I must explain that Alonso is a son of the Church and of the city of Granada and it is of the utmost importance that we disprove this work's authenticity.

"One complication, though, is that the American businessman Agent Pines mentioned was a well-known, and well-documented, collector of Cano's works. In fact, Mr. Francis Wickenhauser had originally secured a number of Cano's pieces now in the church's possession. Mr. Wickenhauser was also a devout Catholic and we would very much like to clear his name as well. So you see, we must have some closure on the matter as soon as possible."

"And are you also suing Hudson County to get it?" Sol asked

"Quite the contrary, Mr. Isistrato. We would like to offer our resources and assistance to ensure a quick and quiet apprehension of the parties involved in these crimes. Even the hint of a scandal is undesirable. Our researchers are reviewing our records of any and all transactions pertaining to Mr. Cano's art. I should have a full report available by Monday or Tuesday. As for the library records, you will want to check everything for the first week of July 1921. That comes from the seller's letter."

Pines handed Lorelei and Sol a file folder, this one containing an overview of the new developments and a copy of the solicitation letter. It was addressed to the Archbishop of Granada, translated from the Spanish.

Your Holiness,

I have something that belongs to your church.

It is a painting by the Spanish master Alonso Cano.

I must warn you ahead of time that it is one of his more explicit works.

If I didn't need the money I wouldn't ask. It was originally looted by the Dutch during the last of the Eighty Years War and continued to change hands until finally it arrived in the United States (again illegally). Ultimately, a Mister Wickenhauser received it by yet another illegal transaction and, by secret agreement, included it in a large group of artworks given as a gift to his friends at the Jersey City Museum in Jersey City, New Jersey, United States. There were pictures of the men and event in local newspapers during the week of July 4th, 1921.

I've included the negative for the photo so that your staff can blow it up and examine it. I am asking $50,000. I'm positive it's worth more to the Church than money. Below is contact information through that city's main library.

Signed,
Keeper Of The Books

N.351.96 v.2 p.98

Yep. Same guy. Or gal, or group. Now they were selling two. They were stepping up their game. Laid low for four months but it was time to unload the merchandise. Same book reference, they wanted a meet on Bastille Day.

"Agent Pines," Sol said slowly, "Bastille Day falls on a Sunday this year. The library is closed on Sundays. The meet has to be somewhere else."

"We thought there was a possibility the librarians would bring the buyers in with their own keys, but you may be right. We have to consider both scenarios."

"The museum," said Lorelei, "It's going to be the museum."

"What makes you so sure?" asked Pines

"The art was always the function of the museum, the theft didn't take place until the museum moved to its new location, and the museum is open Sundays, often with special events on the calendar. If it is a librarian involved, they're still connected to the museum somehow. And maybe the library is a conduit for silent communications. Plus, only four sets of keys to the library are available: the head librarian, Mrs. Savoy; the administrator, Mr. Hughes; the maintenance guy, Klein; and the security desk. The first three are all close to retirement. How seriously can we consider them as suspects?"

"You might be surprised these days, but, no, you're right. Chances are good that none of them are involved. Nonetheless, we'll keep two sets of eyes on the place that day, front and back. Now we'll have to take a second look at the museum. We had originally dismissed the possibilities there as almost the entire staff was comprised of new hires. The director of the museum is independently wealthy and her assistant who went over there with her is very well paid and simply doesn't fit as a criminal type. But again, you never know.

"Well, we do know we have to get into those files somehow soon. The two of you think it over in light of what you've seen this week and let me know what you come up with by Saturday. I'll consult with my partner and together we'll all figure something out. We might be able to get a search warrant for the day the building's closed. Any other thoughts or questions?"

"The guy speaks and writes fluent Spanish," Sol offered, "Or at least one of them, if it turns out to be a group. That translation was a perfect replica, aside from the extra writing, from the first letter, which was in English. No translation software is ever that exact."

"Good call. But that could be any one of the librarians," Pines replied.

"And half of the museum's staff has Hispanic last names," added Lorelei. "I took one of their information brochures when I was there last week and couldn't help noticing that little detail. Right from the first day of my involvement with this case I've been getting this feeling that there's a connection between the two places that has nothing to do with history."

"You do seem convinced. Like I said, we'll take a second look. Anything else?"

Inspector Sebastian gave his business card to the two investigators and told them where he was staying in the event they needed to get a hold of him for any reason. Father Villa hastened to do the same with his card although none of them quite knew how he might be able to assist with the matter.

Outside, the morning rush was audible and the five early risen made their way to their individual cars. Lorelei's mind was racing with calculations and considerations. Something was bothering Sol about the date of the supposed illicit art transaction eighty years ago. It would come to him, he knew.

10.

<u>Reference</u>

"It is art that *makes* life, makes interest, makes importance,
for our consideration and application of these things, and I know of no substitute
whatever for the force and beauty of its process."
- Henry James, letter to H.G. Wells (07/10/1915)

Lorelei could not afford to be predictable in this situation, nor was it in her nature anyway. She used her instinct and took random patrols of the building at any given moment and never in any patterns. She would just appear. She didn't want to be presumptuous in her wanderings or to be looming over anyone, so she mainly stopped at all the main desks and walked only the corridor of the administrative offices. But she did walk the book aisles, as quietly as she could. She'd pretty much met everyone who worked there over the last week, being not too distant and not too accessible. She'd matched faces to files and made initial observations, questions, etcetera, for each.

It was the basement she was interested in right now. They needed to get into those files somehow. What was best? A midnight raid with a squad of *federales*? Too embarrassing for everyone if they got caught. This area was well-patrolled at night by all kinds of cops. Or could she find some envelope of time alone down there during the day? No, a security guard would have no business in those files. Sol would have to do it. But that didn't mean she couldn't do the reconnaissance.

So far she'd noted only one or two staff people ever spending much time down on that level. Everyone seemed to want to stay above ground these days. She had a meeting with Sol that night. She wanted to see where his head was on this. They'd agreed to a regular schedule for the job: Thursday and Sunday evenings she met with him to compare notes and on Mondays they would give Special Agent Pines a weekly report. But things were already moving faster than expected.

It was mid-afternoon on a record hot day. How anyone could doubt global warming at this point was beyond her. The central air-conditioning in the building was meager to begin with, but also concentrated in certain areas and particularly weak in most. The security desk had never even entered into the equation and served as a collection point for humidity.

Downstairs in the basement, however, each room had its own air conditioner in the ground level windows. They were never used. She was going on break in ten minutes. Usually one of the available male librarians or Mr. Klein covered for her for the brief thirty minutes.

She did a walk-through. No one at the request station or maintenance office, the latter of which always had the door wide open and the lights on. Mr. Klein worked enough for two people around here. And then she heard voices coming from one of the farthest rooms. She eased over to listen closer. Laughter. Banter. Curses. Someone was playing cards. Three voices she made out: the boisterous loud guy, an Indian accent and an occasional soft-spoken perfect American English.

She knocked on the door. She heard three emphatic variations of the word 'shit'. She opened into the room and found three librarians, hands frozen with playing cards in hand and all looking as if their mother had caught them doing something bad. With his right hand, the big guy tried to slyly slide a beer bottle behind his seat.

"Hi, guys. I'm not trying to disturb you. I just had to make sure there were no outlaws hiding out in here. Sorry, I'm leaving..." she said.

"Holy cow, Deputy!!" Big John they called him, affable but far ahead of himself. "We thought you were Savoy! She's the only one that creeps around like that! Not that you're a creep, I mean, like, you're not creepy or anything. At all. *Definitely* not a creep. Right, guys?"

The other two rushed to their comrade's aid, apologizing and laughing uneasily. They were all surreptitiously staring at her body and trying to make eye contact at the same time. Nothing new.

The Indian gentleman, Sinha, smiled, "We could use one more player. One hand?"

His accent was so slight you could tell he'd been in this country a long time and he was actually sincere, no preconceptions about female card players. Old school style.

Then the big boss again: "Want a beer?"

The eldest man sat quiet and smiling.

"Seriously," Big John continued, "This is the only day of the week you can get away with it. We've all been here for years and years. This is called 'the quiet hour', only it's actually two; between one and three. There's a big gap in the schedule, nobody comes down here, especially in the summer. And you can't beat the air conditioning for a little while... Huh? Whatta you say? Officer Murray used to hang out with us all the time. One hand, come on..."

She should try to coax whatever information she could get out of them. "Is there a phone in here?" she asked.

"Right over on that column," offered the quiet one, Paterson.

She dialed the law library extension. "Hello, Mr. Isistrato? Hi. So sorry to bother you but I need to take a quick lunch break and no one else seems to be available at the moment. Would it be too much for me to ask you to come down and man the security desk for just a little while?... Well, no, I know but..., even though you're not one of the *regular* staff, I know you don't get a lot of action up there so I had to ask. Yes, yes, I'm just gonna run and get some take-out. Would you like anything, by the way?... Really? Oh, thank you so much. You're a sweetheart! I owe you one. I knew I could count on you... Yes, yes, I'm walking out the door right now. Be right back. Thank you so much!"

They were all staring at her in worship.

"What?" she asked. "He doesn't do anything up there..."

They all laughed in agreement.

"Two hands and I have to get back to work," she said. "The beer will have to wait until I'm off-duty, but you go ahead." She gave Big John a leprechaun wink. He probably fell in love again.

"Prem's a lightweight and Tom doesn't drink anything but special whiskey on special nights. Puritans you all are," Big John concluded, and retrieved his low-calorie lager.

It turned out to be three hands. She wasn't a card shark, but she knew she was lucky and had enough skills to play seriously. She wasn't the big winner, either, but took a nice chunk of small cash from each of them in one round. More than that, she won some pure respect from all of them. Mr. Sinha took the most from all of them, smiling like your wise uncle.

She made her departure. When she got to the first floor Sol looked like he was melting. He practically ran up the stairs back to his precious air conditioned room.

* * * *

Sol was a radio junkie. He didn't like people to know; it was obsessive/compulsive. The news woke him up in the morning, classical music started the day, jazz walked him through to the early afternoon and whatever he found on the waves afterward got him to quitting time. For whatever reason, he needed a background upon which he could

82

concentrate and work smoothly, even, or especially, when it was menial work.

He'd bought his own AM/FM clock radio at ten years old to get himself up for his five-thirty newspaper route and it had never stopped playing.

Here in this new setting he tried getting along without any music or news. He lasted three days before guiltily sneaking in a small portable CD/cassette player radio that he camouflaged in a low shelf of his desk. It helped lessen his current exile.

There was this one local station around here, WSNQ, which was all freeform. There was nothing else like it, at least not in Jersey. WBAI was hard to receive and all about New York. At the Jersey City frequency, the dj's were allowed to play whatever was on their minds. Half of them were community activists, half of them were plain crazy, and all of them knew their stuff when it came to records. There were no commercials, and while most of the shows had some theme or genre or connecting thread, none were programmed for mass consumption.

Sol was partial to one dj in particular and usually never missed his show. It was called 'Wun and Only', but most casual listeners wouldn't know that it was the deejay's last name and naturally assumed it was 'One and Only'. It was two short hours Thursday afternoons. Lorelei's cute little prank had made him miss the first fifteen minutes already.

The thing with Ed Wun was that he was the dj who played exactly what you needed to hear, the kid you paid to make mix tapes for you in high school all grown up now. At moments he rambled after running down the last set list with commentary and just when you'd had enough of his mad babble he blasted you with a barrage of records you never saw coming, from everywhere in the musical spectrum and each fitting the next moment. You jumped, realized that actually you dug what he'd been talking about, thanked him for the songs and all was good. Sometimes God is a dj. Ed Wun was one of those dj's.

While Wun played half-hour sets of music he took phone calls from listeners. Sol was one of the faithful who called in from time to time, to chat briefly and make a request that complemented Wun's selections.

So with his guilty little pleasure going, Sol had more homework to do. The one full volume with Alonso Cano as the subject he'd had to go all the way to the Guttenberg library to get during his lunch hour, with plenty of traffic along the way. Otherwise, there were some short entries in the encyclopedias and various 'Lives Of The Artists'-type series.

The book he did secure was part portfolio and had excellent photos of Cano's work throughout his career, much of it devout. It was an older text and contained a lot of information about the man. Unfortunately, the text was in Old Spanish and it would be slow-moving for him to translate. He gathered what he could from the photocopies he'd made of the other references and print-outs of what was available online.

Tempestuous, indeed. Cano became rich before the age of thirty serving both church and royalty, God and Mammon. He was chased out of his hometown of Granada after dueling with a rival and went to Madrid where he was Painter to the King. In 1644 his wife was mysteriously murdered and Alonso was accused so he took off to Valencia where he became rich again painting for The Chartreuse. All the meanwhile, he was designing cathedrals and painting and chiseling masterpieces. Ten years later, after maintaining innocence of his wife's murder through Inquisition torture he was returned to the bosom of the Church, took holy orders and was eventually listed in the saints' calendar. There was a curious difference of accounts of the man's life between the Catholic encyclopedia and the secular sources.

Sol returned to the pictures. Sheer perfection of form. The artist clearly loved and honored the human body, neither idealizing it nor degrading it. Much of it was of stark light, a lot of chiaroscuro. And then you had to consider the man's personal life. How far of a stretch would it be to imagine him painting sexy pictures for money? He was known to dash off mini-masterpieces for beggars to get back on their feet. He certainly had an expensive lifestyle. Sol wondered what lawyers were charging in those days. Probably the relative same rates as today.

So he examined the photo of a possible Cano work of erotica. You felt it immediately. Our day with all the porno and social emphasis on sexuality was put to shame by a simple painting of innocence only about to be lost. Two young lovers dancing, courting each other like birds. Delicate, devoted, terrified, enthralled. They were petting each other in places, their antiquated clothes half off, eyes locked on each other. You knew they were about to make love and there was nothing evil about it.

The work could very well be a secret piece, Sol concluded. At least he knew what to look for now. The lines were clean, distinct light and darkness, a unique sharpness of detail. *What would a piece like that be worth in today's market? Or the other one by Steen?* More than half-a-million each, he figured. But the seller was asking two hundred thousand.

And yet there's more of them, aren't there?, Sol was thinking. The seller had referred to a multiple number in addition to the first. He or she or they were lining up the buyers. The Dutch royals and the Granada church were only two prospects that were known. Others may not have bothered to go to the police. Sol was making a mental list of tasks for the case when his door opened. No, no one had to knock; it was a public room. He deftly shut off the radio. It was Phoebe Marin.

"Hi, Sol. Did you forget?"

He was drawing a complete blank for whatever she was talking about.

"The reference desk. You said to pencil you in for two-to-four."

Damn! "Oh! That's right! I'm so sorry!" It was almost three o'clock. "Should I still go down there?"

"Well, Meredith's been alone for the past hour but she's got six hands. Still…"

"Right, I'll just grab my stuff. Are you…?"

"I'll be in the New Jersey room keeping an eye on this door but we both know it will be quiet."

He hurried down to the second floor, quick embarrassed waves at those he passed. At the reference desk he caught his breath. Or rather, his breath simply caught.

Standing on a step-stool and reaching high up into a wall shelf was a wondrously curved woman sheathed in a skintight short red dress with no sleeves. Her legs were keeping the universe balanced. It was the redhead, remembered Sol. *What a gorgeous figure!* He snapped out of it, she was stepping down and turning to face him and the patron she'd retrieved a book for (and who also looked a little hypnotized).

He tried not to objectify, but she actually had a pretty doll's face; large, round eyes, softly arced cheeks, tiny nose, pouty red lips. She recognized Sol and gave him a smile that was equal parts reproach and amusement. He walked behind the desk but didn't sit. When she finished with the borrower, Sol was all apologies.

"Do you always keep a lady waiting?" she asked.

He garbled something about running around all day and being distracted. As an afterthought, he introduced himself.

"Meredith." She smiled rainbows. "I'm your partner for a couple of hours. Can you stay until five?"

"Sure…" *Five, six, seven… What time does this place close again?*

"That way we can tell Mariette you completed your full sentence and you can keep me company for the last hour of mine. Deal? I'll try not to let you get bored."

She was flirty and forgiving. He had to fight the urge to say something stupid. A bewitching perfume made that difficult, so he retreated into his regular detachedness. There wasn't a lot to do at the reference desk except wait for the next request, which was every five to ten minutes. Fortunately for him, she enjoyed carrying a conversation and he was able to maintain a calm demeanor while responding to her steady gentle stream of questions and observations. The reference desk was set a good distance away from any reading tables and they were able to talk at a comfortable volume. There was a constant, if easy, flow of people seeking materials but it was nothing as frenetic as the information desk.

She seemed most concerned with the social fabric of the city and dropped names of local personalities and politicians as though she routinely circulated among them. Perhaps she did; she most certainly possessed the requisite urbanity. She was comfortable in her skin and seemed to genuinely enjoy the company of others. Sol didn't mind her company one bit.

At about ten to five Sol said he had to close down the law library. Not an involved process, he didn't explain: it was just turning off the lights and locking the door. The truth was Sol wasn't in the mood for pleasantries with whoever was coming to relieve them in the reference section. He'd about had all the sociability he could stand for one day.

He was at least sincere in telling Meredith he'd had a pleasant time working with her those two hours. He probably imagined it, but as she smiled goodbye he could have sworn he saw, for lack of a better term, a spark in her eye. He thought he was about to be awkward so he abruptly about-faced and marched away. The room was suddenly warmer than it had been the last hundred-and-twenty minutes.

* * * *

The administrative staff on the third floor all exited together promptly at five o'clock every day, Monday through Friday unless there was some special event taking place. Mr. Hughes, the Library Administrator, ran a tight ship and everything on the third floor was shut down by no later than five after. That floor was off limits on Saturdays. The same went for the fourth floor, basically, unless an appointment was made.

Whereas in the past whoever of the librarians drew the short straw had to close the topmost floor, it was now left entirely up to Sol and no one minded. Sol was always eager and ready to leave by five. Alarms were set, areas roped off and a skeleton crew was usually enough to run operations until nine o'clock on the four nights the library stayed open that late. Lorelei closed the doors Monday through Wednesday nights and Friday afternoons, but on Thursday nights it was whoever was available.

Today it was a veteran of the JCPD named Donaldson, who'd been on and off this detail for the past six years whenever it was convenient. Old hat, he said, he could close the library with his eyes shut. No need to fuss. Donaldson only took one or two tours on his shift and then walked everybody out to the parking lot. Sixteen months left for retirement.

Good deal. It was Lorelei's first week and there was no need to make waves anywhere. She was out, good night.

If she hadn't wanted to check out the new gourmet deli on the corner she would have never seen them. Two undercover cops staking out the library, parked in an unmarked car across the street from the entrance. One of them was the bully from the other day. They stared her down openly, lascivious looks. She wondered if they might not have something to do with what she was working on. What were they looking for?

She lingered in the store, keeping their car in the corner of her eye. She knew she wasn't supposed to do any surveillance without authorization but this couldn't have been planned in advance. This was something that required immediate action.

Without looking at them again she made sure they saw her head toward Montgomery Street and turn the corner. The library doesn't have its own parking lot so employees and visitors have to try their luck on surrounding streets for parking. She was all the way down on Barrow Street. She walked as fast as she could without appearing to be in a hurry. In her car she discreetly stripped off her uniform shirt and grabbed a jersey from her gym bag. Throwing on a baseball cap and a pair of sunglasses she drove a wide circle around the plainclothes officers coming up behind them on Jersey Avenue. She found a spot in front of the bagel place on the corner of Wayne Street where she could see their car. She called Sol on his cell phone.

"You remember the new friend you made with Savoy the other day?"

"The cop? Yes."

"What was he doing there, do you know?"

"Trying to get somebody's lending records."

"Do you know whose?"

"No, neither of them ever mentioned a name. But the guy, Sanders is *his* name, probably told Savoy over the phone. I can't exactly go up to her and ask about it, though."

"Did he get what he had come for?"

"No, it's against the law. Why do you ask?"

"He and a partner are sitting out in front of the library right now, eyes glued to the entrance."

"Where are you?"

"Parked down the street behind them. I'm curious as to what they're waiting for."

"What did his badge say?"

"JCPD"

"Have you talked to Agent Pines?"

"Not yet. Thought I'd call you first, pardn'er"

Silence on Sol's end then, "Call me in ten minutes, please. I'll be nearby."

Special Agent Pines confirmed that the two men were plainclothes officers of the Jersey City Police Department, probably pursuing a narcotics case against a local person suspected in being involved with psychotropic drugs. The Feds had already seen Sanders and his partner hanging around twice before, always after the same subject: a young man in his mid-twenties. A completely unrelated matter, Pines said, but told Lorelei that if she wanted to hang around for another twenty minutes or so she could get confirmation on what he'd just told her. Otherwise it was none of their business. Pines described the young man to Lorelei so she could identify him and asked if she'd met with Sol or had anything else to touch base on.

"Nothing other than the files in the basement. There's a nice big cabinet labeled 'Pre-1960'. I'm sure the whole library's history is well organized in there. I think I might be able to get what we need, or at least Sol probably can. We just bumped up our meeting to six o'clock."

* * * *

During his delightful two-hour stint at the reference desk, Sol had remembered that he needed the microfiche rolls of the leading three area newspapers for the week of July fourth, 1921. When Meredith stepped away for a few minutes he quickly retrieved them and placed them inconspicuously nearby. When it got close to five, he merely included them with his belongings and dashed off. The law library also had a microfiche machine that was intended for older law journals and reviews captured on the recording film. He was almost through the last roll when Lorelei called.

Before being shuffled through a few newspaper conglomerates at the end of the twentieth century, The City Journal was originally called The Hudson Daily, and it dated back to the late 1800's. Sol was thanking the heavens for the Eastman-Kodak Company.

He found what he'd been looking for on July 3, 1921. The events covered, of course, were from the day before. Most will remember it as the day President Warren Harding signed an end to the U.S. war with Germany and Austria. But that Saturday night, right here in Jersey City, was 'The Battle Of The Century'. The first-ever million dollar prize fight took place at a place called Boyle's Thirty Acres, a giant wooden bowl of an arena that existed just a few blocks up the hill from here. US heavyweight champ Jack Dempsey was defending his title against the French fighter Georges Carpentier and handily knocked him out in the fourth round. It had been bugging Sol because it was trivial facts like this that he used to know off the top of his head.

The newspaper had done a large four-page spread on the event. There were pictures of foreign dignitaries and international celebrities of the era attending in the front rows. It had been the notorious Jersey City Mayor Frank Hague who had offered the venue to the promoter of the fight and all of the northeast region's gentlemen who could call themselves gentlemen were there. And sure enough, there was a picture of the thirty-year mayor with philanthropist Francis Wickenhauser, Baron Robert Vansittart of England, someone named Remy Durier and Robert L. Heppenheimer… But what did the fight have to do with a donation of art?

Moving forward in the chronology for that week, Sol looked over every little item, event, listing, even the obituaries, searching for some mention of a donation from Mr. Wickenhauser to the library. It was in that Wednesday's 'Society' section. A few paragraphs about the renowned collector's accomplishments and magnanimity and the Jersey City Museum's importance on the national cultural landscape. Next to the article was a photo of Wickenhauser with members of the library's board of trustees (which also served as museum directors), and among them the same Heppenheimer from the boxing match photo. That was when Lorelei called to ask him about Detective Sanders.

Sol printed out copies of the article and two pictures and put the microfilms back in their cases and locked them in his desk until he could put them on the reference returns cart the next day. It was almost five thirty and he ran to meet up with his temporary partner.

She called him again as he was approaching his car and told him to go straight to their meet at the north parking lot of Bayonne park, she was on her way there already. The person Agent Pines had described came out of the library five minutes after their conversation and the plainclothesmen eased slowly into the street to follow after him. The suspect definitely looked like a druggie, maybe a wannabe rock star from the way he was dressed. She was slightly disappointed that it had turned out to be nothing but it was nice to know Sol had her back anyway.

At the park they walked along the water wall discussing what they'd learned thus far. Across the Newark Bay was a horizon of industrial yards, rust, faded gray and black. It was fairly cool outside, heavy clouds above and it would rain at any moment. Lorelei had shed her work belt and worn the jersey over the uniform trousers to look as casual as possible. Sol had left his jacket in the car, loosened his tie and rolled up his sleeves. It was still rush hour.

They came upon a solution of a daytime exploration of the library archives for that coming Sunday. Everyone involved in the investigation could help expedite the search and they had all day to find what they could without worry of discovery. Even cop traffic was light on Sundays. The side entrance of the library was nearly invisible under two overhanging trees and if anyone were around they wouldn't think twice about the swift entries of obviously authorized persons. That part of Mercer Street was all old-timers.

He showed her the copies of what he'd found. What they were looking for now was a corroborating document or dated entry in one of the museum collections logs. They were halfway along the inside park walking path when she asked him if he'd found any of the librarians to be somehow especially suspicious.

"Do any of these people seem like likely culprits to you yet?"

"Hasn't even been a week. I've only met half of them so far and I haven't seen anything obvious at this point. Looks like I'll have to step up my efforts, though. What about you, any leads?"

"I've met them all, and after spending enough time thinking about it, any one of them could have decided to take advantage of a lucrative opportunity. Like you said yourself, people will do anything for money."

"That's for sure. But I've also been thinking about the museum possibilities. It could be a librarian and someone over there working together. I'm sure Pines has started to consider that, too."

The wind whipped up suddenly and a fast, heavy rain fell. They rushed to her car and agreed to coordinate with Agent Pines on Saturday afternoon. There would be more to discuss than they could anticipate.

Sol took JFK Boulevard toward Journal Square and Lorelei hopped onto 440 to grab Tonnelle Avenue into the Heights. It was at the Communipaw Avenue intersection that she saw an unusual billboard. Among all the insurance company reminders and ambulance-chaser promos was something she'd never seen before. It wasn't advertising anything, it was a mural. All she could make out before the light changed was a graphic slaughter of what looked like American Indians by light-haired Europeans in colonial dress. Was it part of some historical remembrance that month? Columbus Day wasn't for another four months. It looked just like an old classical painting you would see in a museum except for one surreal anomaly: amid the massacre, blood and axes, there were peaches floating everywhere, large and small, as if they were falling from the sky. She could see it was all richly detailed but as it was situated on the roof of a three story-building she could only make out so much. As she drove past it she was able to see the large lettering, graffiti style, along its bottom edge: STUYVESANT: 1655. Whatever that meant… The drivers behind her started honking their horns and she hurried into the Lincoln Park crossway.

* * * *

That night at the band 'rehearsal', Sol snuck in some beats and rhythms that made him think of the 'Roaring Twenties'. Nervous, wildly uncertain energy that made the other players cut loose on their instruments. He was thinking about grainy films of great boxing matches, men with bowlers and big mustaches, half-second-fast smiles, pocket watches; the movie just a tiny bit faster than life. He thought of how men associated with one another in those days. Probably much the same as they did today. Haven't they always traded nudie pictures?

When their studio time was up all the musicians were a little sweaty and exhausted. They now had to return to their normal lives, kick up their share of the night's fees. They were all sort of staring at Sol strangely, he thought. Eddie finally had to ask.

"What the hell got into you tonight, Sol?"

91

“What do you mean?”

“You don’t know? You were, like, inspired or something tonight. You took the lead a few times and even did a damned solo! How often does that happen?”

“Yeah... I met the hottest redhead today, man. You wouldn’t believe...”

11.

<u>Meredith Baxbanes</u>

"The axis of the earth sticks out visibly
through the centre of each and every town or city."
Oliver Wendell Holmes ,'<u>The Autocrat of the Breakfast-Table</u>'. vi.

"And we can find new ways of living
Make playing only logical harm
And we can top the old times clay
Make that nothing else will change

But she can read, she can read
She can read, she's bad
She can read, she can read
She can read, she's bad, oh she's bad"
- Interpol, 'Obstacle 1', <u>Turn On The Bright Lights</u>, 2002

Towns and cities are proof that humans inherently enjoy each other's company, give or take the occasional hermit, fistfight or hot-blooded killing. But to see groups of people join together for some worthy cause, as if to rescue others or simply stand united in defense of basic humanity, or maybe even just attend a good concert, might silence the worst of misanthropes. Maybe. Maybe not.

* * * *

She was in love with everyone and no one all at once. She was untroubled, unattached, free. Who knew how long that would last, but she was determined to enjoy it. She was at play in the world. Enough with sadness and disasters, guilt, anger and fear. Just for a little while, please. The sorrows will come again, but not today.

Today she was having chilled mint tea at a sidewalk café with a perfect summer breeze blowing around her short summer dress. She was glad to have short hair again. She watched people from behind her movie star sunglasses. Saw how the men, and some women, gave long stares at her long legs ending triumphantly in beach pumps and brightly painted toenails.

There was an article in a local magazine about a large art event that evening. A gallery crawl would be a nice way to start off the weekend. But who would she take with her? She could think of no one off-hand.

Four more hours stuck inside on such a beautifully sunny day. She glanced around, quickly put on fresh lipstick, kissed a napkin and went back to work. It was finally Friday afternoon and she was smiling at whoever she saw. Except for the loony that was yelling at the lamppost.

After Christopher Columbus Drive, Jersey Avenue has plenty of shade among its just-tall-enough brownstones and regularly trimmed trees. The sidewalks had been renewed a couple years ago all the way down to Grand Street, where NJ Transit had recently completed a light-rail station and where construction had just broken ground on a new medical center. Someone in city planning knew something about new urbanism, she thought. Or maybe it was the architectural firms they were hiring. She would look into it she resolved.

* * * *

A tall, beautiful woman with short red hair entered the library singing and Lorelei remembered she was a librarian. The woman removed her earphones and daintily started up the stairs giving the security guard a smile and a wave and saying, "Hi!"

Rather friendly, thought Lorelei, and returned to her book. She had figured out she could do homework when chained to this desk, and to largely ignore the general traffic, including the suspect that had just passed. No one ever wanted to talk to the security guard. She knew her job was to keep an eye out for any suspicious people entering and so she checked every time someone came in but it was never anyone clearly nefarious. No one but regular people.

So she concentrated on the tedious. She didn't know much about art, but it was becoming easier as she studied it. Different periods, different styles, different ideas in cycles. So far, the works they were looking for were figurative and from the late 1600's. Similarities in line, color and composition. Cano's work was starker and overly serious, Steen's very playful.

Provenance, Pines had said, addressing Sol as if she weren't able to find it just the same. What was so difficult about the line of ownership? Transfer of title, that was all. Which brought her to their plan. From what Sol told her, there should be something tangible they were looking for on that particular week mentioned in the letter. If they were lucky there would be specific references to names and pieces. At least it would be a place to start.

It was far too late for a routine investigation of a theft; looking for fingerprints or other such clues two years after so much activity was useless. The museum was an endpoint; close that possibility and you could close in on the library without doubt. There were two weeks left before the meeting the thieves were trying to arrange. She really wanted a first victory.

* * * *

"Sol!" came the muted shout down the hall. He was coming out of the lunchroom after a roast beef-and-Swiss hero and potato salad. It was Meredith, waving her right arm frantically as if they were across a plaza from one another. "They said you were in there! Hold on a second!"

She walked down the hall as if conquering a country.

"I know this is going to sound crazy because we just met and everything but I, well, you won't believe this, I know, but I don't have too, too many close friends here in Jersey City and I have a number of events tonight I would like to attend, which promises to be an interesting evening in this town, by the way, and you seem like a… a cultural person and it was nice talking with you yesterday and so I thought maybe, if you weren't busy, and I know it's short notice, but if you didn't have plans you might like to escort a lady to some social functions… I mean it doesn't have to be like a date. We could just be co-workers hanging out type thing." An honest smile that brings nations together. *As if he could have dreamt this.*

"Really? Well, I'd be honored, Meredith. I usually just stay home on Friday nights."

"Wonderful! I don't mean that you stay home Friday nights, just that I don't have to look for an actual date. You are so nice! Can you pick me up at 7:30? There are a few little spots that will shut down early and I don't want to miss them."

"What exactly are we talking about doing then?"

"Art, silly! We're going gallery hopping, lose ourselves in rampant imagination, great wasted ideas! Pretty colors, too. Seriously, it's Jersey City's Open Studios tour. Tons of art, chill people, music everywhere, it's a lot of fun. I'll probably have an after-party at my place. But you don't have to stay if you don't want to, I just can't make the rounds without a handsome man on my arm, or a group of girls. And, you know, you're kind

95

of sexy, in a nightly news sort of way. My girlfriends don't like art as much as I do. Okay?"

"Okay! It's a date! No! I don't mean it's a *date* date, I mean Yes, I would love to accompany you. Seven-thirty, where exactly am I picking you up, now?" Why did he feel like a teenager?

"You are simply darling!" She tucked some kind of card into his jacket pocket, gave him a quick peck on the cheek and was off again. "I'll see you later." The earth trembled as she walked away. He was stuck in place when he remembered he had to go back upstairs. He pulled out what she'd put in his pocket: an index card torn in half. On the blank side in a neat, crisp hand script were the words: 'You'd better say yes'. Underneath was an address in the trendy Society Hills community. He started counting down the minutes until he could see this woman again.

When he got to his desk, sitting there was Mariette Savoy looking like a prime minister in wartime, absorbed in thought. She rose as he entered and brightened the room with a timeless smile.

"Hello, Mrs. Savoy! How are you doing? It's nice to see you."

"Hello, Sol. It's nice to see you as well. But please do call me Mariette."

"If you say so."

"I say so. Now, how was your first week?"

"Okay. Not bad."

"Quite a descent after having been up on high, no?"

"Not at all. Everyone here is very nice. It's a pleasant change of atmosphere."

"Well, I'm glad. So, actually, I came up here to invite you to a party next week at my home. We have it every year on the third of July to usher in the summertime. That's next Wednesday, of course, starting around seven, seven-thirty. I do hope you can make it, even if for a short time. It's another one of those silly traditions we have here."

"Next Wednesday? Sure, I don't see why I can't stop by. Thank you very much for inviting me."

"Of course, Sol."

"Should I bring anything?"

"Oh, yes. I almost forgot. Food and drink will all be available but if you'd like to add flavor to it all feel free. What we do ask, however, is that you consider bringing a favorite book. We take turns reading passages to each other, one to three pages, or so. In the salon sometime around eight-thirty."

"Of any kind?"

She didn't say anything, but smiled glowingly and turned to walk with an *à tout à l'heure* hand.

It occurred to Sol that this was the closest he'd been to having something of a social life in years.

* * * *

Why do bells shrill at three o'clock? Sol didn't get many phone calls, he made sure of that. So his cell phone shocked him out of a reverie at the top of tierce.

"Sol." It was Pines. This couldn't be good.

"What's up, sir?"

"You're not going to believe this…"

Another one. Another painting was being offered, some important French museum was involved. Agent Pines sounded stressed, implored Sol to make himself available this evening at six, apologizing profusely. Sol hoped it wouldn't run long.

They were told to go to the lounge of a luxury hotel right outside Newark airport and ask the bartender for the Forteville party. For whatever reason, Sol checked with Lorelei to make sure she'd gotten the call.

"It's getting kind of heavy now, Sol."

"I know. See you in a little while."

The bartender pointed to a pair of doors at the end of a short corridor. Something about all this made her skin tingle. The intrigue, the money. She walked into a room full of men, again. They all stood. Sol and Pines; an extremely well-groomed young man in a three piece suit he should not have been able to afford; and a handsome brown-haired man in his late thirties/early forties, tan blazer, brown tie, brown shoes, looking like someone whose wife was keeping him from an afternoon of golf with his buddies, cross.

Special Agent Pines introduced the young well-tailored Frenchman as Marcel Le Guerroyant, assistant to Mademoiselle Villeforte who would arrive at any moment, and Hudson County Executive Steven Riley, who was obviously being curter than he would ordinarily be. Mr. Riley was wringing his hands.

Though he'd spoken to her only yesterday, Pines made light conversation with Lorelei, casual questions, filling time. No one else was speaking. A few minutes later, Mlle. Villeforte walked in with her bodyguard, or 'associate': a humongous bald man with a goatee and dressed in a suit as expensive as Mr. Le Guerroyant's.

Miss Villeforte was dressed like a tourist. But she managed to make a polo shirt, tennis shorts and sneakers look like inconveniences. Enviously beautiful, stylish and rich, she emanated one hundred percent Bitch.

"Is this everyone? I was purposely late. Marcel?" Marcel nodded yes. "Well, Agente Pines?"

"Lorelei, Sol. I'd like you to meet Miss Francine Villeforte, United States representative of the Geurroyant Museum in Orleans, France. Marcel is a great grandson of the founder and he is on Miss Villeforte's staff."

Her staff? The woman cracked the whip right away. "Why is it taking so long for you to find these people?!" she demanded. "You are telling me you have worked on zis for seex months already and you cannot find an amateur grwoup of thieves? Zee almighty *FBI*?!" If she weren't so attractive, and so French, you would want to walk out of the room. Long free brown hair, an oh-so-kissable face with freckles, an upturned chin. She wasn't done.

"You two are ze ones looking for my painting?" She looked straight at Lorelei and Sol.

They answered 'Yes' in unison.

"Do eizer of you know anytheeng at all about art?" asked Mademoiselle Villeforte.

"We know enough, Miss Villeforte. Enough to get the job done." Sol was already slightly peeved. "So someone's offering an erotic painting to your museum. Let me guess, it was originally yours anyway, right?"

Mademoiselle Villeforte's eyes went wide and livid. She turned to Special Agent Pines who turned a warm red, and then to Mr. Riley, who could only close his eyes, clench his fists and his lips and turn his face to the ground.

"Do none of you barely leeterate Americans have ze slightest idea of what a piece like zis is worth?! Zis is a *Fragonard*! Not some Norman Rockwell print! It eez worth over two million dollars!!"

Lorelei moved forward to give this other woman a piece of what's what when Sol and Pines jumped to intercept. Mr. Riley had to raise his voice. "Alright, already. Where *are* we on this? Please!... We know that the

Guerroyant Museum is claiming a large amount of damages if it turns out Hudson County is liable for any loss to them. What else?"

Lorelei regained control.

"The thieves are going for the biggest bang for their buck," she began. "There may be other offers to other entities coming down the pipeline. So far they won't make a move apart from initial contacts for another two weeks. Aside from offers to the supposed original owners, they may be pursuing other avenues, such as general buyers of erotic paintings by Renaissance masters. And now with your precious Fragonard we can include neo-classicists. It's all in this brief since you're such a big reader, lady." She tossed a packet onto the table. "Special Agent Pines can help it make sense for you. I'll add the details of your situation and see if there's any revision needed." She looked at her temporary superior. "Can I get the rest of this later? I've got something I need to do."

Pines merely nodded with terse lips. Sol was inexplicably pleased with his partner's behavior but did not let it show. He merely faced them all with aplomb, motioned with his index fingers toward the exit and said, "We have to get back to work…" What he really meant was that he had to try to ditch Lorelei and get ready for his non-date.

"Hey!" He caught her in the parking lot. "Are you okay?"

"Yeah, I'm just not in the mood for that kind of B.S. right now."

"Anything you wanna talk about?"

"Nope. It's Friday, just would like to relax." She hadn't seen Anthony in three days and wouldn't that night either. He'd joined the narcotics squad and was working until the pre-dawn hours.

"Alright, then. We're still on for tomorrow, right?"

"Yep."

Jersey City was enjoying a fertile scene of new artists but nothing on the scale of the money and names involved in this case. Around here, you could only get that kind of action in New York City. They'd agreed to take a day to check out some high-end galleries and dealers that might have any possible connection to their case. Each had made a list of targets and questions and together they'd drawn out a route and schedule. They were setting out around nine in the morning.

* * * *

He couldn't resist opening her file. He'd been thinking about her almost obsessively for two days. Some might call it cavorting with the subjects, but Sol argued that he was always able to maintain objectivity and neutrality and thus the question was moot. Besides, what better way to get a close-up observation? And there was nothing in the federal agency contract to the contrary. *And Grandma what big teeth you have…*

Meredith Baxbanes: Thirty-one years *divine*, born and raised in Connecticut but flew off to D.C. as soon as she became eighteen. An apartment in her own name right downtown while she got her degree at Georgetown. Obtained her library master's at Syracuse and is currently working toward a doctorate through New Jersey Institute of Technology in Hoboken. *Wow.* Vice-president of the local chapter of NOW. Single, no dependents. And yet only one living relative listed: a brother fifteen years her senior living in Georgia and with a different last name.

Enough voyeurism, then. He had a little over a half-hour before he had to leave. It would be too cliché to wear black so he found a pair of blue jeans, walking shoes and a white short-sleeved button down. But should he wear his glasses? That was how she was accustomed to seeing him. But maybe it made him look too nerdy for an evening affair. Or maybe she liked nerdy. He was torn over such a small thing. In the end, he kept them on. He could always take them off later.

Navigating the condo map he found her townhouse-inspired unit in a cul-de-sac. Since this was 'not a date', he didn't bring flowers or any such thing but would be as gentlemanly as he could along the way. The front door was pulled halfway open. He rang the doorbell. From inside Meredith shouted,

"Right on time! Come inside, Sol. I'll be down in two minutes."

Her living room was immaculate and what he could see of the brand new kitchen was also. No pictures of friends or family anywhere, only some framed artistic and landscape photography, including a few cityscapes. No hint of any pets, only the smell of fresh flowers and fruit coming from the kitchen.

And then she walked down the stairs.

"Hi, Sol. Thanks again for coming with me tonight."

A short tan skirt, a long cream colored, light fabric jacket whose ends caressed her knees, over a low-cut burgundy blouse, spike heels the color of blood and ruby red lips that made her a vision to behold.

"Well, don't just stand there! Say something nice," she scolded.

"You look lovely," he exhaled.

"Thank you. It's a new outfit." She actually twirled around slowly and for one light second he thought he might fall to the ground. *That's what they meant when they used to call women knockouts.*

"Ready?" She gently touched his arm and eased him toward the door. "Good. You didn't bring flowers."

"No. But now I wish I had."

"I'm sure there will be plenty of flowers on some walls tonight."

The first three galleries were along Bergen Avenue but so far apart they had to drive between them. The first was one of the oldest existing in town, in a former millionaire neighborhood of small mansions with street names like Astor, Brinkerhoff and Monticello, now overrun by crime. But the gallery had been handed down from mother to daughter and had a faithful clientele. Paintings, sculpture, antiques and crafts from all over the world, the proprietress had refined and eclectic tastes and each piece presented was interesting. There was only one other person visiting.

The second place was actually two storefront galleries connected by a corridor at the back of a building a few doors down Storms Avenue just off Bergen. They were owned and run by an upstart with a good eye. The entrance was through an open spaced store painted all black on one side, all white on the other, checkerboard floor. It was a two person show, excellent acrylics. On the white side was the mischievous and imaginative Alex Duque, on the black side was raw emotion and skillful colorings by a woman who called herself Samm. There was a decent spread and fairly good wine in an alcove. Meredith picked out a small plate of noshes, inspected a bottle and poured herself a glass of Pinot Grigio. Sol grabbed a few gourmet (tiny) sandwich halves and a bottled water and they meandered through the warren of assorted works by various artists. The adjoined gallery was more like a lounge with colorful acrylics of shapely women in exotic and provocative outfits, some in suggestive poses. Sol mad a mental note of the place. There was subdued lighting, a mirrored dance floor and a dj station set up in front of a blacked-out glass storefront. There was probably going to be a party here tonight. At the moment there was a thin mix of hipsters.

Their third stop was near Journal Square; an upstairs gallery in an old red commercial building built in the late 1800's. This place was also one of the longest running galleries in Jersey City. It was a group show, all local artists. There were a few standouts, some standards and a couple amateurs. The owner and curator was a friendly and earnest woman in her fifties who rewarded her visitors with a thorough knowledge of the area's art history. A comfortable crowd milled about.

From there they made their way downtown to the newer galleries and alternative art spaces. Everything was represented; the traditional, the experimental, abstract, realistic, mixed-media, photography, installation, miniature, exquisite and weird. All of these spaces were within reasonable walking distance so they had parked at Monmouth and First streets and took a circular course that Meredith had mapped out.

She was an excellent guide, expertly moving among the crowds with an insider's discourse on the scene. He was enjoying himself thoroughly, in his reserved manner. To the numerous friends and acquaintances of hers that they encountered she introduced him as 'my friend'.

"I've saved the best for last, Sol. But we have to drive there. Are you having fun? Do you like this kind of thing?"

"Absolutely. I have the best accompaniment anyone could ask for."

"Awww!" She leaned into him and took his arm. "Let's go. You are going to LOVE this next place."

In a warehouse district, with empty cobblestone streets and lonely loading docks there was, among others, a giant manufacturing building long ago relieved of its original duties. But this particular building had been invaded by artists. Every available square foot had been rented by that odd strain of persons born compelled by unknown forces to share their visions with the world.

One or two weekends a year, during these city-wide events, the majority of the inhabitants opened their studio doors to allow the general public a glimpse of the spaces where their passions were loosed. It was a celebration of art and even the clueless were invited to the party. People came from as far away as Philly and Providence, Rhode Island, and each year the crowds grew larger.

Again Meredith maneuvered deftly through the throngs neither rushing nor moving too slowly. Sol was impressed by the breadth of so many unique talents. But it was impossible to not notice that Meredith knew a lot of people in this sphere of the city. Obviously it made her stand out as a suspect. Somehow it saddened him a little to think about this. But such is life.

On the top floor, the sixth, the walls had all been knocked out and only the building's support columns took any floor space. This was where the big party was. There was a dance band playing. Giant murals were on display in a show entitled 'New Realities'. On the promotional card were listed six names. It was, in fact, a realist exhibit, albeit with many subtle nuances. Some slipped in word fragments, anomalies and absurdities.

Meredith said she felt like dancing, but Sol would pass. Something seemed to be bothering him. After a couple songs she came away from the music to where Sol was and took his hand. Many of the studios downstairs had started their reception parties as well. There was wine everywhere. Some of the better bottles had been brought out. Meredith asked a friendly host for two glasses of chardonnay and led Sol up to the roof where a steady refreshing wind was playing. The night skyline of lower Manhattan bloomed into view.

"But isn't the Jersey City skyline beautiful, also?" she asked him, waving her hand as if making it appear.

"Yes, it is. Just not nearly as big."

"No… Have you ever looked at it from the New York side?"

"Sure, plenty of times."

"Oh…"

There was a moment of sexual tension between them and she obliterated it. "I kissed a girl last week, Sol. Can you believe it? We were at the club and I just did it. I haven't told anyone, I just now felt like saying it. It was actually kind of nice." *Petulance*, he thought. *Like a five year old girl trying to piss off a boy.*She took a deep breath and a last look around her.

"So if you're ready I'd appreciate it if you took me home now. I've invited everyone I'm going to invite. A few of the artists will be coming by as well."

"Of course, Meredith."

Ordinarily, Sol might hang out at one of these after parties for an hour or less, to be polite to the hostess. Or so he remembered. But he had learned long ago that he made people uncomfortable in these settings and had since perfected a practice of slipping out quietly. Tonight, unfortunately, he would have to study what he could of her guests before he wore out his welcome.

"Will you help me set out some stuff, please, Sol? I prepared a snack tray; it's in the fridge with two bottles chilling in the lower rack. I have to get some chairs from the garage."

"Why don't you let me get the chairs?"

"Really? Okay, thank you! They're the wooden ones with blue upholstering. That's the door right there and there's light switches all along the way. Thank you again! You're a doll."

More people showed up than either had expected. Friends of friends arrived with their own contributions to the cause. A lot of people were forced to stand and some of the soiree spilled out onto the front steps. A generous mess was accumulating but Meredith controlled it all with beautiful ease and efficiency. By twelve o'clock she had tamed her gathering to a comfortable level and it drifted casually into the night. She had managed to keep Sol nearby almost the whole time.

"Will you stay for a little while?" she had asked him.

Sometime near two the guests had thinned to a baker's dozen. Sol began discreetly gathering things in the kitchen when Meredith abruptly announced that the party was moving to a recording studio where tonight's band would be playing a surprise set and everyone present was welcome to check it out. She marshaled three frat boys from NJIT to perform an instantaneous clean-up. They didn't know what to make of Sol and looked at him out of the sides of their eyes. But they were tripping over each other to impress Meredith, fawning and panting. Sol would have liked to cuff one on the ear and send them all running home. They were the last people left.

She reclaimed his attention by placing a hand on his forearm while he was rinsing some glasses. She made him look at her.

"Thank you so much for helping, but you can leave the rest, please. I'll load them in the washer later." He assumed she was asking him to leave when she calmly stated out loud, without looking away from him, "Boys, you can go home now. Thank you!..."

They filed out like altar boys and hushed 'good nights'. Sol couldn't bring himself to be falsely genial to them. He also couldn't believe he was feeling territorial. He was losing his head, it was the damned wine.

"Oh, don't mind them, Sol. They're still learning how to bathe alone. They help me out at school and they amuse me. Stay for a little while longer, won't you? We can finally relax. I'm going to change out of these clothes." She didn't wait for an answer.

Try to be cool, will you?!, he chided himself. Her perfume was still in the air, he hoped to never learn its name. He wandered over to the couch where he tried to make some sense of where he was.

How lucky could he get?! Some people fantasize about librarians, but he was probably about to bed the second of two lovely specimens in a single month. Or at least get to make out with her, he hoped. Except... he hadn't known the first was a librarian when they'd met and she hadn't exactly fallen in love with him. Irrelevant, he decided; it was worth the effort and he proceeded with his conquest. What the hell was it that made them so damned sexy? It couldn't be their bookishness. Could it?

She floated into the room wearing only a sheer pink negligee. Sol thought he would have a heart attack forty years too early. He was as stiff as a statue. She was a goddess.

She climbed onto him luxuriously. He'd forgotten he still had his glasses on until she removed them and placed them on an end table.

"Who are you, Sol? You make me want to be bad."

Even had he conjured up some inanity in reply she did not allow it. She delicately placed those rose petal lips to his mouth in a lightly wet kiss, tasting him, as if the first morsel of a meal.

"You pretend to be so aloof but I see the way you look at me."

She began kissing his face and moving her body gently against his. He stopped thinking. She was unbuttoning his shirt. He dared to bring his fingertips to her body.

She tore him apart. He wished for the strength of two men. They savagely made their way to her bedroom where the delicious tortures continued until he was spent. And he had thought he was in great physical shape.

He dozed off somewhere between dreaming and waking. He wondered if death wasn't like some long, deliriously pleasurable sleep.

And then she was stroking his hair and saying his name. So lovely she sounded to him.

"Lover, wake up," she said.

He tried to recall the function for opening one's eyes. "Mmmm….?"

"It's time to go."

They opened. He focused. "What?"

"I'm sorry, baby, I'm not ready to wake up to anyone in my life right now. You have to go."

An embarrassed and bare-assed anger flushed his skin. "Right. Okay." He dressed hastily.

"Please don't be angry, Sol. We're adults, right?"

"Of course. I'll find my way out. Thanks for a great night, Meredith. It was a blast." For an instant he thought of kissing her good night but was terrified of looking even more foolish.

"Good night." He hurried out to his car and remembered to grab his glasses by the couch. There was a thick humidity in the early morning air, cicadas were in symphony. If there were a can or a rock on the ground anywhere he would have kicked it.

Why was he so offended? He'd had casual encounters before. But that was in another life. And he actually liked Meredith. Now he would never be able to be at ease around her again. Was the sex *that bad? Did this chick just use men like toys?*

It was almost five. At least she'd let him sleep for a few hours. He cursed his luck but found it impossible to take himself seriously when he looked in the rearview mirror and saw all the smeared lipstick kisses on his face.

12.

<u>Manahatta</u>

"To the center of the city where all roads meet, waiting for you
To the depths of the ocean where all hopes sank, searching for you
I was moving through the silence without motion, waiting for you
In a room with a window, in the corner I found truth."
- Ian Curtis of Joy Division, 'Shadowplay', <u>Unknown Pleasures</u>, 1979

"I was asking for something specific and perfect for my city,
Whereupon lo! Upsprang the aboriginal name."
- Walt Whitman, 'Mannahatta', <u>Leaves Of Grass</u>, 1855

The moment you touch the streets of New York City you know you've entered a different world. And you can't resist the urge to conquer it, knowing there is nothing you cannot do. You are a crucial electric cell rushing through its arteries, veins that are its subway trains and streets. It doesn't matter where you're from, even if you were born in Manhattan, or if you've already claimed it in some fashion or other, or if you live there today, you want to do it every day. Your spirit soars to tap the top ledges of all those towers.

* * * *

She was radiant, naturally elegant. He was casual, almost even at ease. She'd picked him up at Laidlaw Avenue near the fire station and reservoir, timed to the minute. Her Jeep was better for tight parking. Apparently she liked acid jazz. At least that's what she played in the tunnel.

They could only find a space much further south than they had hoped for and had to walk up Church Street to get to SoHo. There were plenty of tourists and weekend crowds already. Lorelei and Sol were pretending to be a couple, playing it up if and only when absolutely necessary. He invited her to an espresso at the corner of Franklin.

The first stop was technically still in TriBeCa, a tiny storefront on Lispenard Street that stretched deep into the warehouse building it was a part of. One of Sol's contacts had suggested the place if looking for objects out of the mainstream.

A few years ago an expatriate Cambodian man had opened an art and antiques shop specializing in European items dating before 1900 and back to medieval times. The proprietor, Anunt Teyakru, had fast gained a worthy reputation for taste and knowledge. He'd made all the right friends immediately and was routinely consulted by serious purveyors of the trade. He came from money, he showed up on the scene with money and he had made more money very quickly. The investigators were looking for newly arrived hotshots. Then they would look deeper if they had to.

Lorelei must have brought them some luck because they hit pay dirt right away. The man could not stop talking, a nasally high-pitched voice, Asian English, at once conspiratorial and condescending. He was a flamboyant queer, knew his stuff and enjoyed showing it off. He also knew about a rumored stash of 'priceless' erotica being shopped around. The whispers had been circulating over six months now. Genuine Old Master naughties at bargain basement prices. He'd had no substantial information come his way but a few of his clients had made vague inquiries. No, he could not discuss his clients. He could, however, advise them to look toward specialized European dealers, comfortable with these delicate matters. Any suggestions were welcome they said. He named a couple possibilities below Fourteenth Street but stressed what they had already surmised: the Upper East Side. That's where the real money was, and he explained that he liked to be downtown and make the money come to him. He also tried to sell them some racy Chinese silks before they left but they explained that they were only hunting Europeans that day.

Crossing Canal Street through Broadway they walked around SoHo to the few possibilities they'd made notes for. They had both done their homework and found that the first two painters they were looking for were not well represented in the New York Area. The Metropolitan, of course, had some samples but obviously was not a dealer. The Jewish Museum had one Steen, the Museum of the Hispanic Society of America had a Cano. And now they had a third artist to find. The only thing they all had in common was a fullness of color.

Jean-Honoré Fragonard was much more well-known than Cano and Steen, both then and now, but he died poor and forgotten. It was true: at the end of his illustrious life he was almost penniless, irrelevant, and made his exit with a bad reputation because of his standing with the new French revolutionary government. Napoleon himself had kicked Frago out of his apartment at the Académie Royale de Peintureet de Sculpture, named it the Napoleon Museum and it later became the Louvre. It wasn't until decades after he left the earth that the artist started getting the real respect he deserved. And yet, the odds were good that he could not have cared less about what his contemporaries thought of him.

Whereas Cano was very pious and mostly painted Christian mythological scenes, and Steen loved the common folk and loved painting them in their homes and taverns, Fragonard was all High Society, commissioned for grand, sumptuous works, nudes everywhere. He grew up with the arrogance of nobility and by the time he was twenty-four was a wealthy celebrity routinely courted by the aristocracy. He had notorious appetites and delighted in a scandalous lifestyle, reveling in the infamy of his sexual conquests. His patrons were only the wealthy and powerful, they and he who fell prey to The Terror. Frago escaped the guillotine only because of a favor he had once done for someone newly in power. But to the end, he lived in pleasure; died while enjoying a cold flavored ice on a hot day.

It was not a stretch of the imagination to see him painting an intimate love scene for any of the countless businessmen who called themselves his patrons. The photo of the supposed Fragonard erotica showed a work that could easily be the real thing. One had to consider the possibility of a forgery, but why go through the extraordinary effort and danger when such a thing was so easily disproven? The man's work is hard to copy; a mastery of technique and attention to detail. Or, as the art historian Marcel Brion put it: 'Fragonard owes nothing to anybody and imitates nobody.'

The picture was of a *ménage a triose*. Sunlight bathed someone's sleeping chamber, delicious colors tussled everything, flowers and foliage in giant urns throughout, a bed the size of a modern downtown studio apartment, shiny silk sheets, two nearly Rubenesque women, a man with a Greek god's body, all lazing in the proverbial love triangle. And there most certainly was every attention to detail.

If it were genuine, it had to be worth at least a couple million on the black market. They followed their checklists, working as quickly as they could, moving northward through the East Village and Chelsea almost to midtown. They made a good team; proficient, precise. They were bloodhounds on a trail, relentless. Even with a month or two and an expense account to spend in Manhattan, an ordinary person would not get to see all the great and not-so-great art dispersed throughout the island. Lorelei and Sol had to focus on true dealers of a particular time frame. She liked his odd air of authority, he respected her sharp eye. Together they cut through the sea of images and people like a pair of predators.

Noon. It was time to head uptown, past 45th, where the ultra-wealthy shop. After an abbreviated lunch in a deli across the street from Madison Square Park (rich or poor, everyone enjoys a good sandwich), they hopped in a cab that took them to East 79th where they restarted their quest with a top auction house and some of the major galleries. Up here there would be no pretense of being art buyers; real money can smell the fakes. The couple from Jersey was underdressed. Now they had to proceed with their true roles of investigators.

There were evasions, blatantly false statements, completely uninformed speculations and bland dismissals. But nothing tangible. It was already the middle of the afternoon and they'd been chasing vapors all day. On a longshot, they had even stopped into the New York Sex Museum on 47th and Park; two floors in a squat corner building obsessed with eternity's obsession. There was a one-wall display of Continental examples, two pages of text. Much of the whole place was about fetish and kitsch and the attendants all looked like art school interns.

What soon became apparent was that what they were looking for was hidden in a veiled world to which they were aliens. What they didn't know was how to get behind the curtain. They also didn't know that they already had.

There were two stops left on their lists. The last was near the East River and the next was about an eight- or nine-block walk. Moving south they essentially strolled along with the rest of the world, their legs now remembering how much longer city blocks are. Past rows of limousines and picture-perfect people, past Grand Central Station, east along 42nd past the Grand Hyatt and the Chrysler Building, and south again down Third Avenue to Thirty-Ninth.

In a neighborhood once known as Murray Hill (the actual hill leveled in the early 1800's) they caught the scent of their prey. That area, off and away from major traffic in all directions, was an eclectic mix of galleries ranging among mid-level internationals, legacy mainstays, decorative art depots, earnest newbies, and pseudogallerists. Combing through stacks of art journals, magazines, guides, webpages, newsletters and other periodicals, Lorelei had found a small advertisement for a gallery claiming to be "*A foremost specialist in European romantic paintings.*" On a lark, she had suggested to Sol that maybe the 'r' wasn't capitalized for a reason.

Tannenbaum, Ltd. Established 1906.Dealers of Fine Art and Antiques.A large storefront, a much larger store. An excellent display of beautiful lamps, small tables, mirrors, rugs, chairs, candleholders, hutches, bookcases, and so on. Large and small paintings on the wall in gilded frames, all classical. Expensive items but Sol noticed tiny signs of inactivity here and there, dust and little spider webs.

A commandingly beautiful woman with an air of mature propriety made a prim grey dress suit sexy as she calmly walked over to welcome them. Her long, straight black hair was loose and tucked behind her ears, her eyes large black pearls glistening from yards away. Perhaps instinctively, subconsciously, women often check for reactions from male accompaniment when another attractive woman approaches. Often, anyway. Lorelei made no such waste, Sol noticed, but went right to work with the woman after the offer of assistance.

"Oh, I hope so. We haven't had any luck at all today," she feigned. "Nathaniel and I just bought a condo, to see if we're compatible, you know, and we've been looking for just the right painting for our bedroom. One of lovers, of course."

"Yes, yes, you came to the right place, dear. We have sooo many paintings of lovers, I hope you'll spend a little time…" An indecipherable accent.

She ushered them over to a separate gallery toward the rear of the showroom where more paintings hung on two walls and faced rows of prints in utility frames stacked on their sides for patrons to thumb through.

After about a half hour of their perusing through famous reproductions, many indeed lovers through the ages, the woman returned to ask if they had any questions or seen anything they liked.

Sol stepped forward. "Actually, Matthilda and I, Matty, I mean. We were hoping against hope for a classic original. Something a little sexier, maybe. You don't have anything along the lines of a Fragonard in another room, by any chance?"

Impossibly, the woman's eyes became darker. "I'm afraid everything we have available is in this room. We don't keep anything in storage." She paused. "However, if it is Fragonard you are looking for I'm surprised you haven't visited the premier dealer of his works in the city."

"Well, then, so are we," joked Lorelei. "Just who might that be, please?"

With only a hint of superiority the woman replied, "Who else but the Guerroyant museum? They have a showroom and sales office on 57th."

"Who else?!" Sol agreed, though they were definitely surprised. *That's why Villeforte is the American representative for them...* "But we were all along gallery row today, from end to end!" he pleaded.

"They are on the second floor, sir, of number 126, near the park."

"Oh," said Lorelei, not remembering any parks among the galleries. "And what park is that, exactly?" She made the mistake of fumbling for a pocket map.

The woman sighed, "*Central* Park, dear, Central Park. It's two blocks north of 57th."

Lorelei flushed slightly red-faced and the woman regained professional politeness with a gracious smile. "If I'm not mistaken, and I'm sure I'm not, they're open until six on Saturdays. But we, unfortunately, will be closing in fifteen minutes. Was there anything else I might be able to help you with?"

"Thank you, no. I think we'll just head straight there," Sol closed. "Right, honey? Let's get *something* today... Anything you like, even if not for the bedroom." He placed a hand gently on her back.

"Okay..." Lorelei whimpered, "I just hope we can find our way in this awfully big city... Thank you so much, ma'am," the entitlement a younger woman's psychic missile. A long, outclassed walk to the front door, where outside they immediately turned toward the direction from which they'd come.

"*Matthilda*, Sol?! Really?..." she demanded, only partly amused.

"Just call me Nate..."

"After all the names today, Nathaniel was the first thing I could think of! Anyway, do you want to check out this last place or do you really want to go over to Frenchie's?"

"No, the 'Netherfriends Gallery' was just something I threw in because it was nearby. It's actually just an Amsterdam-style bar that hangs local artists. Let's go see Miss Villeforte and ask her a few questions. Just so she sees we're on the job..."

Lorelei looked at her new partner and saw on his pressed eyebrows and taught lips what for him must pass as a smile. "That's more than twenty blocks away. Another cab?"

"Subway will probably be faster, 4 to the Q," he stated.

"Okay... And the nearest station, Mr. New Yorker?"

"We just passed it a little while ago, 42nd and Lexington."

"I knew that! I just wanted to make sure we were on the same page..."

"Sure ya' did, Laura. Sure you did." And they walked briskly back to 'The Deuce', an old nickname for the infamous strip now made family-friendly by Disney and a clean-em'-up mayor-cum-hero. Well, who likes to see someone spitting in front of you?

Down in the tunnels it was slightly cooler than aboveground. For someone so street savvy, Sol was really taking a long time to get a couple of single-ride passes, it seemed to her. There wasn't that long a line when they got there. He'd asked her to wait by the turnstiles to watch what trains were leaving but almost seven minutes had passed now. When he finally came down the stairs he'd lost any air of levity he might have had just a little while ago. He handed her the strip card and said simply, "Let's go," as he moved onto the platform.

When she was near him he leaned in close, showing her some gallery brochure he had picked up along the way. "We're being followed."

She looked only at the paper, asking, "Seriously?"

"Am I the kidding type? Bring that map out again, please."

They made as though they were discussing destinations while he explained to her that there had been a man on a silver scooter with courier signs on its sides pulling out of a parking space, and away from them, up the block at the corner of 40th Street when they left Tannenbaum. The same scooter had been parked across the intersection at 87th Street when they had come out of the William Doyle Galleries. It could have been coincidence but you'd be hard-pressed to find a government or law office open on a Saturday, let alone two. But then the man had come down into the subway with them.

He had kept as much distance as he could from them but everyone in the world knows how hard it is to keep someone in sight down on the platforms, with all the columns, beams and other people. As plainly dressed as could be: khakis, tan/brown/white plaid shirt, black sneakers, he'd put on a Mets cap. He was behind them, at the next staircase. Just look for the cap.

"Lose him or catch him?" she asked.

"Let's prove me wrong. If not, then we say hello. First train that comes is ours."

It was a northbound 6, all local stops. Sol worked off-the-cuff. They waited for the third, getting out at Chase College, 68th Street. Saturdays in the summer a lot of the campus is empty but it remains open. Right outside the southeast subway exit is the entrance to the college's East Building which has a third floor windowed bridge across Lexington Avenue connecting it to the West Building. There was also a seventh-floor bridge, and another third-floor bridge across the intersection to another campus building. It was these elevations that Sol had been thinking about. Even community colleges in the suburbs have art galleries and Chase was the largest college for the City University of New York. So when the security guard asked where they were headed that's what they told him. The Bertha and Karl Leubsdorf Art Gallery is in the lobby of the West Building and they wanted to walk over the bridge.

There below them on the corner was the ersatz Yankees foe, ostensibly checking out the lunch trucks and hot dog stands while really trying to keep an eye on all the entrances of the three campus buildings at the intersection. And then he looked upward. They couldn't see each other's faces but he saw them up there and casually began to walk away. Sol and Lorelei bolted for the stairs. At the bottom, the security guard started to think of questioning the running pair as they flashed a badge and some kind of large ID in passing.

Outside the man had disappeared. He'd walked away from the subway entrances and blended into the scenery. Should they go back to the scooter? No, the guy would let it sit. Or have someone else pick it up. Or it was already gone.

"Let's split up," he said. "I'll take the south quad, three-block radius."

"Right. Look at my shoes, Sol." Decent for walking, useless for running.

"Okay. Stay west on 68th until you hit the park. I'll try to loop around and meet you there."

He took off at a steady pace, not chasing blindly but instead taking in everything in sight and checking down alleys and glancing inside stores. At Park Avenue he zigzagged outward and made the wide circle.

But it was no use. There was no sign of their observer. At the east end of *the* park they reconnoitered. They weren't far from Carnegie Hall, which was approximately the location of 126 57th Street, according to the map. They opted to walk through the park and cool down.

Who was watching them? Were they being marked for a robbery by professionals in the city or did someone know who they were and what they were doing? Or did they pick up a tail along the way, someone who may be looking for the same objects, called in by any one of the dozens of people they'd talked to. Was it Inspector Sebastian's man? Or did Pines put a detail on them? They'd informed him of their outing today.

"I wouldn't be surprised if he did," Sol ranted, his blood boiling. "It would be just like the Feds to overcompensate."

"Whoever it was, now we have to expect it," Lorelei noted.

"Oh, yeah. Even in Jersey City. Or especially."

"Do you want to call Pines and ask him?"

"Tomorrow, in person. I would have just loved to get a hold of that guy..."

"Well, I don't think the librarians sent him..."

It was ten minutes to six by the time they got to 57th Street. When they reached the gallery, the doors were locked and only strategic lights were on. They peered through the glass walls down the length of the opulent showroom but nothing stirred. Suddenly a figure emerged from the darkness. Walking toward them out of a midtown expanse filled only with expensively comfortable leather seating and exponentially expensive artwork was a trim, sure-footed young man in a simple, well-cut burgundy suit carrying a large, dark red leather satchel that matched his shoes. About Sol's height, his reddish brown hair was stylishly combed, longish. Clean-cut, but his eyes were as dark as the corners of the room. Harsh features made his face severe.

He did not open the doors but announced through the slight airspace between them that the gallery was closed. Sol acknowledged the obvious and asked when Mlle. Villeforte might next be in her office, they'd met her yesterday and she'd extended an invitation to visit the gallery (the last bit a lie, of course). The man's visage softened subtly. He lowered his briefcase, reached into his pocket and retrieved a ring of keys.

"Please, do come in," he said as he pulled the door open. "I was actually just leaving, but I'm in no hurry. I can turn on the lights and give you a few minutes if you wanted to look around..."

Lorelei insisted they wouldn't impose on his hospitality and, in any case, had just happened to be in the neighborhood.

"Oh, well, Francine is never here on the weekends. She should have told you that. And unless one makes an appointment with her there's no telling when she'll stroll in. Otherwise, Marcel is here ten to six during the week if you need help finding art."

"Are you one of the dealers?" Sol asked.

"Me? No, I'm strictly back office. Do you know what you're looking for?"

"Miss Villeforte mentioned that there were works by Fragonard available for sale."

The man blinked. A wide smile crept open over gleaming teeth. "Of course," he answered. "Please allow me to introduce myself. I am Louis Efrain Coles. I've worked for the Guerroyant for some five years now, accounting. All of the pieces we have in the US are over in that corner. But we have a large catalogue of prints available as well and we could always have a particular piece shipped from France if you really had to have it...

"Please, take your time. Make your visit worthwhile. I'll be right back."

They had to look around, at least. Mr. Coles appeared moments later with a bottle of wine and three glasses.

"I'm sure Francine would have my hide if I didn't show her guests a proper welcome. This is a cabernet from California. Yes, the French like Californian wines. Aren't they a world's treasure, Monsieur Fragonard's works? Nothing like them." He passed them each their glass.

"Nothing like them," agreed Lorelei. "And you have others..."

"Many. The smaller ones, you know. Was there something in particular you were looking for?"

"The lesser known works," suggested Sol.

"Ah. Then you *will* have to wait to meet with Francine, she's the expert. Are you sure you won't consider other artists? Lesser known?..."

"Such as...?" asked Lorelei.

"Oh, I don't know, I thought perhaps you might have other favorites..."

The man looked Lorelei eye to eye, glaringly lustful, erasing Sol's presence. He was actually a very handsome man. She accepted the volley, and responded in kind, "Only the masters, thank you."

Sol followed his primate leanings and his voice became gruff, "Who else would you suggest, Mr. Coles?"

A reluctant shift of attention, "You never know, Mister..., oh, so sorry, I didn't get your name..."

"Mister will do for now. Thank you, Mr. Coles. We'll come back another time."

Out on the street they didn't speak until they were a few blocks away.

"You kind of cut that short, Sol. Maybe we could have gotten more information from him."

"He'll still be available."

"Mister is my dog's name, by the way."

"How interesting."

"So you don't think this guy might have told us something useful?"

"If he does he's keeping it to himself. If he doesn't, then he was just amusing himself. Either way, he was toying with us. I had to at least pretend I was offended, otherwise we'd look fake. Moreover, he probably knows what Villeforte is looking for and the longer we stayed the stickier it would have gotten. No matter what, he'll tell her we came by."

"We need to find out if she's dealt with these kinds of things before."

"Exactly. Hang on, I'm starving, aren't you?"

"I could eat."

They ducked in to a small Italian restaurant at 54th, off Broadway. Lorelei was semi-fluent, explaining to Sol that she'd started to learn the language last year in anticipation of meeting her fiancé's parents and grandparents.

"The thieves have been everywhere we have," Sol suggested. "They did their research in looking for the buyers."

"Or they're working down some list of original owners?" she asked.

"Where would they have gotten this list?"

"It was with the paintings?"

"A history of provenance…"

"Even for erotic pictures."

"And you think it might still be at the library?"

"Or it was at one time. We'll know tomorrow."

"Meanwhile, we have to expect watchers now."

"Sol, can I ask you a personal question?"

"Shoot."

"Funny you should say that. I noticed you didn't bring a gun with you today."

"Good observation. I'm not a cop, I don't have to have one on me all the time."

"You don't think there was the smallest chance it might have come in handy?"

"You have yours, don't you?"

They finished their meal and hailed a cab back to Worth Street where they'd parked. Coming out of the tunnel on the Jersey side they were stunned by a giant mural on a billboard above the Route 9 gas station. Sol asked that they pull over, mentioning the wall he'd seen painted in the nearby warehouse district. She told him of the one at Communipaw Avenue. They agreed they were all probably done by the same people.

This was one of the largest forms of outdoor advertising allowed by local law, made up of three huge panels. Again it was a classical style painting. Colonial times, small buildings, plenty of greenery left. It was a riot, peasants it seemed. Yes, peasants, as you looked closer. Was it a reproduction of a known painting? No, there was an odd surrealism from where they could see, and large graphic design lettering: JERSEY CITY – A PROUD HISTORY OF RIOTING. Obviously not a work commissioned by the city.

"Let's get closer," he suggested.

The billboard was actually on top of a six-story apartment building next to the station. They eased the car over to a spot in front. Shady neighborhood, but maximum impact on the traffic coming in from the city. The empty commercial buildings began one block over.

It was almost eight. They looked for a super's bell and found a buzzer separate from the others. A small sign taped next to it said, 'Ring bell, go to basement door and wait.' So they did.

There was the noise of children. Just as Sol was about to knock, a squat man with a squat mustache appeared, Hispanic accent, already in pajama pants and undershirt; probably worked an early shift in addition to this maintenance gig. They explained to him who they were and that they were hoping to gain access to the roof for a close look at the billboard. The man was about to have dinner. He asked for identification then said, "Go 'head, the door is open." The building was a walk-up.

On the roof they saw a landscape made to look like old maps, typeset letterings of areas with names like Wyltwick and Bergen, old Jersey City, common-folk being subdued by British soldiers. Definitely the same artist(s) he'd seen on the warehouse wall.

"The other one I saw also had ships in the background, did yours?" he asked.

"Couldn't see it that well, maybe... But it was definitely the same overall style."

"Okay, we'll have to check them both out again. The one on the wall was actually painted but I'm positive it was the same artist or artists."

* * * *

The 'raid' on Sunday went off without a hitch. Pines had secured the warrant, Lorelei had the keys. Special agent Macy was there, as well, along with two nameless 'assistants'.

118

Pines assured them he had not put a tail on them. Despite the general impression, he explained, the federal government doesn't have money for babysitters in these matters.

"No. Just cut-outs," grumbled Sol.

Pines ignored him. "But obviously someone *is* watching you. And I think it's only in Manhattan. You would have both noticed it here on your home ground. So you woke somebody up over there. You said it was before the Guerroyant, so what was on your list at the time?"

Lorelei said it didn't matter, they'd gone to over forty places by that time and more than half hadn't even been on their lists. They had been all over Manhattan.

"Alright," Pines conceded, "Let's find what they're looking for before they do."

Each of them took a drawer full of files from either of two cabinets; one labeled Pre-1960, the other reaching to the present.

Special Agent Pines, of course, had taken the years they'd been directed to and found what they were looking for. Underneath the last section of files, set aside for the museum was a thick, bound journal marked, in handwriting, 'Acquisitions 1901-1929'.

On July 6th, 1921, a 'Special Collection' was formally donated to the museum from Mr. Francis Wickenhauser. A side note was made: 'See Board of Trustees'. The initials were W.C.H.; William Heppenheimer, one of the library's founders.

"We had only looked into the files from the years of the museum transfer," said Pines.

"And it matches what I found in the microfiche," Sol added. "These guys were also seen at the Dempsey-Cartier fight together a few days beforehand. I'll bet the illegal transaction the thief mentioned was a wager."

"How the hell would they know *that*?" asked Macy.

"There's another journal," Lorelei responded, "for the group of paintings they're trying to sell; the 'Special Collection'.

* * * *

Downtown Jersey City has a large Hispanic population. Mostly Puerto Ricans and Cubans, but in the nineties came waves of Dominicans and Central Americans. In the seventies and eighties there existed a large swath of drug and gang activity between Jersey City's Newark Avenue and Hoboken's Newark Avenue, the two of which had only nineteen blocks between them on Grove Street. Bordered on the west by the highways, the area's streets were controlled by the first two groups of people, as was generally agreed by local law enforcement at the time. In the nineties the gentrification around Hamilton Park cut the area in half, the railroad tracks and empty spaces under 78 that led into Hoboken became a wasteland. Today, downtown in the state's second largest city it was anyone's game.

At the corner of 2nd and Coles there is a Honduran *parradillera*; essentially a small restaurant that specializes in roast pig and chickens and contraband beer (often illegally smuggled, usually served without a license, always untaxed; if confronted, the owner could always say it was their private stock served for good friends).

Among all tribes of people there are smugglers and bootleggers. And just like anyone, they have to eat. This place was popular among *traficantes* because of the good number of tables and the pretty serving girls.

The narcotics unit was split in two cars down either side of Second Street, the parking spots having been secured hours ago in daylight. They were watching for a Cuban junkie named Hugo, small and hunched over, long hair, thick glasses. He would be buying from a young group of Mexicans at the restaurant at nine o'clock.

Hugo was a snitch, one with a dominating heroin habit and a three-year prison sentence hanging over his head for a sloppy, jones-driven burglary. Two nights away from his medicine was an eternity in hell for him and these young punks were nothing to him, garbage to be discarded, probably never see them again. He'd come across them last night when he'd been flashing his paycheck cash at a go-go bar on Paterson Plank Road. The deal was he led them to a nice, quiet place a few blocks away where "his" car was parked and Sanders and his people could arrest them all. With the chaos and confusion of the bust the dealers don't often notice that the snitch is placed alone in a black-and-white. Another few blocks and he (or she sometimes) is let out to scurry off with whatever he got, signing an informant's statement later in the week. Hugo only had to do this two more times before they completely cut him loose. Or at least until the next time he got caught.

Anthony was in the unmarked car just off Newark with his new partner Vivian Pereira, a sexy cat-eyed action addict. When the narcs closed in on their targets, one of the Mexicans tried to run. Anthony and Vivian were the ones that wrangled him in. The kid, spiked hair and leather jacket, barely looked the eighteen years his work permit gave him.

After a rundown, Vivian always had to decompress from the adrenaline rush. Out came the pack of cigarettes.

13.

<u>Mariette Savoy</u>

"Somehow I suspect that if Shakespeare were alive today,
he might be a jazz fan himself."
- Duke Ellington, programme notes to <u>Such Sweet Thunder</u>

"And art made tongue-tied by authority."
- Shakespeare, <u>Sonnet 66</u>, line 11

If one is fortunate enough, smiled upon by the heavens, if it is God's will, if we fulfill the purpose of two living cells becoming one, if we are determined to live to the fullest and survive the worst, we get to see the whole world change completely several times over.

* * * *

Mariette had never wanted to be anything but a librarian. As a young girl she lived within canyons of books, her childhood home a valley of open volumes. Her mother and father were her guides through the myriad worlds opened through portals called pages. She was too young, and her family too poor, to travel the way she dreamed of and knew she later would, so she let the words take her there first.

Despite not being of the luxury class her family had made sure to have a library in their home. And once a year her parents gathered her and her sister and brother for a weekend trip to Vienna to visit one of the most beautiful places in the world: the *Hofbibliothek* of the Habsburgs, the National Library of Austria, where all things were possible.

She once imagined herself the last surviving protector of all knowledge against a furious dictator who was in that time slaughtering thousands of people in Europe to rewrite history in his own name. As against all book-burners throughout the story of civilization, she knew she had to be one of those few who would fight to the end to keep truth alive.

And she knew that now, here, where she had decided to make her final home, it was again time to stand up against injustice.

* * * *

It had been a week since she'd seen her future husband. He'd explained that it was a crash course in the narco team, trial by fire. Lorelei was sleeping fitfully, awakening at the slightest sound. Anthony tried to be quiet as he came in but Mister was never off-duty. It was a little after three.

He smelled of cigarette smoke but he wasn't a smoker. She stirred and let him know she wasn't asleep.

"Hi, sweetie," he whispered. "I would've called but it was already past midnight."

"I've missed you," she said, "Is basic training over yet?"

"Pretty much. We made a bust tonight, my first with these guys."

"Nobody got hurt?"

"Nobody got hurt. Perps have a few scrapes, though."

"You smell like smoke."

"That new partner I told you about. He smokes like a chimney. I can't get away from it."

She wondered about his squad and realized she hadn't thought to ask who his CO was.

"Sanders. Detective Sanders," he answered. "He's really old school."

* * * *

At an uncertain certain age, one no longer needs alarm clocks. We simply begin awakening earlier, working, however lackluster or efficiently productive, toward the next hour of sleep.

But Mariette no longer even thought about sleep, either. For her, it had always been another day to be enjoyed. Her mind and her spirit were always ready and her body still jumped.

Somewhere before dawn she was awakened by a dream of absurdity, rooms in the sky, strangers as friends, gibberish conversations. And when in the world did she begin dreaming of cartoon people?

Nonsense, she laughed it off internally as she quietly made her way out of bed. The bear beside her wouldn't stir to rising for another hour or two. The beloved fool still pretended to live a life of luxury.

She moved through the stillness as if moving through time itself, reviewing all the landmarks and bridges in the hallway and on the stairs. In the kitchen is where the world began, not with a bang but with a flicker.

 * * * *

When he got up early enough in the week Sol liked to catch the first fifteen minutes of the BBC news. It made him feel worldly for awhile. Breakfast for his little household and he was at the center of the universe.

A steady drizzle outside gave him the excuse to put the gym on hold today. He sorted through the last couple days' mail, bundled tomorrow's recycling and went about inspecting his building for scenes of the animals' criminal activities. Surprisingly, aside from the usual misdemeanors there was nothing. He'd assumed at least one of them was guilty of something the way they'd followed him around.

Which made him think of other innocents. Today was the librarian party. They would all be there, or most of them, and he'd be on the job. It was time to sniff out the wolf amongst the sheep. He didn't have a top five list but there were contenders. Still, it would be something new for him to catch an unlawful librarian. Or two.

And what about the head librarian? That sweet, dignified old lady? Thinking back, Sol remembered a few shysty senior citizens in his time. Wronged by family, looking to make a plush retirement, or terrified by the thought of an ignoble departure, age had never been a barrier to greed. Far-fetched, maybe, but some things you can't even make up. He pulled her file.

Mariette Savoy: Age sixty, born Torbergin Windischgarsten, Austria; family moved around a lot in Europe until they emigrated to the States in '58, South Carolina, of all places. Graduated state university in Columbia where she also attained her Master's. Early sixties, Women's Liberation times. Married Doctor Savoy, professor, in 1967. Worked as a corporate librarian, legal department of a pharmaceutical giant until 1970, when she had the first of three children; took an administrative position at Princeton in '84, went public in 1989 when she moved to Jersey City. A list of associations from local historical societies to charities to the ACLU. *Certainly keeps herself busy…*

The library closed early this afternoon. There were only a few more of the suspects he had to size up; if he didn't see them at work he would look for them tonight.

* * * *

124

At about ten to noon a good-looking man in a sharp dark blue suit made a superior entrance into the library. The way he strode in like an aristocrat made Lorelei stand up and take notice. He looked like he'd been walking a few blocks in that heat and suit and tie, a bit of sweat dampened his golden brown forelock. He was accustomed to directness and she obliged him.

"In a hurry?" she asked.

He took her in and got in touch with his gallantry, like an Elmer Gantry.

"Not any more… I heard they moved the law library downtown. I'm an attorney with the D.A.'s office. Used to be the building next door. Where's it now, please?"

"Aren't you the assistant DA? I've seen your picture."

"Really?… Actually, I'm one of two, the junior. You saw me in the papers? "

"Sheriff's office, it's on the contact board in the lobby."

"Oh."

"Law library's on the fourth floor. Do you want me to get the elevator?"

"You're the operator, too?!" he asked idiotically.

"No, Mr. De La Cruz, I just call it for you."

"I'm sorry, that was stupid. It's hot outside. And in here…, where's the air conditioning?"

"Fourth floor."

"Right, I'll take the stairs. What did you say your name was, deputy?"

"I didn't, sir."

"Goddamn, Sol!" he exclaimed when he saw they were alone. "Please tell me you're boning the security guard! She's got some serious attitude."

"She's a cop. And she's engaged."

"So?!"

"So you know how I feel about dating cops."

"Who said anything about dating?"

"Why are you here, Paul?"

"Because you don't have a life. And because it behooves me to do some charitable work once in a while and offer you the illusion of a life. Just kidding, you know I love you. Actually, I went to see you uptown and they told me where you were stuck for the summer. I had to see it for myself."

"And now you have."

"Stop crying, you've got twenty-first century Ginger Rogers to look at when you come to work now, in uniform... And you've still got air conditioning! Anyway, it's friggin' Fourth of July weekend! Let's go ballistic! No driving, man, I just need the voice of reason with me tonight. I've got this group of chicks from the Sussex County Public Defender's Office coming to hang out and Caroline says *she's* gonna be around with her friends, too. You know they love the wing man..."

"No can do. The librarians are having a party tonight."

"You're kidding, right?"

"Nope. Maybe afterwards, but I have to put in an appearance."

"You would rather hang out with a bunch of old farts than with your buddies?"

"I'm the new guy. It would be rude not to show up."

"Jeez, Louise... God help me," he moaned. "Alright. How 'bout lunch? My treat, I'm already here."

That afternoon the Jersey City Free Public Library closed at three. Sol, however, returned from his lunch with Paul and closed the law library at one-thirty.

* * * *

It was about twenty after eight, the sun had just called it a day. Tucked into the quiet neighborhood on Lincoln Park's south side are two streets of densely shaded Colonial manors, practically hidden. Sol parked at the top of the hill. The Savoy residence was at 99 Gifford Street, a charming purple manse with a buff front yard and pointy-eyed windows, light violet shingles. A sturdy white-haired man was exiting the house from an arched stone walkway on the side. Immaculate informal master of the house, he had the face of a country boy sneaking off to go fishing, caught by surprise, travel bag in hand. Dressed like an English gentleman, he was off for adventure.

"Oh! You must be Sol. I know everyone else."

"Yes, sir. Mr. Savoy?"

"None other. Pleased to meet you, son."

"And I you. Aren't you staying for the party?"

"Me? Oh, no, I'm not invited. I'm a lowly playwright. Mariette says it's 'a librarian thing' and I wouldn't understand. Decades running now. No, I'm off to have some real fun. If you survive tonight, we'll see each other again" He glanced behind him into the front windows. "Phoebe is in the front room, she'll get the door for you. Be well!"

Where the hell did that Rolls Royce limousine come from? It wasn't there when Sol arrived. It slipped up silently and whisked Dr. Savoy away.

No doorbell, only a big gargoyle knocker. Announce your presence. Four knocks. It wasn't Phoebe, it was Meredith.

His heart only skipped half a beat. Then he was back on track.

"Hi, Meredith. You look fantastic." A short powder-blue evening gown. Torture.

"Thank you! You...um... you've got color in your tie!" she squeaked.

"Special occasion," he replied.

"Is that Sol?!" came Phoebe's shout. "Wonderful! Everyone's here," she said as she greeted Sol with a warm handshake. "We can get started!" She took his arm and led him off to the left inside the house to the salon where everyone else was already gathered. Mild, friendly welcomes.

Mariette came forward to greet him with a light kiss on the cheek and ushered him over to a bar opposite a fireplace. He helped himself to an icy ginger ale. She pointed to a floppy old brown hat on a small table.

"If no one volunteers we pick numbers," she nearly whispered. "So far, Phoebe's going first. You did bring something to read, didn't you?"

"I did." And he picked number nine.

"I chose a passage from Iain Banks' 1990 novel, 'Use of Weapons' for tonight," Phoebe announced. "Appropriate for a bomb-bursting holiday.

"In all the human societies we have ever reviewed," she began, "in every age and in every state, there has seldom if ever been a shortage of eager young males prepared to kill and die to preserve the security, comfort and prejudices of their elders, and what you call heroism is just an expression of this fact; there is never a scarcity of idiots..."

When she finished John jumped up and volunteered an impassioned diatribe about the greatest country on Earth, ungrateful liberals and about how grade-school children are still taught the lie about Magellan having made the first circumnavigation of the globe and eventually read from William Morris's 'News From Nowhere'.

And so it went for their reading: poetry and prose, comedy and criticisms, classics, modern. That pretty brown-haired girl read a hushed recital of one of Rilke's 'Duino Elegies'; the Indian gentleman (Prem they called him) read from Smith's 'Wealth of Nations'; Meredith read a passage from 'The Death and Life of Great American Cities' by Jane Jacobs; Caleb Soter read part of an essay by Edwin Muir, the woman named Cecilia read from the Buddhavacana, Pete though it funny to read from 'Yertle the Turtle' by Dr. Seuss. And then it was Sol's turn. He'd brought 'The Glass Bead Game' by Hermann Hesse, having bookmarked a favorite part. The young Russian read part of a chapter from Chaucer's 'Canterbury Tales' (The Tale of the Man of Lawe). Mariette followed with a few pages from Ursula K. Le Guin's 'The Dispossessed'; the quiet American read from the prologue to Umberto Eco's 'Foucault's Pendulum' and Rebecca finished in grand style with a long, powerful poem she had written herself.

The one-night literary circle broke up and they moved about like molecules with new missions. Now it was getting mixed up. Everyone else was familiar with the large house, comfortable, at home. Sol stayed in the salon for a while like a piece of furniture before drifting through a long hallway where he heard the live sounds of a piano being played.

14.

<u>Dmitri Tovaryetsky</u>

"Why, to what purpose, did He become man, expose himself to injurious mistreatment, ignominious and painful death on the cross? Was it not in order to show man, through His example, that no decision is too hard, that it is worthwhile bearing anything in order not to remain in the womb of the One? That any torture whatever to the living being is better than the 'bliss' of the rest-satiate 'ideal' being?"
- Lev Shestov, <u>Athens and Jerusalem</u>, 1930–37

The universal lottery awards you a bagful of days. You don't know how many you get, you're only allowed one at a time, moment by moment. That's your prize.

* * * *

For him, the whole of human existence was contained in a set of black and white keys. All laid out before you, the numbers perfect, no end, no beginning. Within them was held wonder, fear, joy, hunger, peace, lust, wrath, love, doubt and abandon. Within them were desperation and hope, play and purpose. Without you, the keys are useless, but with them, you may touch eternity.

There was no one in the room. Or maybe there was. He didn't bother to look. He was having a conversation with God. An argument, really, as usual. It was the complaint department and he demanded to speak to whoever was in charge.

With all due respect he began politely; gentle afternoon pleasantries, an explanation of his predicament and a plea for relief. No help. Somehow the rules had been broken; a time limit expired, prerequisites unfulfilled, proof of purchase missing. He insisted on an exchange or a full refund. There was nothing to be done. The return policy is posted but no one ever bothers to look.

And so began an onslaught of reclamations, outraged questions, and crazed insults until an exhausted and wholly unresolved animosity. But this isn't over…

Dmitri loved Mariette's Steinway. It was far more exquisite than his own currently available lover but never given the attentions that only he could offer.

Then he noticed that there actually was someone else in the room. It was the law librarian.

"And just what are you staring at?" he asked his audience.

"That was incredible." Sol answered.

"What was?"

"You're playing. It was amazing."

"I wasn't *playing*. I was fighting. Can't you tell the difference?"

"Well, you know what I mean."

"Yes. Yes, I suppose I do. Forgive me, I get carried away. And thank you for your compliment." He stood and introduced himself. He was about ten feet taller than Sol.

"I don't mean to flatter you, but that was unlike anything I've ever heard before. Is that your composition?"

"There was no composition."

"You made it up as you went along?"

"It makes me up."

"Ah. I know what you mean. I'm a drummer."

But for wildly uncombed black hair, the tall, thin, impeccably attired, blued-eyed Russian attempted to peer into Sol's eyes, possibly his soul, with his own genius-cursed orbs and was rebuffed by an invisible wall. His accent was not too many years old.

"Not quite the same thing now, is it?" he asked snobbishly.

"Sure it is. Drums can be cerebral and piano often becomes primal."

"Well said. Do you like jazz?"

"Only if it's free."

"I think you and I can be friends, Sol. Like Bud Powell and Walter Gieseking."

"What were you fighting about?"

"Why we don't get to choose our own day to die, even if it's two hundred years off. Same old thing. And that if there is indeed a hell, I'll give the devil his due as well."

Rebecca, Mariette and the African woman walked in (Sol still didn't know her name, only that she wore her native clothing). In the chair to Sol's left dropped Rebecca, lightly slapping the top of his hand. "Isn't he awesome?" she asked. Sol conceded by nodding.

Mariette took the space next to Sol on the settee and the other woman huddled into the chair in the corner.

"Aha!!" exclaimed Dmitri. "*Now* I have an audience! Please take no offense, Sol, it *is* somewhat awkward to have only one person watching one practice, almost like an interrogation." An odd smile. He returned to his seat in front of the piano.

"No offense taken, I stole in." Sol answered.

"And so, Mariette," continued the madman, "you were summoned by your unfaithful piano's pleadings to be allowed to come home with me?"

"You do remember what happened the last time you asked, don't you, Dmitri?"

"I was distracted! That traitorous woman I'd brought to your event was on your side! And you know I have the money, what's the point of your stubbornness?"

"That piano means more to me than your money or mine and I tire of telling you."

"Fine! I will show the four of you what a crime that is."

He disappeared them all with a fake bored wave of his hand and returned his gaze to the object of his desire. He closed his eyes and began caressing her, teasing, asking, demanding. He invited her to dance, to swoon, to deny him. But he was her slave, the trick that's played, sworn to perform. He started to sweat a bit, each note of unbearable ecstasy. But he had to stop, there were people watching.

"Voyeurs…," he growled, as he turned to face them: wide-eyed Cecilia, admiring Savoy, stoic Sol and Rebecca with that goddamned innocent smile.

"Right…" he pronounced in British Russian. " And now I am going to punish you all with a song with lyrics in my broken Russian American English."

He began pounding out a tarantella.

Well if someone had been waiting
For an answer to a call
And realized they'd been shouting out
To nothing there at all

And if that someone someday
Were lucky to discover
That what they thought they sought

Was really something other

That the truth so oft elusive
Lay not in what is viewed
Could not be found wherever
But in Paradise renewed

And so what if Jesus had been
Found using carnal knowledge?
Isn't that what all the kids learn
When they're sent away to college?

"Well, that's all I have right now. I'm thinking of turning it into an opera," Dmitri abruptly ended and stood. "And now, I shall go imagine I am in the Caribbean."

Rebecca made mild mock applause. Dmitri bowed and vanished. Without a word, Cecilia, the African woman, followed after him.

"Are you enjoying yourself, Sol?" asked Mariette.

"Thoroughly. Thank you again for inviting me."

"It couldn't happen without you, Sol," said Rebecca.

"That's very nice of you to say."

"It's true."

"Come, Sol, I have a treat for you," Mariette teased. "I've been told you have a healthy appetite." She took his arm and led them to a large dining room where the other women and Prem were setting out the last items of a veritable feast on the longest solid dinner table Sol had ever seen. Cecilia shuffled back into the kitchen. There were dishes of a dozen different cuisines, all of them prepared to perfection.

The slight Indian American, late forties, early fifties, with glasses from the seventies, looked at Sol and with a straight face said, "I'm not really helping. I like to sample everything before it arrives at the table."

"That, and Gods forbid he should be seen doing a woman's job…" insinuated Phoebe.

Meredith flanked her, pinching the man on the elbow, "All the male librarians seem to feel the need to defend their masculinity."

"It looks lovely everyone," Mariette proclaimed. "Thank you so much for your help."

"OOHHH… MMYY… GAAWWDD!!!!" came John's wailing bellow from the salon. "CAN WE EAT NOW, SAVOY?!"

Mariette looked at Sol and giggled. "He likes to call me by my last name because he thinks he knows something about history." For just a moment she looked like a mischievous little girl. "Meredith, please?"

Meredith howled back in the giant's direction, "COME AND GET IT, BOYS!! AND PUT ON SOME PROPER DINNER MUSIC!! PETEY!..."

Like a king with a rook and two bishops, in filed Caleb (bohemian turtleneck scruffy), Thomas (tall and thin) and Dmitri (taller and thinner) with John as a lumbering backdrop. Sol recognized the sounds of Miles Davis, the 'Sorcerer' album. Mariette sat to Sol's right and explained that John was allowed one end of the table because, as he put it, he didn't 'want to hurt anyone'. And that because of his chauvinisms the other end automatically went to a woman. This year it was Rebecca.

"The girls helped me prepare *Lamb Kokkinisto* in your honor, Sol." Of course they had figured out from his last name he was Greek. They'd even brought a bottle of ouzo.

A quick game of musical chairs and everyone was seated. In front of him were Meredith and Dmitri, not directly because there was an even number of settings on that side to his side's odd. The place to Sol's left remained empty until Pete came rushing in.

"Where's mah food? You know these are the only times I eat a good meal!"

"Aw, come off it!" answered Caleb. "You know Grammy takes good care of you!"

"Yeah, she does...," grinned the self-admitted newspaper nerd. "Hey, John, you know there's a band called Me First and the Gimme Gimmes?" He reached a hand past the giant for a turkey leg and had it smacked away.

"No, there isn't. Now, hush. Savoy's gotta give her speech."

"Thank you all for coming tonight," Mariette said with plain sincerity. "And thank you for helping to make Sol welcome to our ranks. Let's enjoy."

Dishes, decanters, ladles and bottles began to fly back and forth. There must have been seven different conversations going on. Phoebe was unleashing on Mariette the hour or two she hadn't been able to converse while helping with the party preparations. There was sports talk at the left end of the table. It'd been centuries since Sol had had a home-cooked meal, aside from his own bland experiments. The meat was faithfully seasoned and tender served over soft, comforting orzo. Amid all the clinking and chatter Sol could hear Radiohead's 'Kid A'.

Something was strange about the music selected for this party. In the short time he'd been there he'd heard a mazurka, flamenco, riot grrrls, a crooner, soca, electroclash, classic rock, a sinfonietta, old-school hip-hop, a folk protest song and Dmitri's crazy piano sonatas. Privately bemused, it seemed excellently chaotic to him. When he had a chance, he asked Mariette who'd made the song mix for the evening.

"Why, we all did. Everyone brings something and we let the player go random. Just another one of those silly little games."

His thoughts were whirling. *Who are these people?* Who of these could be an art thief? How many of them? *All of them…each and every one*, he thought. Together, even, as a group. Yes, as a group. *No, that's nuts*, he argued with himself. *Not a single one of them acted guiltily.* Or was he allowing his personal affinities to cloud his judgment? He questioned his intuition, but he knew. He knew that none of these people showed any of the tell-tale signs. And yet, nobody was that good. Not in real life.

So they knew something.

They knew there had been a recent investigation involving art stolen from the place where they all worked. And then there was a new librarian. And a new security guard.

No. These people were not stupid. Far from it. The feds had underestimated them, but Sol would not make the same mistake. They knew who he was and what he was looking for, even if they were not guilty of anything. So he would proceed from there.

Everyone helped with dishes and clearing the table. John placed one of those massive arms around Sol's shoulder and hustled him toward the rear of the house where there were a dozen patio chairs set out on a deck that could have fit a cruise liner. "Trust me, old boy, I'm rescuing you. If you stay inside they'll pick you apart like turkey buzzards. We're going out for a smoke." The other men followed behind them like cloak-and-dagger ministers.

In a circle around an umbrella table, some of them had an after-dinner tobacco. Thomas, the quiet older guy, lit a pipe, which Sol actually liked the smell of, cherry something, Pete smoked one of his ubiquitous 'reds' and the others, except for Soter, cigars, which Sol could only endure for so long. Cigarettes and their beastly fathers made Sol nauseous.

Thomas explained that he would have to leave shortly but wanted to welcome Sol to stop by a holiday cookout he was having tomorrow. He apologized for the short notice explaining that he had waited to invite him in person and handed him a printed invitation.

"It's more of a guy's party," John assured him. "If you know what I mean. Us boys'll all be there."

"It's a family event," Thomas corrected, "But the boathouse becomes a sports lounge with a grill shack. And there are a few boats available if you want to go out on the lake. Phoebe's got a large van she's taking some folks in if you'd like a ride."

Sol looked at the postcard: a half-hour's drive going west. It might be nice to get out of the city for a while. It might also be necessary to get a closer look at Thomas Patterson.

They all shot the breeze but did not ask Sol any questions. The back lot was expansive, a copse of trees leading to a fence at the property line that looked in to the turn-of-the-century park with revival temple structures scattered here and there. There was a greenhouse on the other side of a large gazebo in the middle of the yard. Soon the cigar smoke was a thick dimension around them and Sol excused himself to take a look around.

15.

<u>Isobel Carrino</u>

"I learned three things in Zurich during the war. I wrote them down.
Firstly, you're either a revolutionary or you're not, and if you're not you might as
well be an artist as anything else. Secondly, if you can't be an artist, you might as
well be a revolutionary.
I forget the third thing."
- Tom Stoppard, *Travesties*, last lines.

in a forest pitch-dark
glowed the tiniest spark
it burst into flame
like me : like me

in a heart full of dust
lives a creature called lust
it surprises and scares
like me : like me

in a tower of steel
nature forges a deal
to raise wonderful hell
like me : like me
- Sjon, for Bjork, 'Isobel', <u>Post</u> 1995

Perfectly imperfect, she concluded, for the thousandth time. Such is life and if you overthink it you get stuck in place and go nowhere. She reminded herself that staying unfettered by doubt had kept her days fluid.

She was the most unlikely of sorts to try to start a revolution, but, hey, you only get one chance.

* * * *

Sol wandered toward the greenhouse. Something beckoned him toward it. The interweaving scents of jasmine and honeysuckle, magnolias and belladonna. It stirred memories of his visits to the American South. Sweet summer nights of aimlessness and temporary freedoms.

He slipped in the door silent by nature. This was a hothouse, flowers from foreign lands, tropical rarities, orchids and delicate fruit-bearers. He walked among vases and vines breathing pure air laced with pleasure.

At first he thought he might be hallucinating. She looked like a ghost. She was glowing. In a loose white dress, at the far end of the long aisle she was perched atop a table, barefoot, her petite goddess legs bridging a river across to the other table. The long brown cascades of her hair like mountain streams at night. Why hadn't he noticed her beauty earlier? She was oblivious to his presence. What was her name again?

He was drawn to her. *I should turn and leave.* She was lost in thought. It was time to find out who she was. He coughed. She jumped.

"I'm sorry, I didn't want you to see me sneaking away. So I'll just say hi and bye." He walked toward her with his hand extended. "We haven't actually met yet."

"I love it in here," she said. "I could just sit here for hours."

"It is nice in here. That's why I didn't notice you were in here right away."

She looked up at him with wide dark star eyes and smiled the night sky, her pale skin illuminated by moonlight. They introduced one another.

"You probably think it's ridiculous for someone to just sit and think about plants," she accused.

"Not at all."

"I was just wondering how curious it is that plants are valued more by people when they're turned into paper or powders." She wasn't smiling anymore.

"Like books and pumices?"

"No. Like money and drugs." She looked so innocent to be talking like that.

"The story of civilization," he answered.

"Greed and fighting. When there are so much more pleasurable things to be doing."

He couldn't help himself, it sprang into erection of its own accord. Her perfectly sized breasts were partly visible from the sleeveless halter. She was a delicious little forest nymph. He eased behind a small cart to hide his commander's abrupt alertness.

"Agreed, agreed," he pshawed.

Suddenly Soter was there with them, came in quiet as a cat.

"There you are!" His face was flush with laughter, nowhere on his brow the usual sobriety. "The dancing's started!"

"Uh oh," grinned Isobel.

"Yup, somebody loosed the librarians. It's officially a hoedown. Come on, you two!"

She jumped off her pedestal and hugged her boyfriend, or fiancé or whatever. Sol probably had an awkward look on his face.

"I'm gonna hang back for a minute," he covered. "I actually came in here to make a phone call. I'll be right behind you." It might have seemed a little unfriendly but better than walking in like the flag bearer at a parade.

When his surge of manly pride had finally subsided, Sol walked into a room filled with the most unusual collection of personalities he'd ever seen in one place, swinging and swaying and whooping it up. There was ragtime blaring. Mariette came strutting over, took Sol's hand and showed him what an old lady can do. It struck him like a water balloon: he was having fun.

Later in the evening, as he drove home, one thought echoed on the streets.

It's the quiet ones you have to watch out for.

16.

<u>Thomas Paterson</u>

"The cause of America is in a great measure the cause of all mankind.
We have it in our power to begin the world over again."
- Thomas Paine, *Common Sense* (1776)

That year the 4th of July fell on a Thursday. It was the occasional situation which inspired American companies, institutions and individuals to find creative ways to justify a four-day weekend. This required shutting down Friday as much as possible and no countrywoman or man would argue against an extended patriotic holiday. In truth, it had been less than two years since the 9/11 horror and the people in this country really needed to try to feel good about themselves again, even if just for a few days.

Privately, for his adult life after the roaring twenties, the Fourth had been like Christmas and New Year's Eve on the same day, but with warm weather. He always bought himself and his family new toys to play with in the outdoors and his wife rekindled her adventurous side. The kids were home from college, safe and sound. Friends and neighbors visited to help celebrate.

So he was thin and balding, so what? Baldness is not a crime, and he was still alive. Alive enough to still give anybody what's what. And despite all its faults, mistakes and arrogance, Thomas deeply loved his country for its triumphs and accomplishments and for its people. Most of them, anyway.

The previous weekend he'd set up the grills, the kiddie pools and slides, picnic tables, shade/mosquito tents, cooling and first aid stations and a modest amount of decorations. This one day of the year he opened his property to casual hikers and boaters from the nearby state park. The two municipalities that shared the lake jointly commissioned a local fireworks company to put on a show on the eastern waterfront where he had three acres and a launch. And in this out-of-the-way area in Morris County just about everyone knew each other to some degree.

An hour after sunrise, while it was still cool, he walked the grounds with his dogs. Though she obviously saw yearly that he enjoyed the Fourth, not even his spouse of nearly thirty years fully understood that on this one day of, by and for the people, he allowed himself to feel like a king.

139

* * * *

Independence Day was not that great a deal for Sol solely because he really, really did not like crowds. That, and the fireworks everywhere made him jumpy. He avoided the beaches and parks, street festivals and other large events. In fact, he usually avoided leaving his house altogether on that day and at nightfall simply went to the roof of his building to watch the rockets' red glare, and all that. In Jersey City the bangs and booms start around noon. And sometimes it's not firecrackers or M-80's.

He considered Paterson's invitation to the 'burbs and while there would surely be a crowd of some sort it would be nothing like the city throngs. Plus, some of the librarians would be there, too, and he could write it off on the FBI's bill. But he would leave it for the early evening.

In the morning he did the household chores and made a couple phone calls. Around eleven he decided to do some casework. It was two weeks now since he had taken this thing on, ten days to Bastille Day and still he couldn't get that old gut feeling, that certainty that he used to count on with these kinds of jobs. He pulled out three of those personal files.

Dmitri Tovaryetski: Thirty-one years old, landed in Philadelphia, PA, by way of Obninsk, Russia, at the vulnerable age of sixteen, after finishing that country's equivalent of high school, then had to do an extra year as a senior in an American high school to be able to attend university here; father was a cellist with the Philadelphia Orchestra; BFA from Villanova, librarian pedigree from Temple; worked at the State Library of New Jersey in Trenton until three years ago when he came here; *No mention whatsoever of his piano playing.* On the advisory committee for the local chapter of Russo-Americans Against Atomic Weapons.

Isobel Carrino: A lovely twenty-seven, bloomed in the wilds of Providence, Rhode Island; another one who ditched her home state after only one year of college, went for the warmer climes of San Diego to study biology; then decided to become a librarian in San Francisco; returned to the east in 1995, first working at a public school in south Jersey for a couple years before coming here; the same note about a recent home purchase that was in Soter's file. *Some guys have all the luck.*

Thomas Paterson: Fifty-five, originally from Knightdale, North Carolina;

140

a Navy man through and through, returning to service twice after graduating from the Academy at Annapolis; survived the Vietnam War as an officer with a few decorations; worked for the US Department of Agriculture for a good ten years when he came home; bought some land in New Jersey in the mid-eighties; four children, two twins, all college age; the only part-time librarian; on the Board of Directors at the Children's Hospital of Hudson County. *Doesn't seem to be lacking money...*

Matter of fact, none of these people seemed to be short of funds, which is usually motive number one for criminal enterprise. And they all engaged in selfless work in their spare time. This wasn't getting any easier.

* * * *

Lorelei was hitting the beach, it was bikini time and she was more than ready. Even crooks get a pass this weekend. She and Anthony had prepped and packed like the professionals they were and beat the traffic down to Surf City as though a daily errand. They'd rented a small beach house months in advance. It was going to be a few days of frolicking, seafood and fun in the sun. Anthony went out of his way to not look like a guido and she pretended not to see or revel in all the gapes and gawks on the boardwalk, but she was, after all, a Jersey girl.

* * * *

Exactly when, or even if, he'd actually agreed to ride with them today was entirely unclear to him, but at one o'clock there they were, outside his door and honking the horn. Except it wasn't a large van Phoebe was driving, it was a small bus. A hippie bus. And not a regular-sized school bus, but one of the short ones, painted all over with psychedelic swirls. It was a very special bus.

"Oh, loosen up already!" she scolded. "It makes the ride fun. You should see the reactions I get on the highway." In the seats of this unique vehicle were Peter, Caleb and John laughing hysterically at Sol's unmistakable mortification, Rebecca, Isobel and a blonde woman trying to restrain their giggles.

"I'll go get my things," he surrendered.

Because they could only go so fast, and with heavy holiday road volume, a normally thirty-minute ride was stretched into sixty-three and a half, like gum under your shoe. And yes, they listened to sixties folk music all along the highway. On cassette tape.

* * * *

Back in Jersey City, a stylish, red-haired young man was pacing the waterfront in a little-known section of Liberty State Park, a tiny peninsula at the bottom of Washington Street. Everyone was out and about and he wanted to be away from all the strollers, cruisers and loungers. While they were all enjoying the luxuries of a military empire, he was busy planning. Forget the party, he had only one thing in his heart and that was vengeance. He was thinking of a different holiday, similar to today's and coming up soon, but much more important to him.

* * * *

When the merry booksters arrived at Paterson's hamlet the celebration was well under way. Spread out over a large tract of idyllic lakefront property were kids playing games, adults at leisure. At a gigantic lodge of a house, the troupe was greeted by Thomas' wife, who knew the others and warmly welcomed Sol to make himself comfortable.

"You know where he is, John..." she hinted, and turned to the women. "Now, ladies, if you'll come with me I'll get you some refreshments. How was the ride over here?..."

John led the men down the hillock like the biggest of a gang of country boys ignoring all the good townsfolk. Sol was taking in the scenery, realizing he'd spent the last couple years only on city streets. The boathouse could have accommodated a small family comfortably. Inside was a group of about six or seven men ranging in age from late twenties to early sixties.

"Left, right, middle... What ever happened to forward?" Thomas was expounding at a restaurant-sized grill as he ruled over steaks and chops with an apron that read 'Dad's Place' on its front and a red, white and blue paper chef's hat. "There's my squad!" he exclaimed mildly as he saw his co-workers enter.

That was the loudest Sol had ever heard the man's voice used. "Plates and utensils are over by that window," pointed the large fork, "and the bar is at that back wall," gestured the tongs. "We were just hashing out the politics of the past year." Sol couldn't help wondering if religion was the topic in the wintertime. Introductions went around between Paterson's

142

audience and his fellow book mongers.

It was, as John had referred to it, more of a boys-only clubhouse for the day and after a while everyone had eased into congenial banter. Some freed themselves a little to use language they didn't let their children hear. Guests came and went. Every twenty minutes or so one of Thomas' sons stopped by to pick up food to bring to the other tables closer to the house, even though there was a large patio grill going out there manned by them. At one point the general discussion in the boathouse wandered toward the subject of gun laws. Some wanted greater freedoms, others tighter restrictions and a friendly debate ensued.

"I think we can all agree that it's absolutely necessary to be able to protect your loved ones and your citizen's rights on your property if and when necessary," said one man.

"That and you never know what random scumbag is packing out there," Pete added.

"So you're pro-gun..." Sol inquired neutrally.

"I'm not pro-gun, I'm anti-idiot," he replied.

"Here, here," Caleb toasted. There was some laughter and salutes to the Second Amendment. After solving a few more of the world's problems the talk branched off to a few tributaries and just general hanging out. By five o'clock women had started swinging by to check on and/or retrieve husbands and boyfriends. Children ran up to the door petitioning their fathers for redress against siblings or other transgressors, or for permissions to go here or there, do this or that. It was the family hour. Sol started to wonder how long his company was going to stay when Thomas came over to him.

"I'm really glad you could make it, Sol," he said.

"It must be horrible to live out here," dry sarcasm replied.

"Almost twenty years of misery now," beamed the older man's glasses. "Hey, there's something I want to show you. It's up in the house."

As they walked up the gentle slope Paterson told Sol the enviable story of how he'd been able to secure all this land for his family at an outrageously low price using full application of Reaganomics.

"John let it slip that you're a fan of radio," Thomas said as they walked inside through the kitchen. "He's got really good hearing."

"That rat fink."

"Relax, nobody cares about that. Not even Mariette. We're just trying to get to know you and I thought you would appreciate this."

On the third floor of this man's castle he opened a door to a small room packed wall to wall, floor to ceiling with a spaceship assortment of dials, antennae, knobs, switches, panels, gauges, meters, interfaces, drives, portals and screens, all apparently part of one machine controlled by a central monitor station at the far wall.

"I built it myself," said the proud inventor. "Radio waves from anywhere in the world and space, including the new digital audio transmissions, without interference or disruptions. Well beyond amateur and I don't have to buy any subscriptions from anyone."

"Well, I am a news junkie myself," Sol joked, "but isn't this a little much?"

"Not at all. I don't spend all my time in here. But if something pricks up my ears I can tune in and listen a lot closer. That way I always know what's going on."

On the way back to the boathouse they were accosted by their female co-workers who used them to infiltrate man land. The perimeter of the masculine fortress was breached and all the day's X-chromosome rules repealed. It was a festive republic.

The afternoon lazed into early evening. In addition to a couple motorboats there were some canoes and rowboats. John suggested they all take a few out on the lake before someone else got the same idea. Because Phoebe was close friends with John's wife, Michelle, she would go with them.

"No worries," stated John. "I have my Walkman."

Caleb and Isobel, of course, took a rowboat for themselves. Pete had become intimate with an outdoor lounge chair and proclaimed that only God would move him for at least another hour.

"Looks like it's just you and me, Sol," observed Rebecca, in her short shorts, tank top and pony tail. He was no longer in any hurry to leave. They opted for a canoe.

It wasn't even awkward between them, they were just two people enjoying the moment, talking like friends. As the sun began to set on the water, a sense of tranquility came over Sol that he chose to let last regardless of how ephemeral it might be.

* * * *

A 60's-and-70's cover band playing in front of an arcade finished their set and announced the start of the fireworks in a few minutes. Lorelei sent out a text message to family and friends. The last one was to Sol.

"Happy Fourth of July!!"

17.

Premdeep Sinha

"The evil of the world is made possible by nothing
but the sanction you give it."
- Ayn Rand, *Atlas Shrugged*, (1957)

In his house there was always hubbub. He liked it that way, though he was the calmest of all. His large family was his life's reward. Children of all ages scampering around, soon he'd have grandchildren, and he was fortunate enough to have his elders with them still. In all, things were as they should be for him.

Almost. There was a shadow that flitted about him that he could not dispel. He would catch a glimpse of it out of the corner of his eye when he was feeling glad of his blessings and then it would just sit on the floor and make things glum. He shooed it away but always knew it would keep returning until its conflict was resolved.

He considered a possible way he could rid himself of this dark thing but it involved a great risk to himself and those he loved. He did not think he would have the courage to take that risk. Perhaps he could simply take the shadow with him when he left this life and no one in his family, not even his wife, would ever have to know.

Except that there were others who knew his secret. And they were very much like family to him. And they also had darkness over them.

He considered, as he was dressing for work, how the world continually reminds us to expect the unexpected. One does the best with what we're given, strive wholeheartedly not to wrong anyone, obey society's rules, try to make the path clearer for those who will arrive after you. And yet, life loves to surprise.

He did not know everything, yet, but he knew a few things. He knew that Life was meant to be enjoyed. He knew that humans are fallible. He knew that in the experience you're presented with it's all merely a series of choices. Some right, some wrong.

He knew he had a decision to make and that the clock was ticking. He knew he would try to make the right call, as with everything else, but he did not from where he would summon the strength.

And he also knew that the new librarian would be coming to visit him today.

* * * *

The skies were oily sheet metal. Perfect for a Monday morning.

There were still two librarians he hadn't had a conversation with. One, he'd been purposely holding off. The other was avoiding him. He decided to visit them both today. But first he would review their files, the last of them all.

Ten years ago, when Sol had just started law school, he was doing freelance work for a law firm in town that handled immigration cases. Most of the time it had been translations (in college he had taken a minor in Romance languages after being forced to learn Latin for his pre-law jurisprudence classes). And although he had a few decent dictionaries of his own, he was on a tight budget and sharing an apartment with a roommate who liked to have a lot of parties and friends hanging out all the time.

So Sol would go to the language section of the public library. It had the best foreign language book collection in the area and that's where he first saw Prem, who was nestled in that warren-end section even then. They never spoke to each other much except that Sol occasionally had to ask for some volume or other that was kept behind the desk. But surely the man would have remembered Sol sitting nearby that year for hours on end; they both still looked much the same as a decade ago.

The woman Cecilia was the children's librarian and Sol could never have a cause or excuse for going into that room. And she had made every effort to not come into close contact with him at the party.

Their histories in this country started with the stamps on their visas, when they were already adults.

Premdeep Sinha: 53, Former accountant in his homeland of Vadodara, India; had to start all over when he got here in 1987; toughed it out in Brooklyn with his family where he got his MLS through Pace University night classes; brought his brood over to safer territory in Jersey by 1990 and worked for a couple years in a prison library until he was hired by Jersey City for his languages; gave his spare time to local immigrant services and associations. *If anyone was slick enough to pull this little heist off it would be this guy, but he was too honest for his own good.*

Cecilia Bangur: 40 years of age, originally a teacher in Kenema, Sierra

Leone; student visa in '95 to Atlanta University in Georgia where she apparently discovered the marvels of librarianship; moved to West New York in '97, married an American in 1998, divorced him in 2000, same year she started at Jersey City Free Public; one child, a daughter; prominent member of a local anti-violence group. *And the body of a 25-year old...*

And both of them guilty, Sol knew. Of something. Maybe not theft or extortion, but they knew something. It was time to find out what.

The library opens at nine and Sol waited until quarter after to walk downstairs. In the stairwell between the third and fourth floor he bumped into Lorelei who was asynchronously in an annoyingly chipper mood. It was the first time she smiled at him. At some other time he might have tried harder to return it but he was back on the job.

To get to the languages section one has to walk through an odd series of back corridors on the second floor, making exact rights and lefts along assortments of oversized-books, ancient and dusty multi-volume collections, portfolios and endless other curiae.

"Oh, Prem doesn't do Monday mornings," explained Meredith. "He comes in some time after twelve." She was covering the languages desk.

"Really... how nice. Well, thank you, Meredith. Hey, why didn't you go to Paterson's cookout last week?"

"*I* don't do mosquitoes, Sol, but I'm sure it was lovely."

"Yeah, it was kind of nice. Mosquitoes weren't bad at all, actually."

"Okay, I just don't like going out to the sticks." She wrinkled that adorable little nose. "Clashes with my wardrobe..."

* * * *

Lorelei was walking her mid-afternoon tour when she came across the young man the detectives had been watching the other day. He was sitting on the floor in one of the aisles with a large book opened on his lap. She could ask him to sit in a seat just to get a close look at the punk rocker but he seemed deep into what he was reading. He turned his dark eyes up to her and she continued on her patrol.

She found ways to discreetly look through windows facing out to the street at the front of the building to see if the undercovers were out there again but saw no watchers this time. It's a short block with a lot of parking activity. They could be farther away but she wasn't about to be obvious by going outside.

$* * * *$

He'd somehow gotten caught up in the law library papers and saw it was already four-thirty. Cecilia would have to wait 'til tomorrow. At five o'clock Sol went back to the languages room. Even in 1992, he remembered, this gentleman often had personal visitors and today was no different. These particular people weren't usually there for Czech novels or Italian poetry, they were friends and acquaintances stopping by to ask for financial advice.

It was rumored throughout town that Premdeep had the magic touch for picking stocks and other investments, that he had a better track record than some indexes. And it was all true. He helped a lot of public sector employees with their planning.

A large black man with gold wire-rim glasses, a corrections officer's uniform and well fed jowls had pulled a chair up to the desk upon which the other librarian, small and unassuming, had his legs propped. When they saw Sol enter, the badge straightened up a bit but Prem remained in repose. Sol waved a hand in greeting and walked over to a rack of foreign film videocassettes, seemingly browsing.

After about five minutes Prem hinted to his friend that he might have to pretend to be getting some work done. The guard, realizing his social call was being cut short due to a nosey co-worker loudly made his departure, grousing about coming back some other day and promising to try that "uh, recipe for that Indian dish you told me about."

Sol finished reading the back of the case for a Mastroianni movie in which he plays a Russian gypsy and calmly walked over to the elder colleague.

"You remember me, don't you, Prem? From ten years ago, I mean," Sol asked plainly.

"Of course.Funny how the world goes in circles, isn't it?" Sinha replied.

"Yes, it is. And yet again I have to ask for your help."

"What are you looking for?"

"Dutch, Spanish, French... Writings by famous painters or their admirers. Do you have anything like that?"

The man understood that Sol had little time to waste. He looked at him unblinking over his half-lens glasses.

"We have a dictionary of foreign phrases and abbreviations with some notable quotations, but it's mostly Latin and Greek. That's about it.

Nothing by or about artists."

"Yeah... What I'm looking for is kind of hard to find..."

"Perhaps you should look somewhere outside the library."

Clear. The man was telling him something.

"I've tried the bookstores and nearby library systems..."

"I was referring to other institutions. I'm sure there are other organizations in the metropolitan area with these interests, but that's not my area of expertise. I'm sorry I can't be of more help."

That was all Sol was getting from this man today, an invisible divider had been raised. He was about to thank him and leave when the man caught him off-guard and asked to see his hand.

"Excuse me?"

"Your right hand, I just want to look at it." And he simply took it, reading Sol's palm like a brief note on a prescription pad. "Not bad," said the man with pursed lips. Sol was asking himself where his normal reflex had been when his hand was already being returned to him. He laughed lightly in amusement. Fortune telling was ridiculous to him. But he asked anyway.

"Okay... so what did you see?"

"Not a whole lot, nothing you can't handle. You had a rough early life but it will get better. And you will have two children."

Sol smirked at this last bit. "Yeah, right. Not likely." He shook the other's hand and bade him good night.

* * * *

8:50pm. - "Sweet's" Indexed Catalogue of Building Construction For The Year 1906, Published By The Architectural Record Co. of 14 and 16 Vesey St., New York City, with 'A Recommendation As To Scope, Purpose And Plan From A Number Of Eminent Architects', was one of those little treasures Sol enjoyed finding in a library. He had grabbed it a couple weeks ago to cross reference materials for a project he was working on in a part of his property built the year before its publication.

Printed by the Herald Company of Binghamton Printers (New York) in the old lithographic processes, when there was still lead and other metals in the printer's ink, it was hardbound, 9" x 11" x 2" and weighed almost ten pounds.

Essentially it was 700+ page-length advertisements for big city material suppliers of the time. While it had been interesting to leaf through, with its drawings and early photographs, it hadn't been helpful for his own purpose, or scope, or plan. He'd almost forgotten he still had it but the fourteen days were up and Sol hated having overdue books.

Since the thing was so heavy, he figured he'd run it up to the fourth floor, check it in himself from the law library and leave it on the cart outside the New Jersey room, where he'd gotten it from the Historic Project. Lorelei was near her desk as it was closing time and people were making their way out. He told her where he was headed and said he'd only be a few minutes.

He stopped to catch his breath on the third floor where he heard a light commotion down the corridor of darkened offices. He moved toward it quietly and heard dull thuds and shuffling. It was the Finance office, down at the end. The door had been pried open and he looked askance to see flashlight beams. He sent a text message to Lorelei: 3 flr now!

He slid in turning on the lights. There were four of them, Asian or Filipino. One had been right near the door, the other three had Phoebe Marin pinned on a desk. They were going to rape her. One had her mouth covered but her eyes were screaming terror.

Somewhere inside him a switch was flicked. With his left hand he clutched the throat of the one near the door, tripped out his legs and slammed him into the ground to land on the back of his head. One came at him from the right and having no other weapon Sol flung the lead weight book like a discus into the man's mouth where it smashed a couple teeth and sent him reeling backward. Sol charged him with one good roundhouse and knocked him out. The one who'd been holding Phoebe's arms behind her started circling Sol's left so he put his foot on a different desk and rammed it into the man's balls, pinning him against a wall, tearily preoccupied. Phoebe jumped down off the desk to shrink in a corner.

The big one who'd already had his pants down for the intended savagery was newly belted and had pulled out a four-inch blade. Sol squared off against him, fists balled, inviting the man to a fair fight.

"Put that away, you don't need that, do you? Look how big you are," he teased.

The Cro-Mag questioned himself and his pea brain told him he could take this geek who'd gotten lucky against his teammates. He tucked the knife in his back pocket (just in case) and raised his log-like arms, foolishly imagining he knew something about boxing.

Sol just started abusing him, slipping in and out, hitting him everywhere with everything, pummeling his face, a whirlwind of blows, then stepped back for both of them to appreciate the moment. The man wobbled slightly, dazed and confused and Sol came in to give him some more. Bull rage came over the larger man and they began pounding each other.

The others were getting up, repositioning themselves around him. They all carried knives and now it was kill-the-pig time. Sol pivoted back for a breath, he could maybe take a few cuts on the way to the hall and he yanked a power cord off a computer to help defend himself.

"Freeze, assholes! I can shoot three of you right away!" It was Lorelei, finally. Seconds are like hours in these situations. She did have the drop on them but when she called for back-up they rushed her anyway.

One was hit in the leg and dropped. Another was clipped on the arm as he lunged past her out the door, knocking her to the side. Sol tackled the one closest to him and Lorelei recovered to get a good aim at the big one's heart. The brute knew his luck was cold tonight so his hands reached up for ceiling.

Sol had taken a couple lumps to the head, glasses knocked off but he was otherwise unhurt. He cuffed two of the men with Lorelei's sets and used the power cord to subdue the one with the hole in his thigh. They quickly sat them all up against a wall.

"Phoebe's in shock. I'm going after the other guy," he said. "Won't need a gun with him."

Lorelei kept her gun on the rapists and went over to the woman in the corner, who was sitting wild-eyed and silent.

All Sol had to do was follow the trail of blood down the stairs. He caught up to him at the first floor landing, where he was clumsily heading for the exit. Chaos had cleared the building once the shots were fired. This one probably had a concussion to go with the bullet wound. He fell to his knees stumbling down the last steps and started crawling toward the door. Sol came up behind him, grabbed him by his hair and might have been about to smash his face into the marble when police officers stormed in and took control of the situation.

18.

<u>Cecilia Bangur</u>

"We do not need, and indeed never will have
all the answers before we act...
It is often only through taking action
that we can discover some of them."
- Charlotte Bunch, 'Not By Degrees', *Passionate Politics* (1987)

"Children's librarians are masochists.
Nobody understands them and nobody wants to."
- Karen Elliot, 'What I Really Learned In Library School'

It was hurricane season, arrived a month later than the official start that year. Tropical Storm Arthur was announcing his arrival with a herald. The winds rattled windows and the rain whipped everything mercilessly.

She was crying again. These days the tears just seemed to overtake her without warning. She'd gotten the phone call about Phoebe last night. She was terrified for her and for herself and all the others.
But she would not give in to fear, ever again.

* * * *

The library was closed to the public the day after the attack. Staff persons were requested to report to work when they were ready as the crime scenes had already been secured or cleared. The story in the media was that a librarian had been assaulted after interrupting a group of vandals, who were ultimately subdued by other library personnel and police. Peter Roque had been forbidden by his editor to go anywhere near the case so he took a leave of absence from the paper and went on a rogue reporter's rampage.

There were a few detectives and a half dozen patrol officers moving about. Almost all of the women who worked on the third floor had taken a few personal days. None of the librarians had failed to show up except, of course, Phoebe, who was at Christ Hospital under psychiatric observation and wasn't talking to anyone.

It wasn't her he wanted to talk to right now, anyway; she would come around soon enough, he was sure from the little he knew of her. She wasn't even supposed to have been there last night. In true form, she had offered to close up the library for Savoy, who was attending a fundraiser. *Busybody woman just had to go through all the rooms.* He had a nervous anger.

The burglars had also broken into a file cabinet with payroll records and were going through the personnel files when Phoebe must have interrupted them. Lorelei said the group never came in through the front entrance so someone else had to have let them in from the basement and they had taken the back stairs to the third floor. In the evenings only a handful of librarians are covering the main desks, no one worked in the back rooms. Sol didn't have to ask the police why those men were seeking what they were. But Special Agent Pines said in a day or two he would get authority over the case as part of his overall investigation and then they would interrogate the assailants to find out who sent them. Sol and Lorelei had briefed him that night.

In the meantime, Sol requested that he be relieved of his duties in the law library for a few days. There was no use pretending to be an innocent bystander anymore. He was going to end this one way or another.

"I need to have the leash removed so I can do my job," he said to his employer.

Lorelei was forced by protocol to take a couple days off after having had to fire her weapon. But she would return to her post on Thursday regardless of what the librarians might or might not know. Sol would keep her up to speed on anything he found. First, though, there was one particular librarian he wanted to speak to in private.

Perhaps she thought Sol hadn't noticed that she always retreated somewhere whenever he walked into the room. Or how some of the other librarians seemed to run interference for her. But he had, every time. And out of all of them, she was the only one who had given away signs of being afraid of something before last night.

She nearly jumped out of her skin when she came out of the supply closet and saw him standing there, rain dripping off his hair and trench coat. He wasn't wearing his glasses today.

"Hello, Cecilia."

She stuttered a 'good morning'.

"You have something to tell me, don't you?" he asked. She was almost trembling.

"About what, Sol? About last night? I wasn't here, this room closes at six." A clipped British accent.

"About what you're hiding. About what you know pertaining to the stolen paintings."

She blinked three times. "I don't know what you're talking about."

"I think you do. And I think you know I'm not asking out of sheer curiosity."

Silence. She didn't know if she could trust this man.

"More people might get hurt over this and you'll feel better after you tell me, believe me."

"I know what everyone else knows. That some paintings were stolen from the museum. We were all questioned and cleared by the FBI."

"Then why are you so scared?" She froze. "I'm a friend, Cecilia. I can help close the matter."

Slowly she sank into her chair, started crying, long heavy sobs. He gently put a firm hand on her shoulder. "Let it out."

"It's not just the authorities looking for these paintings."

"I'm starting to get that... Do you know who else it is that wants them?"

"Yes."

"How do you know?"

She was starting to pull herself together but couldn't seem to start crying. "Last year, in the first week of the school year, a fifteen year old boy was shot and killed by another boy the same age. At school.

"In his grief and in his outrage the boy's father nearly went out of his mind trying to find out how this could have happened, who had given that other boy a gun. He demanded of the police that they tell him where the gun had come from but they had no answers. Instead, he was arrested and spent the weekend in jail for attempted assault on a police officer and disorderly conduct. Those charges were dismissed on Monday when the judge understood what had happened. That Tuesday was 9-11 and the shooting was all but forgotten."

And she kept crying.

"The boy who was killed was my nephew, my brother's son." Embers of rage flared up in her and she straightened her shoulders, shutting off her tears.

"I'm sorry, Cecilia." He gave her a moment before asking the obvious question but she was already answering it.

"The detectives were only able to determine that the gun had been circulating among a Bloods gang here in the city. But it had been involved in a number of previous crimes and soon became shuffled about in various chains of evidence. The police told my brother, Robert, that they would notify him when they had more information.

"But he didn't sit around waiting for them to call. With the little information he had he went and tracked that gun down to its origin. It had come from our own people. It wasn't American suppliers, it was Africans. My brother found out there were African gangs here in America, in Jersey City, who sell guns bought in the southern states.

"Robert tried to build a legal case but kept running into walls. No one would touch it. He couldn't get hard evidence.

"And then he received a threat against his family by the people he was pursuing. He has two other children and didn't want to lose them as well. He had to suppress his agony.

"Nonetheless, he started a local community action organization, of which I am a member, which works to inform people about the dangers that these death dealers present to our children and our neighborhoods."

"Okay, but..."

"Wait. They know who we are and we know who they are but the most we can do to fight them is hold vigils and information events. They laugh at us.

"As for what you are asking me, this is what separates me from the other librarians: In April, two months after we'd been interviewed by the FBI, we all received three phone calls. The first was a gruff, digitally altered voice threatening our lives and those of our families if any of us were the ones selling those sex paintings and did not sell to them. We were given an e-mail address to contact and were told that they would know if any one of us went to the authorities. The second call was from a woman with a heavy Spanish accent who offered to pay double what was being asked for those same paintings, if we were the seller. We were given a phone number to call if we wanted to talk, which one of us traced to an answering service in South Florida. The first two calls had been made to our homes and they knew our names. But the last call had been made to us right here in the library wherever we happened to be that particular day and did not address us by name. It was a low, hushed voice of a man who said he was the one everyone was looking for and that he knew we were innocent of any wrongdoing. He told us all the exact same thing, 'Do nothing and it will all soon be over on a mid-summer's night'. That was it. Mariette called a meeting in late March when she saw how everyone was acting strangely and she realized it hadn't just been the head librarian who had gotten the calls. We decided to wait it out. Even if the calls could be traced, what good would it do? These people obviously knew how to get to us and maybe they did have a way of knowing if we tried to contact the police or FBI. How could we be sure? We all have someone they can hurt."

Sol nodded in understanding. She continued.

"And then in May, the Friday before Mother's Day, I received a visit here in this room. A group of women I'd never seen in the library before brought their small children in for one of our storytelling hours. After a little while I recognized them. They were the wives and girlfriends of the gun sellers.

"I remember knowing they had come to see me and when the other mothers left, they lingered. Then one of them, a real nasty devil of a woman, came right out and called me by my first name. She said that if I knew of any one in this library who was selling expensive European paintings of people having sex that I should call her straightaway and they would give me a nice commission. She wrote a number down on an index card, of all things, and said I shouldn't tell anyone of their visit or they might have to look for me at home. I was so disgusted I ripped the paper into little shreds and walked outside to throw it into a garbage can on the street where it belonged.

"I told Mariette and Phoebe because I was scared but I have a child to protect and to take care of so I had to keep coming to work. Without going into detail, Mariette asked the others to keep an eye on me because there had been an incident connected to the situation with the paintings.

"Things were quiet for a few weeks and we all started quietly hoping that this whole thing really might just go away on its own. And then you showed up. And we knew something was going to happen. And now Phoebe's been attacked..."

"I need to know where I can find the people you're talking about."

"Sol, these people are nothing but killers. They have no souls."

"I'm not tryin' to start a war with anyone, Cecilia. I just wanna find the paintings and put an end to this whole thing so everyone can get on with their lives."

"How do you expect to do that? No one knows where they are or who the real thief is."

"I just need one address. The boss's office, where they operate out of. I'll work from there. You don't have to give me any names."

She vacillated.

"Just the street and the building or house number. Please."

She gave it to him.

19.

<u>Circulation</u>

"I shut my eyes in order to see."
- Paul Gauguin

The house was on a corner, probably picked for the benefit of being able to see down all directions. White aluminum siding, white aluminum fence, requisite two Rottweilers in the front yard. It was a mixed-population neighborhood off Ocean Avenue but there were quite a few West Indies flags hanging from rearview mirrors and on bumper stickers. It was one of the most dangerous parts of the city and Sol would stick out like a cliché undercover cop sitting in a car on that street, as well as be an easy target for any honchos that didn't take kindly to such types.

So he would have to make himself look like a run-of-the-mill local drug addict and do a calculated number of hurried walk-throughs. Then he could know where to set up some type of surveillance.

He tried all different time frames over 48 hours. They were night creatures, which helped a lot. The heavy rain of those two days more than covered him in the daytime.

Half a block down from them on Armstrong Avenue was a vacant 3-floor house. From the attic he could point strong lenses at the entire intersection. A check at the tax assessor's office produced a name and a number.

He called the Mr. Jenkins that was listed as the owner and actually reached him on the line. He was one of those good folk who still answered their own phone themselves.

Sol told Mr. Jenkins that he desperately needed his building for official business over the next ten days. Triple the current rent rate for the period would be paid in advance by the federal government, and Big Brother was strongly suggesting he be open to the offer, considering all those liens on a federally secured loan for the property. Mr. Jenkins was just happy to have that little bit of income in these harsh times.

Sol brought out his old watcher's equipment from their boxes, realizing bitterly that they weren't old at all, that it hadn't even been a full two years since he'd had to use it. Two cameras gave him a close-up on the second floor and a wide shot on the entire corner. He set up camp. A sleeping bag and a large cooler brought him home. When he had to sleep,

157

he programmed four-hour digital recordings which he viewed on fast forward when he woke up.

Nothing stirred around that house before noon. No children lived there. Anytime before lunch an errand boy was sent out for fast food and sundries. No one even cooked in that kitchen. Not food, anyway. And things didn't get rolling until around three.

He didn't expect much, Thursday through Sunday was the basic work schedule for these types. But by Wednesday night it was clear that this was a spot for anything. Guns are hard to move; if they were sold out of this place, it was only a part of the larger operation. Mostly Africans, some Americans that had been accepted. Partying, women, loud music, smoke, lots of drinking; beer, wine, liquor. Par for the course.

And on Thursday evening, precisely at 7:30, there were some unique guests. Japanese motorcycles, young Filipino men, three of them. Part of the Sterling Boys, same as the animals from the other night. This town wasn't that big after all.

Sol knew these guys from the ten years working here. Every immigrant group has its necessary outlaws and the new community from the Philippine Islands had these jokers. It was more show than strategy, they dabbled in drugs and gambling but were mostly late on arrival so had to make a niche for themselves off West Side Avenue in the West Bergen neighborhood. They had seized upon Sterling Avenue and tried to capitalize on the inference to the famous guns despite the difference in spelling.

They came out fifteen minutes later. It was no use trying to follow them on their crotch rockets and Sol knew where to find them anyway. Better to stay put for the moment, see if anything happened with his current target.

Somebody was putting up a bounty for these paintings and these two groups, seemingly worlds apart, both had an interest in it. They already had a connection: the way these boys had dismounted their bikes said they'd been here before. They were here for a regular transaction, drugs, guns or both. But they had a higher connection: a bigger boss who liked expensive European erotica.

* * * *

When she told him about what had happened Anthony was inscrutable, irritable. He suggested she consider opting out of the assignment. This surprised her since he knew she was not one to shrink from danger.

"Yeah, but it seems to be getting kinda messy now," he said off-handedly from in front of the television.

"And it's my job to clean it up," she reminded him.

"I'm just saying maybe it's time you started considering other options."

"Like what? A more ladylike profession? Or the barefoot-in-the-kitchen thing? What are you saying?"

"I don't know, forget it."

She didn't feel like letting it go. They argued. He stormed out. She was left confused and frustrated by his attitude.

* * * *

Friday morning, a little after three, Sol went looking for a house on Sterling Avenue with particular motorcycles in the front yard. It's usually a quiet residential area so he was able to cruise. A six-block stretch, only took a few minutes. There was at least one light on for each of the three floors. Even the basement had that familiar blue glow coming out from its little windows. They'd been getting high all night.

These guys were hardly an organized outfit. They were more of local bad boys. But they had been motivated to come out of their environment to sneak into the library just for files on the librarians. The gun runners also had taken a big risk with their move on Cecilia. There was something more than money pushing these guys. Felt like they were trying to buy cred; credibility, credentials with someone they needed to impress.

In a few hours he would be meeting with Lorelei and their overseers. He would tell them what he had and ask for FBI surveillance on both houses so he could move around. They had to work quickly now, it was forty eight hours to Bastille Day.

He went home to wash up and get a couple hours of sleep on a bed.

* * * *

By six the sun was already lighting up the Manhattan skyline. At the southern end of the New Jersey Palisades in the little town called Weehawken there sits on a cliff an old greystone mansion on Kingswood Road. A nearly solid bulk and unadorned, one might mistake it in passing for an embassy building or even a mortuary. In fact what it served as these days was actually the offices of a private real estate investment firm. In former lives it had been a Masonic lodge, a Jewish temple and a Polish cultural center, among other odd jobs and some long periods of inactivity.

And on that day it was also their next meeting place. She had arrived half an hour early (to beat the boys this time) in a dark blue compact borrowed from a friend and parked at a high point on the inclined street where she could see the entrance. She watched agents Macy and Pines meet with a thin, cow licked man in a brown cardigan sweater on the front steps, and they all quickly slipped in. Inspector Sebastian followed a few minutes later, alone.

At 6:25 she saw movement in her rearview mirror: Sol was coming down the sidewalk. He was walking like a man late for work.

She ducked down and as he passed she honked the horn lightly. He turned as if he'd set off a car alarm. She leaned over and opened the passenger door for him.

"Why aren't you answering your phone?"

"I'm in a very bad mood," he answered.

"Gotcha coffee just in case I caught you... Black and sweet, right?"

"So you did. Thank you. Laura." He tasted the coffee.

"Okay, so let me tell you what I think."

"By all means. Coffee's pretty good, where'd you find it?"

"Right on the boulevard, Cuban place. Anyway, from what you said last night, this thing is bigger than our superiors had anticipated. I believe they were taken by surprise."

"I agree."

"And you're one hundred percent positive it's not a librarian that's the thief?"

"Ninety-nine point five. There's always that possibility. But I'm pretty sure these people were set up. And still there's that slight chance that it was one of their own who would do something like that. More importantly though, it's not just an art heist. It's about to get above our pay grade. Now might be a good time for us to ask for a raise."

"Is money your only motivator?"

"No, just the top two. Wanna get going? It's time."

Door was open, no reception. Everyone was to go straight into the main hall. The man who had greeted the federal agents was Charles Bennett, a British national and principal of Bennett International Holdings, as well as current owner of the building in which they now stood.

Mr. Bennett had received one of those letters of offer for a painting by William Etty, a British painter best known for his nudes. Again there was a photo of the work being sold. But Mr. Bennett had received something none of the other entities solicited had: an old thin accountant's log, leather cover worse for wear but still proudly embossed with 'Waltham's of London'.

"Also, this time the letter doesn't make any claim of wrongful ownership," Macy informed them. "So we don't know why Mr. Bennett was selected as a potential buyer aside from his being a patron of the arts from England. The letter simply says they thought he'd be interested, that the painting belongs to the people of England."

"Why do *you* think they contacted you, Mr. Bennett?" Sol asked.

"The agents have already asked me that but I haven't the slightest idea," said the man.

Bull. He was lying. There was a reason he was approached but he wasn't telling.

"Our company and my family buy art, but certainly not this kind of thing. I was rather offended by this parcel. I called the local police but they told me over the phone that matters concerning the mail are a Federal affair and that I would have to call a postal inspector."

"Their offices are in Newark," interjected Agent Pines. He was looking through the little book. "They've also been instructed to contact my unit if there are any instances where artwork or artifacts are involved. This is the first we're meeting Mr. Bennett in person."

"What is Waltham's of London?" Lorelei asked Bennett.

"It's one of those stuffy old gentleman's clubs. But it's been defunct for over twenty-five years."

"How do you know of them then?"

"Everyone knows that name. Sort of like your Yale Club."

"Any connection to them through your family?" Sol suggested.

"None that I know of."

"If you'll forgive me, Mr. Bennett," Inspector Sebastian offered delicately, "You may want to look into that possibility. Perhaps someone in your family was a member?"

"And how the blazes would some art thief know that if I don't?!"

His feathers were ruffled. Everyone gave him a moment to smooth them. Pines had handed the book to his partner, who was now giving it to Lorelei.

On the first page, printed for identification data to be filled in were only the words, 'Book of Private Exhibits' inked in black letter calligraphy.

Inside were dated itemizations of acquisitions, sales and occasional auctions of nothing but paintings. For each listing there was an artist's name and title of the piece, as well as a detailed description including dimensions, materials and, of course, subject matter. It was all erotica. Among the artists listed were the names they were looking for.

The dates begin in 1885 and were closed out in the summer of 1914. A thirty-year book.

"At the start of the first world war," noted Inspector Sebastian.

"But seven years before they show up on the library's books..." mumbled Pines.

"Okay," asked Lorelei. "So what do these people expect to happen? The sellers, I mean. They're basically trying to extort a royal family, a museum, the Catholic Church and, and... a random businessman?"

"Why not?" responded Sol. "They've all got money. And they all have a reason for wanting the pieces offered. Except for Mr. Bennett, of course. And while he may not know why he was selected as a potential buyer, the sellers know who he is."

"They had to know someone would go to the police," poised Pines.

"But if anyone were interested in buying, they wouldn't. The thieves took that gamble," Sol replied.

"How would they know it wasn't a trap?" countered Lorelei.

"They may or may not have made preparations for that. Either way they have to take a chance if they want to get rid of what they have," he concluded.

"When did you get this package, Mr. Bennett?" asked agent Macy.

"About two weeks ago but I've been rather busy and I wasn't able to call the postal inspectors until this past Tuesday." There was a collective groan for the lost days of possible clues.

"Can I see the box?" Lorelei requested. It had a Jersey City postmark. All the other letters had taken bumblebee international routes. But they had to have all originated here.

"Sol," as Pines looked at his watch, "I'm definitely taking you up on your request with those two locations. None of them from the other night are talking. Lorelei, looks like you'll be putting in some overtime outside the library. Inspector Sebastian has something he'd like to share with you two before you all walk out together. We just want to talk to Mr. Bennett for a couple minutes. I'll be in touch."

Just inside the front entrance, the dapper Inspector offered a colleague's knowing smile. "Now is when the real work begins, hey? I just wanted to let you know that we were not able to find anything in our records for the painting in question, but that is not surprising. *Tambien,* it does not say anything either way.

"So, Agent Pines mentioned that there seems to be some kind of drug and gun connection to these objects. You know... stolen and forged art are often, if not regularly, used as collateral for drugs, guns, all types of merchandise. We have seen it in Brazil and a few other countries."

"I was wondering about that," Sol told him.

"And, of course, it is very useful for the purposes of money laundering. As untraceable investing." The man gave them both a hard look, as if saying something without words. Was it about Bennett?

"Well," Sol answered, "the guys I've seen are nowhere near sophisticated enough to be on that level. They were put up to their actions by somebody higher up."

"Someone with the kind of money that these others have, no?"

"Exactly."

"Well, please let me know if can help you with anything at all. I am at your disposal night and day. My powers might be limited in this country but I steel know how to do research."

"Actually," Lorelei looked at Sol and then at Sebastian. "I had an idea that you are invaluable for. I'd like to discuss it with you later today. After I go over it with my partner."

"Oh, absolutely! I am starting to wear out the carpet in my hotel room!"

Lorelei followed Sol into Secaucus to a diner on the side of an industrial road where the dirt wheeled into the air by the passing trucks was a permanent fixture.

"What's your idea?" he asked over muddy coffee and beat-up cherry pie.

"Just a hunch. Put all the known would-be buyers in one room, like tonight, tomorrow. Ask for a volunteer to take the bait for a meet with the sellers. Except the good inspector is not an inspector, simply a representative of the church. We have to try to draw out the thief."

"That's true. But why not just ask Sebastian to do it? He'd be the best suited for the job."

"But the church is the least likely to negotiate with thieves."

"Good point. Okay, so if you'll clear it with Pines and coordinate, let me know when you need me. I have a hunch of my own to follow up on."

* * * *

Lorelei showed up to the library early as well. The neighborhood residents were all heading to work and she grabbed a parking space across the street and just a couple hundred feet down the next block, where she could see the front entrance. She was still in the borrowed car.

She sat looking at the old building with a wholly new understanding, an unfortunate intimacy with it. Who could have imagined that such a revered institution would be the site of a crime, now or ever? Let alone two. And she could have killed one of those men the other day. That's not like winging somebody. Maybe she wouldn't have even felt bad about taking out the trash. Maybe she should have mentioned that to the police psych she'd had to talk to.

Yesterday this place had felt like a funeral home. Visits had dropped noticeably. Even the regulars were avoiding one of their favorite hangouts. It wasn't just the shooting that had everybody scared. It had finally gotten in the news that a woman had almost been raped here.

At quarter of nine she saw Mr. Klein pull up in a wood-paneled station wagon that had somehow survived the 70's. A few minutes later, Thomas Paterson rounded the corner at Montgomery, looking around him cautiously as he walked briskly. Klein got out of his car and they greeted each other like Cold War border guards. She exited her car to meet them. Out of safety concerns female staff persons would not be opening or closing the library. But the maintenance manager and the librarian were glad to see Deputy McSherman there.

* * * *

Sol couldn't wait the eight or more hours it would take for Pines to get authorization and personnel for the broader surveillance. He went straight back to the crow's nest, entering through the side alley wearing a hardhat, goggles, overalls and a tool belt.

If he was right, today being Friday, the African house would be stocking up on merchandise for the weekend customers. At some point in the mid-day a small group would go shopping with a grocery list of illicit goods.

He was not wrong. They got up early, around ten, and there was a

164

clear buzz of activity. Sol hurried to his car which he had parked around the corner from the target. He laid low and started sweating the minutes that no one walked by. At ten-thirty a team of four loaded into a dark green truck in the garage.

Sol knew these streets too well for his own comfort. He was practically able to predict all the turns the driver would make as they made their way out of the city. They caught the Turnpike extension off Garfield Avenue and headed west toward Port Newark. He almost lost them in a staccato set of jug handle switches that brought them out into a distribution zone of giant shipping warehouses. He had to be careful with his distance now as there were fewer cars out here and he was completely unfamiliar with the territory.

They reached a desolate area of freight rail tracks and a single stretch of road, a Doremus Avenue. They turned onto a dirt road and Sol could no longer follow without being made. He tucked his car behind one of the small utility buildings dotting the landscape and set out on foot. Keeping the truck in his sight, he ran along the space between two sets of elevated railroad tracks. There were only highway overpasses ahead so they couldn't be going much farther.

The road ended, the truck slowed to a crawl over the rocky ground until it stopped directly under the interstate it had just gotten off of. Sol found the best spot to observe them from a starving mound of dirt with a few skinny trees, as well as to see if anyone else came behind them. He used a zoom lens on his camera to watch and snap shots.

A dark burgundy sedan came out from behind one of the massive concrete columns. A man and a woman. Young, but unless drug dealers started dressing like cops and driving standard unmarked cop cars, those two were cops. There was no license plate on the front, which is illegal in Jersey. Except if you're an undercover cop. They all shook hands like old friends.

The couple invited the gangsters to the back of their car. There was an exchange of small, square travel bags. Money and drugs. Sol took off as fast as he could back to his car.

Once there he found a patch of meadowlands marsh nearby where he lay prone to watch the road and wait for the vehicles to exit. It looked like there was only one way in or out of that area.

First the green sport truck, going back the way it came. A few minutes later the sedan, turning left to leave in the opposite direction, north on Doremus. He waited another minute and jumped in his car to follow, driving part of the way through his binoculars.

He watched them enter the on-ramp for Truck 1 & 9. He couldn't get close enough to read their back plates but he hoped they would somehow show him the town they worked out of. Instead they took him all the way up to 'Motel Mile' in North Bergen where they pulled into the Circle Inn Express.

Sol found the next u-turn and pulled into the parking lot of an auto parts store across the highway from the motel. He watched as the man came out of the office, they parked their car and the pair, teasing and laughing and groping, went into a room on the second floor with nothing but the clothes they had on, which would presumably soon be less of a burden as well.

Sol had to try to get that plate number. He got back on the highway and came around to the northbound lanes. He pulled up behind the motel and parked in front of a side exit. In the shade of the little corridor he pulled out his binoculars and took a mental photo of the license plate. He drove away and called the number in to Pines who ten minutes later told him they came back as fakes, no such record in the DMV.

Back to the motel. He parked outside and walked around the front to the office. He asked for a room on the north side, explaining that he wanted to be away from the noise of the intersection with Tonnelle Avenue. A short stay, he was on his way to the airport, he said.

He watched their door for two hours before they came out. He got a good look at their faces but was out of film. When they got in their car and pulled up to the office Sol tried racing to his car to go after them. He watched them osmose into the midday stream of traffic before he'd even gotten to his door. Pulling out of the lot he was slapped with a red light and cars in front of him at 36th Street. The trysters had caught all the greens and were long gone. He tried to catch up but it was futile.

He returned his room key. He would have to get a warrant for the motel manager to show him the rental card of his lost subjects. Another four hours of waiting. He went home to try to make sense of it all, stopping off at his usual one-hour photo place.

At 5:30 Pines called him with another brick wall. The driver's license number the man had used belonged to a convict currently serving a five year sentence in state prison. Sol faxed the photos over to Pines' office though the agent was out in the field.

* * * *

On the evening news Jersey City was on all the local channels for something besides another murder. A group of activists was blocking traffic on Marin Boulevard and First Street. The TV reporters said the group was protesting the sale of the building where Meredith had taken him to the art parties.

It had started a half hour ago and a few arrests had already been made but the protesters stayed in swift, rotating motion and supporters were pouring in.

20.

<u>Gentlemen and Villains</u>

"I turned the volume up this morning
'til there was ringing in my ears
I haven't felt this good in years

another villain on the cover
of every major magazine
the victim somewhere in between"
- Brian Vander Ark of The Verve Pipe, 'Villains', *Villains* (1996)

"Now
Your attention, please
Now turn off the light
Your infection please
I haven't got all night

Understand, do you understand?
Understand, I'm a gentleman, I'm a gentleman"
- Greg Dulli of The Afghan Whigs, 'Gentlemen', *Gentlemen* (1993)

William Etty's paintings are extraordinarily beautiful, though his personal life was rather unremarkable. He was a shy, reticent man. He did not spend his nights loudly carousing or counting the women he bedded. Not even a mention of a wife anywhere. He was never a part of any great movement and he never killed anyone (that we know of). Proper English education, modest financial success, died where he was born, relatively comfortable and untroubled.

But his nudes shall be eternal. His colors are mesmerizing and he was one of the few artists of his time to excel in painting classical motifs. Yet to this day he's still one of the most underrated. And though he could be rather preachy with some of his themes many of his works had a strong natural eroticism. *Two Girls Bathing. Musidora* (a buxom woman with her hand on her flower). *Nymph and Satyr. Candaules, King of Lydia, Shews his Wife by Stealth to Gyges, One of his Ministers, As She Goes to Bed.* All of these pieces burn with sexual intensity. His *Diana Standing by a Waterfall* would give any of today's lingerie models a run for their money.

In his time, his work shocked the status quo and was often referred to as indecent. *The Times* (London) declared them 'entirely too luscious for the public eye'.

Etty once wrote, "Finding God's most glorious work to be Woman, that all human beauty had been concentrated in her, I resolved to dedicate myself to painting".

The piece being proffered to Bennett, *Sappho in Exile*, was just slightly more graphic than the better-known works: two timelessly voluptuous women kissing and pleasuring one another out in nature, a field of wild flowers.

Sol was no art expert, but it seemed these four paintings causing so much trouble were simply parts of the artists' repertoires that were not spoken of in polite society. No, these kinds of works were only seen in 'Private Exhibits'. In places like gentlemen's clubs.

These days in the US, the term 'gentlemen's club' is only a euphemism for stripper bars. Even in London, where the true first clubs were founded, this had become the trend. The originals were city retreats for the aristocracy, places where the gentry could gamble (still illegal in public then), eat fine meals and relax away from their families. 'Clubland' on the West End used to mean something entirely different.

After England's series of Reform Acts from '32 to '85 by the late 1800's almost anyone with decent credentials and sizable funds could obtain membership in one club or other. Women started their own clubs. Waltham's, however, staunchly maintained its strict criteria of pedigree and status right up to its demise amidst the rampant liberalism of the nineteen sixties and seventies.

So what was Bennett's connection to Waltham's? That's all it could be, he'd gotten the book. Maybe he really didn't know, maybe it was buried deeper in his family's history than he'd bothered to look. Or maybe he did know and didn't want anyone else to know. But then why go to the police? He couldn't have been *that* offended... *But he could have been that threatened...* If he did have any connection to these paintings, and he really was so insulted, a capture of the culprits would put a lid on it for him. Any which way you posited it, this guy knew more than he was telling.

Sol flung the files down on the coffee table and started pacing. His place was a mess. His regular life had been thrown into disarray. He was being mean to his pets, dishes stacking up, unanswered phone messages. He hadn't checked his mail in days.

There was an invitation. To a party. Tonight. Union City.

It had arrived five days ago. Fine parchment paper, thermo graphic gold print. Addressed to his full name, "Please be Welcome and Invited to a Celebration of Independence".Food, music, dancing. No host, just a time and place. A 'plus one' and a handwritten postscript: "We can discuss art".

* * * *

Somewhere near Danbury, Connecticut.

He leaned back after an excellent lunch. His cooks had surprised him with Mediterranean sea fare. Normally, fish and such were routinely for dinner on Saturdays. But of course, he wouldn't be home tonight. And they knew how to read him by now. He no longer ate anything substantial anywhere away from home but tonight he would be sitting with his countrymen.

He pushed away from the table and stepped out onto the balcony. Two of the girls of the house were in the pool. Even more delicious. One was sunning, the dark-skinned one, and the other, the blonde, was doing laps. Both naked. A beautiful way to start the day.

But today had made itself a damned workday. He began going over the schedule in his head. It was almost eleven-thirty. He went upstairs to change out of his nightclothes and run a few miles on the treadmill. He would need two suits later; one for the meetings and one for the party.

He hated going into Jersey. If only for all the traffic and dirty industrial gloom and the teeming masses. And because it reminded him of harsh times in his youth. He would have his driver take the roundabout route, through the border at lower New York State with all those scenic lakes and hills.

* * * *

It was by the purest of coincidences that Sol should get a brief close look at Mister Llewellyn Yeshevin, one of the most successful real estate developers in the New York metro area, down in the old factory district that was rapidly being transformed.

The protests had subsided for the time being and Sol was checking out the area on foot, noting quite a few new upscale businesses since the last time he'd passed through here in the daytime. He'd stopped to rest in front of the new Golden Newport building, sat at a nice little bench when he'd noticed the rich man, him stancing peacock proud at his newly completed luxury residence tower, perfect scam of cheap property, cheap labor, cheap materials and lots of cosmetology and marketing. The skyscraper was a month old, like a newborn baby. Llewellyn had parked his best Mercedes Benz right on the promenade, next to the fountain.

Yeshevin had appeared like a robin on the lawn, swooping over the sidewalk to pop out of his car, eyes in the sky.

The artificially bronzed little white-haired man had his hands on his hips surveying the newest conquest for his kingdom. There were only the two of them out there that morning but Yeshevin thought he was the only person on the planet. Sol made a mental note of the man and continued his study of the neighborhood.

* * * *

Louis Efrain Coles stepped out of his house on Mercer Street to a glorious afternoon in his beloved Jersey City. This shady old lane of brownstones could be any town in Europe for him. Pigeons and terra cotta are the same everywhere. He was maybe a bit overdressed but didn't care. He was feeling empirical, unstoppable. There was a fire inside of him and it was growing.

He walked downtown ready to challenge God Himself, looking upon the streets as if he owned them, which, perhaps, he did in a way. He passed by the only real cafe in town, saw it was crowded, and headed for the Vietnamese restaurant a few blocks away. They had outdoor seating and it was the only place to get the powerful Lotus tea at the time.

This town had come a long way in the seven years he'd been here. He'd arrived when it was still unsafe to hang out where he was sitting now. On any given day you could have seen a fistfight or some other violent altercation on this street. There used to be open-air drug dealing on these corners.

In the late nineties, when the financial companies came they brought with them the flood of young urban professionals that all the real estate developers had been waiting on and salivating for with their newly-built but as-yet vacant apartment towers. They'd been planning for the market trend that had begun in Hoboken a few years before.

He'd seen it plenty of times elsewhere, most recently Alphabet City and the rest of Loisaida (LowerEastSide-uh). He supposed it was only natural. Artists, condemned to poverty, look for places they can afford to live and work in. They're an insular breed, they tend to congregate and help each other out. Word gets around in their community that there are districts that are artist-friendly. They make their neighborhoods more interesting and vibrant. Realtors actively seek out these artistic types for exploitation. Once a scene is started, young people with money and a sense of adventure want to live in these edgy areas. Lease rates rise steadily. Then people with even more money want to live at these fashionable addresses. Finally, the artists and the older residents get kicked out. Merely a financial cycle.

But sometimes money gets carried away, blind and ravenous with greed, taking more than it needs. And sometimes someone has to stand up to it, even if all you've got is a slingshot.

He finished his tea and ordered a spicy vegetarian lunch. He still had a lot of work to do later.

* * * *

Lorelei had arranged with Special Agent Pines and Inspector Sebastian a conference of sorts. The young Duke, the charming museum director and the squeaky clean Englishman had all agreed to be available for a half hour in the evening. Inspector Sebastian was simply Mister Sebastian, of the Granada Archdiocese Office of Art and Artifacts. To put everyone at ease, instead of FBI offices in downtown Newark, a banquet hall of a famous Italian restaurant on Avenue C in Bayonne was hastily secured for the hour before their regular business got going. Pines was alone.

Sol and Lorelei had gotten the okay to come in a few minutes later than everyone else. They sat together in Sol's car at a good angle across and down the street from the entrance. Neither was in a talkative mood. The sun was still shining warmly as it began setting over the bay and locals were out in droves. No one even looked twice as they passed them.

She would have told him if she had received any such type of invitation as he did. He had thought about it long and carefully. If he took her with him and it got nasty, it would be his fault for letting her come along. If he didn't tell her and went alone she would think he didn't trust her or her abilities. She was, after all, his partner, right? But she was a fledgling. A fledgling who'd earned her stripes already and certainly wasn't a frail little thing, he reminded himself.

And if something did go wrong and something happened to her how could he live with himself? Obviously someone knew who he was, but maybe they didn't know who she was and it should stay that way.

At exactly six-thirty, two entourages arrived. Mademoiselle

Villeforte stormed onto the scene with her SUV limousine and a small army of assistants. A more subdued luxury sedan pulled up across the street and out stepped the Dutch Duke with a devilishly good-looking black-haired girl in a burgundy dress and a large boulder-faced man in a suit, presumably a bodyguard.

They'd been asked to be discreet. Apparently the degree of discretion was unclear to them. Two minutes later the extraneous personnel were returning to their cars, no doubt swiftly dispatched by a certain federal agent. Both cars disappeared to park somewhere else. Right afterward, Mr. Bennett squeezed into a parking space with a two-seater sports coupe and rushed inside.

"Gang's all here," said Lorelei without any mirth. Pines would be handling the introductions and updated overview of the matter at hand. Once in the event room, Sol and Lorelei explained to their guests that it was now time to catch the thieves and retrieve the paintings but that it would help if one of them were to feign interest in making the purchase they'd been presented with. Of course, no one volunteered.

"Certainly not," scoffed Bennett. "Do I look like someone who has time to be playing cloak-and-dagger?"

Villeforte was disgusted. "Or do *I*?! Is this what you dragged me down to this heek town for? These people could be dangerous!"

Royal Chase was bored. "Perhaps Mr. Sebastian could extend his services to you, considering he's the only one getting paid to be here..."

"Or perhaps the Duke could make amends for his country's having stolen our painting in the first place," responded the Inspector.

"Oh, please," snorted Villeforte. "What would the Catholic church want with *real* art?"

"And why can't one of you special agent men or detectives pose as a buyer? Isn't that what you people do?" demanded Bennett.

"We suspect they know exactly who you each of you are and what you look like," Sol answered him.

Silence.

"They began by looking for moneyed buyers in this area," Lorelei explained. "That's how they found the Guerroyant. They had less luck with the Steen and the Cano, so they went down the lines of ownership."

"They'll have at least one document of provenance for each of the paintings." Sol was addressing Agent Pines. "The book from Waltham's came part and parcel with the whole donation to the library from Mr. Wickenhauser."

"Mr. Bennett," Lorelei picked up. "You and your family don't just buy art; you invest in it, as does your company. The sellers were looking for someone with enough cash and possible interest in a British painter."

"These people are working out of Jersey City," Sol continued. "So that's how they conducted their strategy. Because of their long connection to this area, the Dutch government maintains a small office of heritage and cultural affairs which lists the Duke as the official representative of the royal family in the United States. They know you live here."

"As for the Cano painting," concluded Lorelei, "the Catholic Church is a global entity but they had to start with the Granada Diocese."

"Why, because Spain has no money?" Chase lobbed the insult.

"Because that's where he was from," Sol answered. "And because the church has plenty of money."

"Fine," said Mister Sebastian. "I'll do it. The Duke is right. I am getting paid to look for this painting and so I shall do whatever I must."

Villeforte already had her cell phone in her hand. "Come get me. Now." She turned to Pines. "Special Agent Pines, I expect the next time you call me it will be to tell me you have my painting or you were all," she arced an eyebrow at Lorelei and Sol, "incapable of apprehending some petty street hustler." She bid farewell only to the Duke and Bennett.

"Just a second, Miss Villeforte," Sol stopped her. "Quick question: If we do get your painting back, what would the museum do with it? Sell it or store it? It's certainly not a piece that could be put on display..."

Her nostrils flared. "That is not for me to decide, nor for you to know. The museum's directors will do what's appropriate." And she could be bothered no more.

"Please," said Mr. Bennett as he prepared to also exit. "I would really prefer not to have any more to do with this whole thing. I personally don't care what happens to these paintings, so unless there's any other information you need from me I would appreciate not being called at all." He gave each of the men a fretful nod and extended his hand to Lorelei. "Detective McSherman, I wish I could say it was a pleasure." Off he went.

"You know, this is not terrible." The Duke was examining and finishing his glass of Italian table wine. "Well, I wish I could be of more help to you all but obviously I can't participate in such sleuthing activities. Now, if it were television that would be a different story. Otherwise, as I said before, feel free to call me to let me know how it turns out, yay or nay." Not exactly regally, he paused at the buffet table to gather a couple of items on a paper plate as he left.

The four investigators waited a few moments before any one spoke.

"What was your hunch, Laura?" asked Pines.

"I'm not even sure anymore," she conceded. "I thought maybe at least one of them would be a little too eager to help."

"We're going ahead anyway," Pines said. "That little break I told you about when we started was that someone else has already taken the bait. We've been periodically monitoring the book being used for the first letter. Last month a reply had been made on page 119, as opposed to page 98 as indicated in the Duke's letter. We asked him and he assures us he never had anyone make any type of response. This confirmed that there were other buyers approached who we know nothing about, as the two of you had already guessed. We looked for likely prospects and canvassed them but nothing panned out. Two weeks ago the Inspector made the response for the church but no one's contacted the offices in Granada. Obviously we don't have any more time. We've scheduled round-the-clock surveillance on the library starting at midnight. Laura, you and the Inspector will be attending tomorrow's panel discussion incognito. Sol and I will be watching the outside of the museum all day."

* * * *

Paul had called him earlier in the day and was parked outside his place when he got home. It wasn't a social call. The young D.A.'s assistant had a concerned look on his face. He'd been assigned the burglary and attempted rape at the library.

"Any news?" Sol asked him when they were inside.

"You were right. It looks like they're part of the Sterling Boys but none of them are talking. All of them had priors but it's all petty shit, no real weight or serious violence until now. The oldest one had a gun possession charge as a juvenile. Looks like he's more careful these days, nobody had anything but those knives on 'em. So you held them off, huh?" He managed half a smile. "What's it like to have your ass saved by a hot chick with a gun?"

"Very refreshing. Those guys were about to carve me up."

"So I read. And if these guys don't take plea bargains you're going to have to testify. They're saying they were only trying to scare that lady and that they had been invited into the room by her, that they hadn't broken in. The library was open and they're saying they'd wandered up to the third floor. *And* they're saying that you assaulted them first."

"They have a private lawyer, don't they?"

"Two. What do you think they were looking for, Sol?"

"Anything they could steal, maybe payroll checks, stored cash. The library has a few cash registers. Ms. Marin had the bad luck of stumbling onto them, like me."

"So how can they afford attorneys?"

"You'll find out they're wannabe gangsters. I guarantee the mouthpieces are local ambulance chasers, probably Filipinos, too."

"How did the officer know to come upstairs?"

"We were making a whole lot of noise while we rassled."

Paul was scrutinizing him. "Anything unusual happen since then?"

"Like what?"

"Like anyone strange hanging around?"

"Nobody outside the usual weirdos, why?"

"You never know. Sometimes these people try to get revenge, you know that."

"I wish they would..."

"Easy, now, killer.You said you became a librarian to stay outta trouble, remember?"

"Trouble seems to be the only thing that loves me."

"Leave it alone, Sol. The D.A.'s office will take care of these lowlifes."

"You'd better."

* * * *

Saturday night

The protests downtown had started up again and become a riot by nightfall. Local youth and visiting rabble rousers had decided to get in on the fun. The police were starting to set up barricades to enclose the four-block area but the crowds kept growing for lack of anything else going on around town.

At nine o'clock Sol set out for Union City taking Kennedy Boulevard. He was there in less than twenty minutes. 47th & Cottage Place, an old lyceum. Its parking lot was overflowing on to the narrow street. A thick humidity had emerged. It would be a scorcher tomorrow. He found a spot two blocks down in front of an outdated shoe shop.

The people heading toward the large hall carried small flags and bands of the same three colors: gold, blue and red. Colombians.

There was a guest list. Sol figured there was an asterisk next to his name as he was ushered in and shown to a small table for two. The place was jam-packed. On the stage were a live band and young dancers in traditional costumes. The music was sort of like rainforest country western, accordion-heavy with conga drums and some kind of scraping instrument.

Sol helped himself to some empanadas and champagne cola. He looked around. Colombian women are something to behold. He considered brushing off his Spanish, then thought it best to wait at his table for the inevitable summons.

It came ten minutes later, from a beautiful hostess with an apology from "the doctor", and a request to be patient another ten minutes. She came back and escorted him to a private room in a separate part of the building where a lone man in a tuxedo, early forties, sat behind a desk. There was a man at either end of the hallway outside. Sol recognized an office, but it wasn't this man's office, too messy. The man's taurine head was neatly laurelled by short curls shined and tight. A little too much cologne, his eyes were those of someone who wouldn't be getting into heaven.

"Thank you so much for coming, Mr. Isistrato. I hope you find the setting agreeable."

"Pretty women, good food, music's nice. Sure."

"Do you know who I am?"

"No, but since you know who I am I can guess."

"I know that you are someone who is looking for something I also seek. And even though you are not the librarian who has it, perhaps you will find out who does."

"That's the goal, right? But how do you know I'm looking for this?"

"*Un pajarito*, a little bird told me you're not just a librarian. It's really irrelevant to me who you are, no offense, except that you would give these treasures over to the authorities, who would in turn place them in storage where they would languish for years and years buried under tons of litigation and red tape."

"Probably."

"Or, and this is why I am imposing on your time, you could somehow manage to get those paintings to me and I would pay you much more than anyone else is asking or offering."

Sol had to be diplomatic. This guy could put a hit on him for cheap.

"Thank you for the compliment but this is just a job for me."

"There's nothing wrong with a few bonuses now and then for work well done."

"Don't you care that eventually some tracks will start leading to you?" Sol risked.

"Not at all. I'm not worried about anyone coming after me. I haven't actually committed any crime and I don't even exist as someone you could look for in this country."

"Nonsense. Anyone participating in modern society in any way can be found. But maybe I have no interest in you at all, no offense. You're not who I'm looking for. No one will ever be able to stop the flow of drugs and guns, certainly not me. I'm not a crusader and I very much enjoy being alive. I just want the thief and the merchandise. The trail sidelined to you."

The man smiled somewhat patronizingly. Sol asked him, "How did you hear about these paintings, if I can ask?"

"I have several dealers throughout the country. The grapevine started talking about them months ago and then the buzz became concentrated here, in the Manhattan area. The sellers started courting certain buyers directly, sending notes for contact through the library. I had already made offers to all the other librarians. You're the new addition. All eyes are on you now."

This man was not even afraid of the FBI. He had to be high up on the food chain, well protected. Sol couldn't help feeling resentment at that kind of power over other people.

"Doesn't it bother you at all what all these people do to each other just so you can have your expensive erotica?"

"People do horrible things to each other for much less. You know as well as I do, obviously, that it's all just business. Corrupt cops and politicians come and go, guns are distasteful most of the time. But drugs are forever. People will seek them out until this planet is just another cold, dead rock. Beyond all that, Mr. Isistrato, for some of us, art is even more eternal. It gives life meaning."

"You'll forgive me, I hope, but it's not that simple for me. Besides, those paintings just might find a way to you on their own, before I can get to them. But thank you for the invitation, it's a nice party. Happy Independence Day, by the way."

"We're celebrating early. The official date is next week, but who's counting? Here's my card if you should change your mind."

Just a phone number, probably an answering service, fake name. Doctor Lazarus Knowles.

* * * *

It started out clear and sunny. A mild breeze kept it comfortable.

At the Hudson Yacht Club, off Washington Boulevard, near the mall, a coterie was enjoying drinks and sharing laughs on the outdoor deck. A woman and three men, all dressed for boating. They had the whole veranda to themselves; everyone else was watching the regatta from the piers. The patio revelers' own race wasn't for another hour-and-a-half.

A thin, nervous man with a British accent was addressing a gleaming, tanned, green-eyed man wearing island-beach-style dock shoes.

"... and they ask us if someone would care to volunteer as bait for the thieves..."

And they all laughed again.

"Worse," the French woman said, "As I am leaving, your pencil-pushing frwend actually asks me what I will be doing wis ze painting!"

They laughed more. Then the green-eyed man grew slightly melancholy.

"Yeah... About him... I think he's taking this whole thing personally now. Those stupid Philippine pigs have jeopardized everything. If Sol hasn't found the paintings for us yet, it might be time to take him out of the equation."

"What do you mean?" asked the naive Dutch nobleman.

"Not quite sure yet, just somehow put him on ice so he doesn't get in the way. I've seen a couple of the cases he was involved in. He might be hard to get rid of later on."

A waiter with spiked black hair came to ask if they were in need of anything. He was off-handedly dismissed.

* * * *

At three o'clock the museum doors opened. Slipped into the stream of hipsters, intellectuals and senior citizens were Lorelei and Inspector Sebastian. They each took a seat on opposite sides of the center aisle in the auditorium, both toward the rear. Lorelei had camouflaged herself as best she could, aiming for Plain Jane.

Nothing nefarious revealed itself, no one acted suspiciously. Those who arrived accompanied were with friends or family. Your standard wallflowers and loners were represented, clearly there for the talk. Many of the attendees seemed to know one another. None of the librarians showed up but Lorelei did recognize someone from the library: the punk rock kid, mocking culture in a loosened white shirt and black tie. He was there with a few of his friends, the group looking like an experiment in American multiculturalism, all of them proudly decked out in their rags and flags of youthful rebellion, contemptuously sprawled out along the fifth row.

The discussion was entitled: 'Art and Money: How Worth Is Determined'. The panelists were a handful of well-known area artists, a successful gallery owner, an art consultant and a university professor. After a prosaic and generalized introduction to the theme by a professional moderator, a young Asian woman, the panelists weighed in with their own experiences and opinions. Then the forum was opened to questions and comments from the audience. Not too obnoxiously, but the group of young rebels were being slightly disruptive with audible disagreements to statements by the speakers and challenges to "the commercialization of art", as one of them put it. When one of the artists on the panel, also a local civil servant, admitted to being seduced by the lure of celebrity the band of idealists stood in unison and filed out. After another forty minutes of polite debate the event concluded without incident.

Lorelei and Sebastian lingered outside with the other people, pretending to have a conversation about their favorite artists and styles, both surreptitiously taking stock of their surroundings. Sol was around the corner on Monmouth Street and Pines a few hundred feet down on Montgomery. None of them noticed anything unusual. When the crowd dispersed Lorelei went to Sol's car, the inspector to Pines'.

They waited for the staff to come out. A tall, middle-aged African American man in jeans, sneakers and a peach polo stepped out holding the door for a chubby young Hispanic woman in all black who then locked it. They lowered the security gate and he walked her to her car a few spaces in front of Pines. The girl pulled out and the man walked off toward Newark Avenue. The team repaired to a makeshift command center Pines had set up in an abandoned pharmacy at the end of Jersey Avenue.

The library had been quiet as a crypt, the street traffic minimal, all neighborhood people back and forth through Van Vorst Park. Lorelei mentioned to the others that in the lecture hall she had seen the young man that the narcotics detectives had been watching. She described him and his friends.

"You mean Generation Y that spilled out of the museum halfway through?" asked Sol. "The only thing they're guilty of is lighting up a couple joints in public. I saw them walk by."

"Then why would the narcotics squad be so interested in him?"

"Could be a small-time dealer for the artsy crowd."

"Psychedelics," Pines interjected. "The East District Commander told us the kid's mixed up with LSD and ecstasy."

"The way they all dress that's no surprise," observed Sol.

"Other than that," added Sebastian, "There didn't seem to be anything unusual."

"Any possible bathroom meetings?" asked Pines.

"Negative," answered Lorelei. "No synchronization between people getting out of their seats."

"People changing seats?"

"None."

"So what was the big deal about Bastille Day?" Sol wondered aloud.

The answer came a few hours later, around five, while they were clearing up the last of a few pizza pies. As the sun came searing in through the windows, Villeforte could be heard screaming out of Pines' cell phone from fifteen feet away. Once he had calmed her down somewhat and concluded the call, he told everyone that the Guerroyant's showroom in Manhattan had had its glass walls and doors shattered, its offices ransacked. The building's security company had called her when a guard on patrol had come across the scene. The alarms had never gone off and no was seen near the area on the security cameras. Nothing had been stolen or vandalized, just the front facade destroyed. He was going to have to go into the city to check it out. Lorelei suggested she, or they, accompany him.

Just then the FBI techie on Pines' team summoned him over. A police dispatch had gone out to Harborside for vandalism at the luxury high rise, the penthouse.

Pines dispatched Sol and Lorelei to the waterfront while he headed to the tunnel with the Inspector.

The Duke's lavish apartments had been entered into and completely ripped to pieces. All of his expensive furniture had been destroyed, any and all glass in the place had been smashed and there was one word of graffiti on almost all his walls: SLAVER.

He sat despondent amidst all his ruined belongings.

"Now it really does look like someone doesn't like you, Chase." She had to force the issue. "Are you sure there isn't anything else you might want to tell us?"

He was saved from answering, ironically, by Pines. They'd already gotten the emergency page, now on the phone they only had to walk out onto the Duke's balcony to see the blazes raging in the dark of the warehouse district at the foot of the hill. First-responding sirens were only now converging on the scene.

The building Bennett International used as its offices was in its origin the mansion of industrialist William Stowe, the second. The shrewd businessman, in a time without escalators, had ordered a connecting elevated tunnel with both a walkway and a safely slow-moving conveyor belt, from the manufacturing plant to his house high on the cliff top. The house, the connecting tunnel and the unused factory had all been firebombed.

When they arrived they were kept back by JCFD about a hundred yards as thick black smoke filled the area. Some ancient waste chemicals in the rear of the building had caught flame. A fire chief stopped to talk to them briefly, he knew Lorelei. Definitely no accident he confided.

A large blast went off in a pitch-black part of the inferno. Hellish flames roared against the firefighters as they were slowly, steadily extinguished by a newly amped-up response coordination in the region. Heavy duty helicopters in the air, monstrous trucks on the ground. Then the media, with all their antenna vans. All the nearby residents had come out to see, cars pulled off the highway.

Lorelei and Sol decided to casually canvass a four-block radius, maybe see something the cops might have missed. The arsonists could still be around. They often liked to watch their handiwork. But the pair saw that futility right away. The fires had become an event on this hot summer night, the crowds were growing. It would be a long one for everyone.

Pines met them back at the scene with a handful of local officials. A few firefighters had sustained some smoke-related injuries but so far there was no indication of any people inside any of the structures. They wouldn't know for sure for another hour or more. Smaller explosions were still going off here and there. Fires had been started at all the entrances of the expansive production facility.

Pines was calling in federal forensics teams. Bennett wasn't answering his phone but had to be located. Sol and Lorelei were sent to start looking for him at home. Pines said he wanted to have a look around the Duke's penthouse.

21.

<u>Sugar On My Tongue</u>

"I didn't have enough strength to resist corruption,
but I was strong enough to fight for a piece of it."
- Joe Morse, *Force Of Evil* (1948)

They were meeting at Pines' office in downtown Newark at eight. Sol was sitting by the window in Ark's Gourmet Deli, two doors down after the old church, by quarter of seven, having coffee with his sugar. Wild thoughts were drag racing in his head. All night it had been, through fitful patches of rest. He couldn't even give attention to his newspaper.

Just before all the traffic and hustling and shouting gets started, when the sun is only hinting at its approach, Broad Street is a wide phantom avenue with empty historic buildings gaping at you, questioning, confused. Sol just stared back at them, merely acknowledging that he, too, was one of the sleepless. He'd been up all night half his life.

The new security measures around the federal building required drivers to circle a narrow set of one-way streets and two inspection posts for access to the government parking lot at the southeast corner of the complex. By seven-thirty there's a long line of cars. Sol merely parked on a side street across the boulevard from the front of the Peter W. Rodino Government Center. He preferred not having to enter through basement levels. At ten of, he folded his Star Ledger and strolled through the lobby.

Special Agent Macy was there today. Presumably he and Pines alternated as leads on different cases. Sol wondered what other art crime files they were working. His clothes disguised a taut frame. The man was like a sharp axe in a soft leather carrying sheath.

Bennett had never been located last night. He was a bachelor and his house staff said he hadn't been home all weekend. Villeforte had summoned the Guerroyant's legal department and initiated a second lawsuit. The Duke took the time to arrange a press conference to announce the need to bring in a team of Dutch security forces to keep him protected as the Americans had failed to do so.

Sol handed Pines a folder with the film and prints of yesterday's surveillance.

"Let's go over what we have." The G-man was pressed for time, as usual. "Preliminary reports conclude no thievery of any kind at any of last night's attacks. There were also no fingerprints or footprints found. The alarms were disabled at the gallery and the penthouse, and the cameras around the house and access way to the empty plant below show nothing. Only the back of the house had been hit. It was all Molotovs."

"They walked *over* the sky bridge!" remarked Inspector Sebastian.

"These were professionals," contributed Macy, "Like damned ghosts, and they weren't looking to steal anything."

"They were sending a message," said Lorelei.

"So it would seem. But to say what? 'Buy what we're offering or else'?" he answered.

"Or perhaps someone believes these people already have the paintings," offered Inspector Sebastian.

"Why not take some of the many other valuables that were everywhere? And why all the destruction?" asked Pines.

"Because they only want the erotica," answered Sol. "It's not a question of money, it's personal."

"Another buyer?" Macy was skeptical. "How would they know who else had been approached?"

"The sellers might have let everyone know who was in the market," Pines postulated. "To start a bidding war."

"Or an actual one," suggested Lorelei.

"Sol," said Pines, "I'm going to authorize surveillance on those two groups you've identified but it'll be pretty limited. Hopefully something will come of it. I have to tell you all right now that we're already starting to stretch our resources on this case."

"I have reached out to some friends in Europe to see if anyone might know anything about known traffickers of stolen art in this area," offered Sebastian. "I'm expecting to hear back from them later today."

"Alright," Pines was fidgety. "We'll meet back here in 48 hours. Laura, anything you want to add?"

She bristled at the perceived slight, feeling a lack of contribution. "Well, I'm hot on the trail of an overdue book fiend, I suspect a shady group of teenagers has been using the biography section as a make-out spot and there's a strange old man who keeps ripping pictures out of the Newsweeks and might be one of last night's vandals. Other than that, no, I've got nothing."

None of the men said anything until Sol responded.

"I was going to bring it up, Laura, but you beat me to the punch. Richard, it's time Laura joined me on reconnaissance."

"Fine by me, that was the deal from the start. But you have to keep your schedule at the library, Laura. You're our front line there. You, too, Sol, we need you to maintain a presence there. You never know when one of the librarians might suddenly feel the need to open up about something. The two of you work it out and keep me updated, as usual."

* * * *

Inspector Sebastian had been extended, through Pines, the international law enforcement hospitality of temporary use of some non-sensitive federal offices; fax machine, copies, internet, phone, the staff lounge. It gave him some anonymity and also benefitted the FBI's thinly staffed new unit.

Sol and Lorelei walked uneasily out onto the slow-burning asphalt together.

"Not a little bit of sarcasm upstairs. Getting antsy, Detective?"

"You try playing security guard for a while."

"No thanks. Hey, do you have your files with you? I know you do..."

"So?"

"Something occurred to me upstairs. I just want to jot down the call numbers specified in those letters."

"How much are you not telling me, Sol? What are you finding and keeping to yourself?"

"Listen, I might not like it any more than you do but in this little partnership I happen to be the quote-un-quote senior operative. Or didn't you read the letter of subscription as closely as you did my file?"

"It's only 'cause you're so much older."

He started to protest but saw she was just busting his chops.

"You were supposed to have me with you on the surveillance work all along?" she asked.

"That's what they told me. But some things I do better alone. Obviously I'm not the most likeable fellow in the world."

"No, you're not. Here..." She gave him the copies of the letters. "Jot away. Now, where's your car and what's next?"

"Next we have to do some digging."

* * * *

On Tuesday Inspector Sebastian asked his new colleagues to meet him down at Port Liberte, an enclave of millionaire gated communities of

185

condos and townhouses still under construction at Jersey City's southern border on Upper New York Bay. Undeveloped at the bottom of Chapel Avenue there remained a parking lot and storage facility of a stubbornly slow dying barge dock. Several small boat carcasses littered the yard.

In the warehouse office, Sebastian introduced them to four lanky, droopy-lashed men dressed like gloomy Mod models, two of them with cigarettes dangling from their lips.

"They're Interpol. New York office," said the inspector. "We've just crossed paths."

One of them moved the dirty blonde hair from his eyes. "We're looking for drugs," he said laconically. Took a drag. "Heroin and cocaine."

After a moment or two when no further elaboration was made by the international secret agent man, Inspector Sebastian played the diplomat. "They've traced a supply line from the Caribbean, the Dominican Republic. Two weeks ago there was a cargo bust right across the water there, at the port. Customs stamps indicated passes through Senegal and Miami but there's no logged point of origin."

A less mysterious member of the group, short curly hair and right hand fingers twitching, laid it out. "Someone around here is piggybacking commercial shipments to the area. Crates within crates, that sorta thing."

In the back of the room an agent with a wide grin was gazing at the ceiling and slightly bobbing his head rhythmically.

"Rum," he laughed. "Hefty little care packages of coke an' 'eroin snuck in the center of pallets of empty rum bottles. Only one bottle maker on the island and all thirty rum companies use 'im. It's like a shell game. This crate was sent to a liquor distributor in Secaucus that doesn't exist. Someone would have shown up to claim it with fake paperwork."

"The Port Authority wanted to keep it quiet but it was New Jersey DEA that had gotten the tip and they wanted their interception all over the television" Pines added.

"How does all this help us, Rich, Inspector?" Lorelei asked.

The Inspector answered, "These gentlemen would like to keep an open line of communication, an exchange of any information possibly relevant in any way to someone they are looking for here in the Northeast."

"Interpol not only deals with drug trafficking," Pines said, "They also have a division for art crime. They started the first comprehensive list of the world's stolen and missing art in 1947."

The one Interpol agent who hadn't spoken yet, a dark-eyed, dark haired wraith of a man had a voice of gravel. "The person we're looking for is also a collector."

* * * *

Outside the sun glared angrily at all of them as they made their way to their cars. Pines and Sebastian were going into Manhattan to talk to Port Authority officials and pay another visit to MissVilleforte and the Guerroyant galleries. Sol and Lorelei were to give the Dutch nobleman and the British businessman one last chance to remember something they'd somehow forgotten to tell us.

"One last thing, Hudson County is asking for a status report and general statement, I need some kind of paperwork from the two of you in the next couple of days. The D.A.'s office is putting together a defense against the suits by the Dutch and the museum."

"Who's got the case, do you know?" Sol asked.

"Paul De La Cruz. Do you know him?"

"Yes. Do they know my name?"

"No, just that we have a team of undercover investigators and they don't know where."

"Steven Riley knows."

"He signed off on confidentiality."

"How much is that worth?" Sol snarled.

"We have to take the man at his word."

Sol had to wonder how often Paul and the county executive got together for drinks or golf.

* * * *

He asked her to meet up him with him at Lincoln Park, by the lake. When they were alone in his car he showed her the list of titles for the call numbers in the letters.

973.049 FRA - <u>From Slavery To Freedom</u>, by John Hope Franklin

641.259 WIL - <u>Rum: A Social And Sociable History Of The Real Spirit Of 1776</u>, by Ian Williams

633.61 ABB - <u>Sugar: A Bittersweet History</u>, by Elizabeth Abbott

306.097 YUPP - <u>Yuppies Invade My House At Dinnertime: a tale of</u>

187

<u>brunch, bombs, and gentrification in an American city</u>, by Joseph Barry

"Don't you think the feds went and checked the same thing?" she asked.

"Of course, but it wouldn't have made sense to anyone who hadn't seen the murals. Remember, they don't live here like we do. And who's to say those murals were around when this thing started?"

Something clicked for her. "These people WANT to get caught!"

"And we're going to oblige them. Let's go downtown."

* * * *

Meredith was at the circulation desk looking like she was about to rap somebody's knuckles with a ruler, the collars of her stiff shirt sharp enough to cut. She was wearing glasses, but they were definitely not sexy today. She actually seemed relieved to see him.

She told him exactly what he'd come to ask her about: a group of rebel artists called the Art One Collective.

"They're the ones who started the protests on First Street."

* * * *

They parked a block away from the building, outside a place called Uncle Jack's, which was one of the only places in town that offered live music. They walked down the cobblestone street to a grand red factory building now grown over with vines and random artist touches and oddities. Just approaching it, the building took you to another time, another place, the only sound your own footsteps.

A green-grey alcove entrance that could have been a magical mystery portal, a landfill pile of unanswered letters and parcels. For a placed filled with artists, there were no kind of normal sounds anywhere. There were no smells whatsoever, no signs of life. The only things moving were dust specks in the waning sunlight. As they walked down the hall to the nearest staircase they could see why: most of the doors had eviction notices on them.

On the lonely, haunted fourth floor the walls had all been cleared except for the very farthest. Even from where they came in they could see it was one of that series of murals around the city. Confrontational, subversive.Antagonistic.Beautiful.

A landscape like a historical map, the subject a slave market in New York City. Though the background was deliberately juvenile, cartoonish as the actual classics, the figures were disturbingly realistic, intensely detailed from their rags or riches to the pure hatred or sheer terror in their eyes.

British merchants selling African captives to the American colonists. Again, ships on the horizon; the English flag and one more they couldn't immediately identify.

Below the auction blocks on which people were displayed as merchandise lay stacked the burlap sacks of sugar and triple-x jugs they were being bartered for.

From all the nearby buildings and houses blood seeped from windows and doors.

In large black stencil letters, like those on shipping crates, along the bottom edge of the painting were the words, "WHAT PRICE HUMANITY?"

* * * *

Through a combination of books and internet research Sol revisited a curious background of rum that he'd already forgotten in middle school. Not only had the liquor been a major factor in the American War of Independence, it had been both a product and catalyst of explosive growth in the North Atlantic slave trade.

With a long history as 'sugar wine', true rum was first distilled from molasses by slaves on sugarcane plantations in the Caribbean; Barbados was the place say the old tales.

The American colonies immediately fell in love with the drink and every man, woman and child there had their share. As its popularity soared, along with the European affinity for sugar, so did the need for more slaves to work the cane fields. The infamous triangular trade was established between the colonies, West Africa and the Caribbean. Molasses, sugar and people were routinely exchanged as currency.

American reaction to the British Sugar and Stamp Acts of 1764 and '65, respectively, sparked the flame of dissent and disrupted the colonies' participation in this abominable business, allowing the islands to dominate sugar and rum production for decades. The Haitian slave revolt of 1791 shifted the balance of rum power to Cuba and Jamaica, which by the mid 1850's were the two leading suppliers of both sugar and rum for the known world. But while Cuba had the protection of the Spanish navy and army, Jamaica was soon besieged by pirates as a favored stronghold, thereby providing the British Empire a whole new source of strife.

Cuban plantation owners, alarmed by slave rebellions throughout the Caribbean, petitioned their Spanish rulers for broader powers over their human chattel and were rewarded with an augmentation of slave shipments and the imperial military presence. There was too much money at stake to allow the subhumans to interfere. While the abolition of slavery gained momentum in North America and Europe, Cuba was the last country in the Western Hemisphere to accept captive Africans, in 1860.

The largest island in the Caribbean completely dominated the world's sugar and rum production through the late 1800's with most of its rum companies based in the city of Santiago de Cuba. The internationally famous Bacardi brand, for example, now known as a Puerto Rican product, was originally a Cuban creation.

It was the Great Depression and the separatist movement on the island that were the undoing of the rum hegemony. Right up until the end of World War I Cuba provided 80% of western civilization's favorite sweetener. When General Gerardo Machado of the Cuban War of Independence imposed a nationalist rule, the majority of the capitalist rum companies fled to the newly formed Dominican Republic. The most famous of Dominican rums, known as the three B's (Brugal, Bermudez and Barcelo) are all of Cuban origin.

But there were dozens of other, smaller, rum companies that had followed in their wake. One of these was De La Cruz, a company owned by Paul's family.

22.

<u>Fiction</u>

"Come right over
I'll knock on your shoulder
This is a story and this is what I've planned
An angry man, an angry man
Nothing is more fatal than an angry man

Tell me
Will I make it home tonight?"
- The Knife, 'Neverland', *Silent Shout* (2007)

She called him around eight, asked if he was busy. Never too busy for her, but he couldn't say that. He was just glad to hear her voice. His eyes were bleary from a few hours of reading back and forth between paper and liquid crystal. He needed to get some air and they agreed to meet in Little India, where few outsiders go. Lorelei suspected Sol didn't have a girlfriend at the moment.

There was a popular informal restaurant tucked off the main street, on Liberty Avenue. They each had an enormous Naan bread and various bean and vegetable dishes to dip it in. It was cool enough for the sweet tea and half the place was an outdoor courtyard. Summer rain was teasing with small gusts of wind and there were a thousand spices in the air.

She was excited, almost giddy with the sureness of breaking this case.

"Portuguese is the other flag in the mural," she informed him.

"Makes sense, the Portuguese were the primary carriers of slaves during the North Atlantic slave trade. How much do you want to bet that the freightliners pull out somewhere around Lisbon?"

"We should call Pines and have him or the Interpol boys check it out. That had to be part of the reference on the Duke's walls."

"That's not all. Here are the pictures of those two possible narcs I was watching last week. They can either be delivery kids or be building a case against someone, but maybe they can lead us to whoever is offering up the big money for these paintings and we can make an interception." She looked as though someone had just smacked the back of her head.

"That's Anthony," she said. "My fiancé." She studied the pictures

191

closely, going over the sequence of the exchange under the bridge. Hadn't he said his new partner was a man? Maybe they just switched up for this operation. Then in the last shot she could see the woman bringing a cigarette to her lips.

She looked at Sol. He hadn't told anyone except Pines about the motel room.

"Looks like they're running an operation," she surmised.

"Yep. Probably stacking charges," he added. "They might be looking for the same people we are."

"I can ask him about it..."

"No, not just yet, anyway. It may not be necessary and you could jeopardize our own investigation. We just want the paintings, remember?"

"Right..."

"We'll let the bigger kids play with the guns and the drugs. All we have to do is find that stash of old nudie pictures, our parts are done and we can go back to our normal lives."

She wasn't so sure about that last part but had to agree that they'd only been hired to find stolen art works. And to go undercover in a library, of all places. So it probably was best just to close out their end.

"What about the aristocrats, then?" she asked. "Don't you think they know more than they're telling?"

"Definitely. We'll ask Pines to get their financials."

He reached Pines on his cell immediately and explained why they felt their request was necessary. The agent answered that he'd already obtained those records that morning. His team had been going over them and found an unsettling connection. More checking was needed tomorrow and the next briefing would again be Wednesday morning. Also, the two people Sol followed last week are Jersey City narcotics officers.

"Yes. I just found out. The man is Detective McSherman's fiancé."

* * * *

Wednesday, July 17th, 8:30am

Paul De La Cruz's grandfather, Adolfo, had moved his sugar and rum operations to the Dominican Republic amid the Central American tumult of the mid-1950's, though the family had continued to live in Cuba. When, in 1958, it was becoming evident that the young Fidel Castro and his Communist revolutionaries would be taking power on the island, the aging patriarch hurried his brood to the sanctuary of the United States, landing in Miami where he ultimately retired, never to return to his beloved island.

Paul's father, Ricardo, had chosen to move to New York with his new bride in the early sixties. He currently ran the De La Cruz businesses with the help of Paul's two older brothers. And though Paul had opted for a legal career, he naturally had a stake in the family fortune. Sol needed to know how big of a stake that was before he jumped to any conclusions. The math had started formulating; it was possible his friend had a hand in all of this. Even the largest of cities, or perhaps especially these, still have to play hometown politics. And Hudson County, Jersey City in particular, has long been notorious as a prime example of corruption in local government.

Sol never put it past anyone to give in to greed. He already had Paul's home security code from the countless nights he'd delivered him from inebriation. He had no warrant and probably wouldn't have been able to get one anyway with just the hunches and ideas that were guiding him. He simply waited up the block and watched as Paul left for work.

It was accessing his personal computer that was the gift horse. The answer for the password question was the name of his favorite band. Obviously Paul had never imagined anyone having the gall to raid his home computer.

Sol spent nearly two hours snooping through the files. Aside from a few thousand shares of stock in the family enterprises Paul didn't seem to have much involvement with their functions. His investment portfolio looked like a million bucks, all the big names, only a handful Sol hadn't read about somewhere. However, Paul did bring home plenty of work from the D.A.'s office: calendars for different courts and pending dates, daily schedules, relevant case law citations and numerous contact lists.

And buried beneath seemingly innocuous directory labels as - 'Local Property Taxes' and 'Neighborhood Safety Initiative' was a document marked 'Clean Sweeps'. It was a spreadsheet, comprised of what Sol recognized as Jersey City street names and dates filling a calendar for the next eight weeks. There was also a column for an indecipherable alphanumeric code of eight characters and one for personal notes, which were the clinchers.

    - 2 brick H - for exch w/ No. 1
    - 5 oz C - recirculate [sic]
    - 1# M - dismantle 'Darkside' (favor for No. 6)

Kilos, ounces, pounds. Heroin, cocaine, marijuana. Either Paul was overseeing elaborate, city-wide sting operations or he was running a criminal enterprise of his own.

'The Darkside' was a name Sol recognized and confirmed with the address. They were a small-time clique of Greenville rappers who sold weed out of a house on Bergen Avenue to maintain their ghetto fabulous lifestyle. They weren't gangsters so much as a junior Wu Tang Clan. Sol had investigated them in 2000 in connection to an insurance claim on a vacant property that was destroyed in a fire under dubious circumstances. The owner was a family relation of one of the members and ultimately no arson could be proved; it had been made to look like trespassing junkies had accidentally burned it down. The claim went through but not before Sol had learned everything he could about this group. Now it looked like they wouldn't be so lucky. The narcs were coming to shut 'em down.

Sol copied all the files in the 'Neighborhood Safety Initiative' and investment folders onto a CD-ROM and swept his tracks away from Paul's apartment. Once home he made a couple copies and pored over the data like an entomologist.

* * * *

She had to stop kidding herself. Anthony had been too often unavailable the past couple months. He was working too closely with his new partner for her liking. And now Sol had made some connection tying them to the stolen art. Would it be wrong to follow her would-be husband around one of these nights? Should she just ask him? And ask him what, exactly? Are you sleeping with your new partner? Or, can you help me find the stolen paintings you know I'm looking for because *my* new partner thinks you might know where to find a certain drug kingpin who's also an art lover? Or better still, remember those librarians I told you about? Yeah, they're actually a secret criminal organization covering up their involvement in the international art black market by targeting wealthy competitors with violent intimidation tactics.

No, but she could ask him his new partner's first name by now. She could have very easily seen them at work somewhere on the city streets. And maybe she would soon.

* * * *

194

He was hunting again. The night welcomed him back.

Undercover cops and street criminals obviously keep the same general schedules, depending on your shift. Sundays are somewhat sacred on both sides; everyone is resting from Saturday night's madness and wild adventures, business for them both, and the civilian world is trying to relax in anticipation of the work week. Mondays are pretty much a scrambling reality check for most all of us and by Tuesday things are in full swing again.

Narcotics detectives can be anywhere in the city at any given time, though they are usually assigned rotating territories or are in an active operation for a target area. Sol was guessing his persons of interest were working according to the schedule. There was nothing specific for this night but the listings for that week were all in the Duncan Avenue hot zone. This quarter-mile strip was dominated by six housing project towers bordered by the interstate, a sprawling cemetery, the darkest part of Lincoln Park and a section of West Side Avenue known for hookers and all-night grease pits. All around dead ends for unwitting wrong turns, predators in the shadows.

He cruised around in wide circles, not too fast, not crawling. To all observers he was just another plainclothes cop making the rounds. He got dirty looks from the bad boys, slight nods from the black-and-whites. He saw a few of the real narcs but not the ones he was looking for. It was a slow night. Even the hustlers were doing little more than hanging out.

She was right on time, again. This graveyard shift would begin at eleven, maybe go to four or five.

"Still awake or just getting up?" she asked as she got in his car. They were near the university.

"Still awake. Not alot going on but I want you to get a good look at some friends of mine who might be able to help us. We're gonna cruise around for a little while."

This was the first time for her, just roaming the night like this. Any busts she'd participated in had been perfectly scheduled, timed and executed. They made small talk as the street life moved in the dark about them.

As you leave town on 440 there's a Greek diner that stays open 24/7. Years ago Sol had been a regular at a certain hour of the night and had come to get to know a group of men who also visited the place at around the same time. Midnight was lunchtime for these gentlemen who were the four members of the city's South District Violent Crimes Unit; the patrol officers who carried automatic rifles and submachine guns in a big window-tinted black truck. They had taken to that guy at the end of the counter specifically because he didn't talk much. Over half a year's time they had learned some of what Sol did for a living, and he they.

The Outpost Diner was a local mainstay while its surroundings were constantly changing over the past fifty years. Sol was greeted warmly by the owner and staff who still remembered him. He asked for a booth next to his old counter spot, introducing Lorelei simply as his friend Cynthia. The crew was at their usual seats, reserved for that hour by the manager. Sol salooned up next to a crew-cut burly mustache man in a light olive military jacket seemingly saying prayers over a small bowl of macaroni salad.

"Man, it's a good thing no bad guys are around," Sol said quietly to the Formica. "Who would save all these old people?"

"Saw you when you came in, shitbreath. How ya been?" said Lieutenant Gallo, a deadly calm sort.

The truth was the job required the men to keep their heads low for as long as it took to finish what could always be their last meal. While the streets were quiet, the eatery was bustling on a hot night. Next to Gallo a beefy man in a leather vest and t-shirt, mean blonde spikes, leaned backward and muttered,

"Jeez, they still let anybody come in here. We need to find a classier joint."

Sol greeted him and the others along the counter, "Nice to see you awake for a change, Ronny. No good soap operas today?"

The man gave him the finger, friendly-like. They had to be discreet.

"Who's the pin-up? And please tell me you're working private security for her," hummed the lieutenant.

"She's a cop." That's all he had to say. They spoke quietly for a few minutes of mundane workaday things like local drug lords and African gun-runners. He thanked them firmly but without handshakes.

"Be safe," was the usual goodbye.

* * * *

Wednesday briefing.

Inspector Sebastian was busy getting chewed out by church superiors sent from Spain to light a fire under him.

"We're getting very close, Richard," Sol told the stressed-out crime-

196

fighter. "These rich people are withholding information."

"They know each other, and they're not that rich. How well they know each other we don't know, yet. But they're all minority shareholders in a real global-operating development company called SDS that has holdings in this area." 'Bennett International' is actually mostly local with a branch office in London, no doubt just a desk at the elder Bennett's office building. Villeforte has more authority with museum funds than she has any personal money. The Villeforte name carries weight in academia but not in the financial world. As for the Duke, he's only wealthy because he's royalty. A wonderful lifestyle, but everything's budgeted and accounted for. He hasn't exactly helped fill the family coffers. His most creative enterprises are old mansions in Orange and East Orange rented out to Section 8 recipients.

* * * *

It was 5:19 when he checked his watch that afternoon. As he pulled onto his driveway, a bulky bald man got out of a car parked across the street and started toward him. Sol hadn't installed his remote opener yet and had to get out and insert a key to raise the old warehouse rolling bay door. Out of the side of his eye he examined the interloper: a heavy weightlifter, legs too big to walk normally. He was wearing a short-sleeved polyester shirt that showed off his huge biceps, specialty khakis and leather sole loafers. He was overdressed for this interview.

"You Izzis, ...Izzistrato?!" he demanded.

"I am. Who are you?"

"That ain't important, who I am. I got a message for you. Back off. Go deaf, dumb and blind and nobody'll bother you. They said you'd know what that meant." The man cracked his knuckles and neck bones in a pathetically routine display of musculature.

As the garage door completed its lift Sol listened for the expected trotting of heavy canine paws.

"I know what it means and I'll ask you again who you are." The man took a step toward him with his right hand raising.

"Get 'im!" Sol commanded the 120-pound street-born pitbull, as they'd practiced so many times.

"Wha?" The oaf didn't know how to react. He tried punching the dog who was faster than he was and had a skull like a riot helmet. Sol had inherited this monster from a neighbor who couldn't take care of him. He'd been less than a year when he'd got him. He'd been trained well, lockjaw onto the thug's arm, trying to tear it off. The guy fell backward, panicked.

"Getimoffa me!" he screamed.

"Hold, boy!" The dog stopped to a growl and held tight. Sol grabbed the collar put didn't pull the beast off.

"Who sent you?"

"I dunno!"

"I can have this dog tear you apart before you get to the holding cell. Who sent you?"

"I DON'T *KNOW*!! Guy I work with sometimes said this was a favor for a friend, no names."

"Who's this guy you work with, then?"

"Me." A voice from between parked cars." Now let him go or I shoot you *and* the dog."

Shit. This guy had come out of nowhere, had to have been watching nearby. The back-up, another guido, medium build, t-shirt, trying to keep a .22 low, pointing it at the dog. Curious bystanders at either end of the street could see something was going on and kept their distance. Sol had no weapon on him. He commanded the dog to stand down and they eased backward.

"Get in da car, paisan. You, gimme yer keys..."he said to Sol. "Toss 'em. Your phone, too."

The man stepped on Sol's cell, picked up the keys and flung them far into the parking lot across the street.

"Do yourself a favor and mind your own business, you'll live longer." They climbed into their car, the smaller one still pointing the gun at Sol from the back seat as they screeched away down 139. Sol seared their faces into his memory.

They'd come to threaten him at his home in broad daylight. All bets were off.

* * * *

Thursday morning, in the silent darkness, he wanted blood. Again he'd only been able to sleep a few hours. He'd looked for Paul at his place but the playboy was spending the night elsewhere. Sol didn't want to talk on the phone.

The District Attorney's office was in the grand old court building, bastion of occasional justice. Paul's parking spot was right near the entrance. Sol was waiting for him, slightly unkempt and pissed off, in front of the steps as he pulled up around eight forty-five.

"Did you send somebody to my house, Paul?"

"What are you talking about? You look crazy, Sol!" Paul wasted no time getting them away from there. "Let's talk in my car."

The old Harsimus Cemetery is three blocks down the hill on Newark Avenue. They drove to the end of the inlet and turned around to park face forward. It was still early, no visitors yet and the maintenance guys were not about to go up and mess with those official plates.

"Did you send a couple guys to my house to push up on me?" He asked again.

"Why the hell would I do that?"

"Because you know what I'm working on and maybe you don't want me doing my job. How long have you known about my assignment?"

"I was the one who recommended you. But the boss made all the final decisions for the DA's office."

"Until now."

"Yes, I have the case now. So what?"

"So you know there's other elements besides stolen art involved here."

"And? Crime is crime, it's all against the law, etcetera, etcetera. What's your point?" Paul was smooth and polished, this is what he lived for. More than ready.

"My point is maybe the DA's office, you, in particular, might know who some of the other players are and might be co-mingling cases."

Paul's eyes narrowed.

"You were only supposed to find the paintings, Sol. What do you know?"

"I know guns and drugs get people killed on a regular basis. Innocent people."

"People who deal in these things are not innocent, Sol."

"You know what I mean," Sol growled.

"No, I don't. This is life in the city, grow up. Street people are a waste of life and that's how they treat each other and their surroundings. Law and order has to try to contain their disease and they will naturally resist. Along the way, so-called innocent people are going to get killed."

But maybe you help make that happen.

"You know I'm not going to stop until I'm finished."

"I know, Sol. You're just doing your job, right? I have to get to my office. Can I drop you off somewhere?"

"No. I'll walk."

* * * *

Friday.

When you're sneaking around behind your girlfriend or boyfriend or spouse's back, your time frames for infidelity are usually limited, especially if your secret lover is also betraying someone. Often, there needs to be a schedule for sexual deceit.

Such was the case with Anthony and Vivian. The Friday morning exchange was one of their regular chores that gave them a few hours to themselves, on the job, "investigative time". The rest of the squad also took long lunches and they, too, had their own agendas.

Undercover narcotics officers are often the most susceptible to temptation. Chasing after and consorting with drugs and big money is like dancing with the devil. You have to really hate drugs or be purely indifferent to money to be a hundred percent dedicated to the task.

Sol walked Lorelei through the scenario up to the underpass overture. He had set up their perch early in the morning on top of one the unused mini-buildings at the farthest edge of the rail yards. He'd gambled on leaving it to her to start their tail at the house and scored: it was a routine thing. One hour earlier today but they'd been prepared for that. He wanted only for her to see the exchange and they would jump back in his car, this time tucked even deeper into the high meadow grass. Once again Sol followed them to this week's love nest, the luxurious Sandy's Lodge on Route 3 outside the Mill Creek Mall. The cheating hearts had stopped for fast food on the westbound side of the highway and Lorelei had already been able to see far-too-friendly French fry games.

This motel had only one way in or out, a secure square of property. Next door was an apartment complex, where Sol parked. He loosened his tie, took off his glasses and ruffled his hair. He slipped through the front entrance nonchalantly and began a short-term relationship with a nearby vending machine. When he saw Anthony and Vivian enter a room he strolled into the front office and secured one of his own.

It had become all too clear for Lorelei. By the time Sol got back to the car she was numb. They slipped quickly into the number Sol had drawn and set up the camera.

"I'm sorry you had to find out this way," he told her. "It wouldn't have been enough for me to just tell you."

She said nothing, only stared through the lens silently praying her man and his partner would come right back out after having logged evidence or whatever other police business they had to do in a highway motel operations room. Five minutes went by. Fifteen. Sol could only sit quietly nearby as each expired moment tore deeper into her. He wanted to suggest leaving, perhaps tell her that their subjects had stayed in the last place for over two hours but held his tongue. When a half hour had elapsed the truth was excruciating. Her hands and shoulders began an involuntary tremble. She stood up abruptly.

"Fuck this! I'm gonna shoot them both!" She started for the door and Sol was forced to block her way. She instinctively dropped back a step into fight mode. "Get out of my way, Sol…"

"Can't do that, Laura." He was probably sparing the cheaters from a righteous licking but he couldn't let his partner cause herself harm that way. "It's not worth it, he's not worth it, and you'll blow our surveillance."

"I don't care! Get out of my way!"

He just stood there.

And he was right. What was she thinking? That she would just go berserk on them and plead passion to the court? She knew she had to get a grip on herself. She looked at Sol and saw he was serious. Maybe she should shoot him, too.

Instead, she turned away from him, suddenly feeling dead, dropped like a stone onto the bed and covered her eyes with clenched fists. When she was sixteen she had solemnly swore to herself that she would never, ever, again cry over a boy. And this bastard had convinced her that they weren't all the same. He had made her believe in true love again and now it was clear she was not enough woman for him. And he had been lying and smiling and kissing her and having sex with her all along. And all she could do about it now was cry.

Sol was not the best qualified candidate in the consolation department. He certainly wasn't about to put his arm around her or offer a shoulder. He simply sat down next to her, a couple feet away, to give her silent support and simultaneously block the door. She cried for about ten minutes until she could think straight. They had to get out of there. Then he did put his arm around her as if they, too, had just been romping; he had to cover Lorelei's face as they took the hundred-mile walk to the car.

As they drove away he tried to keep her focused on the job.

"Those guys they met with are the ones whose wives came by to see Cecilia Bangur about the paintings. If someone is dangling a prize out there for the paintings you're fiancé might know about it. May have to ask him soon."

"Oh, I'll ask him alright..."

He took her to her car, knowing she had the pm shift at the library later. He'd been abusing the interns the past couple weeks but if something didn't give soon he'd be condemned to the fourth floor again.

"We have to hit the streets tomorrow night, remember?" he reminded her. She simply nodded. She had to go on automatic just to finish out her hours at the stupid library.

* * * *

He kept telling himself that it would not have been enough to just tell her about her fiancé but he still felt lousy. It never ceased to amaze him how men throw away the world when they have it in their hands. Laura was obviously a good woman, had a good head about her, a good heart, and so damned good looking. He shook his head. She didn't deserve this... crap, this kind of thing, this mess.

He had to pick up their trail again and couldn't risk Lorelei being seen. Where were they going after they were done? Who were they giving what to? They'd be back on the job, professional-like; alert, watching the clock. They'd have to finish out their daytime duties, details, then go home or wherever to rest up for Friday night's features.

He cruised by the motel entrance, saw their car was still there, then planted himself at the far end of the weedy remnant of what was once a 29th street, ready to ease into position behind them when they pulled back onto 1&9. But they didn't. Instead, when they appeared a half hour later they turned right on to the tiny, two-building block where he was and they were coming straight toward him. If it hadn't been for a slow moving delivery truck they would have seen his car. This severed limb of a street was a shortcut to Columbia Avenue, which joined 495. There was still a huge parking lot between them as they drove past and away from him and Sol had to wait until they approached the on-ramp to wheel around and go after them.

They used the quick Marginal Highway to get to Hudson County east and took the picturesque drive along the cliffs to eventually get back to Jersey City. They were headed straight toward police headquarters on Erie Street where there was no way Sol was going to be able to sit on their car. So many cops around, Sol knew enough of them personally that one might see him, and aside from that, around there the streets are always watching. He decided he only had a couple hours before the bureaucratic file office people ran for their lives on a Friday afternoon. If he was swift, he could get everything he needed by 3:30 and no one would be griping to him about his last-minute requests.

* * * *

She could not look at him again without wanting to kill him. She packed a weekend bag, grabbed Mister, turned her phone off and started driving. She didn't know where she was going, only that she couldn't be home when that dirty sonofabitch eventually showed up.

Sol had offered a spare room at his place, said he'd be out most of the night in case she didn't feel like being home. But she wanted to be completely alone, very much alone. She couldn't go to her parents or any of her brothers because they'd know what was wrong right away and probably want to go shoot Anthony themselves. She didn't feel like commiserating with any of her friends. And she sure as hell wasn't sleeping in a damned motel room. But she knew there was some serious work to do tomorrow.

So she drove. First west, then south, blindly, oblivious to time until she found herself deep in dark Jersey farmland. Some back road, she had no idea where she was. They got out of her jeep to look around. Peering into the black, she made out the silhouettes of barns and houses with lots of space between them. But the sky had exploded for her. No moon, all the stars were shining brightly and she remembered how small she actually was. She started crying again and couldn't stop this time. She had let herself believe that she was part of something greater than themselves, that there had to be something of fate in their union. Now she felt nothing more than a foolish child. She screamed inside of herself at his betrayal. She sat against her bumper and let it wash over her, rolling currents of ache and drowning.

When at last she was drained of her hurting they got back on the road. Mister had never seen her do anything like that and he'd remained quiet and still. She was prepared to sleep in the car if she had to, just not on the side of the road. Soon she came upon signs for Allaire State Park. New Jersey operated on the honor system: if one arrived after park ranger office hours, you could still snag an unreserved camping site and make nice in the morning. She scored an unclaimed yurt, threw a beach blanket on the thin bunk mattress and collapsed exhausted. Mister was on high alert, his senses amped up. The sounds and smells of the forest kept him awake most of the night as he kept guard over his best friend.

203

* * * *

Saturday morning.

He got a call from Rebecca at his house phone. She had kept his number, was his first thought, from that night they spent together. Then he remembered they'd never exchanged their exchanges.

"I got your number from the library directory, I hope you don't mind me calling you at home..."

"Right, no, not all. What's up?"

"I was wondering if you were very busy today. I thought maybe we could find some time to talk..."

Yes! She digs me! "Not too particularly busy, no. Just some errands to run, should be done in a couple hours. Everything okay with you?"

"Yes. It's not about me, though. It's about the other librarians. I... I just... I'm worried about them and part of it has to do with you. I think there's something I need to tell you."

"Do you want to meet right now?"

"No, no, it's not an emergency, it can wait. Would you mind coming over to my place, though? I really don't feel like going out today..."

"Of course, how's about twelve-thirty?"

"Perfect. I'll make us some lunch."

She was in hang-at-home mode. Just as sexy. Sweats, t-shirt, fresh-faced pretty.

"I hope you don't mind I'm dressed like a slob."

"Nonsense. Your place is really cool..."

"Isn't it? I love it. Come look, there's actually a courtyard with a garden that these elderly women take care of."

She'd made a great salad, including some tomatoes from the garden, and a light chicken pasta dish. The day called for lemonade and they sat near the fire escape, chit-chatting until they came to the reason she called. She hesitated, searched his eyes.

"I don't really understand everything that's going on but I know the librarians are scared. And I know you're involved, obviously. We all do. Maybe not exactly *how* you're involved but we know you're not one of the bad guys. So I've decided to trust you.

"I care very much about these people I work with and I don't want to see any more of them get hurt. So if no one else is stepping forward, I will. We think we know where those paintings are."

* * * *

Officer Ramirez was working the security desk at the library that day. He'd been volunteering for a lot of hours there.

A heat wave had invaded overnight. It was 92º at opening time, a hundred by one o'clock. But he was prepared, he'd brought a cooler filled with ice and water bottles.

He was thinking of nothing but Lorelei. He practically worshipped her now. He was worried that she hadn't returned his phone calls yesterday or this morning, or at lunch. She usually got back to him within the hour whenever they had to confirm scheduling. He was fit to burst with the information he had for his new heroine.

She descended upon his earth and ripped open the front door an hour before closing time. Tight white jeans, hot red sleeveless top, black assassin heels. Her hair was a little wild, which was unusual. And she had a strange look in her eyes, like when mommy used to get mad. As she walked up the stairs he didn't know whether to be turned on or scared.

"All right, Ramirez, what is so earth shattering that you couldn't tell me in the four messages you left?"

"Well, Deputy, I'm sorry I was so insistent but what I have to tell you can't wait. Check it out: you know I'm new to the force but I grew up around cops my whole life and a lot of my family and friends are cops, or they have been, and I've always wanted to be a cop and nothing else, you know what I mean, right? So, like, right here in Jersey City I know a lot of cops, and I hang out with a lot of them. I know, like, a lot of higher rank people like sergeants and lieutenants and stuff and, you know, they like me and everything so sometimes they, like, tell me things, you know?"

"Uh huh..."

"Well, anyway, some of my friends have been crackin' on me saying that I have to be careful now 'cause I'm working such dangerous territory here at the library and that I might have to take the lead on the Great Library Caper and stuff like that, and whatever.

"So, like, this past weekend I'm hanging out with my boys at this club in West New York that a lot of Jersey City cops hang out at. I don't know if maybe you've heard of it, Club Odyssey? But I don't think I've ever seen you there..."

"No..."

"So, anyway, later in the night I meet this smoking hot chick, I mean, not as hot as..., well she was *okay*, you know, good looking. And we're dancing and doing shots and hanging out, whatever, whatever, when all of a sudden she says she knows who I am! I'm like *what*? And she says 'I know who you are and I have what you're looking for.'"

"Really..."

"*Yeah!*... This trips me out and I tell her I don't know what she's talking about. I thought she was joking until she said she knew I sometimes work here. And she goes on to say she knows what those rapists were really doing in the library that night and that she had it."

"Which is what?"

"She said I should ask you, you would know. She mentioned you by name."

"And this woman's name?"

"Said it was Terry. I didn't get a last name."

"Did she say how she acquired what she's talking about?"

"Nope, I didn't think to ask."

"What did she look like?"

"Medium length brown hair. 'Bout five-six, 'couldn't really see the color of her eyes in there, you know what I mean? So do you know what she was talking about?"

"No, but I would definitely like to find out. Did you get a phone number?"

"Well, yeah, but that's why I was trying so hard to get a hold of you. We were trying to set up a meeting for this afternoon, after the library closes. She's like really anxious to get rid of this thing, whatever it is. I offered to meet with her alone but she said she would feel better if you were there. So now that you're here you wanna go or what?"

"Go ahead and make the call."

* * * *

He was in his work suit, and strapped up. He wasn't going anywhere unarmed anymore.

The librarians were only slightly off the mark. What Rebecca told him were the last few details he needed to lead him straight to the target. The Internet, solely through news threads and two years before MySpace and Facebook, helped shape a picture of the subject and provided his possible whereabouts for that Saturday. But it was the reliable, supposedly outmoded white pages that gave him the home address, right under their noses the whole time.

It took almost two hours to get an actual visual fix on the guy in the crowd. He was where he was supposed to be, an outdoor concert at the Hoboken waterfront that would be finishing soon.

Sol had no time to waste, the man might head home at any moment. He rushed back to Pavonia, where he slipped on a pair of leather gloves and into an alley at the corner of Mercer and Barrow Streets. He waltzed right through a long shared courtyard and found his way in through the second floor of a turn-of-the century brownstone. He didn't even care if anyone had seen him, he wanted the cops to arrive, just after he was finished with what he needed.

He had his gun drawn, but no one was around. All over the living room were framed photos of this man with a lot of friends and family, too many beautiful women for one man to deserve, but it looked like he was single, nothing feminine in the house.

Sol was done with the place in seven minutes, found what he was looking for right where he started on the top floor, some kind of sanctum sanctorum. All four, boldly displayed on easels. He had to brush off the sense of awe. He looked them over quickly, carefully, knew what he had. He took one of them; removed it from the holding frame, rolled it up, tucked it in a strapped tube he'd brought, threw that over his shoulder and stepped out the front door ready for anybody. A couple was crossing at the corner, away from him, no one else around. He hustled to his car down the street.

Sol had just committed another B&E but it was worth it. The case was closed, the danger was over, everyone was safe. And then Lorelei called.

She knew her partner would want to be present at this thing. Neither of them knew that they were only a few hundred feet away from each other at the moment.

"Believe it or not I was just about to call you." He was breathing fast.

"I have a surprise for you," she said.

"And I for you."

She gave him an address out in nothingville off the Turnpike, said it was happening in a half hour, a meet they couldn't miss. He had to stop off at home first, then he would map out the location and meet her out there as soon as he could. Whatever it was she had for him, he hoped it wouldn't take long. It would only be an hour or so for Special Agent Pines to get the search and arrest warrants for Mr. Louis Efrain Coles, thirty minutes more for the federal government to lower its wrath.

"It's not a 'Keeper Of The Books'," he exclaimed to Pines. "It's the damned bookkeeper!"

* * * *

New Jersey is globally infamous for its wastelands. This holds especially true for its torso in the northern half. Throughout the world there linger the retread jokes of 'that smell'. Having once fueled the industrial revolution, hundreds of manufacturing and petrochemical plants were conveniently erased from the national collective memory as clean technology gradually revealed how dirty we'd gotten ourselves.

One of the truly desolate and abandoned regions in the most densely populated and second wealthiest of the fifty states was a two-mile tumor on the spine of the Turnpike between the city of Linden and the township of Carteret, the latter of which had, in the late 80's, tragically demonstrated for the rest of the northeast how a whole town can just up and die.

Giant empty tanks, snaking oily rivers, dead poisoned ground, crumbling husks of all manner and size of structures. Not even vagrants or other scavengers came out here. There was nothing living here.

Yet, around the edges of these once vital and peopled plants and refineries there used to be tiny little pockets of business districts. Some of these businesses were either absorbed or left to die by neighboring communities, some simply survived, scratching out an existence like the hardiest of desert dwellers. One of these such anomalies was once a tavern, and it once had a name. These days it was just a place that existed but was never spoken of.

Usually only urban dwellers know what a 'blue bar' is. It's just a watering hole for cops and friends of cops. If you are neither of these and should happen to wander into this kind of an establishment unknowingly, perhaps traveling through a strange town, to wet your lips and relax for a moment, you will quickly begin to experience a sense of abnormality. The bartender asks if you need directions and the patrons all have you under surveillance. If you still decide to have the one drink you're allowed, you finish it and leave quietly.

If, by some inexplicable chain of events, you should find yourself in one of these places out on the edge of nowhere, with no cop friends, you have every right to be very nervous.

Such a place existed just fifteen miles away from Jersey City's big

208

happenings. After hopping off I-95 at exit 12 and moving past the main local byways, taking you past a couple cemeteries, the Linden airport, a bridge over marshland, under the highway and past the first mammoth metal fossils of a bygone era, a dusty broken road brings you to a small boxy building covered in toxic grime from the Plasticine Epoch. It was relentless afternoon summer heat and the brown misplaced place looked like a giant wounded and hungry nightmare. Blackened windows, no signs or lights except the burned out neon tubes of the High Life. And it was here that Lorelei and Ramirez had been invited to break bread and sip champagne. The woman called Terry had told Ramirez it was a cop bar. Apparently she had a thing for cops. Lots of women do, he slyly reminded himself.

Lorelei would only go in her jeep. The rookie cop who thought he was a badass driver was shaken in the rumbling open-air passenger seat. She'd changed into running shoes and drove like hell on wheels. A cloud of dust caught up to them when they blew in to what was once a parking lot. They had come upon a place out of an unholy past.

No one else around, no cars. They wondered aloud if they were at the right place. Maybe around back, where she eased her jeep behind the building to find a single Harley. The back door, an old rusted metal one, was slightly open. Her skin was jumping. They walked through a black-walled hallway, past a couple bathrooms and into the large dimly lit barroom.

A white-haired, crew cut biker in a dark grey t-shirt was at the bar. Except his tattoos were all Christian and patriotic. He pretended not to notice them walk in.

"Hey, man!" Ramirez, still in his basic issues, knowing it was a cop bar was trying to get cool with the bartender. "Kinda quiet around here today, huh?"

The man just nodded slowly.

"We're supposed to meet somebody here," he added. "Anybody been by in the last hour? A woman named Terry?"

"Nope." The man didn't bother to look up from the sink where he was wiping some glasses really slowly. "Sure she'll be here though. Sumthin ta drink?"

"Um, okay, well, I *am* off duty now. Yeah, I'll take a Cool River Light and, uh, and whatta you say, Laura? Can I call you that? A glass of white wine? Laura?"

"Nothing for me," she said. Her hairs were on end.

"Are you sher?" the biker drawled.

This bartender was somehow not right, she thought. "Okay, bottle of Guinness, please," she said. Without even knowing why, under the bar she deftly removed her service pistol from her purse and tucked it in her jeans at the small of her back.

Seven long minutes later the front door blew open in a shock of sunlight. Sol's silhouette stood in the frame for a second as his eyes adjusted to the darkness inside. He looked around, saw Lorelei and parted the dead sea between them. "What is going on?!" he said a little too loudly. On the way here he knew this couldn't be good.

She tried to shush him. She was looking like a femme fatale and with this kid in his baby blues, waving hello and smiling, in a place where people come to forget things or to do things they later try to forget. And this goddamned bartender was giving him the creeps.

"Can I get you something, sir?"

This guy had surely been a policeman at some time or other. Not allowed anymore. Sol smelled brimstone all over him, nothing good. "Shot of whiskey, brother, American, okay? No chaser."

"Right," said the leatherskin, who poured two doubles and helped himself to one. Then he walked away toward the bathrooms.

"Sol, you know Officer Ramirez from the library. He's been in contact with someone who says they have what we're looking for." She had compromised them both, convinced that it was worth whatever the boy scout was talking about. Sol quickly looked the young cop over. He appeared honest, sadly and very inconveniently clean.

"Can I talk to you over here for a second, please?" he said at her, not in his normal calm.

"What is your problem?!" she demanded away from the bar. "We're about to get closer to the paintings!" she hissed.

"I already found the paintings!" he pressed out if his teeth. "Pines is getting the take-down together right now and we have to be there. Look around you, this is a set-up. We have to get out of this place!"

Too late.

They'd been watching from somewhere nearby, waiting for everyone to get inside. Car doors were slamming outside. Sanders led the slow charge in through the front door, letting his belly be the first to enter, sure and easy. Behind him were his gaunt black partner, then a hefty Arab-looking beast and the ersatz Mets fan from the other day in Manhattan (now wearing a Phillies cap), followed by the Hispanic vixen and Anthony. Then the sound of the loud motorcycle out back, roaring away.

The narcotics unit fanned out in front of them.

"Hey, look, people, it's the fuckin' library police," Sanders announced. "Hope nobody has any overdue books!"

The rookie actually laughed at this. Lorelei saw Anthony and the other woman and jerked into reaction.

"What the hell are you doing here?!" she shouted.

"Relax, honey, why haven't you been answering my calls? We just want to talk to you." He lined up with his squad. "It looks like our investigations have overlapped and we all need to find a way to work this thing out." Then he tried to step toward her.

Blood filled her eyes. "I don't wanna talk to you, you bastard." The Irish in her rushed to the scrimmage, every nerve sparking. "I already know about you and *puta* over there! What is this?"

"Bitch!... Who you calling a *puta*, Pippy Longstocking?!" The tough Latina moved forward and was stopped by the man between them.

"What do you mean, babe? She's my work partner..." he said.

"I can see why you told me she was a man, but you can't lie to me anymore. And don't call me 'babe' you pig!"

"Relax, relax, everybody," Sanders commanded. "This is just business."

Ramirez had no idea what was going on. He looked to the woman named Vivian for some kind of explanation. "What's up, Terry? What's the deal?"

The baseball enthusiast spoke for her. "Ferget what she told you. We need those paintings." South Jersey accent, good ole' boy.

"What paintings?!" the twenty-two year old newbie shrieked.

"He doesn't know anything," Sol stated, addressing Sanders directly. "What do you want?"

"So you're the guy. Yeah..., you're the pencil-dick at the library the other day," the oaf realized.

"That's not what you called it when it was in your mouth, fat boy."

They lunged at each other but Sol had been two steps ahead of him. Like a machine punch, he clocked the bully a solid jab across his big mouth. Everybody stepped back for a moment, unsure of where this was going. They really had only come to talk.

Sanders was the first to try to draw. He'd foundered backward like a trust exercise onto his boys, punk ass surprised and instinctively reached for his .45.

Lorelei was pure action in response, faster than the fat detective, Sol was a split second behind her. Sanders' team started to pull but Sol calmly waved his gun around. "No, no, no..." he said. "You don't wanna do that."

Ramirez froze. Sanders had only been able to get his hand on his revolver.

"Aim at the woman, Laura," Sol ordered her as he swept across the men's faces. *Gladly*, she thought, and aimed at Vivian's chest. "Ramirez, listen carefully," he said without looking behind him. "You don't have anything at all to do with this. But if you wanna make it out of here clean and alive you'll draw your weapon and point it at the guy with the baseball cap."

The kid was motionless until ballcap moved for his piece and the young man's hand was a daily reflex, practiced in the mirror. They were outgunned but the only ones aiming.

"We," Sol said slowly as he backed away, "are going to leave now and nobody's gonna get hurt, okay?"

Not very likely, but he had to try. They had no radios to call for help.

"Laura, darling," Anthony appealed to his fiancé. "Baby, please, calm down. We're just here to talk, put the gun down. Sanders, c'mon, tell her..."

Sanders composed himself but kept his hand where it was.

"Look, sweetie, people...," he said, "This is just a big misunnerstanding. We're workin' a case that only partially has something to do with those paintings you're looking for. But we need them to catch the bigger fish, y'see? Of course Anthony was gonna tell me they assigned you to look around, we were there first. But we can still work something out. Yer buddy there, with the glasses, he ain't what you think he is, an' he ain't worth stickin' yer neck out for, believe me. He's only in it for himself an' he's already got his hands dirty. Did you know he was friends with the DA? Oh, yeah, he's tryin' to make himself look good at your expense. He's a nothing, a has-been. There will be other cases, kid, and we can help you with them. You just gotta let this one thing go."

"Don't listen to them, Laura, they're messing with your head. They're not about to let us walk out of here." Sol stated flatly.

She was confused for a second until Anthony opened his mouth again.

"Honey, this is me, your fiancé. Look at me. I love you, I would never do anything to hurt you."

She didn't even glance his way. "Ramirez, whatever you do, don't lower your weapon. We have to leave now."

They were cornered. Their only chance was the back door, far enough away that they were widely exposed to their enemies' fire. But her jeep was out there, and hopefully the biker hadn't done anything to it.

"I'm parked out back, Sol," she told him.

"Then you should probably go and start the car, dear. I'll be right out."

Time stopped as the three of them inched toward the exit, guns directed at the narcs who were just waiting for their chance, trained to expect gunfire and all they needed was a few more feet to lessen their chances of getting hit. Sol and Ramirez had just reached the back wall and Lorelei burst out the door when the barrage of bullets came at them. They each managed to squeeze off a couple rounds against triple their firepower.

Sol had made it into the hall but the kid was pinned behind a small extension wall in front of the utility closet. Sol dropped to the floor and fired three quick shots around his end of the hall. He was answered by six guns clapping. They wouldn't survive another round. Ramirez was crouched, scared to death. He looked at Sol with pleading eyes. Sol held up three fingers for a lifelong moment for the young man to focus, then started slowly counting them down. On one, the rookie found his courage and came out shooting as he crossed the canyon gap to the hallway where Sol was adding cover fire. A scream erupted from the bar.

"Go!" Sol pushed the kid out the door and fired another couple shots before making a break for it himself. They threw themselves into the back of Lorelei's jeep and were tearing away as the narc squad rounded the side of the building trying to shoot at them past Sol's defensive blasts. But there were only four of them: Sanders, Vivian, Anthony and Jimmy ballcap. When the jeep was out of range they ran for their cars to give chase.

If you can't leave from here the way you came, there's only one way you can go. It doesn't even exist on maps; it's the one service road along the CSX railroad, a narrow route built for slow-moving industrial vehicles. Even more abandoned than where they running from was a place called Tremley Point, a dead man's journey across marshland and two deadly little tributaries of the Arthur Kill. The chasers was taking pot shots at the open air jeep, the three riders crouched for sheer life.

That nameless road ran desperately through the void for an infinite eleven minutes before they could see the Goethals Bridge in the distance. It suddenly becomes an Amboy Avenue, where Lorelei scrambled around desperately to find a way onto the bridge. Miraculously they came to a spaghetti swirl of ramps and climbed up to the span named after the Major General who oversaw the building of the Panama Canal, now a saint in

Sol's book. They bounced into the traffic of the Staten Island Expressway, with so many other wonderful cars and people. They'd lost their pursuers, but not for long. The narcs knew they were headed back home.

The panic over for the second, Ramirez begged for understanding.

"Those're dirty cops, kid," Sol shouted above the motorway din. "They were just using you to get to me and Laura, Deputy McSherman. It's a lotta shit involved, right now the less you know the better it is for everybody!"

"But that was her *fiancé?!...*"

"EX-fiancé!" Lorelei yelled from the steering wheel. "Whatta ya doing this weekend, Ramirez, you free?"

Sol couldn't believe she was cracking jokes as they were racing for their lives. But it was her way of trying to steady her nerves as she looked in her rearview mirror. Off the rough off-roads, the cops' modified Crown Vic's had caught up to them. They had their lights and sirens on. License to kill. The other drivers were moving out of the way. A couple of well-timed bullets pyuned past them, one cracked a corner of the windshield.

She looked back at Sol in a do-or-die instant.

"Let's switch!" he shouted.

Was she smiling as she jumped into the passenger seat with one hand on the wheel and the other on her gun? Yeah, she was, but it was a wicked smile. She started shooting right back, hitting both cars, forcing them to fall back.

A couple seconds respite. She looked at the newbie, still afraid, still not sure what to do. "Those guys are trying to kill us, Ramirez! There's nothing to think about!"

He nodded slowly and lifted his gun again. Sol reloaded on his lap. When the narcs came up on them again, the young gun and Lorelei kept them at bay.

"Get your belts on," Sol shouted. "And hold on tight!"

Sol took a good look behind them. Anthony was coming up fast on his left, ballcap and Sanders staying in his blind spot. They were going to try to squeeze in on them. Time for a hockey move. Sol suddenly slowed just enough to find Sanders' car and slam it into the guard rail, dragging it along with friction sparks. The front end crumpled on the right and the car spun away backwards where it was hit by a vehicle that couldn't stop in time.

Sol sped forward to confront the other car, the burgundy sedan with Anthony and the woman. This time they were the ones on the offensive. Sol drove with his right hand and had his gun in his left. They all took insulting shots at each other. In the jumpy, open-aired jeep it was hard to get good aim. They were able to hold the line until Sol screeched out onto the exit for the Bayonne Bridge, the jeep tilting onto two wheels and the sedan tight on their tails, sliding into Martin Luther King Jr. Expressway going north into Jersey.

The souped-up police car was much faster on the highway than the jeep, of course, and Anthony had made his decision. He'd crossed the point of no return. He was going to have kill the woman he'd asked to marry him or go to jail for the rest of his life, however long that is for a locked-up cop.

On the stretch leading up to the next bridge he began speeding up and slowing down around them like Cassius Clay in the ring, playing with them. Once on the bridge, when he was just close enough behind them he zoomed forward and rammed into them, knocking them off balance, and then fell back out of their range again.

Every single one of them was familiar with this entrance into Bayonne. The highway abruptly narrows and runs smack dab into a residential zone. This is where their pursuers would close in on them. Sol took the only chance they had left and holstered his gun. He pushed the jeep forward to 100 mph knowing Anthony would also speed up. Then right where the road touches mainland again and a divider appears Sol veered left into the southbound lanes swimming frantically past the oncoming cars and right off the road, bouncing down the small hills into a mixed-use zone of houses and commercial buildings. He did the 4x4 through some suburban patches of greenery, a few backyards and over yet another set of railroad tracks to land in a strip mall parking lot where they were slammed into by a minivan whose driver was talking on her cell phone.

When the shock wore off Sol and Lorelei clumsily made their way out of the car. She scooped her gun off the floor of the car. The air bags had gone off but Ramirez had no such protection in the back of the jeep. He was unconscious, but alive, and bleeding from the side of his head. Sol checked on the other driver who was in mild shock but essentially unharmed. Anthony had quickly found the police turnaround and they could hear his siren coming toward them. A crowd of shoppers was gathering around them and some people came forward to see if they could help. The mall's security patrol was speeding toward them across the lot.

"We have to keep going, Laura, get security to take Ramirez to Bayonne Medical."

She pulled out her badge and ordered one of the mall cops to take the kid to the nearest hospital in their SUV. She told the other one to call 911 and stay with the minivan lady until the ambulances arrived.

Sol looked for the fastest automobile around with a driver present: a silver Nissan Z with a college brat staring out in amazement. Sol walked up to him with officialdom, flashed his investigator's permit with the state seal on it and faked a sequester.

"State police, son, we need your car."

"Whu..., what?"

Had to flash the damn gun in his jacket. "Get out!" Sol ushered the boy out of his prized sports car. "Let's go," he said to his partner.

The sound of sirens was everywhere now. They raced through the back streets, zigzagging northeastward to find 440 again. Once back in Jersey City he drove breakneck maneuvers through the Greenville and Claremont sections to sneak up the hill to Journal Square where they ditched the stolen car behind the Lowe's Theatre. As they walked Lorelei left a haphazard message on Pines' voicemail. On the boulevard they hastily picked up a couple t-shirts.

They knew it wasn't safe for either of them to try to go home right now. There were sure to be some kind of cops there already or on their way. It was impossible to know how many were under Paul's and Sanders' control. Forget going to any local station house, at this point it was shoot first and ask questions later. The narcs had the upper hand right now, they got their story in first. There were squad cars and black-and-whites racing and screaming everywhere like a horde of banshees.

Through the afternoon crowds Sol and Lorelei casually hustled down to the New York Sports Bar on Sip Avenue, an anonymous sort of place where they nursed a few O'Doul's as they got their wits together. Fortunately for them few people out drinking on Saturdays like to watch the evening news, especially in this neighborhood, heavily Hispanic, Middle Eastern and Pakistani. Football and futbol on the screens.

Sol told her about locating the paintings and about Paul, how Anthony and his crew had to be working for him.

"When the hell were you gonna tell me?!" she demanded under her breath.

"I only knew for sure about Paul on Thursday and I only figured out where the paintings were this morning. I didn't want you to have any knowledge of what I did to confirm."

He told her how he had stashed the copies of Paul's files (and the painting) he'd stolen in a lock box hidden in a large hole he had carved out of the rock underneath his building. He'd learned very early on about having good hiding places from the countless poor examples he'd had to find.

The old warehouse that Sol had made into his home was situated on a cliff of a rail canyon; the northern end of the structure ended at an old fence between the second garage and an unnoticed concrete overpass. This entrance to the descent is camouflaged in summertime by untrimmed foliage covering both ends of the small bridge. It's only in the winter that anyone ever sees the ragged little stone steps to a steep drop. He would have to take hard way up.

They waited until it started getting dark, walked steadily down to the end of Van Wagenen and then made their way along the Norfolk-Southern train tracks, ducking into the shadows whenever a train approached, until they were right below his building. She waited for him as he climbed up the rock wall to retrieve the CD's, painting and his emergency kit: cash, false ID, another gun and two clips.

Under cover of darkness they crouched on the side of the tracks for three hours before a slow-enough freight train came through and they were able to hop a ride over the rail bridge into the big blind city as the rain started coming down. There would be no sleep for them tonight.

* * * *

They were being referred to as 'cop killers' in the news reports. One of Sol's bullets had put Sanders' partner in a coma.

Sol, Lorelei and Ramirez weren't supposed to have left the bar without a satisfactory understanding between all parties regarding those paintings. The story Sanders and his crew delivered to everyone was a slightly modified version of the one they had prepared before going in; a plan B if Sol and Lorelei wouldn't wise up.

Lorelei was having an affair with Sol behind Anthony's back. Worse, Sol was a drug dealer: almost two whole ounces of cocaine were 'discovered' in the trunk of his car. He'd recruited Lorelei as his partner and they were being investigated by Sanders' unit. They'd managed to set up what they thought was a buy with one of the undercover officers and were about to be arrested when they recognized Anthony and had drawn their guns. A firefight broke out and Sol and Lorelei managed to escape. Ramirez was an off-duty cop who'd simply got caught up in the operation. Someone would be coming by to check on him in the hospital tomorrow.

Special Agent Pines didn't immediately know how to react. He'd executed the warrants for Coles and found the paintings, arrested and charged him with grand theft, possession of stolen property and a few other things to hold him but the man made bail within the hour it had been set at 100K. Federal bail judges are available on weekends.

But why hadn't Laura and Sol been there? Some crazy message about her boyfriend and a set-up. Had his two new hires started fooling around? And where was the fourth painting?

23.

<u>The Dark Side</u>

"In all men is evil sleeping;
the good man is he who will not awaken it,
in himself or in other men."
- Mary Renault, *The Praise Singer* (1978)

"I ain't a killer but don't push me..."
- Tupac Shakur as Makaveli, 'Hail Mary', *The 7 Day Theory* (1996)

We all of us have secret lives, real or imagined. Some are fanciful, some are necessary or convenient, some are inescapable.

* * * *

They'd been underground for a week, moving from place to place among Sol's contacts and the cheapest motels in New York City. They had to keep moving. He had no kin on paper and Lorelei's family would definitely all be watched. In two brief calls to assure them of her innocence and let them know she was okay they had begged her to turn herself in to them, but she couldn't do that just yet. She was afraid to tell them everything about Anthony, afraid he and his cronies would go after them. They just might anyway. She hated him even more now, it burned inside of her.

Pines had offered them federal protective custody until all the facts were straightened out but they'd still be in custody, unable to act for themselves.

Paul had fast-tracked the indictments and they were now wanted for attempted murder of a police officer as well as a multitude of other false charges.

A national law enforcement alert had been issued: armed and dangerous. Their pictures were on heavy rotation at the local TV stations for three days.

They were hunted animals. You can only run for so long before you're taken down or arise victorious. They were out of options.

It was somewhere in Queens, a Greek neighborhood where Sol'd spent half his childhood, that they made the decision to stop running. In this city headlines and attention spans are brief, but memories are long.

An old friend, now an old man still working as a superintendent and oblivious to the English-language news in Jersey, lent him a basement apartment that was vacant. He knew Sol was in some kind of bind but assumed it was over the woman.

"Aren't you glad you gave up fighting, though, Sol?" he had asked the young boxer he remembered.

The place was devoid of furniture, except for a couple of new mattresses and some milk crates the old man had secured. At least it had electricity, though, hot water and a couple of small air conditioners sweating away valiantly against concrete heat and humidity. They sat on the floor with their backs literally against the wall.

She was too young to be mixed up in this kind of thing, he thought, really nobody deserves this. But for some reason she trusted him. He wasn't the most charming of men but he was up-front, take it or leave it. She was resolute. Her steady green eyes told him she knew what had to be done.

"We need proof, Laura. We have to hit them. We have to hit them hard and fast."

"I can do that."

"Can you do it without killing anyone?"

"I'll do my best."

* * * *

Tuesday, named after the god of war. It was a half-moon rising.

Paul controlled a good portion of Jersey City mid-level drug and gun operations, with cooperation and blessings from various larger criminal organizations of all local ethnic groups which paid him a type of retainer to either ignore or protect parts of their more expansive endeavors in his sphere of influence if and when necessary and feasible. The presiding District Attorney was old and in the way, a figurehead with her mind on a permanent vacation. The First Assistant was a do-gooder with aspirations toward capitol halls and arcades. The other towns comprising Hudson County were essentially small fiefdoms, easily managed by local tribal leaders and judges. But in Jersey City, where all the real action was, he was the man in charge. And he had a small army of followers, including a tight and loyal narcotics squad and a few groups of runners, all of which benefitted immensely from his largesse.

No one in the public domain questioned his wealth or his integrity. He was a shining example of civic leadership. But he was actually a businessman at heart, focused on the bottom line. His father had instilled in him the law of the jungle. He saw himself as something of a cross between Joe and Jack Kennedy, but with a subtle Cuban flavor.

People like Sol lacked the vision of the greater good, of bigger pictures, and they lacked the essence of leadership to move humanity to new levels of prosperity. They served merely as minor functionaries of progress. And if they failed to contribute to the great march forward, or, worse, attempted to impede it, they allowed themselves to be trampled underfoot.

Paul had been told by #1, Doctor Lazarus Knowles, that Sol had accepted his invitation to their brief conversation. That the good doctor knew who Sol was and what he was looking for would have confirmed for Sol that he was on the right track somehow. No doubt he'd taken it upon himself to sit on the Sterling Boys to see what he could find. He knew Sol had arrived at his rung on the ladder but he didn't know that Sol had the list.

* * * *

To carry out their intentions they needed a few things. Not least of these were more cash, more weapons and ammunition, some tactical equipment, a whole lotta luck and a little help from some friends. Sol was going to have to ask for a few favors and call in a couple.

You'd be amazed at what you can buy in a police supply store with the proper identification. These places can verify that you are an out-of-state officer of the law but they don't receive police bulletins except from their own state, usually about criminals impersonating police and these were still being done by fax.

Licensed gun shops, on the other hand, were now by requirement being connected to their state's police databases and routinely received electronic alerts about armed fugitives in their area or nearby states possibly looking to re-up on arms and bullets. For the things they could no longer obtain legally, and to be smuggled back into Jersey City, they would have to go see a man Sol knew from long ago.

As they walked down the darkened stairs from the restaurant to the private night club, Sol's past embraced him with cruel remembrance. Low lighting, and only for the few tables that wanted it. People still smoked in places like this, the hell with what the city health department had ordered. There were always a lot of people here visiting from the old country, the islands. They had no use for so many American rules and regulations.

The young girls dancing in authentic outfits on a lit stage in the center of the room were often vacationing with their families and brought their people's traditions to their new world cousins and nostalgic elders. The people around them threw rose buds, handfuls of petals and dollar bills at the girls as the band played feverishly off to the side.

Sol never thought he would have to come back here, especially not under these circumstances. They made their way over to a table of men flanking Joseph Kotrotsiou; fat, bald potentate of Greek Astoria. The other men left him alone with Sol and Lorelei. The man spoke in his native voice to Sol in a lowered tone.

"You see, my boy, you should have stuck with boxing," he said, "You could have been rich and retired by now and not gotten into all this trouble. You didn't believe me when I told you you might someday have to come ask me for something, you remember? So, anyway, what is it that I can help you with?"

* * * *

The Greeks had gotten them what they needed, including a harmless white minivan used to deliver them back over the Hudson, complete with clean plates. They worked out of a small apartment right across from the Hoboken Terminal. Here the trains, overland tracks as well as tunnels, converged with ferries, light rails and a highly popular district of restaurants and bars.

Sol's alias had an unusually pristine credit rating but the realtor just needed the commission. They would scarcely be noticed now that they'd changed their appearances. Sol had a buzz cut, plain t-shirts and jeans and plenty of scruff, Lorelei's hair was now a medium-length dark brown and she was dressing like a pissed-off butch.

Next on Paul's list of city 'cleaning' operations was a modest little buy of Vietnamese heroin out of a sundries store on Montgomery Street, at the top of the hill and a couple blocks away from the National Guard Armory.

They had been watching and waiting on the roof of the small building since before sunrise wearing black POLICE t-shirts, caps and fatigues. Two mini cameras had been strategically placed in the alley with motion sensor triggers. Shortly after the store opened at nine o'clock the team of three Philippine cocaine cowboys rolled up on Baldwin Avenue, parked on the sidewalk and walked through the garbage alley to the back entrance of the grocery, where someone unseen let them in. Sol and Lorelei quietly made their way down the fire escape. A few minutes later they could hear the Sterling Boys make their way out and they snuck up behind them.

"Ay," Sol whispered. The three whirled around to see two cops pointing their guns at them. Except they quickly realized who it was: those two wanted for *shooting* a cop.

"C'mere," Lorelei cooed, motioning them closer. "You already know we'll shoot."

They walked over reluctantly. This needed to be kept quiet just a few moments more and Sol was keeping an eye on all the windows and doors around them.

"Strip," she said firmly. "One at a time, you first," she pointed her gun at the leader, a bulky Buddha-looking guy with pointy black hair named Pete Luan. He scoffed with his eyes. She aimed at his groin. "Now! Or bleed, it's up to you." He started to unbutton his shirt. "Nice and slow. Just to your shorts. Don't worry, you're not my type."

In his waistband was a nine millimeter pistol. Sol found one on each as he had them in turn handcuff one of the others. In Luan's queer little fanny pack was a couple thousand dollars worth of poppy powder.

When they were stripped and cuffed Sol and Lorelei taped their mouths shut and moved them into a corner of the small concrete yard. Sol opened the back door of the store and shouted "Police! Everybody on the floor!" He didn't bother going inside.

There was screaming from a woman inside and somebody crashed out the front door. The Filipino boys tried to shout things out but were immediately silenced by the guns still pointed at them. Sol and Lorelei marched them through the alley and out onto the street. Around the leader's neck, along with the fanny pack, Sol hung a hand-made placard with black marker block letters that read: COURTESY D.A.'s OFFICE.

With plastic ties Sol had the boys play ring around the rosy on a utility pole. When they were secured, Lorelei called the police non-emergency number and said there were some men dealing drugs at this corner. They waited two minutes then she and Sol picked out one of the motorcycles each and rode off down the hill through the office plazas of Mill Road and disappeared.

Pete Roque had been left an anonymous tip at the Hudson Journal to wait for a phone call today about the people who had attacked Phoebe. He'd gotten that phone call with a time and location ten minutes ago. What he found when he got there made the next day's front page.

* * * *

The new recruits on the porch, young boys, didn't know how to react when Sol just walked right up to their house in the 'hood asking for their head guys by name.

"I'm not a cop. Tell them it's the guy about the fire a couple years ago."

At first the crew leaders hadn't believed him. It's hard to trust someone who once had you under investigation and appears out of nowhere to offer you help you didn't know you needed. Especially when he's a white man.

But when Sol told them exactly what day they were supposed to have how much reefer in the house they had to give him the benefit of the doubt. That, and he was now a wanted criminal just like half of them.

"I'm not being altruistic, I need a favor," he explained to them. "The truth is it was none of my business until now."

"Go on," said a mouthful of gold. He called himself Black Sun, real name Marcus Winston.

"Look, if nothing else, you know that these people who want to come down on you, as a favor for some crack dealers, by the way, they're destroying the youth. Everybody's. We've all been kids. We all know what it's like. It's hard enough by itself. There's no need for guns and drugs being shoved down their throats.

"I actually listened to a few of your songs, by the way, when I was checking you guys out back then. And I know you're not down with the bullshit. All I'm saying is do what you have to to have this house clean tomorrow night. Then you'll see I'm telling you the truth."

On Thursday night, when the narcotics raiding team swarmed over the darkened house they found it completely empty, devoid even of any human presence for over twenty-four hours. Thanks to an associate, The Darkside was able to watch from a house across the street while Sol and Lorelei recorded it all.

* * * *

Friday morning

Despite occasional interruptions, life and business must go on. So far it was only a rumor that Sol and Lorelei were back in town. Sanders' people hadn't been able to get close to the Sterling Boys for all the attention and Paul made sure to appear oblivious to all the developments. Nonetheless, he'd quietly put out the word to his people to be on alert. Not to stop what they normally did, but just to be extra careful. And while Anthony and Vivian took a few additional precautionary steps to ensure that they weren't being followed at any point on their way to the weekly trade-off with the Africans, they failed to consider that there could already be someone waiting for them.

They backed into their usual cubbyhole in the high grass to wait. Lorelei and Sol materialized at their windows like ghosts in the bush. Man on man, woman at woman. The two in the car scarcely had time to think as they were helped out of the car at gun point.

After making her reveal and disarm herself, they had Vivian cuff Anthony to the tie-down pin in the trunk, which contained five ounces of confiscated cocaine. The usual reserve guns were also there.

"Sit down," Lorelei told both of them. Then she walked over to Sol and handed him her gun.

"You," she said to Vivian. "Stand up. Walk over here with me."

Sol pointed his gun first at Anthony then at Vivian.

"I have no hesitation in shooting either one of you right now," he said

"Throw your hands up," Lorelei said to the other woman.

"Whut?!"

Lorelei showed her what she meant with a quick left faster than a rabbit. And the chica understood quickly.

Girl fights can be fun to watch if it's not serious, if there's skimpy clothing involved and no one gets hurt.

But a real fight between two women is actually rather ugly. Beautiful creatures trying to savagely destroy each other is not a pleasant sight.

The hardened Elizabeth native and JCPD trained narcotics officer was no weakling but Lorelei had been training and fighting since she was a twelve-year old tomboy. It had come natural to her. She was like a cat toying with a panicked mouse.

She hit the zone, destroying her opponent as if a dream sequence. Her rage only gave her strength, she had focus. The other was only reacting, trying to keep up.

Judge not, call it what you will, a woman's wrath shakes the world.

When Vivian could take no more and was falling to her knees Lorelei slapped the living daylight out of her and dragged her by her hair to the front of the car where she handcuffed her to the steering wheel. She asked for her gun back and Sol quickly took a few pictures of their captives and the cocaine. Then he threw the drug bundles into a satchel and they took off into the marsh leaving their beaten opponents for the Africans to find.

* * * *

Saturday night

They didn't care that much that he'd saved them from being arrested, they weren't afraid of jail. It was a solid he'd done for them, though, and so they had agreed to return the favor. And they were getting paid. Still, they worked out of and practically lived in this Caddy and the back seat had a hump. White boy had to ride bitch.

Sol cared even less than they did at this point. They were an armed escort. The metal of their guns clinked against his, nobody paid it any mind. The heavy bass vibrations of their pumped up speakers drowned everything out. They were all getting into the apt mindset, ready to die and coming down the road.

The job was to take this guy around a few stops in Jersey City and one in Union City, the last. Just watch his back and get him out if there's any trouble, which could come from all sides. Those dirty cops might still be looking for them. And one of those stops with this guy involved going into enemy territory, an actual street gang that just didn't like the Darkside boys and were the ones they were supposed to have been sold out for, so it balanced the deal.

First stop he just popped out and slipped a note to a skinny, freckled waitress, at the back of some diner off the highway, whispered in her ear and she gave him a kiss on the cheek.

Second stop was back in Greenville where they parked across the street from a ruined playground. Dude pulled out a camera with a zoom lens and for about a half hour took pictures of a drug spot run by their

226

rivals, South 36 Crew.

Third stop was an apartment building on Garrison Avenue on the West Side. He said he'd only be two minutes, they were to double park and keep the car running.

The last stop was some big old church-looking building on the corner of two jam-packed tiny streets. Sol had them park on the sidewalk at the rear of the lyceum. This was where they all had to get out except the driver, who was to remain low, lights and engine off but ready to take off at any moment. They were meeting with some Colombians. The rap boys assumed it was for drugs.

Fifteen sweaty minutes later the driver thankfully started the car when he saw his people and that crazy white boy come swaggering out.

About ten blocks away Sol simply asked that he be let out of the car and said they were done. He thanked them and wished them luck. He vanished into the busy crowd of Bergenline Avenue.

* * * *

They only had thirty-six hours left. She'd gotten stuck with the last of the paperwork. The fee for taking care of personal business on company time, he'd joked dryly. He was out doing the last of the legwork.

They'd had to put the case together; charges, evidence, summary. She was to wrap it up. It was her first, after all. Everything had to be tightly bound, waterproof; i's dotted, t's crossed. They'd agreed they would turn themselves into the Feds on Monday, after one last thing.

She was empty. Her hands, her body hurt. Her mind hurt. She could barely see straight but she had to keep going, typing out the timelines, long list of suspect's names, involvement, histories. That was mainly for their benefit as a guide. Afterwards came all the forms and citations.

* * * *

In the two weeks that Sol had been watching him, he had learned a few things about Samson "Lion Man" Olaperi. The leader of the African Ocean Avenue gang was a man of habit, in various ways. Perhaps as a counter to, or some sort of imagined compensation for, all the criminal acts and vices he engaged in, the man went to church on Sunday. Basically, though, he went because his mother made him.

She was a faithful member of the Mount Zion A.M.E. Church on

Clinton Avenue in Newark, across from the Divine Riviera Hotel. This congregation had a tradition of marching the Holy host through the streets after Mass as they prayed and sang and shouted hallelujah. To an outside observer it was a lovely little spectacle: all the parishioners in their Sunday best, a mix of Westerner and traditional African clothing, clapping and chanting, rhythmically raising their voices to the Most High.

Samson did not walk with the procession but followed slowly behind them in his gleaming white Infiniti, his lieutenant driving. It was an hour-long duty after which he would usually take mama and her friends out to lunch.

The section of High Street at the crest of the hill where the Essex County Courthouse presided was usually quiet and still on Sundays, with the neighborhood pilgrimage the only thing moving. 'Lion Man' normally dozed in the passenger seat, waiting away the residue of the previous night's festivities. This particular Sabbath he was stirred to waking by the sound of motorcycles having suddenly come up behind them on either side of the car.

From the bikes and the leather riding gear he'd thought it was his Philippine associates. Except… Oh shit! They had guns drawn.

Sol and Lorelei had taken them by surprise and forced the driver to unlock the doors. They left the bikes where they were and got in the back seats.

"Don't make us kill you. Turn the car around and start driving," Sol commanded.

“You are making a big mistake, brudder…” Samson threatened with forced calm.

Sol put the barrel of his gun against the gangster's head.

“I am not fucking around! I prefer you dead. Now you're gonna take us to where you keep the guns or I'm just gonna leave your bodies right here and call it a day.”

The faithful flock was left standing in shock as the rich man's car pulled off. It took a few minutes before someone thought to pull out their cell phone to call the police. By then it was far too late. Lorelei was telling the driver how to drive.

They were brought to a house on Prospect Avenue in neighboring East Orange, just past a block that looked like a bombed-out war zone. Sol had them pull into the driveway to the back yard where he and Lorelei ushered the front seat occupants out at gunpoint.

Expecting to find some heavily armed thugs, they used the Africans as meat shields to clear the entrance into the kitchen. The smell of high-grade marijuana smoke, scrambled eggs and pork sausage filled the air.

A voice called out from the living room.

"Hey, Lion Man… Whatchudoin' here on a Sunday? Oh…"

Lazing around a giant flat-screen television and an X-Box video game console was a group of three young black men stoned off their asses, two of them wearing Seton Hall University t-shirts. It took them a few moments to process the sight of their handcuffed benefactor and his right-hand man being walked in by a white dude and chick holding guns at their backs. Even then they were frozen in place.

Sol and Lorelei sat everyone down.

"Who else is in the house?" she asked the gamers. They glanced at each other nervously. There were more of them somewhere inside.

"Keep an eye on the doorways," Sol told her. He picked the most frightened of the kids to plasticuff the others, then bound him as well. Lorelei babysat while Sol cleared the rest of the house. Behind the only closed door on the second floor he found a pair of young lovers sound asleep, black boy, white girl.

"Wake up, sleepyheads."

Roused, then startled to see a strange man holding a gun.

"What the fuck?!" the young man spit. The girl started to scream but Sol barked them quiet.

"Shut up! Both of you. Get some clothes on."

He brought them down to join the others and told Samson to accompany him to the basement where was stored about a dozen assorted handguns, an Uzi, three automatic rifles and two shotguns.

The Lion Man and his pride of African criminals were using clean-record American college kids to smuggle up guns bought in the South. No doubt these kids had some local gang affiliation as well.

They took pictures of all the suspects and firearms and then Lorelei grabbed the keys to a dark grey Honda Accord belonging to one of the boys. She put a call into the Essex County Gunstoppers hotline while Sol summoned Pete Roque. The Garden State Parkway was right nearby. Before they left they hung another of those placards around a murderous captive Lionman: COURTESY HUDSON D.A.

* * * *

Monday morning

Paul called him promptly at the start of the business week. He used a disposable number and a voice modifier. Sol knew it was him anyway and had been expecting the call. They only needed a few seconds to talk.

"You've got three days to get your affairs in order, Sol. Even you have some kind of family out there somewhere. It may take me a little while but I'll find them. And one by one I'll have all those innocent librarians killed, over a careful period of years. Disposable is what they are and all their deaths will be on your hands, Sol.

"I have all the time in the world, unlike you. Besides, it's not what you know, old boy, it's *who* you know. You're the only one pushing this, man, and you're risking that woman's life. She can play ball or she can get it, too. Makes no difference to me. But it's you that I want.

"Give yourself up for them and everything goes back into balance. I leave everyone else alone. It's not an offer, Sol. I'll start with the women and McSherman's family tonight. You know very well I always keep my word. With you, it would just be more details. You have one hour to understand and tell me how you want to die. You'll have to get your own dinner this time, though, okay, buddy?"

* * * *

Only a handful of people knew that Sol had a son. Those few did not include Paul. The child was four years old and he was the only thing that mattered in Sol's otherwise non-descript life. He only got to see the boy one day a week. That was why Saturdays were sacred to him and why it was painful for him to see or be around other people's children.

He and the mother had split almost two years ago and she had moved down the shore with their son. At the time Sol had been working long nights and odd hours for a criminal defense firm. There was nothing he could do about it then. It was what the job called for and no one else was hiring legal gumshoes at the time. She wanted nothing less than a husband with a normal 9-to-5, home for dinner every night and without the all-too-frequent mysterious phone calls or unsettling cuts and bruises. That, and Sol's philandering in the early days of their relationship (her excuse for not marrying him) had made it impossible for her to ever fully trust him.

Nine months after she left him Sol had tried to reorganize himself to please her and ensure a strong presence in his son's life. But it was too

230

far gone. She had started dating a stock broker and it looked like it was getting serious. All for the best, he supposed; he really had only ever wanted her to be happy anyway.

And look how it had ultimately turned out. She was right to have left him. He wasn't even going to make it to his son's fifth birthday.

He had called her last night to ask for a brief visit. He told her he'd be going away for a long while and she had assumed he meant prison. She only acquiesced when he assured there wouldn't be anyone coming to arrest him at her apartment.

The child was delirious with all the toys that 'pop-pop' had surprised him with. It was a mild evening and the three of them went to a nearby park to play with a remote controlled car and kick around a new soccer ball.

Sol told the only woman he had ever loved that he'd made out his will to leave everything he had in their son's name, under her authority until he turned nineteen. She objected some but it was already a done deal.

He watched as the boy scrunched up his little face figuring out new tricks with the radio transmitter and wondered what kind of man he would grow into. The failed father studied every detail of his only son's features for the last time. Cherub cheeks and curls, long eyelashes like his own, tiny lips pursed in scientific discovery. When he figured out how to make the toy car jump over some rocks he turned to his parents with wide-eyed wonder and delight and Sol felt something crack inside of him.

At the mother's apartment Sol held the boy in his arms, talking to him until he fell asleep. He put him in bed and felt a bottomless guilt at what a failure of a father he was. He said a brief goodbye to his once true one and hurried out the door. On the drive up the Garden State Parkway he began making mental preparations to meet his fate and the pollen in the air made his eyes water.

24.

<u>Jersey City</u>

On the day of September 11th, 2001, amid all the panic, confusion, fear, horror and death Jersey City had been called upon to help survivors get out of lower Manhattan. There had been a staff meeting scheduled at the library that day. Instead, with the Twin Towers burning before them, they had all marched (only police and emergency vehicles were being permitted to operate downtown) to the docks at Exchange Place to offer medical help, hand out water and supplies, guide the lost to communications and transportation, and to unload bodies. They never spoke of it afterward but none would ever forget.

That day all the librarians knew who the others were and what it really meant to sacrifice yourself for strangers. And on this particular day they had to act as one again for one of their own, despite his unclear objectives.

They knew that organized crime was involved in this whole mess. But they also knew a few other things, too. Each of them. They were little things, to be sure, seemingly inconsequential at the time but enough to fit like pieces of the larger puzzle that they thought they had almost solved.

Mrs. Savoy had inspected every inch of the library, including the basement and administrative offices, on a yearly basis since the second day she was given the mantle. This was a decade before the museum moved to its new building. And never once did she come across any paintings of nudes. In fact, the permanent art collection was primarily dedicated to regional art from colonial times to the library's opening and forward to the middle of the last century. Everyone knows the nude was never a popular subject in traditional American painting (excepting occasional pieces like John Vanderlyn's 'Ariadne') until after the Sexual Revolution. It was Mr. Savoy, in a phone call from Italy, where he was on a research trip, who suggested the library was only being used as a red herring.

Pete Roque knew the gun runners were untouchable in Jersey City because he'd tried to follow up on the gun-control group's work as a story and been shut down.

Caleb Soter knew the punk rock kid had something to do with the paintings but couldn't figure exactly what except that he only hung out in the Fine Arts section and that whenever he was around there was a low

232

hum of unusual activity around the library.

Isobel was a painter of landscapes and she rented a tiny studio in the #11 Arts Building. She knew there was talk floating among residents of a movement to purchase the building from which they were all being evicted.

Meredith knew it was still a nascent art scene in Jersey City, with less than a handful of high-end dealers. These would have been easily screened by the FBI.

Tidbits of information like that were all they had. Together they'd come up with a possible scenario, which Rebecca had revealed to Sol.

They now knew that he and Lorelei had also been looking for these paintings, presumably in a governmental function, and now they were being pursued as criminals. Not a single one of them bought the story being sold by the police.

The day Sol and Lorelei had been forced to go on the run, a special meeting had been called and at its conclusion they had all resolved to take immediate action.

They would use everything in their powers to bring the truth to light.

They hit the streets, door to door, from public to private, high and low, through everyone they knew or could think of asking, looking for answers, information and some kind of justice.

In downtown Jersey City, at the corner of Bay and Erie Streets and directly across from JCPD Internal Affairs headquarters, there is an old bar. It was originally Irish-owned until a Puerto Rican gentleman bought it in the late seventies.

In that bar, between all the neighborhood know-it-alls, they knew it all. The retirees and other relaxed regulars spent their abundant free time discussing and arguing the goings-on in town even though most of it was none of their business. The later it got in the night, the more loose information rose in the air. All you needed was a little Spanish. Pete Roque was fluent. You didn't even have to talk much, just listen closely. Word had it that that librarian cop-killer had a bounty on his head, no questions asked.

* * * *

Sol had told Lorelei that they needed to postpone their surrender for a few days. He said that he and Paul had come to an understanding and a truce had been reached. They were not to make a move until midnight

Thursday.

"Is he going to run?" she'd asked.

"He's not going anywhere. And neither are we."

That Thursday morning, August 8th, it seemed to her that Sol was strangely serene. He'd arisen and gone out well before sunrise. When she got up she'd found a note instructing her to hold her appetite.

He returned around eight with an elaborate gourmet breakfast, a rich assembly of items from the best shops on Washington Avenue.

He was unusually talkative. Over the course of a few hours, as they killed time in the apartment, he asked about her childhood, what her family was like, and what she planned to do once this whole thing was over. At noon he asked her to take a walk with him to the waterfront where they bought ice cream and he uncharacteristically divulged bits and pieces of his own life.

She couldn't contain her curiosity.

"Why are you acting so strange?"

"I'd like to return to a state of grace. And you're the only person I have to talk to."

An odd answer, and then he added, "We might not ever get to work together again."

For the very first time she saw him smile. It was sincere, but it scared the hell out of her.

He spent the afternoon listening to what he said was his favorite radio show, even called in a request, as if this were any other day. At four o'clock he said he wanted some time alone and was going out to catch a matinee.

* * * *

The alert went out at five. A local radio station had issued a distress signal to its listeners looking for anyone who knew someone named 'Sol' in hopes of preventing what the disc jockey was convinced could be a possibly imminent suicide. He didn't give his reasoning right away but repeatedly advised his listeners that he was not joking and that he would serve as a clearinghouse for any and all serious information about a man in his late 20's or early 30's who lived in Jersey City and listened to a lot of radio. He continued to play upbeat, positive music, interjecting little 'life is good' snippets hoping Sol was still listening, and took calls but made constant interruptions to repeat his alert, 'find Sol'.

Calls started trickling in, people asking if it was the same Sol that was the fugitive librarian. No one knew for sure, until a couple of his friends called in.

* * * *

Half of the men already had guns, but so did Mariette and Meredith, ladies' pistols. John grabbed his hearty shotgun, Thomas his faithful sidearm and Pete a Saturday night special. Prem was sworn to non-violence but if he had to he would defend himself with a family heirloom sword. Cecilia, Rebecca and Phoebe had military-strength mace cans. Caleb pulled out his aluminum baseball bat and could not dissuade Isobel from coming along with her sacramental dagger. Dmitri summoned his Russian pride and armed himself with a large, heavy mallet hastily bought at a big box home improvement store. They all brought the strongest flashlights and lanterns they could find.

The sun was going down. They gathered in the library basement.

Cecilia begged forgiveness for her sin of wrath and prayed for God's righteousness.

Premdeep knew there was strength in numbers and he'd already been cleared by his own conscience and his gods.

Thomas had had to leave his family twice before to go to war.

Isobel had always wondered what it would feel like to stab someone.

Dmitri was scared shitless but couldn't imagine missing out on all the excitement.

Mariette had faced Death on plenty of occasions before but this time she was not afraid.

Meredith always stood up for her friends.

Pete was ready to rock.

Phoebe had maternal instincts and she wanted revenge.

John really liked combat mode (you only live once).

Rebecca truly cared about Sol and was dedicated to her newfound family.

Caleb would not have been able to live with himself if he did not try to help.

* * * *

235

He'd met them off Burma Road as agreed. He got in one of two cars that drove to a secluded parking lot off Freedom Way in Liberty State Park. They were to walk into the woods for about ten minutes to a hill that looks directly upon lower Manhattan between Liberty and Ellis Islands.

Just for the fuck of it, after they had frisked him he fought them all, with shots they never saw coming. A good old slugfest. He was gonna get his licks in and he did. They didn't know what was hitting them but it just kept hitting. He hit them all, at least a few times, but there were just too many of them. At the end it was a pile-on. These guys had plenty of training and experience in beating on people.

* * * *

The librarians had left their cars in the main visitor's lot on Jersey City Boulevard. Lorelei had snuck into the park on the Hudson Bergen Light Rail, jogging from the Jersey Avenue stop. In the thicket of a service road they came upon each other, her one mag light met by their dozen lamps. It was fifteen minutes before the supposed killing time. She was running blind, they had the coordinates. They gave her authority but insisted on backing her up. All they had was each other. It was enough, they could do it. They charged forward.

* * *

"You're the biggest mistake I ever made, you know that, Sol? But I know how to make corrections."

Paul was rambling madly to Sol, who was about to be the first man he'd ever killed by his own hand, a hand he had to hold against his hip for the trembling. "People like you are just always in the way, man." On and on he went. These guys never shut up. Sol was just trying to focus through the ass-whupping he'd just been handed. *They actually brought a body bag*, he found himself thinking.

Last night he'd tried to sum up his life for himself. What a paltry contribution to the world, to the future he'd done nothing toward securing for the next generation.

Paul was droning on about fulfilling potentials and he was probably right but it was the last thing he needed to hear right now, he'd already condemned himself twelve hours ago.

He somehow shut everything out, the ranting, the grunts and

snickers from his deliverers.

As they practically dragged him along the wet ground he thought of only the good things he'd known, the good people in his life. He remembered his gentle, all-giving mother, his crazy big-love father, the adoring little sister now a good, strong young woman. He could taste the salt of the ocean waves he battled every summer, refusing to get knocked down and rising immediately if he did. He thought of long walks in surreal winter storms. He thought of all the pretty girls he'd beheld everywhere, what had made life worth living for him. He could see all the strange and wonderful places he'd been to, the pure glories in nature, the triumphs of human aspiration. He heard the words and the music, flashed through all the incredible images. He saw the faces of all the endlessly fascinating people he'd come across, low and high, humble and great. He felt again the quiet joy of earth and grass under bare feet, the electricity of cold mountain river water, the power of the wind, the sun that warmed him, the moon that mystified.

And nothing had ever been better than the touch, yes, the scent, the sight, in dark or light, the ecstasy of a woman's body.

Etty was right. About a theoretical god's masterpiece, and an honorable vocation painting pictures of it. But it was too late for that for Sol.

"Alright, man, we're here." Paul was huffing from the long walk. The full moon in the clear night illuminated them. "This is where you said, right?"

Sol squinted around through swollen eyes. There she was, the bitch that had birthed him. New York City. The only one who had ever fully accepted him for what he was. Yeah, the last sight he wanted to see before he died. The virgin at the door, in gown and crown, with the torch forever lighting welcome, warmth and warning. That dark empty hole where the twins had been. The lights all around never dying down. The city where any one of us could be anything we wanted...

"Yeah, this is it," he answered. "The box you want is over by that mound."

Paul upped his chin at Sanders. Sanders eyebrowed the fake Mets fan and his fat partner. The two started walking over as if expecting a land mine.

A low growl came from the dark.

"The next person who moves is gonna get shot." Lorelei. Like Joan of Arc.

Anthony recognized her voice, held up his fist to hold everyone. "It's her," he whispered, "Relax, don't shoot. Let me talk to her."

"Laura! Lorelei, baby doll! We can work this out. Trust me, babe, we can make this thing right for everyone."

The defenders turned their lights on their enemies like a UFO.

"There's no working this out, Anthony, you're all under arrest!" she answered him, though they were clearly outgunned.

"A bunch of fucking *librarians*, Deputy?!" ridiculed Paul. "Grizzly Adams, fashion chicks, geeks and an old lady with an antique? Really?!"

"I keep it clean and I am a good shot," answered Mariette.

The cops all start laughing until Paul silenced them with deadly seriousness.

"Alright, alright, everybody calm down. This is no longer funny." The dirty law enforcers all knew that Lorelei would probably have to die if she didn't stand down. The others could once again be pressured to keep their mouths shut and go away. Or, though highly inconvenient, they could slaughter them all and keep the bodies in the woods while a couple guys went to get trucks to load them in.

"I'm going to give you good people one last chance to walk away. If you even think of me or this whole disaster again I'll erase you and your families, every single one of you. And you, Deputy McSherman, I'm going to give you the opportunity of a lifetime."

The cops all raised their weapons at the librarians and the sheriff's deputy. Suddenly there was an ugly applause of click-clacking from the darkness behind them. When the narcs turned toward the unmistakable sounds of guns being cocked, the librarians took aim.

"Who's out there?" demanded Sanders.

"Yo mama, *aaasshole*... Drop y'all guns and you don't die tonight."

The cops all kept their guns drawn around them but no one fired. Now they were getting nervous.

"Sol! Sol! Hold on, man, I'm comin' man! Hold on!" Running screams coming from the direction of the road. Sol recognized the voice. It was his friend Eddie, the poor fool, probably coming with his old beat-up .38 to save the day against a professional squad of killers.

"Hold your fire! All of you!" came an amplified voice from yet another direction. "This is Jersey City Police ordering all of you to lay down your weapons! Now!"More click-clacking, this time from real heavy guns. "Sanders, order your men to stand down! This is over and nobody has to get hurt." A high powered spotlight shone the corrupt narcs in a cold blue light. They were all sweating. They were surrounded.

"Gallo!" Sol bellowed. He knew it was the VCU. "Gallo, the guys in the dark came to help me..."

"I said EVERYBODY put your fucking guns down!" There was an automatic rifle from Gallo's team trained on each of the groups, two at Paul and the corrupt officers.

Eddie stumbled out into the fracas waving an old revolver and yelling hysterically, "Who's first?! Who's first, goddammit?! Who wants some?! Let my friend go!"

"Eddie!" Sol called out, "Put the gun down. You're late, as usual."

The well-intentioned musician looked around and slowly took a couple steps back, gun still pointed aimlessly skyward. Loud sirens blared out of nowhere and a white SUV roared onto the scene, megaphone blasting, "Sheriff's Department! Nobody moves!" Out jumped Sheriff Cottington, Mitnaul and Carlotti." Three pump action shotguns raised high. The Sheriff called out, "Laura, you alright?!"

"Fine, Sheriff! The guys with the rifles are police!"

One life-long silent moment as everyone hesitated. Paul attempted to take control again. "I'm the assistant D.A., people! I'm ordering all of you to stand down! This is a highly classified investigation and you are all interfering!"

"Not the way it looks like from here, De La Cruz!" Gallo raised his sights directly at Paul's chest. "Why don't you let him go? He already told us what you're doing. Give it up."

Paul looked down his arm to see his hand still clutching Sol's bloodied collar, holding up a battered man on his knees and in handcuffs.

Lorelei called out. "Sheriff! De La Cruz has that narcotics unit running drugs and guns for him! Including Anthony! And now they're trying to execute Sol!"

Mitnaul zeroed in on his former friend. "I always knew you were never good enough for her you piece of shit! G'head an' move, stupid! I'll blow your legs out right from under you!"

"You don't know what you're talking about, officers!..." Paul shouted. "This man and that deputy are cop killers. You should be helping me take them down right now." He put his gun against Sol's head. "I don't know what the hell those other people are doing here!"

"We're taking you down, De La Cruz!" Pete Roque answered. "We know all about how you're killing Jersey City's people! It has to stop! This is a goddamned citizen's arrest."

"Let him go!" Big John boomed.

A helicopter suddenly thundered above them in blinding, all-exposing light.

"FBI!" an amplified megaphone commanded. "There are snipers all around and above you. Everyone is to hold their fire. All Jersey City narcotics officers are to lower their weapons immediately. Sanders, that means you and your crew."

Pines and Macy were on either sides of a mounted machine gun and a G-money searchlight in the open bay door. They could see a small group of men in hoodies easing away into the darkness but had to concentrate on the center of activity.

They were bluffing, there were no snipers. They'd come alone with the pilot and an FBI desk clerk they scooped up along the way, had grabbed all they could carry from the small armory at a certain hangar at Newark Airport. Back-up was on the way, but it might have been too late.

They circled tightly around Paul and his corrupted officers. Sanders was the first to raise his hands. The others followed suit. Paul couldn't move. He couldn't believe what was happening to him. This wasn't the plan.

"Only leaves you, Mr. De La Cruz," said the helicopter. "Be smart, drop your gun and step away from Mr. Isistrato."

He thought of pulling the trigger and blowing Sol's head clean off. But he'd be shot dead himself. Or worse, he could survive and then spend the rest of his life in prison, maybe even as a cripple. He panicked. He would decide his own fate, not these idiots. He could still get away with it, he deluded for a second. *No, they'll get me. On the street or in prison. All of them. The criminals I locked up, the people who want me silenced. They'll get me either way. Or I can keep Sol as a hostage and try to get out of here.*

Sol was counting. If he wasn't dead already there was only one thing Paul was gonna do.

There's too many of them. There's no way out.

He could feel Paul's hand tremble on his neck and the barrel shaking pressed above his temple.

Fuck it.

The hand on his collar released and the gun lifted. Sol swung and lunged upward with everything he had left and slipped a right hook hammered onto Paul's chin. The gun exploded between them and then he was blind and the thunderous roar of death was all he could hear. And then the blackness and the silence.

25.

<u>Last Night A DJ Saved My Life</u>

"He forc'd his neck into a noose,
To show his play at fast and loose;
And, when he chanc'd t'escape, mistook
For art and subtlety, his luck."
- Samuel Butler, *Hudibras*. Pt. iii, canto 2.

Death is merely the shedding of flesh. You wake up and assume a new form.

* * * *

When you take a beating, it's nothing like the movies or other pulp. There is no getting up the next day. After the short sharp shocks, the world of hurt opens up to reacquaint you with every piece of your rented body. It might let you sleep for a while, here and there, if the punishment is severe enough, but then you begin to pay for every blessed second of unconsciousness hours before you even fully awake. Every cube inch of you is roaring with pain and there's nothing you can do about it.

So he slept. For a long time. Almost two straight days. He could only mutter, in and out of waking, whenever he sensed someone trying to come too close, "No damn drugs!"

Sleep of pain is filled with wild dreams and horrible nightmares. All of your latent, dangerous thoughts are purged. If and when you make it out of your anguish, you emerge as something wholly different.

It was dark when he knowingly opened his eyes and he knew he wasn't home. At first he panicked when he couldn't sit up or make his limbs move right away. *Had they paralyzed him?!*

That's when all the knives of electricity stabbed at him to let him know that wasn't the problem. He could still tilt his head straight forward a few inches, though, without too much punishment. And in the eternal dark he could make out all the sterile white walls and trappings of the old cursed familiar hospital room.

He was in some sort of torso brace, which meant broken ribs. His right leg was elevated (*goddamned disgrace*) and there were bandages all over his face and head. And the fucking intravenous pumping who knows what into him. Those fuckers had done a number on him. He indulged himself with a few barbaric revenge fantasies while he took a thorough inventory of all his working parts and where the damage had been done.

He called for a nurse and got the detailed list of breaks and lacerations. They were keeping him at least through tomorrow. There were two federal police officers outside his door.

He allowed himself to be spoon fed, tasting nothing but bitterness, until the growling in his stomach stopped. Well, he *was* lucky to be alive...

As there was no one else in the room, Sol asked that the lights be kept on for a while. When the orderly left, he plopped his head back on the pillow and familiarized himself with the ceiling he'd be staring at all night. Then he tried to recall the details of what had happened that night before he'd blacked out.

* * * *

Paul had concocted his plan long before he'd ever gotten to Jersey City. His personal dream and ambition had always been to become a man of immense political power, through any and all means available, a fantasy fueled by his times and circumstance. He'd already been born rich, but had always wanted to make a name for himself apart from his heredity, apart from his father. Hudson County was only supposed to have been a stepping stone to larger arenas. It had seemed so easily attainable, he'd believed it his destiny.

He'd been playing Sol for a sucker, as a pawn, the whole time, for years. When they'd met at Columbia as would-be lawyers, Paul's first instinct was to calculate how he might be able to use someone so useful. His second reflex was to note that Sol was a good guy, kind of a nice guy just not nice. Just another angle, it was a weakness he could exploit. He kept Sol in his network as if in his pocket, as with so many others. They'd lost touch for a few years; Sol had dropped off the face of the earth. Then he had conveniently re-emerged as a diligent little legal beagle right here in Jersey City, just when Paul had begun building up his hidden empire. He'd been inadvertently convenient for unique bits of information about the goings-on around town.

But Sol hadn't been as easy to figure as he'd figured.

Sol had prepared to give up his life for the others, kind of a no-brainer, but he had never been one to give up without a fight. Few people get to pick the time and place of their leaving this world.

And if they were forcing him out, he was gonna take a few with him.

The deal was he couldn't go to the police or the Feds. But there were plenty of criminals in Jersey City who leapt at the opportunity to take an easy shot at a bunch of dirty cops and a dirty DA who'd put them all in jail at some time or other. Sol even put a cherry on it, planting a small pile of extra cash exactly at the location he'd given to the group who'd won the job.

Lieutenant Jay Gallo was a smart man in a town just starting to wake up again. He heard everything, he was always listening, always watching, always waiting and ready. People cannot help but talk too much, especially on the street. He'd figured it out by the time the VCU had gotten the call to be on the lookout for the fugitive. Sol had given him and his team a heads-up weeks ago to expect some gun busts. Then the waitress had passed him the note in which Sol outlined the African gang's connection to Paul. He'd started keeping a close eye on the young D.A.'s assistant.

Faced with hard time in a cop's worst nightmare, Paul's flunkies all started singing like a big city boys choir. The younger ones struggled to scavenge what little self-respect they could spot on the floor but Sanders had long been prepared to save himself; he'd been collecting evidence against everyone involved, especially his unofficial boss, for just this type of eventuality. For the first day or two he tried to portray himself as the undercover hero but his natural stupidity, a couple too many sports cars and gambling debts and twenty years of alcoholism nixed that. The Feds just took what information he had stored in his swank condominium and didn't bother to offer him any kind of deal; he was just that kind of vermin.

With Sanders' accumulated dirt, the case that Sol and Lorelei had prepared, and more files seized from Paul's computer, another two dozen arrests were made reaching everywhere from traffic courts to local businesses operating as fronts for illicit gains.

Sol and Lorelei were cleared of the false accusations leveled against them and had become something of local celebrities.

* * * *

By that Sunday Sol was recovered and cognizant enough to receive visitors. They were allowed in groups of four and he actually had to revise his approved registry a few times. He wondered morbidly to himself if all these people would have come to his funeral.

The first to see him, superseding his guest list, were Special Agents Pines and Macy, Inspector Sebastian, and his partner Lorelei. They updated him on all the developments and reminded him that there was still plenty of work to do. He asked them how they had known to be there when he'd only informed his hired guns.

"For that," Lorelei told him, "you can thank your… eccentric friend and the librarians."

When Mariette Savoy, John Claasenburger, Phoebe Marin and Pete Roque came in he asked them.

"How did you find me?"

"Dear, boy," Mariette chided. "Didn't anybody ever tell you that librarians are the secret masters of the universe?"

"No, seriously..." he implored.

"We'll let your buddy tell you," Pete said.

Through the rest of the day a few of Sol's acquaintances and some of the other librarians passed by. Late in the afternoon Rebecca arrived alone. She'd only been there about ten minutes when Meredith strutted in.

"Well, if it isn't the happy booker!" Rebecca mocked.

"Hello, Sister Sunnybrook. How's the spinster life?"

Sol couldn't remember getting this much attention since he'd fractured his elbow playing high school football.

Just before the end of visiting hours Eddie finally blew in.

"Oh, man, I'm sorry I couldn't get here sooner. I have to keep a low profile now. I think I'm being watched. Listen, you gotta get outta here and take your little zoo back. They're driving me nuts! I mean, the cat's alright, keeps to himself and does his thing, but that beast you call a dog and that damned rabbit, all they do is run around my house like shit machines and they chew on anything they can find. I swear, I almost had fresh rabbit stew the other day when that thing ate my computer cables. And-"

"-Eddie," Sol cut him off. "How did you know where I was that night?"

"Oh, yeah! That radio dj you like so much. He got the whole town riled up looking for you. He told me off the air that you requested a set with Nirvana, The Doors and Joy Division. All suicides. I was hanging out downtown when my boy Keith asked me if it wasn't you they were talking about. The dj was telling everybody that your library friends were asking anyone who knew you to contact them. Seems one of 'em is a radio head like you and they were monitoring all the police frequencies. And who knows you better than me? I called in, told them it had to be you but that you were no suicide, except that this time you kind of were, but anyway, I remembered that spot you had shown me when we were kids, where you said you'd be happy to die. It was getting dark and they told me they were getting together with your lady partner in crime. Man, she is *smoking* hot! Please tell me you two did the nasty while you were playing Bonnie and Clyde!..."

"Wasn't like that. But listen, thank you, man. You saved my life."

"Don't even mention it. I know you would've done the same for me…" He paused to consider. "You would, right?"

"You know I would."

"Right, right! I know that, I'm just kidding."

A nurse poked her head in to announce the end of visiting hours.

"Hey! Almost forgot!" Eddie rummaged through a canvas briefcase. "I brought you some videos to keep you company!"

"Come on, man, you know I don't like porn!"

"Yeah, but you're cooped up in here!"

"See you in a few days, bro..."

Sol laughed to himself when he was alone. *Looks like you were right, Paul: it IS who you know.*

26.

<u>Art One</u>

"First I dream my painting,
then I paint my dream."
- Vincent Van Gogh

PRECEDENT MAKES LAW
IF YOU STAND WELL
STAND STILL
- Inscription on the William J. Brennan Courthouse
583 Newark Avenue, Jersey City, New Jersey, USA

He would always remember August 19th of 2002 vividly. Not only because of the events of the day but also because it was one of the few good Mondays he'd ever had. He had just cheated the grim reaper one more glorious time and made a nice sum of money off the dare.

He was able to dress himself by now after more than a week of invalidity and despite the appearance of a wounded soldier he took pure pleasure in donning a tailored charcoal three-piece suit he reserved for special occasions. The jacket comfortably accommodated his shoulder holster, which he would unfortunately need to wear today, and probably for the foreseeable future.

He'd been offered a police escort but Sol just couldn't live like that. His freedom and his privacy were all he could ever really have or take with him.

It was a beautiful morning for a walk anyway, even on crutches, and the courthouse was, after all, a mere three blocks away. The arraignment was scheduled for nine o'clock, at which time all the state-level charges and penalties would be read to Paul and his minions; everything from abuse of office and corruption to assault with a deadly weapon and attempted murder, not to mention drug dealing and illegal firearms trafficking.

The following week at the federal courthouse in Newark the United States government would illustrate for them what was meant by crime and punishment. The RICO Act was being invoked. But today they had to answer to Jersey City.

Newark Avenue was overflowing with traffic and a crowd of people. From the corner Sol could see the herd of reporters being addressed by the Mayor, the County Prosecutor, Sheriff Cottington, and the Chief of Police. He continued nonchalantly along Central Avenue to the rear entrance of the courthouse on Pavonia.

When he reached the looming stair-count he noticed Paul being helped out of a limousine and into a wheelchair near the disabled-persons ramp. His family had posted the 1.5 million-dollar bail bond, both in the Superior Court and the U.S. District Court. He was with his lawyers and a few supporters, but they were obviously also avoiding the media. Sol could see Paul reach behind him and pull his assistant closer to him, whispering something in his ear.

As Sol began the clumsy ascension he could tell Paul's entourage was hurrying up the long bi-level incline to beat him to the entrance. A handicapped race ensued.

Sol tried to establish a methodical pace but the high, unforgiving steps scorned his ambulatory aids. He looked like a water-borne insect trying to climb a wall. Paul and his wheelchair pusher resembled a celebrity mommy jogger, with handlers and fans trailing behind them.

Near the top Sol slipped and almost fell flat on his face but at the last second thrust out his right crutch against the wall, simultaneously stopping his fumble and blocking Paul's advance. He straightened himself up, turned his back to Paul and his people and proceeded toward the door. They weren't supposed to be allowed within such proximity to one another, but these things happen. One of the purposes attorneys serve is the prevention of direct interaction between opposing parties in a court action.

Without looking behind him, Sol greeted the court officers at the security gate with extra friendliness and handed over his weapon to be checked into the basement firearm registry. He took his sweet time removing his jacket and belt, wallet, keys, phone and loose change in his pockets. His colleagues were already upstairs in the courtroom.

Paul pleaded Not Guilty that day and would do the same the coming week. He was taking everything to trial. Sol was serving as both a material and an expert witness for the prosecution. It would take a year or more before a date was set for the legal battle but Sol was a patient man.

* * * *

If you go down to the Jersey City Free Public Library today, walk around and take a really good look at the whole building, you might still get to see something rather peculiar most people never notice.

Shortly after it was completed, one of the founders (who shall remain unnamed) had the first of that city block's townhouses built directly adjacent to a corner of the library. A small walkway was constructed between the two and the house was used as a gentleman's retreat for all the founders and their guests. For a time, it also served as a private salon and gallery. In the days of the events portrayed herein, 103 Mercer Street existed as the home of Louis Efrain Coles.

Though it was walled over in his new home, Mr. Coles had early discovered the curious connection upon taking possession of the townhouse and confirmed for himself that it was nowhere mentioned in his ownership papers. When he'd managed to pinpoint the corresponding location within the library building he'd found the doorway blocked by an old-fashioned wooden bookcase in the archives section of the first floor. Noting that there didn't seem to be any type of alarm system installed on either side, he'd let it be until the time came when he found himself with a heaven-sent purpose for the secret passageway.

Louis was not only the bookkeeper for the Guerroyant's New York galleries, he was also an artist himself. His well-compensated daytime position afforded his comfortable residence and lifestyle, while the income from his artwork allowed him to rent a proper studio for his outsized oeuvres.

For six years he suffered Francine Villeforte's daily belittlements and disrespect, a seemingly eternal deluge of insults and piles and piles of receipts and invoices. For the first couple years when Louis was still trying to do a good job and would from time to time ask about discrepancies or incongruences with certain accounts, he was immediately lambasted and reminded that he was only there to worry about the math and not the reading. Francine never tired of pointing out that the final checks and balances were the province of real accountants, specifically a French firm with which she dealt directly. Afterward, for the last four years of his tenure, Louis Efrain simply did as he was told.

That is, until the day he came upon the knowledge that Villeforte was using museum funds and accounts to privately invest in a development corporation that was trying to purchase and tear down the building where he had his art studio in order to build a luxury hi-rise, of which there were already plenty in the area. Then Mr. Coles began conducting closer examinations of all the ledgers and notes and realized that all was not kosher.

In late 2000, about the time Dubya Bush, a ggod ole' Texan boy from Connecticut, had himself anointed King Of The World, the billionaire real estate mogul Llewellyn Yeshevin had decided to slum it for a night and visited the Open Studio Tour in the #11 First Street arts building he'd been eyeing for the past year.

He found himself enthralled by one Isobel Carrino, an adorable little thing. Her landscapes were pretty enough to adorn any of his countless walls, but it was the artist herself he wanted to possess. An intuitive creature, Isobel sensed that this arrogant snob had no real appreciation of her work but was only trying to impress her with his affluence.

When she declined to sell him the three pieces he'd selected, he was affronted and demanded to know why. Never the loquacious type, she could only explain herself by saying, "I just don't like you. You're a dead soul."

Yeshevin had never been so insulted in his pampered life. He vowed to himself that day to raze that building to the ground and to only ever pay attention to commercially successful artists.

As it is with us, those who have serious ambition must plan. The bigger the ambition, the bigger the plan. The bigger the plan, the more planning and planners are necessary. And in the early 1990's, when it had finally dawned on the moneyed what an amazing view it was of Manhattan from the Jersey side, the feeding frenzy started gaining momentum. Remember, the Twin Towers were born in 1973, and all the surrounding spires also took twenty years to come of age. Previously, the skyscrapers were all uptown.

Whoever was in business in Hudson County in the last decade of the twentieth century had to look to the future. Commerce, construction, politics and all the other machinations must synchronize. A plan must be formed. And in the all-too-valuable Jersey City waterfront, a Grand Plan had begun to take shape.

Paul had inserted himself and his personal blueprint into that larger design a bit late in the game. He'd met his upper-crust accomplices at the yacht club in 1999, all drawn to each other by their mutual love of boating and their identification as the city's new young elite. They had partied together all that year just as the whole world had been instructed to by the artist formerly known as Prince.

It was on the eve of the millennium, ecstatic with the bewitching power of expensive sparkling wine and an assortment of smart drugs, that the group of friends had sworn allegiance to their little group and the mission to secretly rule the town. What Paul lacked of the culture and refinement the others possessed he compensated for with connections and influence.

Through unscrupulous dealings and ill-gotten gains they'd begun purchasing properties in the area and exploiting them for all they were worth. Paul and the Duke had investable capital, Bennett was the licensed broker, and Villeforte was able to wash dirty money through the convenience of art sales.

The circuit kept them happy for a while but they soon realized they needed a major deal to leap frog to where they all really wanted to be: the billionaire echelon, Trump Tower "class".

They'd decided to hitch their wagon to the strongest engine in Jersey City redevelopment: SDS Corporation, Llewellyn Yeshevin's behemoth.

The #11 First Street building happened to be smack dab in the center of the line of new construction envisioned by the Planners, and it was next in line for transformation. That the artist residents were putting up a fight was of little consequence. Eventually such aesthetic concerns could be placated by allotting a small percentage of the newly developed property for artist work-live spaces; presumably the kind of art more appeasing to the wealthier, genteel sensibilities that would be present in the new version of the Arts District. Such a formality would satisfy any pesky community-requested requirements for zoning.

Paul et al., only needed to come up with a nice big chunk of cash, one million dollars to be exact, and they could get a piece of the action. It just so happened that one of their premier clients, a certain doctor, was offering roughly that amount for a particular set of paintings said to be up for auction on the black market in Jersey City.

Except that complications arose. Those paintings proved to be harder to obtain than anticipated, and those damned artists in the building just would not go away quietly.

* * * *

At Sol's suggestion, Special Agent Pines had kept Louis Cole's arrest and the seizure of the paintings completely quiet. Mr. Coles was more than willing to cooperate with the authorities and divulged all the information he'd collected pertaining to Villeforte's wrongdoings, which in turn led the FBI to the illegalities conducted by her associates. In fact, that had been Louis Efrain's intention all along. He'd been trying hard to get everyone's attention.

Inspector Sebastian and his people were able to ascertain that the Cano painting was a forgery despite an incredibly painstaking effort to simulate authenticity. The Feds followed suit and proved that the others were also fakes. Since Coles could not be charged with stealing something that never existed, the point was moot. There was no physical evidence whatsoever linking him to the destruction at the Guerroyant, the Duke's penthouse, or the Bennett buildings, and he had an airtight alibi: he was present with a pair of dates at a performance of Stravinsky's *The Firebird* at Lincoln Center. The most he could be accused of was attempted fraud and forgery, both crimes which were third degree and carried maximums of three-to-five years. Coles was a first-time offender and in light of his contribution to the greater overall indictment he was absolved of his creative crimes. By his request, he was allowed to keep the fake Cano.

The other two paintings, the 'Fragonard' and 'Steen', were used to set up a sting operation by the newborn FBI Art Crime Team to solidify their case against Villeforte and company. The 'Steen' had been turned over to Royal Chase, who actually arranged to have the reward money paid to Sol and Lorelei.

Within a few days Francine was arrested on the Upper West Side trying to sell both pieces to an art dealer who specialized in Latin American works. The Grand Jury Indictment was then handed down. Bennett was captured at Newark Liberty Airport attempting to board a flight to London. The Duke seemed to somehow perversely enjoy being taken away in handcuffs in front of his apartment building; he smiled and made sure to show his best angles for the cameras. They were all charged with a multitude of crimes including money laundering, lying to federal authorities, embezzlement, tax fraud, and accessory to a long list of crimes on Paul's part.

When asked about the would-be Etty painting, Sol said he'd used it to entice the buyer into purchasing the other three for payment at a later date. Predictably, Dr. Knowles had vanished into thin air.

* * * *

Sol was parked in front of #11 First Street in the late morning.

He really liked this old building. Something about it sparked his imagination. He'd seen some truly wonderful art here and met some interestingly original people. That hundreds of artists had gathered in this old factory to forge something so transcendent was a phenomenon in and of itself, something you didn't find in many places.

Turned out, that was what it was all about. Art against money, politics and power. Everybody was fighting over scraps of land and trying to justify their claims. Except that the artists didn't have to justify themselves. They were just doing what they were compelled to do, following their passions, creating instead of destroying. Showing how beautiful and beautifully terrifying life is and can be. Where would we be without our artists?

Here they had taken over land that nobody wanted, that had been discarded, and made something great of it. Then the money wanted it back and tried to brush away the ones who'd made it valuable again.

Maybe a little black-and-white, but that's what Sol was like. It took fifteen years for this community of artists to make people want to visit the area again and profit had not been the purpose.

The Art One Collective had somehow miraculously come up with almost half a million dollars toward much-needed repairs for the building which Yeshevin had been citing in his efforts to have the property condemned by the city. They hired a heavyweight team of lawyers and were able to secure designation as a Historic Landmark Site, which halted any talks of demolition. They would keep the struggle going to the end.

Yeshevin was determined to have his way, because that's what spoiled children are like. He gobbled up all the plots of land around the site and modified his plans, confident that he would see this antiquated eyesore leveled before finishing out his compensatory Napoleonic existence.

Sol was rooting for the poor artists but he was also a born cynic. He looked around and got out of the car, then pulled his crutches out from the back seat.

He took the freight elevator to the third floor, where he knocked on Louis Coles' partly open studio door.

"Come in…" floated an echo.

Coles was lounging in an arm chair at the far end of the immense studio, surrounded by four youths in various settees.

Sol tried to downplay the supports as he made his way over to them, making an effort to walk as upright as possible. When he was about ten feet away he grabbed an available straight back chair and straddled it, propping the underarm cushions of the crutches on his lap.

Coles stood but kept his distance.

"Can I get you something to drink?"

"Nope."

"Right." He sat back down. "Well, then. People, you all know who our guest is." He gave Sol a devilish grin. "You might say he is of the *esprit de corps*."

Sol was not amused. Coles looked almost saddened.

"I thought you might like to meet some of my fellow artists."

He gestured with an upturned palm to a pale young woman with shoulder length wheat-colored hair and forest creature eyes. She was dressed somewhere between off-off Broadway actress and French resistance fighter. She wore a violet scarf and a black beret.

"Mr. Isistrato, please meet Honore Fragonard. She and her family emigrated from Poland a few years ago so she could study art in the U.S."

His hand moved to the straight-backed young black man in the gold plaid thrift-store three-piece. The kid actually had a derby on his head.

"This is Alonso Cano. He was born in Brazil but ran away from a lack of a home and made it here by the time he was fourteen and learned painting on the streets."

Cole's left hand presented a tan-skinned girl with long raven hair and pitch-black eyes with white-fire irises. Jeans, sneakers and a Kill Rock Stars t-shirt.

"Here we have Jan Steen. She is one of the last point zero one percent of Native Americans still in Jersey City. And over there," he flourished a wave toward a handsome hostile-browed Asian youth lounging in an armchair, brown v-neck pullover and khakis. "Say hello to William Etty. First generation Chinese American and also the creator of the leather books we made for you. His family has been book makers for centuries."

It was the crew of rebels at the museum in July.

"And what did you do, Coles, just offer adult moral guidance to these young people?"

"Who do you think did the drawings?"

"Where's the punk rock kid and what did he have to do with all this?"

"Ah, our anarchist historian has taken off for his new adventure already. He gave us the providence."

"You mean 'provenance'."

"No, I don't. I know what I said."

"All of this because you were getting kicked out of your studios?"

"Yes."

They stared at each other for a hard moment. Louis Efrain fidgeted, then elaborated.

"That's how it started, anyway. I really did need the money. To buy this building. And then I understood fully what those people were doing and how we were just a few of the many victims. I, and then we, wanted everyone to know. Hence the murals. Eventually someone would have figured it out. You just happened to expedite things. Nice work, by the way."

"You could have gotten someone killed. Myself, for example."

"I apologize for that. I never intended for anyone to get hurt. But you seem to handle yourself rather well."

"A woman was almost gang raped!"

No one could face him, they all looked away. Coles nearly whispered to the floor before him. "I needed to shine a light…"

"That's nice. But I believe you owe me some money." Sol pulled back the left lapel of his jacket to reveal his weapon. "That's what I came for. Nothing else. Fifteen percent, cash, like I told you. You give that to me and I will instantly forget I was here, as I expect you will also."

"Of course. I've had it ready for some time now."

"Good thing."

Coles turned to the Brazilian kid and nodded. The young man pulled out an old leather medicine bag from behind a couch and brought it over to Sol. Once he'd inspected the contents, Sol removed his belt, looped it through the handle and slung it over his right shoulder. As he stood to leave he took one last good look at each of them.

"Kindly remain seated until I'm gone."

As he started to step out the door he turned halfway behind him.

"By the way, for what it's worth I think you all paint beautifully. I'll keep an eye out for your original works."

* * * *

He met up with his ex and their son in Manhattan.

"Pop-pop! What happened to you?!" the toddler shouted upon seeing Sol bruised, bandaged and crutched.

"I was slaying dragons, son."

The child pursed his lips and nodded sagely. "Wes, I know what dat's like."

For once Sol was not uptight and didn't nitpick the child's behavior, even in the restaurant where they had a late lunch and he was standing on the seat and exclaiming about everything he saw in the window. She was even more beautiful than he remembered, shining in a brightly colored sundress.

The boy liked boats. From the little he knew and understood about his two grandfathers, they both loved the ocean. He didn't know that much about Pop-Pop since he didn't see him as much as he did Grampa the Navy sailor and Poppy the old fisherman.

They'd brought a couple RC's to take out on the lake in Central Park. A slight admonishment had to be made when the excited boy shoved aside a couple of slow boats but otherwise it was a perfectly pleasant afternoon. Mother and child had taken the train in, Sol was driving them home. The two adults pretended to not remember how attracted they'd once been to each other. His son wanted to see him tomorrow, too. He insisted. Sol could think of nothing more he wanted to do the next day.

* * * *

Lorelei was exquisitely dressed for dinner. A dangerous black evening gown. Even had her hair up and wore tiny diamond stud earrings and a sexy jade necklace. She had accepted Sol's invitation to a celebration dinner. He'd had to rent a tuxedo, something he vowed to change that very week.

"You look unbelievably beautiful, Laura. I can't help but wish we'd met in a different way."

"Why? We'd still be the same people."

"True... Well, I'm glad I met you, no matter the circumstance."

"Me, too, Sol. You're not half as bad as you want everyone to think."

"That's debatable, but I'm glad you think so. Can we make a toast?" She'd picked out a boutique champagne. "To making it out of this one with our skins intact."

They clinked glasses and sipped and looked into each other, her green into his black. Each thought of a kiss, the thoughts swiftly dismissed.

"There's something I want to talk to you about," he said seriously.

She was one of the very smartest, bravest, honest and most professional people he had ever come across. He could only hope she regarded him in the slightest similar fashion.

"You are the best partner I've ever had."

"You've never had any partners, Sol."

"Not everything is in my stupid file, Laura. I'm telling you, it's been more than an honor working with you."

"Well, maybe sounds corny but I'm glad you were my first."

"Really?"

"Yes, Sol, I actually learned a few things from you."

"No kidding..."

"Yeah, like what *NOT* to do in certain situations."

"Well, that's something..." They shared a good laugh and he inevitably became serious again.

"I have a proposition for you. I have a couple hundred thousand dollars I'd like to invest in a private investigative firm. Top of the line offices, equipment, staff. I want you to be a managing partner."

"Wow," she asked cynically, "You've really managed to save that much with a librarian's salary? Or are you *nouveau riche*?"

"Ask me no questions and I'll tell you no lies..."

"I don't know... I'd have to seriously think about it."

"That's all I ask. We can choose our cases, accept only the ones we're comfortable with. No shady clients, no craziness."

"That *does* sound good..."

She agreed to consider it and they enjoyed the rest of their meal.

* * * *

It was getting late in the night. Eddie had been over for a few hours to shoot the breeze. They were finishing a long game of chess. On the stereo Cannonball Adderly was playing 'One For Daddy-O'. Almost empty beside them a large bottle of Sauvignon Blanc, smoke in the air. Eddie liked reefer, said it took the troubles away for a while so he could concentrate on the beautiful. He was the only person allowed to smoke in Sol's house, just not cigarettes.

And what troubles, Sol would always ask, since Eddie was a fairly successful musician.

"Aw, you know, man... Everybody wants your money, try'n' 'a screw you one way or the other... Women are all crazy and they try to make you crazy with them..." His eyebrows arched, his eyes glazed over as he recalled one of his greatest stoned revelations. "And as I have always told you, my government-aligned friend, no one seems to notice that we're all still just slaves to the landowners, to the one percent, man!"

"C'mon, man, it's not *that* serious... It's just history, humanity in the making. And we're *all* crazy in some way, some more than others…"

Eddie missed the indirect poke.

"Yeah, well, I'm looking to the future, man, to brighter days. Check."

"Amen to that. Checkmate." Sol was a mediocre chess player but once in a while he got lucky.

They were shouting amiable insults at each other when the doorbell rang, a very rare occurrence at Sol's place. Eddie backed him up, just in case. He knew where Sol kept the anti-dummy stick.

It was Meredith.

What in the world?

She was wearing a pocketed white blouse, a short white skirt, white stockings and white sneakers.

"Hi, Sol! You forgot again didn't you, you self-absorbed man?! Or, okay, maybe it was the medication... I told you last week I'd be over to take check on you, silly! I have a few vacation days, remember?... You really don't remember do you?"

Eddie became a wisp o' the will and disappeared.

She took over his place like she owned it, criticizing his Spartan decorating. "*And* I told you it would be late because of my Monday night reading group, but whatever, let's have a look at you."

He thought he was dreaming.

"What are you waiting for?" she asked. "You like to play pretend, don't you?"